Broken Horses

Kate Beales

2025
Linen Press

Published by Linen Press, London 2025
8 Maltings Lodge
Corney Reach Way
London
W4 2TT

www.linen-press.com

The time line of the workers' strike, and the vast distances covered in
the narrative have been compressed for the sake of story.

A CIP catalogue record for this book is available from the British
Library.

Cover art: Django Pinter
Cover design: Django Pinter & Leigh Forbes
Typesetting by Blot Publishing – blot.co.uk

ISBN (paperback): 978-1-0683417-5-5
ISBN (hardback): 978-1-0683417-9-3
ISBN (ebook): 978-1-0683417-6-2

About the Author

Kate Beales is a freelance writer and theatre-maker working with communities across the UK and around the world. She is a Senior Artist and Freelance Associate with National Theatre Learning, where she has worked for 29 years.

As an Associate Artist at Project Phakama, she worked with refugees on the streets of Paris and Athens, collaborated with a photographer to build pop up darkrooms for pinhole photography and storytelling projects, and made participatory shows with 2-5-year-olds in a giant bed. She's co-devised theatre-based workshops for doctors in Osaka, and taught storytelling for the Medical Humanities course at Bristol University. For twenty years she was a visiting lecturer with New York University's Tisch School of the Arts London, teaching Storytelling and Shakespeare Studies.

Kate currently creates theatre, storytelling and writing projects with wounded veterans throughout the UK for The Drive Project. She is a proud member of the Routes for Women facilitation team, working with female refugees and asylum seekers. She teaches storytelling to senior executives, and devises creative workshops for writers and other artists.

Praise for Broken Horses

*A haunting story of love, rebellion and betrayal. Broken
Horses is a powerful retelling of a forgotten struggle for
workers' rights set in a land of harsh beauty, where the
fight for dignity is a fight to the death.*

—**Tim Robbins**
Academy Award-winning actor and director
(Mystic River, The Shawshank Redemption)

*A finely crafted, compelling love story with Patagonia
at its heart, exquisitely evoked in all its wild beauty and
brutalities.*

—**Avril Joy**
Author of *Sometimes A River Song, The Silent Women*

*I loved it; timeless, windswept, the writing as brisk and
wild as the horses. Patagonia is alive in the pace and
soaring landscapes.*

—**Eleanor Anstruther**
Author of *A Perfect Explanation*

*A gripping tale of love, courage and brutality as a young East
Anglian woman sails away from the grievous aftermath of
the First World War to seek employment on the other side
of the world. Luminously beautiful, Broken Horses is deeply
researched, full of historical detail and shimmers with a sense
of justice and redemption.*

—**Katharine Quarmby**
Author of *The Low Road*

Broken Horses is a haunting, exquisite novel that will stay with the reader long after they have closed the back cover. Beales writes from a place of tender even painful instinct but never at the expense of her pulsing plot that offers buckets of drama and substance so that the novel is never overshadowed by the story's epic geography. I loved it.

—Fiona Melrose
Author of *Even Beyond Death*

Richly evocative of cruel times in a place of stark beauty, Kate Beales' debut novel tells a gripping and cinematic story of women's courage in a world fighting to recover its humanity after the Great War. Its epic sweep teeters between tragedy and hope, as Georgie Carruthers is taken from a life of domestic servitude to fighting for freedom and justice far from home.

—Emma Claire Sweeney
Author of *Owl Song at Dawn*

A compelling story, beautifully told. Kate Beales' debut is a must-read.

—Stephanie Butland
Author of *The Woman in the Photograph*

A wonderful, evocative novel. Kate Beales is a hugely talented writer with a vivid sense of character and place that draws you in from the very first page.

—Danny Scheinmann
Author of *Random Acts of Heroic Love*

For my father, Kim.
Born 1910, Kimere Aike, Magellanes, Chile

We respectfully recognise and acknowledge the indigenous peoples of Patagonia – the Tehuelche (Aonikenk), Selk'nam (Ona), Kawésqar and Yaghan – who inhabited this land long before the arrival of European settlers.

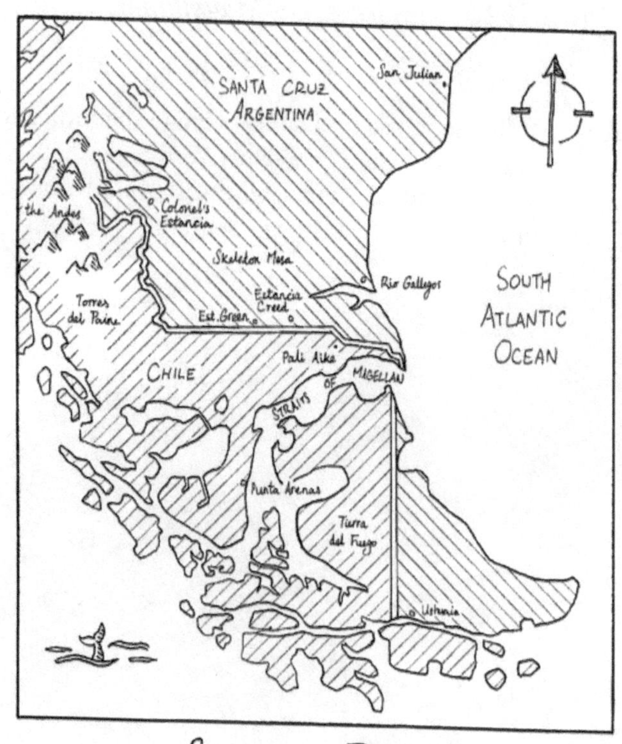

SOUTHERN PATAGONIA

PROLOGUE

Marta, Part V
Second winter, June 1921

Punta Arenas

I never thought to hear a voice like that again, an English lady's voice. Neat as the buttons on her fine silk dress. I wanted to rip those buttons from her skinny throat.

I could see she was afraid, though she held herself upright, like a lady. Thin, but not because she was hungry, those arms never had to lift anything, and her skin so pale you could see the blood beneath. Blue blood they call it, in the English houses. Her hair, I'd not seen hair like that before, all blowing around her head. The English ladies I used to know pulled theirs back out of the wind, neat as their dresses. Except just once, the time my mistress's yellow hair spread out around her head like branches waving.

This new one, at the port, her hair was a nothing-colour, the colour a ghost's hair might be. A ghost, come to find me. I wanted to twist those curls between my fingers. To take her hair and pull it. I wanted her to be more afraid than me.

PART ONE

1.

Punta Arenas, June 1921

*Sandy Point: grey and cold all the year round, prone
to katabatic winds and violent storms. A convict set-
tlement grown rich on the wealth of sheep farmers, a
scurry of low wooden buildings studded by the grand
colonial mansions of these powerful ranchers, the region's estancieros. Gateway to the Straits of Magellan
and Southern Patagonia, a land named by Magellan's
sailors for the oversized feet of its inhabitants.*

From *Travels in Patagonia*, by Henry O. Chambers

I scan the ragged shoreline. A wrecked ferry rises from the
sea, watchful as a haunted house. Waves slap the rusted
hull, seabirds squabble on broken railings, their shrieks lost
between wind and waves like the cries of drowning men.
How many mothers lost their sons that day?

Sailing into port past a shipwreck seems a grim sort of
welcome, like gargoyles on a church. But now our ship's horn
sounds, passengers press forward to lean against the railings,
and excitement quivers the crowd. My own heart quickens at
the sight of Punta Arenas, a jumble of houses clustered over
the hillside, a ring of dark mountains beyond. This is a new
world, uncrushed and hopeful. Ghosts have no place here.

Fellow travellers gather to shake my hand and wish me
luck. You'll be alright now, they tell me kindly, you'll get

over it. If they knew I had chosen to break off my engagement, I doubt they would have been so generous. I say my goodbyes with almost indecent haste. Most of the friends I made on board have already disembarked into northern cities with heavily scented air and exotic names – Rio de Janeiro, Montevideo, Buenos Aires – where dinghies selling souvenirs bobbed among the ships and boys dived for silver into blue water shimmering with sunlight. My turn now, though there's nothing exotic about Punta Arenas. Just grey sand, grey sea, and a biting wind so strong it tosses spray into the air and rocks the small boats against their moorings.

But this is no time for self-pity. I've read the Creeds' letters so often I could recite them by heart: *Everything will be arranged, you will be met at Punta Arenas and accompanied to the estancia.* Now I wonder if Ian Creed – veteran, widower, estanciero – has come himself to meet me. I tug my shawl tight around my shoulders and lift my face to scan the waiting crowd.

The air stinks of fish. At the top of the jetty, a stream of travellers flows around me, indifferent as the sea. Dogs fight over piles of filth. Seagulls swoop at fallen spoils and disappear upwards, lost against the whiteness of the sky. Never have I felt such a ghostly separation from my surroundings, as if I have been superimposed onto the wrong canvas. Have I crossed the world for this?

I grip my bag. There is no reason to be anxious: I am twenty-three years old, and soon to be a governess. I've been a nurse in a hospital and lived through a war. I may be at the very end of the earth, but someone is here to meet me. There must be a waiting room, as there would be at an English railway station. Why did I not think to enquire when I was on board? I must find the shipping office. Someone there will tell me what to do.

Three women walk arm-in-arm along the broad street that runs beyond the quay. From the ease and freedom of their gait, they seem about my own age, and with a burst of optimism, I run after them – perhaps they will speak English. But when I draw closer, something in the bold sashay of their hips, the current of attention rippling through the crowd around them, gives me pause.

A man calls out and they spin round, coloured ribbons fluttering against bony angles of rouged and cavernous cheeks. Before I can look away, the nearest, a girl of about sixteen, catches my eye.

She stops, narrowing her eyes in concentration, tilting her head as if trying to place me. Her thin face is ravaged with scars. "What do you want, English lady?"

The hostility in her tone skewers me. My feeble Spanish withers on my lips. The girl leers at my discomfort and hitches up her skirt, thrusting her hips in an obscene dance. Her companions laugh as they take her by the arms and pull her away. One of them looks back over her shoulder with a wink, rolling her eyes, tapping a finger against the side of her head as they disappear into the crowd.

The girl is mad. It shouldn't matter: I have seen worse at the hospital, much worse. Yet there was an expression on her face, not just of hatred, but of recognition. As if she knew me, and I had done her harm.

Beside me, someone is speaking. "Miss? Miss Georgiana?" A young man, my own age or thereabouts. Hair shiny and black as a crow's wing, skin the colour of a maid's fingers at walnut time. Two deep lines furrowed between his brows.

He must have witnessed that stupid, humiliating scene. When he makes to take my arm, I jerk myself away. "Who has sent you?"

"Señora Creed. I have brought the wagon for you." His English is slow, awkward, but at least I am not expected to muster a reply in Spanish.

"Where is she?" Please, God, let Mrs Creed be at hand. Let her be warm and kind and motherly and welcoming.

"The Señora is waiting for you, Miss. At the estancia."

You will be accompanied to the estancia. My new home, waiting for me somewhere under this vast white sky. "You will drive me?"

"Yes, Miss." He is walking towards a covered wagon, a pair of horses already harnessed, snorting their steamy breath into the chilly air.

"I see." What was I thinking, expecting Ian Creed? I am a governess, not a guest. Still, I am empty and stupid with disappointment. "How far is it to the estancia?"

"Two days."

"Two days?" I must have misunderstood. "You mean two hours?"

He shakes his head, his face serious. "Dos días."

I am to spend two days on a wagon with this stranger? "But who is to come with us? I can't..."

"We must leave now. Because of the snow." He spreads his arms wide, as if to apologise for the weather.

In my bag, along with my Spanish phrasebook, is the letter from my father.

I assure you, Mrs Creed, that Georgie has exactly the kind of character you desire in a governess. She may be only twenty-three, but she is sensible and dependable. For all her tender years, she has been a resolute and doughty support, not only to me in my parish work, but more importantly to the village hospital, when she was old enough to join the war effort.

Most of his parishioners would take issue with the sensible and dependable part – my mother too, no doubt. But what else could he say? That his daughter is the sort to break her promises, and this at a time when virtually every young man in England is either a hero or dead? No wonder he was prepared to bend truth into hoops to see me gone.

Resolute and doughty, on the other hand, I can do. "All right. If we must." The young man does not answer, but tosses my luggage into the back of the wagon. I point to the bench behind the horses. "I want to sit there."

Something like impatience passes over his face. "The wind."

"I want to see." My voice sounds high and querulous, not resolute at all. No matter. I cannot sit for two days alone in that dusky interior, listening to the thump of my own heart.

He raises an eyebrow, but leans into the wagon for a sheepskin and blankets, tosses them onto the bench. My hands are trembling as he helps me up. He must have noticed, though he keeps his eyes down and says nothing. There is a knotted cloth at his throat.

"What's your name?"

"Raúl, Miss."

Raúl. Long, soft vowels. I turn the name over in my mind, its unfamiliar rolling intonation. All the strangeness of this place resides inside that sound. I want to weep. I want to jump down, run to the ship, and beg the captain to carry me home. I want my parents to take me back, and Eddie to forgive me for not loving him enough. I want to go home. I sit perfectly still on the bench and stare straight ahead as Raúl whips up the horses and the wagon rolls forward out of the port.

*

The great ships have given way to smaller ferries and fishing boats when an obstruction appears on the road ahead, a small group of men in workers' clothes gathered around an old man who is shouting, punctuating his words with a newspaper he hits against the palm of his hand. Raúl curses softly to himself.

"What's happening?" He is jumping down from the wagon. "Raúl. Wait." But he is already at the edge of the gathering. The men part to let him through.

The driver of a motorcar has descended from his vehicle, now he too marches into the crowd with an air of expensive authority. Those closest to him shrink inside their shabby jackets, avoiding his eyes.

Onlookers have swelled the crowd. I can no longer see Raúl. A wiry figure with ragged black hair beneath an odd little black-and-white cloth hat is shoving his way towards the driver. Despite his poor appearance, he moves with an arrogant swagger quite equal to the other's confidence. Dirty rags confront a fine sheepskin coat. The driver's lip curls. He raises his walking stick and jabs it hard into the other's chest. The black-haired man recoils. His right hand moves to his belt. There is a flash of metal and the expression on the driver's face turns to fear. Someone lunges at the ragged man, knocking the knife from his hand, pulling him away.

Everyone is shouting. The horses throw up their heads, stamping and whinnying. A stone hits the side of the wagon, then another. I scramble down from the bench and run around the edge of the crowd, searching for Raúl.

By now the street is a roiling mass of bodies. I pause to get my bearings, relieved to see a handful of policemen running towards the fight. One of them raises a rifle and fires a volley of shots into the air.

The street holds its breath. Then, with a shout, the crowd takes flight. At once I am surrounded, tossed between elbows, chests and shoulders, my face rammed against leather and coarse wool, thick smells of lanolin and sweat. People are screaming, horses shrieking. I clutch at coat tails as my knees scrape the ground. In the distance I hear a whimpering sound and realise the voice must be my own.

Through the confusion I hear shouting in Spanish. A rough hand pulls me to my feet. It is Raúl, his face tight with worry.

"Are you alright, Miss?"

Am I alright? I remember the thud of stones against the wagon. "I couldn't see you." My knees slacken. I am afraid I might fall.

He takes my arm, gestures toward the wagon. The snow is coming. There is nothing for it but to go on.

2.

The wagon

Raúl was right about the wind, it howls about us, dragging my shawl from my shoulders, flapping it behind me like a pennant. I clamp my skirts tight between my knees, clutching the shawl to my neck with one hand, clinging to my hat with the other. What would my parents think if they could see me now, disappearing into the wilderness beside this taciturn stranger, the wind tearing my hair from its pins, my best dress, carefully selected for meeting the Creeds, hopelessly creased beneath my useless English coat?

I have tried to ask about the fight at the port. "Who were those people?"

"I don't know, Miss. Union men, maybe. Revolutionaries."

Dear God, is this how revolutions happen? A walking stick, a flashing blade. I remember the driver's face, how his anger froze to terror when he saw the knife. "What do they want?"

He shrugs. "What revolutionaries always want." A pause. "The estanciero did not help himself."

"You mean the driver? He was an estanciero?" Like Ian Creed. "But that man wasn't English, was he?"

"I don't know, Miss."

He turns his attention to the horses, and we lapse back into silence. I dare not ask any more.

The afternoon wears on. Slowly, imperceptibly, the events at the port begin to fade. I am lulled and then mesmerised by the slow undulations of the landscape, mile upon mile of flat, brown earth, extending as far as the eye can see. I raise my face towards the wind and imagine it lifting me like a kite, high into the thick white clouds. Beneath me lies the whole of Patagonia: the port, the wagon, all pin-pricks on the vast carpet of the plain, thin threads of road, running alongside the narrow ribbon of the Straits towards the ocean, smaller than a puddle, dotted with tiny ships, and far away, on the other side of the earth, my parents, alone in the vicarage. My heart twists. They would have given anything to have their sons returned to them; their daughter, it seems, they can do without. Well, if they are glad to see the back of me, then I am happy to be gone. The war cannot touch me here, not the souls of the dead, nor the judgements of the living. In this place, I can make my own beginning.

The horses jingle at their bits. Raúl sits silently beside me on the bench, solid beneath his heavy cape. The heft of his shoulders, the tension in his forearms. Only his hands move on the reins as he steers the horses around the rocks and potholes that litter the track. We drive for hours without speaking, edging the ragged coastline, and I gaze at the rusted skeletons of abandoned boats washed up along the shore. When we pause to water the horses, I climb down to stretch my aching legs on the beach. Tiny hurricanes of sand sting my face, loose strands of hair whip my cheeks. I lean my body into the wind and run with arms outstretched as far along the empty strand as I dare. In a thick patch of reeds out of sight from the wagon I squat to relieve myself, clutching my flyaway skirts in one hand, praying Raúl won't come searching for me.

When I return to the wagon, he is crouching beside the rushes, lighting a fire. I perch on a rock, watching as he boils water, wondering how many other pioneers have stopped in this place before me.

"What is your work on the farm, Raúl?"

He answers without looking up. "I am a horse breaker, Miss."

"Did you break in these horses we are driving?"

"All the horses." A pause, then, "The horses on the farm belong to Señor Creed, but here" – he touches his fist against his heart – "they belong to me."

He sets aside the kettle, unknots a small canvas bag and tips dark grey-green herbs into a bowl, taking his time. When he has poured the water, he puts a silver straw into the bowl and passes it to me. I sip gratefully, only to recoil at the bitter taste.

"What is this?"

"Maté, Miss."

"I expect I will get used to it." I cup the bowl between my hands. "And this?"

"It's a calabaza, Miss."

I hold the bowl at arm's length, examining the rough-hewn interior, the stained pattern around the rim, beautiful and wild. I have never imagined drinking from such an object. When I set it down, he reaches over, and my eyes widen as he takes it up and drinks through my straw, before topping up the bowl with water and passing it back to me.

"In England, everybody drinks from their own cup." I regret the words as soon as they are spoken. What does it matter? England is behind me now, tea at home, my mother's ancient willow pattern, the old milk jug with its cracked, familiar handle. Was it Harry's fault, that crack, or Hugh's? Neither of the boys would tell, and now I'll never know. My memories of my brothers are forever attached to a cracked milk jug, a flat pebble perfect for skimming, the sudden fizz of sugar in my mouth. Tiny discoveries, passed back and forth to hold and stroke and taste. How often did we say to each other, Look! Feel! See what I have found! Now, the taste of maté drunk from a calabaza belongs to me alone. My father would say, tell them anyway, Georgie, talk to them, the dead are always listening. I have pretended for all our sakes that it is true.

Anyway, I am supposed to be a pioneer. I steel myself for another sip of maté, composing my face against the bitterness, trying not to think of the young man's lips closing around the straw. Raúl merely raises his eyebrows and turns aside to scoop handfuls of sand and throw them on the fire.

The wagon weaves its way between the inky waters of the Straits and the open plain that stretches in brown and purple waves as far as the horizon. Wind burns my cheeks, my lips dry until they crack. I huddle inside my blanket, shifting on the wooden bench to ease the numbness in my legs. Occasionally the emptiness of the landscape is relieved by great flocks of geese wheeling above our heads, or ostriches – real ostriches! – racing across the flat scrub. Herds of muscular deer-like creatures gallop alongside the horses. I forget my stiffness and twist round to watch as they unfold away from the wagon, their brown backs vanishing against the hills.

"Oh, look! What are they?"

"Guanacos."

I clap my hands and the lines around his eyes deepen with amusement, but later, he nods towards the sky and I lift my face to discover a pair of condors, swooping so close he can show me the tilt and steer of their fingertip feathers. In my excitement, I jump up to look and lose my balance. He catches my elbow, holding me steady.

"Watch the horses, Miss," he tells me. "They see more than we do. Watch their ears, they will show you everything." After that he is silent for a long time, as if he has said more than he intended. I watch the horses and strain to see more than shadows of bushes and scrub, but I understand what he is trying to tell me: that beneath its unbroken emptiness, the plain teems with life.

"How will I know when we cross into Argentina?" It seems a miracle that the wagon can simply roll from one country to another.

"You won't know, Miss. The plain doesn't change from one side to the other. The sheep and the guanacos, they don't notice a difference."

His face breaks open when he smiles, creasing tiny lines at the edges of his eyes as though he is looking at the horizon, or into the wind. The village girls at home would be captivated.

"Are you from Argentina?"

"No, Miss. From Chile. My uncle brought me."

How much easier to come here with an uncle. "To work?"

"Yes, Miss."

Like me, I think, marvelling. Here to work. "Is the estancia your home?"

"Yes, Miss."

Home. The very word aches with longing. No matter how hard I try to push it away, I am borne back again into the past, helpless against the current of my thoughts. Wisteria and crumbling red brick. My little attic room with its bumpy walls and views over the clover fields. Dust gathering on cufflinks and cricket bats, the paraphernalia of boys, darling boys, trapped forever inside the frames of photographs, never to grow old. Beneath the wind, the whispered condolences of neighbours passing in the lanes, the murmur of bereavement in the churchyards. Calamitous outpourings of grief behind the closed doors of quiet Suffolk villages.

When I gave up Eddie, I gave up everything. If I'd understood what it meant to leave, carrying nothing but disgrace and hurt and outrage, perhaps I would have stayed. But it's too late for that now. I lift my face to the sky, letting the wind sting tears into my eyes.

The young man is watching. "What does your uncle do at the farm, Raúl?"

"He died, Miss."

"Oh. I see. I'm sorry." So Raúl, too, is alone. He says nothing more, but calls to the horses, as if comfort is to be found there. Perhaps, for a horse breaker, it is.

When we stop to rest, I gather soft ostrich plumes caught in the bushes, turning them between my hands, stroking the down against my cheek, tucking them away inside my coat. The consolation of tiny things. My childhood collection of treasures is gone, all the books and shells, coloured pencils and china animals packed up and donated to the Sunday school. I used to imagine myself married, carrying them with me to a new home, saving them for my own children.

In the evening, birds circle overhead, shrieking in the gloom. "Caranchos," he tells me, pointing. "They eat guanacos, the sick and the small ones, in the night."

I shake my head, cover my ears with my hands. He gives me a sideways glance, and I fear I have offended him. When we pull up in front of a small guesthouse fronting a shingle beach lined with sedge and rushes, he jumps down without a word, at once busy with the horses. I hover beside the wagon, not knowing if I am to wait, to follow him, to knock on the door. But moments later he returns, a puppy cradled in his hands.

"Oh," I cry, lifting it into my arms, smelling the warmth of its soft paws. "Who does it belong to?"

"It doesn't belong anywhere." He carries my bag into the vestibule and disappears. I am left alone.

It seems I am the only guest. My taciturn host will not meet my eye: I follow him through a maze of corridors to my room, and dine alone at a bumpy table, my first night in Patagonia, picking at mutton and potatoes left out on a tin plate, listening to the splash of waves on shingle. Through the window, I search the inky darkness of the Straits for signs of Tierra del Fuego, and fancy I see fires flickering on a distant shore. But perhaps it is nothing more than the reflection of my own lantern in the glass.

I will not be afraid. I will show them all. And the child will love me. More than the cold, or the emptiness, it is the howling voices of the wind that shiver through me, reminding me of my own loneliness, of everything I have left behind.

3.

The Creeds

We arrive, as Raúl predicted, in the evening of the second day. The wagon turns off the road beneath a painted sign barely visible in the gloom: Estancia Creed. Dogs bark at our wheels, the shadow shapes of horses canter along fences lining the track and veer away into the darkness. In the distance, I make out the pale outline of the house, windows punctuated with pinpricks of yellow light, a row of tiny eyes watching for us.

"Stop. Stop, Raúl." Anxiety makes me snappish. "I need to get in the back."

He helps me down without a word, his hand strong beneath my own. For a moment I have an absurd longing to close my eyes and hold on. I jerk myself away from him, stumbling into the dark interior. My coat is crumpled and inadequate, the wind has made a bird's nest of my hair. By the time the wagon pulls up in front of the house, I am fighting tears.

"Goodnight, Miss." Raúl holds out his hand again to help me down. I dip my head to hide the wetness on my cheeks. When I recover enough to look back, he has disappeared.

*

The Creeds are waiting for me in the hallway. Maud Creed, the widow, is nothing but dust and memory in her black dress, dark hair turned to steel at the temples, deep furrows in her forehead. At her side, her pale-faced son. His story has already captured my heart: a widower in his twenties, his wife and baby daughter buried not twelve months past. Ian Creed was buried himself once, too, in the Great War, up to his neck in the mud of a French battlefield. His body has recovered from his wounds, but the internal shape of him must surely be unfathomably altered. In the flicker of the lamps, his shadow trembles in impossible angles on the stairs. When my eyes adjust, I see a small boy in his dressing gown, hiding behind his father. Leo.

"Ian," Mrs Creed says sharply. "Help the poor thing with her luggage." Her son shoves his floppy hair back from his face and steps forward, proffering a hand.

"No, no, it's fine, please." I am too weary to smile.

"How was your journey? I hope you were comfortable?"

"Yes. Thank you." I picture the endless hours of flat, unchanging landscape. She nods, satisfied. "The port's a bit grim, though, isn't it?" The words are out before I can stop myself. I feel, rather than see, her raised eyebrow. "There was a demonstration."

"A demonstration?"

"People were fighting. The police came and chased them away. Raúl said they were revolutionaries."

"Raúl?" Her voice is chipped ice. Too late, I realise another mistake: I have as good as told her I was sitting with the driver. At least I didn't let slip the dreadful episode with the mad girl.

"I'm sure it was nothing serious," Ian puts in hastily, and my heart quickens with gratitude. "Probably just some dock workers. You don't need to worry," he continues. "We are quite removed from that sort of thing here."

"I think you must be quite removed from most things here."

Mrs Creed does not smile. She cuts past me to the door, thrusting the bolts across. In the lamplight, her mouth is a grim streak across her face. Nobody speaks. I shove loose strands of hair behind my ear and crouch down beside the silent child. "Hello Leo," I say, smiling. "I'm Georgie. I've come to live with you, and I hope very much that you will play with me and show me everything. Will you do that?" The little boy shrinks behind Ian. I had hoped for more. But what could I expect from such a small, motherless child?

"You must be tired," Mrs Creed says. "There is a tray in your room. You can go upstairs now. We will show you everything in the morning." And so, it seems, I am dismissed.

*

I am to sleep next door to the nursery, in a small wood-panelled room, decorated in the style of any old-fashioned country house: heavy walnut dresser; turned wooden washstand with Chinese blue jug and bowl; creamy wool and starched linens. The familiarity should be comforting, but Mrs Creed's abrupt dismissal has crushed what tiny spirit I had left. Wind rages through the corridors, banging on walls and windows. I wonder how anyone manages to sleep in this house. On my bedside table lies a book: *Travels in Patagonia*, by Henry O. Chambers. Holding my candle close, I flick through the pages to a chapter entitled *Life on the Estancias*.

Faced with the privations of life in Southern Patagonia, a woman of good family derives some comfort from creating conditions as close as possible to those of her original home.

Mr Chambers might as well have been writing about Maud Creed, though whatever privations I am to face in Southern Patagonia, they will surely be a relief after England and the war.

*

The fire has burned down in the grate and the room is shrouded in darkness when I am woken from a fitful dozing by a long, desolate wail rising above the wind. I think of Leo's wan little face and frightened eyes: he must be having a nightmare. The sobbing continues. No one, it seems, is coming to comfort him. But I am resolute and doughty. I push back the covers and wrap myself in my shawl.

Cold air stings. I follow the sound out of my room, but by the time I reach the nursery, the crying has stopped. Leo lies fast asleep, bedclothes tucked neatly around him, no sign that he has stirred. I lean over his sleeping body, feeling the gentle rise and fall of his breath.

As I slip back into the corridor, a figure appears in front of me, holding a candle. Both of us cry out, and the candle gutters. Shadows bounce wildly off the walls.

"Georgie? What are you doing?" It is Mrs Creed.

"I heard crying. I thought it was Leo."

"Leo has a nursery maid. It is not your job to get up in the night."

"I'm sorry. I thought..."

"It doesn't matter. Anyway, it's just the wind – listen. You'll get used to it. Go back to bed."

She is right. There is only the wind. I feel her eyes on my back as I creep away, and a familiar sick, humiliating sense of shame, undercut by a tiny flicker of defiance: I don't care what she says, I would do the same again, even if it is not my job. I climb back into bed, shivering in my inadequate nightgown, and it occurs to me that, despite the lateness of the hour, my new employer is still fully dressed.

4.

The estancia

I wake with the peculiar emptiness that comes with forgetting where you have fallen asleep. Nothing but stillness, cool air, an impression of open space. It is all over in an instant. I know where I am: the estancia. Now it is safe to open my eyes.

The room already seems familiar. Only the light is different: it has a heaviness, a dull quality. An end-of-the-world light. The house has not yet shaken off the stillness of night-time, but my heart is beating too fast to go back to sleep. I slip out of bed, shivering, and splash icy water from the jug, a lick and a promise, my mother would say. Wrapping my shawl tight around my shoulders, I ease open the bedroom door. Floorboards creak beneath my feet, loud in the silence. Passing the nursery, I peep through the door and listen to the soft breath of the sleeping child. He has not stirred. I tiptoe downstairs, taking in surroundings I'd failed to notice in the lamplight of my arrival: mahogany bannisters, high-backed chairs gathered stiffly around low occasional tables, family photographs in elaborate silver frames, the glowing red and gold of thick Persian rugs. Not a single ornament or furnishing that would be out of place at home. So much for pioneering.

The Creeds' presence lingers at the foot of the stairs: the ferocious widow with her thin, fierce mouth, the angled shadow of her widower son. Grief is here, I feel it as surely

as if the dead still lay across the furniture. I shake it off and
pick up a photograph, holding it to the light. A much younger
Maud Creed stands in front of a tall man in a dark suit. An
ostrich feather is tucked into her hair, the curve of her neck
pale against the dark shadow of her dress. She is beautiful.

*

A black marble clock ticks on the mantelpiece in the dining
room. Unsmiling portraits line the walls. Winter light turns
candelabras into twisted shadow-fingers. In daylight, Ian is
still pale. He seems older than his twenty-nine years, tired
skin and crumpled forehead giving his face the appearance of a worn linen shirt. His eyes are clear, though, and
thoughtful, the same soft blue as my father's. He raises an
eyebrow and I realise I am staring.

"I hope you have an excellent morning," he says.
"Mother will show you everything."

"You won't have breakfast with us?" I don't relish the
prospect of being alone with Maud Creed.

"I had mine a while ago, in the kitchen."

So Ian too has been up and about the house. He might
have found me examining his photographs. "What will you
do today?" I ask, to cover my confusion.

"Oh, I'll be out on the farm. We're rather behind this year."

"Are you riding out today?" Mrs Creed is behind us. I
spin round, stifling a cry.

"Mother. I didn't see you. You made me jump." Ian
sounds uncomfortable. "Yes, I'm afraid so. It's necessary."

"Lali can go."

I glance from one to the other, like an unhappy spectator
at a tennis match. I would like to ask who Lali is, but between
mother and son runs a current too powerful to interrupt.

"We'll see." Ian pulls out her chair, waits for her to sit.
"It'll take more than just Lali."

"Well, surely there are some men left who will do as
you ask."

The air prickles. A flush rises from Ian's neck into his cheeks. My voice, high and silly with anxiety, fills the silence. "What does Leo like for breakfast? Can I help?" They are both looking at me. Am I really speaking over the Creeds? I reach across the table, sloshing porridge into Leo's bowl. Grey milk pools outwards. "Oh goodness, I am sorry, I'll just… No, no, please let me…"

Ian's hand is on my arm. "It's alright," he says, throwing a napkin over the soiled tablecloth. "Look… it's fine."

With pointed precision, Mrs Creed sets down her coffee cup on the other side of her plate. "You seem very young for your age," she says icily. "Are you really twenty-three?"

"Don't be ridiculous, Mother. Of course she is."

My heart thumps against my chest. On the ship, trying to forget how far I was from home, looking out over the impossible vastness of the sea, I told myself, over and over, like a prayer, the estancia is waiting, the estancia will be my home. But on my very first day, I am humiliated.

Leo comes to my rescue. "Look, Papa, look! It's snowing."

The sky is blank as a sheet of paper. White flakes rest on the dark earth. Already, the horses in the corrals wear dappled snow-blankets across their haunches.

"How jolly," I cry, my voice loud with relief. "Please, after breakfast, might I take Leo to play outside?"

"I suppose so." Mrs Creed frowns. "Just in the garden, though, no further. Not the camp." She stands back, appraising. "You can borrow one of my dresses."

I search my skirt for stains. "Is something wrong with mine?"

"You'll need Pilar to sew something heavy into the hems."

"What? Why?"

"To stop them blowing over your head. I'll find you something for now. You're rather thin," I wince under her unsmiling gaze. "We'll have to be creative. Now. You must tell me something more about yourself. Weren't you to have been married?"

"Yes. Yes, I was."

I was to have been married. One week after I saw my brothers off to training camp, I walked Eddie to the station to join his regiment. Soon, he would be at the front. His slender fingers rested over mine on the handlebars as we pushed my bicycle between us. The early morning sun cast shadows across the lane. Eddie unbuttoned his coat and shifted the rucksack slung heavy across his shoulder.

"You should have let your father drive you," I said.

"Oh God, no, it would have been awful for him. Anyway, I wanted to be with you."

As if it wasn't awful for me too. I shoved the bicycle into his hands and crouched at the side of the road, pretending to tie my shoelaces.

"I'll be back soon," he said. "It's only France."

"I know."

"And you'll be so busy. You won't even notice I'm gone."

He waited for me to say something light and kind, but my mind was thick with dread and the words caught in my throat. Instead, I knelt in the grass, tearing at knots of bindweed ravelled around the dog roses. Eddie threw down the rucksack, leaned the bicycle against the hedge, and sat beside me in the slanted sunlight.

"Come on, Georgie." He brushed broken petals from my fingers, held me against the rough wool of his greatcoat until I gave up and wept into his shoulder, then kissed the tears that ran down my cheeks into his cupped hands. When he put his mouth to mine, I tasted salt between our lips.

"How sad," Mrs Creed says and I jump at the sound of her voice. "But you are young. You have plenty of time."

I stare at my hands. I should commiserate with the Creeds for their own losses, but I am afraid to speak for fear the tears will fall. Outside, the snow, silent and expressionless, continues to cover the ground.

*

After breakfast, Mrs Creed scans me up and down like a tailor, then leads me up a narrow staircase, past a corridor of servants' bedrooms to a box room at the top of the house where strange objects shrouded in dust sheets loom like ghosts, sighing as we pass. Cold winds its way around my limbs and grips my bones. We reach a heavy chest, and Mrs Creed pushes aside piles of clothing folded into layers of tissue paper. With a little click of satisfaction, she holds up an expensive-looking dress in thick, slubby silk. A faint smell of mothballs drifts in the chilly air.

"It's very small," I say, doubtfully. Mrs Creed must have been a great deal thinner when she bought it. Or optimistic – despite the mothballs, the dress looks fresh and not particularly old-fashioned.

"Nonsense." She stands back and scans my frame. "It's only for today." A pause. "So what did happen to your fiancé, Georgie? Did he die?"

Her bluntness takes my breath away. On the boat, everyone assumed Eddie was dead and I did not tell them otherwise. Not a lie so much as an act of omission. Protection from pursed mouths and sideways glances, murmured conversations. But Maud Creed is my employer, and I am to live in her house. I can't answer a direct question with a lie.

"Actually," I try to speak slowly, "He didn't die. He was injured. Terribly injured. So badly... it was impossible."

The silence lengthens between us. I brace myself for more questions, but in the end, she says simply, "I see. Well, you wouldn't be the first." She turns back to the dress. "I think this will do very nicely." And for now, at least, the conversation is over.

In my bedroom, I shiver and curse in my petticoat as I wriggle into the bodice. The weighted hem knocks against my shins. The dress is beautifully cut, by far the most expensive garment I have ever worn, but the heavy silk grips tight around my waist and hips. Just for going outside, I tell myself, I'll take it off as soon as we've had our walk. I try not to think of the sealed trunks and pale shapes in the box room. At home we lived among our dead, but I never felt their eyes the way I feel the ghosts of this house watching.

When I appear on the landing, Mrs Creed turns me around, gives the tiniest of nods. "Yes. Very good." Trapped inside the straining fabric, I feel a glow of pride. "Run and get your coat," she adds. "I'll tell Pilar to send Leo down when you're ready."

"I can take him with me now."

"No. I'd like to see him first. Go. Put on your coat."

5.

The sticky gate

Leo's little face is rosy with cold. "Come."

I try not to breathe too deeply into the taut seams of Mrs Creed's blue dress. "Didn't your grandmamma say we were to stay in the garden?" But his foot is already on the gate. "Oh goodness, Leo. Please get down." Now he hops down on the other side and stands watching through the bars. "Oh. Well, just quickly, then. Can we open the gate?"

"It's sticky."

I tug at the latch. It is indeed sticky, the metal ice-cold under its dusting of snow. But nothing ventured, nothing gained, I had brothers once, and they taught me how to vault a gate, so I hold my heavy skirt in one hand, step onto the lowest bar, then lean forward, swinging my legs up and over. The thick hem drags, catching on a hinge. I slip on the patina of frost covering the top of the gate and there is a dreadful ripping sound as I tumble forward into the snowy grass, leaving a jagged shred of material behind.

I sit up, rubbing my arms and legs. No damage, except for the wretched dress, its hem hanging in ribbons from the gate. The dark windows of the house gaze down on me. For a second, I sense movement, high up at a casement, perhaps the very box room where the dress was stored, but surely it is just a catch of the light.

Leo has disappeared. I can hear him shouting. My insides curl at the thought that someone will find me sitting in a puddle of snow. Sure enough, a figure emerges from the out-buildings: a boy, about twelve years old, with the pinched look of working lads whose bony shoulders already carry the responsibilities of adulthood, and a sly expression, which might be amusement.

"I'm fine. I don't need help," I say in English as I pick myself up. His eyes darken in confusion and immediately I feel guilty.

"What's this? Georgie?" To my horror, Ian has appeared on the path, Leo dancing around him. When I look back, the farm boy has disappeared.

I stand to attention, pulling my coat close. "I'm so sorry. We were just... I..."

"Papa," Leo shouts, waving flurries of snow. "I want to show Georgie the farm."

"Of course you do. And what about Georgie?" Ian's eyes are warm and hopeful. He seems not to have noticed the damp patches on my coat. I stuff the torn silk deep into my pocket, and look around for something, anything, to show that I am interested.

"What is this plant here?" It's a small, gnarled bush, thick with thorns and not very promising, but Ian looks pleased.

"That's calafate. In summer, we make jam with the berries. You probably had some on your toast this morning." He drops his voice to a theatrical whisper. "They say that once you've tasted the fruit of the calafate, you'll always return to Patagonia."

"Really?" I am whispering too, entranced. "Why?"

He smiles. "Honestly, I don't know. Some old legend or other."

A couple of workers lean against a nearby fence. I wave a greeting, but they stare back, unsmiling, until I lower my eyes. Ian says something abrupt in Spanish, and they coil languidly away. One of them spits sideways into the snow. Ian takes my arm, steering me past icy puddles until we reach the corrals. When he stoops to clear loose stones from the path, I sneak a look back across the yard. The men are gone, but a faint whisper of hostility hangs in the air.

"My father built this place. The house, the farm, all of it." Ian's eyes light up when he speaks about his home. "These posts are made with spars and masts he salvaged from wrecks in the Straits." I imagine drowning fingers clutching at these beams and wonder what happened to Ian's father.

Leo tugs at my sleeve. "Shall we go riding, Georgie?"

"Oh, I don't know how to ride." I laugh. "My father is a great believer in bicycles." Eddie's father kept a stable. If Eddie and I had married, our children would have learned to ride.

"That's strange." Leo's little voice breaks across my thoughts. "Papa, Georgie can't ride."

"What?" Ian feigns shock. "Well, she can always go out in the car."

I detect a hint of pride. "You have a motor car?"

"Indeed we do. She couldn't make it all the way to Punta Arenas at this time of year, but we can go for a tour in the spring."

"That sounds fun."

"Oh no, no!" Leo's pale hair flops against his face, a miniature version of his father. "No, Papa. Georgie wants to ride."

Ian looks at me. "Would you like to, or is Leo teasing you?"

Isn't this why I am here, to become somebody new? It's what a pioneer would do. "Alright, then. If Leo would like it."

"You're quite the spirit, aren't you? Consider it done. I'll teach you myself." Ian smiles, and I feel myself quivering with delight, like a small animal being stroked, knowing he is pleased with me.

We walk through empty sheep barns to the shearing shed. Dust and scraps of old wool blow across the darkened floor.

"Where are the sheep now?" I am embarrassed by my ignorance.

"Not far. On the coironal. The winter grazing. You see that spiky grass? That's coirón. They can always find some sticking up out of the snow."

"So they can survive outside all winter?'

"Most of them. They have to."

"And the shepherds?"

"They stay in the huts. They hunt and watch the sheep. It's a wild sort of life, but it's what they know." There is an edge to his voice, as if I am accusing him of something.

"Why do they come here?"

"You do like questions, don't you? Oh goodness, don't look so worried, I was joking. Why do they come? Big things, small things. The war. The revolution in Russia. Nasty little family histories. Chaps who've fallen into disgrace back at home. All looking for a new life. In this place, nobody asks questions."

Fallen into disgrace, looking for a new life? It seems I will fit in well here after all.

6.

Blue cuffs

We reach a broad puddle, silvered with ice. Ian takes my hand. "Gosh, you're cold. Your hands are freezing." Then, looking closer, "you're all wet. Did you fall?"

"It was nothing."

"Why didn't you say?" He is still holding my hand. Beneath my coat sleeve, he can see the blue cuff of Mrs Creed's dress. For a second, his grip tightens. "We should get you home," he says. "You'll catch your death." There is something careful in his tone that was not there before.

Leo's face falls. Ian squeezes his shoulder, the smile back in place. "I've got work to do, old man. Lali will be after me."

I can't contain my curiosity. "Who is Lali?"

"Lali's our manager. He came here with my father. Loves this place as we do, knows everything there is to know about farming. Sometimes I think he knows everything about everything."

I picture my own father standing on the platform, his face in ruins as my train pulled away. He knew everything about everything, until the war came, and all our hopes were lost.

"Anyway," Ian says. "I'll walk you to the gate. Mother will look after you." A pause. "She's kind, you know. She comes across a bit fierce, but that's because she's had to be, living here." He spreads his arms wide, showing me. Beyond his fingers the plain stretches in all directions, vast as an ocean. My old world was all edges and boundaries: narrow lattices of village lanes, rows of tiny cottages, fences, gates, walled gardens, hedgerows and headlands. Crossroads. Corners. Nothing I have ever seen has prepared me for such enormity of space. How must it have been for Maud Creed, arriving here as a bride? From across the garden, the house's shuttered eyes stare back into mine, unwilling to answer.

"Have you always lived here?" I ask, as we set off again towards the yard.

"All my life, apart from the war." A quick glance at Leo, who is running in circles with his mouth wide open, lifting his face to falling snowflakes. "Alice and I never intended to live here full time. But when my father died…" He stops, leaving me to imagine. "I used to take her away, before the war. She liked Buenos Aires." He gives me a wan smile. "She was always very clear about what she wanted."

"That sounds like a good thing."

"Maybe."

So Alice had strong opinions. I wonder how she got on with her mother-in-law. Ian passes a hand across his eyes and loneliness seeps out of him. "I'm so sorry," I murmur. "For your loss."

"Yes. Well. You know how it is."

"Yes. I know."

Something passes between us, a kind of recognition. "Right," he says abruptly, and the spell is broken. "You must have had enough. And I need to get a move on before the morning's gone."

"Where are you going, Papa?" Leo asks.

"To the puestos along the north road." I detect a note of rebellion. It makes me like him all the more. He steps back, as if to take his leave, then hesitates. "Look, I'm sorry, but I have to ask…" He is staring at my sleeve, so hard it makes me want to put my hands behind my back like a child. That awful sinking feeling as I remember the shreds of silk in my pocket. "I couldn't help noticing. Your dress… the cuffs?"

Not the hem then. Relief makes me want to laugh aloud. "Oh, it's not mine. Your mother lent me one of hers. Were you wondering?"

He takes my wrist in his, turns it, staring at the little cloth buttons, the white scalloped edge.

"My mother said it was hers?" He drops my arm.

"Yes, of course. She lent it to me because…" The words wither in my throat. How could I not have guessed? No wonder Mrs Creed insisted I put on my coat before Leo saw me. How could I have been so stupid as to think this dress ever belonged to Ian's mother? My skin shrivels inside the silk as if it has been poisoned.

He has seen the horror on my face. We both know. Although he doesn't yet know, and neither does Mrs Creed, about the ragged hem, hiding in my pocket like a curse. Alice's dress, so fresh, so carefully packed in its tissue paper, is ruined. I want to tear it from my body and stamp it into the ground.

"I'm sorry," he says, with a tiny shake of his head. In his voice, there is only kindness. "Where was I? My mother's dress. It took me by surprise." I stare at him in stupid gratitude. "Not that I know an awful lot about dresses," he continues. "Honestly, they all look the same to me."

He has rescued me. I am helpless with relief. "Right," he says. "No more delays. Look, why don't you wait here if you're not too cold? I'll get Rajah, and you can wave us off."

7.

The riders

Leo and I wait hand-in-hand at the edge of the yard. Alice's dress clings tighter than ever, a vice around my ribs. A trap set without my knowing.

With an effort, I wrench my attention back to my small charge. "So, what do we do in winter, Leo, apart from play in the snow? Can we go into town sometimes, or pay visits?"

He shakes his head. I look out over the paddocks to the plain: no roads, no woods, no fields to punctuate the landscape, no buildings or settlements as far as the eye can see. On the horizon I can just make out the indistinct shadows of the hills. My heart sinks.

There is a sudden clatter of hooves in the yard. Dogs circle the horses. Breath steams in the icy air.

I bend down to whisper. "Who are those men riding with your Papa?"

"There's Lali." Leo points to a weather-beaten figure with a thick grey beard.

"Leo! Please," I pull at his arm. "Don't make it so obvious." But Lali has noticed, is leading his horse across the yard to greet us. He does not smile, just bends to kiss the top of Leo's head, before bowing over my hand with a murmured greeting. His grey hair hangs in a long thread between huge, bear-like shoulders. His forehead is criss-crossed with wrinkles like a map. Thick eyebrows lie heavy over deep-set black eyes. A man to rely on, but not to cross, I think, as he straightens and turns away, whistling to his dogs.

A little apart from the others, a rider thin as wire is mounted on a black pony with a mane that flows over its neck like a creature from a fairy tale. His sallow face is long and angular, his mouth moves without ceasing, muttering either to himself or to his horse. The shuttered gleam in his eyes reminds me of the mad girl at the port, and my grip tightens around Leo's hand. I must be careful. I can't start seeing hostility everywhere.

"Who is that one, Leo?"

"His name is The Talker. He's from Entre Ríos. Between the rivers. That's far away. He brought me an ostrich egg once with paintings on it."

"Oh my." I feel my eyes grow wide. "An ostrich egg? Really? Do you still have it?"

"I broke it."

"I would like to see an ostrich egg." But now I have forgotten The Talker. "Oh look, Leo, is that Raúl at the back?" A tiny beat of excitement at his familiar face. Before I realise what I am doing, I have lifted my hand to wave. I drop it again, quickly, hoping no one has noticed.

"We don't say Raúl, we call him Horsebreaker."

"Do you?"

Raúl sits very still, his face muffled in scarves, the wicked tines of his spurs glinting against his boots. On horseback he is proud and upright, no longer a servant. My first gaucho.

Ian leans over to ruffle Leo's hair, then pulls the reins high across his horse's neck so the animal ripples and wheels round on its hind legs. He whistles up his dog, Loca, and digs his spurs into Rajah's sides.

"See you soon," he calls over his shoulder. "Take good care of Georgie."

The Talker salutes and says something as he passes, but his words are lost on the wind.

The horse breaker pulls up beside us.

"Hola, Raúl."

"Señorita." He salutes me, and I am glad I was brave enough to greet him. He leans down, beckoning Leo, his face so close I can see the tiny lines at the edges of his eyes. Peeping out over the collar of his shirt is the puppy. I lift Leo up so he can stroke the small velvet head with his fingertip, feeling the warmth of the horse as I stand against its shoulder.

"I'll bring her back to see you, little one," Raúl says in English. "Hasta luego."

"Hasta luego, hasta luego," Leo sings after the riders, as one by one the horses leap over the ridge and disappear, leaving only their hoof prints in the snow.

The story of Calafate

Calafate, the beautiful yellow-eyed daughter of an Aon-ikenk chief, fell in love with a young man from a rival tribe. When the chief learned his daughter was planning to elope with her unsuitable lover, he commanded a powerful shaman to prevent her from leaving. The shaman obliged by turning the girl into a bush, covered in yellow flowers – and the chief requested the addition of sharp thorns, to protect her from her suitor. The young man sat down near the calafate bush and wept. When the shaman saw this, he felt terrible guilt for inflicting such grief on the young couple. He turned the young man's heart into the purple berries that cover the calafate bush, and in this way, the two lovers could always be together.

From *Travels in Patagonia* by Henry O. Chambers

8.

Pali Aike

The riders thread their way in single file along the narrow track, following snowy hoof prints. Ian is at the front, separated a little from the rest. The Talker follows Lali, his mouth shut. He knows better than to bend Lali's ear with his prattle.

Raúl, on his Hero, rides last-but-one. Behind him, Juan Sant, the new shepherd, a man so insignificant as to be almost invisible, a scrawny frame beneath the loose folds of an ill-fitting jacket. Juan Sant arrived at the estancia pushing an empty cart. Bad luck hangs over him like a shadow. He has a reputation as a union man. These days they are everywhere, already there is talk of telling him to take his cart and move on. But the old man's face has no sharpness in it, the bloodshot eyes are soft. Yesterday, Raúl surprised himself, telling the Englishwoman about the uncle who brought him here. Now he wonders if the uncle, long forgotten, looked something like Juan Sant.

When they reach the open plain, Sant spurs his horse forward and trots alongside Raúl, hooves spraying snow.

"So where are you from, Horsebreaker?"

Of all questions, this is the one Raúl most hates. But there's always trouble in lying. So he squares up, looking Juan Sant in the eye. "My mother was from Chiloé. I was born there."

"Really? We're neighbours, then. I'm Chilote too. From Castro."

The pressure drains from Raúl's chest. "I'm from Ancud. But I don't remember. I left with my uncle when I was small. He was from Argentina."

Juan Sant laughs. "Ah, maybe one day you'll go back and see for yourself where your ancestors caught fish."

"Maybe."

"What news from Punta Arenas?" Sant asks lightly.

Raúl takes another long breath. The demonstration at the port, the Englishwoman falling among the workers. If he is a union man, Juan Sant might want to know about these things. "No news, che."

"What about your Englishwoman? She must be desperate to come here."

"She's not my Englishwoman."

"Still. What's she like?"

What is she like? Curly hair whipping her face, veins like blue shadows beneath her pale skin, eyes flickering with anxiety. "She's young. Like a girl. She..." How can he put it into words? "She liked everything."

Sant laughs, and the horses lift their heads. "That won't last long." He lights another cigarette. "Why won't you tell me what's going on in Punta Arenas?"

"Why do you care?"

Sant puts a finger to his lips. "Shhh. I don't want The Talker knowing my business."

Raúl laughs, but he lets the others pull ahead. When they are a safe distance from The Talker, the falling snow a soft curtain between them, he kicks Hero closer to Sant's horse and lowers his voice to a whisper.

"Is it true they put you in Ushuaia?"

Ushuaia. The word falls between them, grey and hard and heavy. At once Raúl wishes he hadn't spoken. He would take it back again if he knew how.

But the old man doesn't flinch. "It's true."

"Why didn't they just send you back over the border? Is it because you were in the union?"

"Oh no. Back then, I was just a carter." Sant laughs. "It was Ushuaia made me a revolutionary." Raúl can't help but look round, as if the snow itself might be listening. "I had some savings," Sant continues, "and I bought a piece of land. Just a little place I could have some sheep and a few cattle. Plenty of good grass, big fish in the stream. It was beautiful."

"Good for you." Raúl has plans of his own. Horses. Land. Reputation.

"But there was a rich farmer," Sant continues. "He said the place was his, that I had stolen it. The land had cost me everything. There was nothing left to pay for a lawyer." He shrugs. "They could have sent me back to Chile, but they put me in Ushuaia."

"Is it as bad there as they say?"

"Those who say have no idea. Imagine a giant star. Five long corridors all spreading outwards from the centre. In the middle, one huge stove. Thieves and murderers, they get cells beside the stove. The revolutionaries are farthest away." An odd little smile. "The cold is like nothing I've ever known. Cruel as a knife. Outside, cold smells like trees and grass and earth. A man can run, or ride. Look for ostrich eggs, kill a guanaco, light a fire. In Ushuaia, cold stinks of fear." Juan Sant's eyes harden. "When I arrived, they took away my clothes. No blanket. No bed. I begged for water. The guard came back laughing. By the time I saw the bucket, it was too late to get out of the way. He threw snow water over me, then left me naked for a week. I thought I would die."

Raúl pictures the frailty beneath Sant's shabby clothes. "Who else was in there?"

"Everyone you'd expect. Men who, if their knives were taken away, they'd kill each other with their teeth. There was an estanciero, you know." Raúl can't help himself; he glances ahead at Ian Creed, shrouded in snow. Sant has noticed, his face twists once more into that odd smile.

"Even for the rich, sometimes there is justice. That one in Ushuaia, he killed his wife too."

"Shut up," Raúl says. "Shut up. I don't want to hear that kind of talk." Rumour spreads like manure on your boot, and the smell sticks just as strong. He digs his spurs into Hero's side and the horse lunges forward, leaving Juan Sant behind.

The little troupe stops under a circle of twisted ñire trees. The men busy themselves making a fire, boiling a kettle for maté. The light is already beginning to fade. From here, Lali and Ian Creed will continue along the north road, while Raúl and Juan and The Talker follow the border towards the lava fields.

By the time the three men reach the edge of Pali Aike, the snow has stopped falling. They select a small dry cave and light a fire in front of the entrance. The Talker takes his rifle and disappears into the dusk, slithering over rocks. Raúl's eyes droop.

There is a shot, then footsteps, and a thud as The Talker hits his head against a rocky outcrop. He curses and throws a rabbit onto the ground beside the fire. "That's enough. There are puma here."

Raúl cuts the rabbit's throat and drains its blood into a tin cup. The Talker picks up the cup and swallows the contents in a single gulp. Blood runs down his chin. He smears it across his face with the back of his hand, then leans against the wall of the cave and closes his eyes, humming and muttering to himself. Raúl skins the rabbit, skewers it onto a spit and balances it over the fire. He puts the pelt in a bag, and sits back again, listening to the pop and sizzle of fat, watching the firelight flicker against the night sky.

Later, when Raúl wanders away from their little camp to piss among the calafate bushes, Juan Sant follows him.

"I want to tell you about the real revolutionaries in Ushuaia," Sant says in his soft voice.

Raúl shrugs.

"The Angel was there. Radowitszky?" Raúl shakes his head. "The one who blew up the police chief in Buenos Aires during Red Week."

"I don't know anything about that." Raúl turns back towards the camp, but Sant puts a hand on his arm.

"I swear to God that man is an angel." He breaks off and wipes the back of his wrist over his eyes. "Everybody loved him."

"Who else was in there?" Raúl asks. Sant's words have curled around his mind like woodsmoke. He curses himself for wanting to know.

"There was The Piemontese— that's the name he went by. They let him out the same time as me. Nothing like The Angel, though, he'll die killing, that one. They say he still wears his prison hat." Sant pauses. "He'll be out there somewhere. There's work to be done."

Raúl shakes his head. Enough. The old man smiles, puts his hand lightly on Raúl's shoulder. Together, they pick their way back through the snow towards the camp.

The Talker crouches at the fireside with the maté bowl. In his other hand is a flask. His breath smells of whisky.

"You chilotes have a lot to say to each other."

"Not as much as you, che," Juan Sant says.

The Talker laughs, and the sound is a sneer. He takes a long swig from the flask, keeping his eyes on Juan Sant. Raúl reaches over and tears a leg from the rabbit, but The Talker has not finished. "You've heard the rumours, stranger?"

"I've heard," Sant replies, wiping his knife against his trouser leg.

Raúl grits his teeth. The rumours are everywhere, slipping like smoke between men's thoughts. He tries to block his ears to such talk. He has no appetite for picking at the scab of whispered accusations that accompanied Alice Creed's body into the ground.

The Talker is quiet, as if sobered by Sant's silence. He takes another gulp and sets the flask on the ground. "You carry a few stories yourself, they say." His eyes glint in the firelight. "If the jefe hears you're a revolutionary…"

"Why would he hear that?" Sant's knife lies still against his leg. Raúl pictures the old man crouched among the murderers and revolutionaries of Ushuaia. Despite his age and emaciated frame, Sant is a survivor, his body taut as wire. His knife glitters in the firelight.

The Talker leans back, pretending to stretch, his hand sliding toward the rifle. Two wary dogs circling each other. Before either of them can spring, Raúl is on his feet.

"Go ahead, kill each other. And me too, if you like. You think anyone would care? You got someone waiting for you?"

Silence. No one would care. All three of them know it to be true. The land would swallow them, the snow would fall, and melt, and fall again. Sant shrugs, lowers his blade to the ground. The Talker narrows his eyes at Raúl, then throws back his head and tips the whisky down his throat. The three men listen to the crackle of the fire and the hiss of sparks shooting out into the snow.

"We are doing well on this farm, Mr Revolutionary," The Talker says, eventually, his voice low and even. "And Don Ian is good to us, whatever they say about him. We don't need anybody stirring up trouble."

"You're right," Juan Sant replies, that same wry little smile playing at the corner of his mouth, perhaps nothing more than shadows thrown there by the firelight. "Nobody wants any more trouble. As long as your estanciero sticks to the agreement, he's got nothing to fear."

"He's your estanciero now," The Talker mutters under his breath.

Juan Sant nods. "So he is. And he's made some promises to his workers. Promises the unions would like him to keep."

"He keeps his promises." Raúl says, suddenly furious, and Juan Sant smiles.

"So all's well then, che. All's well."

The three of them lapse once again into silence. Sant turns away, digging at his fingernails with the knife. The Talker mumbles softly to himself and passes his flask to Raúl. The liquor spreads through Raúl's body, warming his insides. His face is burning from the heat of the fire, his back frozen in the night chill. He wants to close his eyes. When he looks up at the sky, the stars have disappeared and once again, the snow is falling.

9.

Magazines

Being Leo's governess is not arduous. In the morning, lessons. After lunch, Leo takes a nap, then we play together in the garden, if the weather permits. Mostly it doesn't. The winter days are so short, so grey and so cold, that by mid-afternoon the nurserymaid, Pilar, is already drawing Leo's bath and making preparations for his supper.

And so the days pass. I had expected – wanted – to be busy. At home, once the trickle of wounded men became a steady stream, and then a torrent, each day was a whirlwind: pedalling to the hospital, shoving my hair up under my cap as I ran onto the ward, cycling home after every shift to accompany my father on his visits. On my days off, I worked in the garden with my mother or carried milk, vegetables, murmured condolences to widows the colour of ashes with hollow-eyed children clinging to their skirts. At night I collapsed onto my little bed, too tired to stir even when I heard the soft tread of footsteps, the creak of a door opening, to Harry's room, or Hugh's, the inevitable muffled sobs as my mother sat on one or other of the empty beds.

The war took everything. Even the living felt like ghosts. Later, on the long sea voyage, when I sat alone in my tiny cabin, or on the deck, crushed by the weight of sea and sky, when I could not move for the sorrow of all that was lost, I felt I might shatter into tiny pieces. But idle hands make the devil's work, and the devil had done enough already, so I shook myself off and set about exploring the ship. I offered respite to a beleaguered mother with too many children, and read novels to an elderly lady suffering from seasickness. I took exercise with the wife of a retired colonel who called me Little Miss Eyre, and dined with the captain, an old friend of my father's, trying not to feel pleased that I was the only young lady to be invited. When I asked questions about navigation, I was allowed to visit the bridge.

Here at the estancia, there are only the Creeds. Pilar, the nurserymaid, is gentle and doe-eyed, and I wish we could be friends, but the girl speaks no English and when I try to talk, she is overcome with shyness. The other servants look at me with suspicion and duck their heads to avoid my eyes. I am afraid to approach them with my hopeless Spanish in case they laugh at me behind my back.

Days follow their pattern. While Leo sleeps or plays with Pilar, I tidy his little toy box, hoping Mrs Creed will be impressed. I line his books in alphabetical, then height order, then pull them all off the shelf and arrange them on his bedside table. I sit on the floor, surrounded by stories, pressing my face into the pages, breathing the familiar smell of childhood classics, or study my Spanish dictionary, testing new words on Leo and Pilar, trying not to lose heart when the two of them glance sideways at one another, stifling giggles.

Through the long, grey hours of solitude, I live and relive each moment that has brought me here: memories of home taken out and examined, held to the light then wrapped away again in the back of my mind, out of my own careless, clumsy reach.

*

One afternoon when Leo is asleep, I drift downstairs looking for something to do. The door to Ian's study is ajar: with a sudden impulse of curiosity, I slip inside.

The room smells of tobacco and old leather. A gun cabinet in the corner contains a pair of rifles, several silver knives in ornamental sheaths, a length of rope with leather-covered balls hanging at each end, and a small collection of skulls and fossils. At last, something exotic. I turn a skull between my hands, marvelling at the arrow sharp jaw and tiny, jagged teeth. A puma, perhaps. I glare into its empty eye sockets and give a little roar, then return it hastily to its place on the shelf.

Above Ian's desk hangs a map of Southern Patagonia. Tiny, familiar names: Punta Arenas and Río Gallegos, the immortalised horrors of Última Esperanza, Isla Desolación, Puerto del Hambre. Ice fields and frozen lakes, mountains and ragged coastlines. I follow south with my finger: the Beagle Channel, Cape Horn. Antarctica. The great explorers, Magellan, Fitzroy, Scott breathe over my shoulder. The map is elegant and beautifully drawn – my brothers would have been impressed. I feel the familiar prick of tears and turn my attention to the desk.

Ian Creed, it seems, is busy but not well organised. The desk is overflowing with papers, mostly accounts, the figures unimaginably high. I am tempted to tidy the desk, instead I pick up a copy of the Magellan Times. Among the advertisements for legal advice, farm machinery and automobiles, an announcement catches my eye: *A gang of revolutionaries made an attack on the Estancia Blythe, but were driven away with shots.*

I stand, staring at the newspaper. Before I can recover myself, the door opens. The newspaper falls from my hand.

"Georgie? Whatever are you doing?"

"Mrs Creed. I was just…" What? "I was writing to my father. I needed a blotter, and thought perhaps…" My voice trails off. Since when was I so quick to lie? Is this what it means to be beholden to somebody else? How can a governess say to her employer, I'm bored, I'm lonely, I can't bear the company of my own thoughts?

"Well, next time, come to me." Her eyes flick over the newspaper. She picks it up, folds it, drops it casually back onto the desk. "Did you find one?"

"What? Oh… I hadn't looked yet. I just came in. I'm sorry if I startled you."

"You made me jump out of my skin. But never mind."

Somewhere beneath the awkwardness it occurs to me that Mrs Creed was not the one who had jumped. But already she is waiting at the door, whatever she came into the study for apparently forgotten.

As I slink past, she lays a hand on my arm. I am terrified she is going to ask for the letter, but she says merely, "Come."

I follow her along the corridor until she stops at a door beside the kitchen, which turns out to be a small sitting room. On a table at the window sits a sewing machine. My heart stops. She must know about the dress.

But she ignores the sewing machine, bending down instead to rummage through a basket of newspapers. "I do believe there are some ladies' magazines in here," she says. "Yes, look! I was going to put them on the fire. Perhaps you would enjoy them."

I am lightheaded with relief. The magazines are years out of date and comically démodé. They would be fun to read if only there was someone to laugh with over the old-fashioned styles. In several places there are small windowpanes, tiny squares and rectangles, where the illustrations have been cut out. Someone has been making collages.

I wonder if Alice's hands flicked through the pages as mine do now. Besides the wretched dress, I have seen no evidence of Ian's dead wife, at least not in the rooms to which I am admitted. All I know is that she was slender, with beautiful taste in clothes. Even the thought of her snipping out illustrations is nothing more than my own imagination. I have tried to repair the ragged hem of her blue dress, but I'm a terrible seamstress. The dress lies hidden now, stuffed into the back of my wardrobe. Perhaps Mrs Creed did show me the sewing room on purpose, but she says nothing, her silence a gaping hole in the fabric of the household.

At night, when my bedroom is dark and the wind rattles at the casements, I am haunted by a worse fear: that Alice herself is watching, and she knows what I have done.

10.

Pig day

Time ticks. Leo and I are working our way through the nursery bookshelf: Andersen, Grimm and Lambs' Tales from Shakespeare. We are especially delighted by a book of English Folk Tales, and spend hours poring over the adventures of Childe Rowland, Jack and the Beanstalk, and the Laidly Worm. We agree that neither of us is keen on ghosts, but we love strange beasts and rides to the rescue. I commission Leo to draw me a dragon.

As he labours over the paper, an unfamiliar stirring undercuts the morning, an energetic rumble, coming from the deepest part of the house. Leo shifts in his chair and cocks his head. Before I can stop him, he has thrown his book aside and jumped to his feet.

"Leo, wait! Where are you going?"

He catches himself mid-flight and swings round to answer, his face a picture of urgency and delight.

"Georgie! Come on! It's Pig Day. Pig Day. Pig Day. Pig Day."

"Pig Day?" But he is gone, leaving only the sound of footsteps running down the stairs, jumping the last few, sprinting across the hall. By the time I reach the kitchen, he is already in the garden, skipping along the cinder path with the cook. One of Cook's fat hands is folded around Leo's small one, the other holds an enormous curved knife.

Someone has followed me into the kitchen. When I turn, Mrs Creed is at my back. "Hurry up," she says, giving me a little push. "Stay with Cook and don't go near the men."

The sticky gate is wide open. Peons are hurrying across the yard with sticks and pails. I search in vain among the unfamiliar faces for Raúl. Men duck under fences into the pig pen and advance with arms outstretched. Their wooden staves pin each shrieking animal in turn. The smallest are allowed to slip through the circle, and these gallop around the pen, absurd and panic-stricken, then stop, panting, in the farthest corner. I find Leo pressed against the fence and reach for his hand. "Leo, I don't think..." but he wriggles out of my grasp and disappears into the slaughterhouse. The peons fall back to let me through. Too late, I remember Mrs Creed's instruction: Don't go near the men.

Inside the slaughterhouse, Leo stands transfixed. I pull his face into my skirts as the huge blade flashes silver before hurtling down. The pig twists and collapses onto its side in a single contorted arc of movement. The farm boy, Álvaro, darts forward with a bucket. Blood spurts over his arms and splashes, steaming, across the wooden floor, out onto the snow.

I turn away, one hand still clutching Leo, the other pressed against my mouth. I am in the hospital. Open wounds and raw stumps. Eddie's soaked bandages. Bloody cloths, bright red, rinsed and wrung, pink water circling into drains.

I mustn't faint. I hurry Leo outside and stand in the yard, gulping cold air. Too late, I notice Lali watching with an amused smile. Leo comes to my rescue. "Pig day, Lali," he sings, pointing to the shed. "I saw the pigs."

"I know." Lali's face softens. "But you know what? I don't think your Miss Governess likes it so much."

In the hospital I learned to hold my breath and stop my ears, to keep a breezy smile on my face. Yet here I am, caught unawares by a pig. I make an apologetic face. "I know we need the bacon," I tell Lali, "but I can't help feeling sorry for them." He stares, uncomprehending. "At home we kept a pig as a pet."

His grey beard shakes with laughter. "You English. You're all the same. I've seen Englishmen who love their dogs and their horses more than their wives and children. And now it's pigs. The slaughterhouse isn't for you, Miss. Go, get yourself back inside with the Señora."

"No." The word comes out sharper than I intended. "I'm learning, Lali. Can't you see?" If I was expecting respite from blood and guts and death, then apparently I must think again. But it's too late to be squeamish. "I want to be... part of things. How else am I to be useful?" The tiny break in my voice is a betrayal.

Lali shrugs "Did the Señora say so? In that case, be my guest. But not in there." He stands back for the men as they shoulder the vast carcasses and points across the yard. "They can make use of you in the smokehouse." He hoists Leo onto his shoulders. "Why don't you come along with me, little one? Go," he adds with a nod. "Help if you must. We'll be back soon."

I hover outside the smokehouse door, hoping someone will notice. The men handle great cuts and slabs, passing them along to be rubbed and salted, ready for curing, smoking and storing, or parcelling them between blocks of ice hacked from the water butts. When I can bear it no longer, I take a few faltering steps inside and slip into a space at the end of the counter beside the cook, who nods a curt welcome. Some of the men glance sideways. My skin is crawling with self-consciousness, but they've all seen me, I can't back out now. I roll my sleeves to the elbows and set my jaw.

Cook tasks me with wrapping and packing. It is light work compared to the rest, but soon my back is aching and my fingers are blue with cold. The counter tops run red, hands split raw from salt and freezing water. From the ceiling hang hams, coils of sausages, sides of bacon. Barrels of salt pork lie alongside resident tubs of bacalao, cod, salted and dried, quite unlike anything I've ever eaten at home. Buckets of blood are stirred and thickened into slabs of black pudding.

I have no idea how much time has passed before Lali returns. He is alone.

"Where is Leo?"

"Don't look so worried. I took him home. He's with Pilar." A pause, and a small nod of approval. "You've been here all this time? You've done a good job."

His praise makes me forget the cold and the discomfort. I long for the Creeds to hear his words. Álvaro fetches a kettle, and I watch as the maté bowl passes along the counter. Always with the right hand, as Mr Chambers has written, to show the drinker is not holding a knife. When the calabaza comes, I take the straw and drink with the others.

"Look at you," Lali says. "You're a daughter of the estancia now."

If only my father could see what I have become, how in so short a time I have proved myself worthy of his faith. With the stirrings of a lost happiness, I beam at the line of workers and they stare back at me, uncomprehending. One of them nudges his neighbour. But I will not be daunted. In time, I will earn their trust.

Ian appears, framed in the smokehouse doorway and the workers fall quiet. When he sees me with Lali, he raises a hand to wave. "Georgie?" There is surprise in his voice. "Well, well. I do keep finding you in unexpected places."

Lali rescues me. "She's done well," he says, his tone jovial, approving. Cook nods in agreement. I feel the heat rise in my cheeks as the workers' eyes flicker over me, then back to Ian and away.

"Well done, Georgie. Quite something. I'm impressed," Ian says, and I breathe out in relief. He glances around the peons, his smile fixed on his face. "Looks like you've finished. Gracias a todos. Buen trabajo. Good work, every-one."

Nobody speaks.

"Right. That's it." Lali slaps his hands down onto the counter, challenging the silence. "You're done here." He nods his head toward the doorway. One by one, the men slip past him out of the smokehouse and disappear.

Afterwards, Ian and I stand together in the empty yard. "Let's get you home," he says. "You must be frozen."

My teeth are chattering with cold, but I don't care. Today I have earned my place.

"I'm terribly impressed." He steers me through the sticky gate and into the garden. "What on earth made you muck in like that?"

"I wanted to help. To be part of things. It's what I would have done at home." The word falls between us. Home. His eyes flicker, though he says nothing. Suddenly my triumph seems ridiculous, my behaviour beyond unseemly for a governess. He must have been appalled to find me in the smokehouse, up to my arms in blood. "I hope you don't mind?"

"Not at all," he says, and then again, as if convincing himself, "no, no, of course not." He falls silent and I wait, afraid to speak again. "It always used to be like that," he says at last. "My father and mother, when they first came here, they did everything themselves. It was a wild place, back then. My mother never lost the habit."

What happened? I want to ask. Where was she today, your mother?

"She would have come herself," Ian continues, as if he has read my mind, "if it wasn't…" He pauses. A little furrow forms between his brows. "Things haven't been the same since my father died." He speaks slowly, as if the words hurt him. "You must have noticed the men." I remember the peons' watchful eyes. "Times are hard, we've all had to tighten our belts. I've invested in new stock. It'll be worth it in the long run, but the unions won't wait. They want returns now, they pile on pressure, as if that helps, and turn the men against me." A mirthless laugh. "Honestly, you'd think I was the devil incarnate. My mother... it hurts her. She shouldn't take it to heart, but she can't help it. It upsets her."

We have reached the kitchen door. He takes my arm, guiding me up the steps. Inside, I stop to lean against the hearth, grateful for the warmth. "You know what, Georgie," he says, "you've impressed all of us today. Even Lali, and that's no mean feat. You're a trooper."

So the day has been a success after all. I wonder about Alice: was she a trooper? Did she roll up her sleeves and stand among the men? My heart gives a little skip of pride.

11.

The cemetery

After Pig Day, the farm becomes our playground. Leo runs among the animals, prattling in his baby voice, collecting hidden treasures: feathers from the hens, golden brown or green-black and streaked with iridescence, a speckled eggshell or a tuft of soft, grey rabbit's fur, catches of colour and light. In the yard, we lift our faces to the falling snow-flakes, or roam the fields, following tracks and footprints through the snow.

We see fresh puma prints near the corrals. "I wouldn't care if she took just one lamb," Ian tells me, "but she's teaching her cubs to hunt. They'll kill fifty between them. It's a massacre." He and Lali ride out with shotguns, but return home empty-handed.

One afternoon Leo and I wade through the snow to the tiny cemetery beneath the hill. Furthest away, a series of rough-hewn stones bear the names of half a dozen servants. Next to them, a slab of marble, cut with the name of Ian's father, Stephen Creed. At the end of the row, the earth still mounded and hard with frost, a new headstone is marked with the image of an angel and inscribed with the words *Alice and Emily Creed. Beloved mother and daughter. Angels gone to God.*

Leo is looking at the angel. "Pilar says el bebé está tocando."

"Leo. Whatever do you mean?"

"The baby knocks at night because she was left out in the cold. She wants to come inside."

"That's nonsense." I hide the tremble in my voice with sternness. "Pilar shouldn't say such dreadful things." A chill breeze, softer than cobwebs, brushes across my cheek. The gravestones seem darker now, as if a shadow has been cast over them. "Come on, Leo, let's go home."

But Leo slips his hand from mine and runs ahead through the snow to the tiny farm office. Before I can stop him, he has thrown open the door.

"Well, hello," Ian says. "To what do I owe this honour?"

"Leo." I try to sound firm. "You've said hello to your Papa. Now let's go home. We mustn't disturb him."

"Of course you're not disturbing. This is delightful." He pushes aside the heavy ledgers and gestures to a chair beside the desk. His gentle manner reminds me of my father. "Don't you love this contraption," he says, busying himself with the water heater. "Hot water on tap. Just the ticket." His face is bright with expectation. I can hear the pride in his voice.

"It's very modern." I smile admiringly, remembering Raúl's little fire among the rushes, my first maté. His hands passing the calabaza, his mouth on the straw.

"We're bang up to date here," Ian is saying. "I'm thinking of installing one of these in the bunkhouse." He laughs. "It's filthy work, farming."

His men will be happy if he gives them a water boiler. Perhaps that's why he wants to do it. "How many sheep do you have?" I ask.

"Well…" His eyes light up and I feel a rush of pleasure. Already I have learned the way to his heart. "As it happens, I've just expanded. What would you say to twenty-five thousand?"

I do my best to imagine such numbers: sheep as far as the eye can see, on the coironal and by the river, scattered across the plain and over the far-off hillsides. He pulls out pen and paper and sketches a rough map for me: roads and rivers and boundaries. I watch his hand create a world.

"Look, it's the history of everything that ever happened here. Old Man's Ford. Puma Creek. Skeleton Mesa."

"Tell me about that one," I say, leaning over to point, feeling the nearness of him.

"Oh, it's not a pretty story, I'm afraid. Lali found the remains of a dead horse out at the boundary. And the following day, about thirty miles away, at the foot of the mesa, another skeleton." His eyes flick towards Leo and he lowers his voice. "Human." I gasp, feeling my eyes widen. "It must have been the rider," Ian continues. "After he lost his horse, he would have walked as far as he could. He probably headed for the mesa so he could climb up to look for water."

"And then what happened?"

"Nothing. He just couldn't walk any further."

I shudder. "I don't ever want to go there."

"It's worth it. It's a beautiful spot."

"How can it be beautiful, knowing what happened?"

He tilts his head to one side, considering. "That's a good question. But still, I think, it can. It's not as if the land is any different, it's only the humans passing through who change things." His eyes drift away and I wonder if he is thinking of the war, of humans passing through, changing things.

"But there's a legacy, surely," I insist. "When we know someone has died?"

"I suppose so... I'm not sure. It's not like Europe here. The land is so vast, it hardly notices us. When a person dies, it just, I don't know, flicks us off, the way you flick an ant off your sleeve."

I wince, thinking of the graveyard behind the house.

"I'm sorry," he says quickly. "I meant it as a good thing. As if the land keeps its innocence, however brutal that seems. You're a good listener," he adds, pressing the map into my hand. "Keep this. When the days seem long you can take it out and look at all the places we'll explore when the weather gets better." I tuck the map inside my coat, and fancy I can feel it next to my heart.

Ian settles deeper into his chair, telling stories of sheep in the frigorificos, trucks and ships; sheep on their way to England, amassing fortunes along the way. Twenty-five thousand sheep yielding almost ninety thousand kilos of wool, hauled in vast bales to the port at Río Gallegos, shipped across the Atlantic towards the European winter.

"The war was good for us in that respect," he says. "The army needed winter uniforms. It was cold in France."

I frown, imagining my two brothers dressed for war. Eddie's greatcoat against my cheek.

"Oh, I don't mean there was anything good about the war," Ian continues hastily. "But it's nice to have one's work rewarded. They needed wool, and we were able to provide it. I liked to think I was wearing my own sheep when I was in France."

*

I lie in bed, my mind drifting with the flakes of snow that whirl against the blackened windowpane. Why should it matter that Ian profited, if the war was fought in God's own name? At first, when it was going to be over in just a few months, I truly believed that God was on our side. But when the months dragged on and the telegrams started to arrive, a new and terrifying idea occurred to me: what if God was listening to someone else's prayers?

There was a dull-eyed woman who came to church with purple bruises on her face. Her smallest girl wore callipers from the polio, the oldest boy, not more than eight or nine years old, was known already as a troublemaker. Once, she came leaning on a stick, wincing with every step; the parish tutted and sighed its sympathy as she struggled up the path. Her name was Sarah Gerard, but she was known to every-one as 'poor Mrs Gerard,' or simply 'that poor woman'.

When poor Mrs Gerard's husband left for France, the bruises disappeared. A stranger, known to the children as Uncle, moved into their cottage at the end of the lane. Sarah Gerard continued to come to church, but the air around her grew thick with condemnation, the congregation held her apart, as if her prayers might contaminate the rest. I prayed with everyone else for the safe return of all our soldiers, including Sarah Gerard's husband. I dared not imagine what Sarah might be asking God.

How strange that of everyone in our small village, all the gossips and do-gooders, rich and poor, bereaved and bereft, the memory of this sad woman has followed me to the other side of the world. Sarah Gerard didn't even stay in the parish. Uncle disappeared and the little girl with callipers died of the Spanish flu. Sarah's belly grew round, protruding from her scrawny frame. This was the final straw: a message was sent from the parishioners via my father that she must stop coming to church. One night, she packed up her remaining children and vanished. Nobody ever heard from her again.

Tonight, the house is alive with thuds and whispers, it moans as if its timbers are still at sea. Downstairs, Ian Creed sits alone in his study. The war is over. There is nothing left to pray for but the sorrow of the living and the souls of the dead. I am about to blow out the candle when I catch a tiny sound beneath the wind. Knocking, gentle and insistent. Once, at home, my mother's eyes emptied and she swore, shrieking, that she could see my brothers. My father took her outstretched arms and fought them to her sides: There are no such things as ghosts. I believed him. I never felt them in our house. But this is different. My skin is cold, my hair stands on end. I tell myself it is not knocking, it must be the wind, a tree scraping against a window, but the thought of someone outside my room is more than I can bear. I have to see for myself. I summon every ounce of courage I ever had and open the bedroom door, holding my candle high.

The knocking stops. Chill air blows through cracks in the windows, lifting the curtains. My muscles move of their own intent. I fly back inside the room and leap into bed, pulling the pillow around my ears, waiting for daylight.

12

Ángel

In the morning, a vague feeling of unease hangs over the dining room. The Creeds seem listless. Perhaps they too have been disturbed by the noises in the night.

Leo is pulling at my hand. "Georgie, I want to go out. I want to play on the farm with Papa."

"Why don't you skip lessons this morning," Mrs Creed says. "You could all do something together."

Ian opens his mouth to respond and she holds up her hand to silence him. It is impossible to decipher the unspoken communication passing between them.

"You're right," he says at last. "I don't have much to do today."

"Excellent. Have a good morning." With a nod of encouragement, she is gone.

"Here's an idea, Georgie," Ian says, turning back to me. "The weather's not bad today. How about we go for a ride?"

"Oh no," I say, before I can contain myself. I am not sure I have the gumption to attempt a riding lesson. "If it's not convenient…"

"Why would it not be convenient?"

How can I tell him I see exhaustion in the lines around his mouth, the dull glaze of his eyes? That I recognise the way he pushes his hair back from his forehead and rests his cheek against his hand? "I'm… I didn't sleep too well."

"Really?" Now he is looking at me solicitously. "Why couldn't you sleep?"

"The wind, I suppose. It was particularly loud, don't you think?"

"Was it? I didn't notice. Actually…" He glances at Leo, who is puttering in the corner, making tiny growling noises at the dog, "I had rather a bad dream. I get them, sometimes." At once he turns his head away, as if regretting that he has spoken. How lonely he must be, to have revealed even this much. "Anyway." Another forced smile. "The weather's set fair. What do you think, Georgie? Are you game?"

How can I refuse again without giving offence? "If you're quite sure…"

"Of course I'm sure. I promised, didn't I?"

I catch the crack in his voice and dare not question him further. "In that case…" I try to muster some enthusiasm.

"It's very easy. The saddles are like armchairs and the loose rein is much simpler than the English way. We'll get you a steady animal. A good pingo. Horsebreaker can choose one for you."

We find Raúl in the saddle room. The sharp winter air has shivered me awake, and I begin to feel a tingle of excitement. I draw deep breaths of the rich, comforting smells of horses, mixed with linseed, leather and bran. Raúl puts aside the bridle he is oiling, wipes his hands, and hoists Leo into his lap. The child leans against Raúl's chest, his small body softening. No wonder this man wins the trust of horses. The strength of my opinion takes me by surprise.

"We need something very steady," Ian is saying, in English. "A good personality for a lady. Not dull, but trustworthy. Utterly reliable."

Raúl looks at me with his head on one side, considering, and it occurs to me that Ian's description is a good fit for the horse breaker himself. A slow flush is creeping up my neck, and over my cheeks. It must be nerves. I lower my eyes to avoid his gaze, but he has already turned back to Ian.

"Yes, Señor. I have one we could try out for the Señorita. He is coming along very well. His name is Ángel."

Ángel. Leo jumps up and down beside me shouting, "Ángel, Ángel," and Raúl laughs, tousling his hair. "Hush, little one. You got to be calm. You'll frighten him."

We walk through the tangle of barns and outbuildings to a paddock where a dozen or so horses graze together.

"Why not him?" Ian points to a pretty chestnut.

Raúl shakes his head. "Not that one, Señor. He is good, but… escarciador."

I look at Ian, who shrugs. "Chews on the bit, apparently. Horsebreaker thinks he's not good enough for you."

Raúl has slipped through the fence and is pushing between the group towards a small grey with a broad, wise forehead. The horse lifts its head at the sight of him. Its nostrils flare.

I experience a sudden shudder of dismay. Faced with a real animal, my limbs seem to separate from my body. Raúl throws pads and sheepskins over the little horse's back, pulling down leathers and tightening straps. My own chest tightens. But it is too late to back out now. I remember Raúl's words as we sat together on the wagon: Watch the horses, Miss, they see everything. I watch Ángel, trying to interpret the flicker of his ears, but understand nothing except that I am afraid.

Lali has joined us.

"Look, Lali." Leo dances in front of him. "Georgie is to have Ángel. Papa is teaching her."

"Is that so?" Lali raises his eyebrows and I force a smile, trying to quell the churning in my stomach. Raúl is waiting at Ángel's side. They are all watching, but the saddle is impossibly high. Raúl cups his hand. I take a deep breath, put my toe into his palm, and he lifts me straight up, like an acrobat. With a lightness I had not thought possible, I hover in the air, my other leg swings up and over, and I am on top of the horse, looking down at Raúl as he stands back, wiping his hands.

"I'll take care of Miss Georgie now." Ian holds out his walking stick, and Raúl takes it with a nod. Ian pulls himself up onto his Rajah, reaches for the halter, and leads me through the yard, where the farm boy, Álvaro, drops his buckets to stare. Out on the ridge, Ángel throws up his head and I clutch at the mane with a little shriek as we break into a trot. Ian laughs.

"Sit back. Relax. You're making him nervous."

"What do you mean? I'm the one who's nervous."

"Sit back," he says again. "Don't try to lean forward, this isn't the English way. Let your legs stretch out. And the reins just in one hand, see?" He shows me how to swing the reins across Ángel's neck, how flexibly the little horse can twist and turn, how responsive he is to my hands.

"The horses are all broken to work with sheep. They're used to changing direction. Look, it's easy once he understands what you want."

It is astonishing to be part of another living creature, to feel its breath, its power. I am giddy with excitement. "I can't believe it, Ian. This is wonderful."

"You're easy to please," he says, smiling.

A coil of hair blows across my face, catching the corner of my mouth. I shake my head, lift my hand to tuck it behind my ear, and there, in front of me, is Eddie, the old Eddie, winding loose tendrils between his fingers, brushing my face so lightly, so tenderly that I have to bite my lip to prevent myself from crying out aloud. Remarkable how the detail of his pale, slender hands can fill my whole mind, and at the same time I can pull away and see the two of us together as if from above, like looking at myself through a telescope. I am there and not there. I am watching from above and I am leaning against him, feeling the pressure of his body against mine. His twisting fingers send a shiver through me. If I move, he will disappear.

"Do you know," Eddie says, "this is the part of you I'm going to miss most. You carry your whole self in your hair."

He laughs and the sound makes me ache with delight and desire. "Soft, and pretty, and never quite under control. Reckless."

"Reckless? What on earth do you mean?" I am astonished.

"Oh, I wasn't being serious. Anyway, it's a compliment." He cups my face between his hands. As I lift my lips to his, a breeze flutters the curls back across my mouth. He blows them aside with a smile and a little flick of his head, the gesture so perfectly Eddie, so light and funny and entrancing that I want to throw myself into his arms and smother him with kisses.

Ian is still talking. He hasn't noticed anything. "You look marvellous, Georgie. You'll be charging all over the place in no time. We won't be able to stop you."

"What? Oh, yes." The excitement has drained from my body and the cold bites through my bones. Eddie is gone. Only the plain unfurls before me, bright with snow. Nothing but empty space, and the end of the world itself. "Yes," I tell him. "You won't be able to stop me."

13.

Raúl and Georgie ride

Out on the plain, Ian seems to recover a missing part of himself. His cheeks glow and his eyes sparkle. He points out plants and tells me the names of birds that fly up from under the horses' hooves. Sometimes he stands in his stirrups to gaze over the drowsing sheep. They lift their heads and scatter as the horses pass, then shoal back together into a shifting grey mass that flows across the snow. To my great disappointment, I am not a natural horsewoman, at least not yet: both Ángel and I know I am entirely dependent on the little horse's good grace. I squeal with fear and cling to the saddle when Ángel snorts and swerves at hares zigzagging through the gnarled stalks of the calafate. Ian reaches over, laughing, to grab the bridle, and our mingled voices vanish into the wind, the grasses whipping our legs as we fly side by side across the plain.

I carry Ian's little map wherever we go, adding names and symbols for each new discovery. The first time I jump down from Ángel, resting the paper on my knee, Ian leans over my shoulder.

"My word, that's rather good. Where did you learn to do that?"

"My brothers," I tell him. "Harry was a surveyor, in the war. And Hugh…" I fall silent. My mother wept for a week when Hugh joined the RFC. But someone has to go up and take the pictures, he told us. Otherwise, what's old Harry going to draw on his maps? And in the end, it was Harry who died first, his beautiful drawings inadequate protection against a perfectly targeted German shell. Someone on the other side must have drawn accurately too. He died a whole four months before Hugh, even though it was Hugh who flew his plane so low, like a daredevil in the circus, that none of us could believe he would survive a single night. But that was Hugh. If he hadn't been lost to the war, perhaps he would have been a pilot anyway.

Harry, of course, would always have been a cartographer. While Hugh ran around us making engine noises, Harry and I pored over the atlas, discovering oceans and continents, poles and capes, the meridians of longitude and parallels of latitude. We persuaded our father to invest in a pantograph so we could copy maps to scale. Later, Harry studied trigonometry, and talked about the principles of topographic field-work. The first time he saw a theodolite was probably the happiest day of his life. We were visiting a friend of my father's; I wanted to see the theodolite too, but my mother pulled me away. Don't be selfish, Georgie. Today is for Harry, not you. Later, Harry drew me a picture to explain how it worked. I read his textbooks, trying to make my sketches look like real maps. Mixed burnt sienna for the contours. Black for culture. Prussian blue for drainage. If I had been born a boy, I too would have been a cartographer.

"Well," Ian says again, "it's terribly good. I wish you'd told me. You could have drawn us a much better one to begin with. In fact, I think you should."

I shake my head. "No, no. I love this one." But the idea takes shape in my mind: I will make a map for him. A map of the estancia.

*

Ian says, "I've got an idea. Horsebreaker is going up to the winter pastures to check on the horses. Why don't you go with him? It'll be an adventure."

A quiver of excitement, followed at once by doubt. "What if I can't keep up?"

"Oh, he'll take care of you. And it's not far, only a couple of hours. You'll enjoy it. You can do some of your drawings."

*

I am queasy with nerves as I follow Raúl over the ridge. But he sets out at a gentle pace, the softest gaucho trot, turning round to check on me, sometimes reining back to whisper a few words to Ángel, who snorts and tosses his head in response. The puppy snuffles the snow and barks at rabbits. When Raúl whistles, it falls in behind and runs at our heels.

We reach a long stretch of flat, open ground and Raúl gestures: shall we go faster? I take a deep breath, ignoring the butterflies in my stomach, the anxious patter of my heart. Raúl spurs his long-legged Hero, and Ángel kicks up his heels with a little whinny, stretches his neck, and sets off in pursuit. Snow flies, whipping our faces. By the time we reach the river, my cheeks are hot, and I am gasping for breath.

"Güen? Alright?" he asks, leading us along the path beside the frozen stream, twisting round in his saddle to check that I am following. The horses pick their way in single file along a narrowing track until we reach a steep, rock-strewn ridge. Hero leaps upwards in a churn of snow. I let out a shriek, terrified Ángel will slip on the icy rocks. Raúl turns, laughing, but when he sees my face, he jumps down to hold Ángel's bridle as the little horse lunges up the path onto surer ground. Sheep lift their heads, watching with cautious eyes.

At the far side of the meadow, the track dead-ends in an impenetrable barrier of scree and undergrowth.

"To the neck," Raúl calls, in English, ducking to avoid the tangle of branches, and I drop forward, my nose pressed against Ángel's mane, trusting the little horse to follow in Hero's footsteps.

On the other side of the trees, Raúl stops to hoist the puppy into his lap. "Señorita, we have to go in the river now."

His soft accented English makes it sound like a question. As if I have a choice. I grip the reins tight as Ángel slides down the bank towards the freezing water, hesitates, finds his feet, and jumps down. I cry out, lifting my legs clear as the horses slosh over pebbles, breaking ice with their hooves. I am almost disappointed when we round a curve in the river and Raúl leads us back up the bank. My heart is still beating from the adventure. I feel brave and strong, like a real gaucha.

He stops to let me rest, and I sketch the snowfields, the river and the copse. Later, I will add the drawings to my map, retracing my journey across paper, laying down the memory.

"So where are you from then, Raúl, in Chile?"

He looks at me through narrowed eyes. "My father was Argentinian. But my mother was from Chiloé. I was born there."

I have spent hours poring over maps of Patagonia. I have seen the jagged peaks of the Andes, the jigsaw puzzle of fjords along the Pacific coast. I have seen Chiloé.

"I'm from an island too, you know. What's it like, Chiloé?"

"I don't remember, Miss." His voice is flat, final. A memory rises, unbidden, from Mr Chambers' travel guide: *Chilotes are generally considered a brutal and inferior race, only marginally more developed than the Indians.*

The puppy noses against Raúl and he runs a gentle hand over its head. He doesn't seem brutal or inferior.

When we reach the top of the hill, Raúl stops, and holds out a hand.

"What?" I whisper. "What is it?"

"You see them?" I squint at the horizon. Dark shapes moving on the hillside. Horses. "We must go slowly," he says, "or they will run away." He whistles softly and the puppy falls in behind.

"Are they wild?"

"No... and yes. I know them. They were born on the estancia, but they have not yet been tamed."

The horses have gathered, heads raised, poised for flight. There is an electric stillness in their watching. Raúl points at the herd, his voice low. "You see the leader?" The stallion stands in front, pawing the ground.

"He's protecting them, isn't he?"

"Yes. But they are curious." He puts a finger to his lips. Watch the horses.

Hero whinnies, and a reply ripples back from the herd. The horses move closer, stopping to sniff the air. I can feel Ángel trembling beneath me. His ears flicker. Then the leader throws up his head and wheels round. The herd follows.

"Oh. They are so beautiful. It's like – I don't know – it's like magic."

Raúl says nothing, but he is smiling. His face is rapt. From a distance, the horses lift their heads and gaze back at us with calm curiosity before they drift away, nosing the snow for food. Raúl waves a hand. "You see that one – dark, with the white nose? Malacara. I like him very much."

"And you'll break him in?" I ask. "How do you do it?"

"I will show you," he answers, and his eyes are shining. "I will show you in the spring."

He will show me. I could hug him for his promise. I am dreaming of horses. Already I am dreaming of the spring.

We ride on in silence, listening to the wind in the long grass. From time to time I twist in the saddle, hoping for one last glimpse, but the horses have vanished. The memory of them, so perfect and so wild, has sparked new life in me, as if a great weight has lifted from my heart, as if I have witnessed Eden itself. Tears prick my eyes.

Raúl rides close to the fences, checking, jumping down to twist a sagging line straight, or set a leaning post upright. In one place he examines two lengths of wire, snapped exactly in the middle between the posts, as if cut with a pair of scissors.

"What's the matter?"

"Nothing." He drops the wire, frowning.

Further along, we find the body of a baby guanaco caught in the fence. "The herd jumped over," Raúl explains. "But this one is too small."

"It must have been so afraid." I try not to imagine its desperation.

"They don't understand fences," he answers with a shrug.

"You're not leaving it there?" I can't bear to see the tiny creature's arched throat and empty eyes, its slender legs trapped in the pitiless wire.

He looks surprised. "You want it?"

"No… I… I thought you'd take it down, that's all."

He turns back, pulling out his long knife. I close my eyes as he cuts the guanaco free and throws the little brown body into the trees.

When we reach the steep path, Raúl dismounts without a word to lead Ángel, his back braced against the horse's shoulder, slipping on rocks and scree. I cling to the saddle and throw my own weight backwards. At the bottom of the hill, Raúl is breathing hard, I can see his chest rise and fall beneath his cape. He reaches down and puts a handful of snow to his mouth, then swings himself back up onto Hero and kicks forward into a steady trot.

Ángel, recognising the road home, pulls alongside, and where the track narrows, the horses' flanks touch. My knee brushes against Raúl's leg. I try to turn Ángel away, but he tosses his head and takes the bit between his teeth. Our legs are pressed together between the two horses. Raúl glances down and kicks Hero forward. "I'm sorry, Miss," he says softly. Mortified, I haul on the reins, trying to look as if I haven't noticed. All the way home, I feel the echo of his knee against mine.

By the time we reach the yard, I am stiff with cold and weariness. Raúl catches me as I slip from the saddle. His hands are warm through my coat, holding me.

"I'm sorry," I say. "I'm so cold. My legs are giving way."

He looks down at me gravely, his face very close. His breath blows like smoke across my face. "You did well, Miss."

"I'm only a beginner, you know."

His forehead is broad, his black eyes liquid beneath those straight brows and thick, dark lashes. Eyes the girls at home would have gossiped and squabbled over like sparrows. He smiles, and the seriousness gives way to a flash of something warm and kind. "Yes, Miss. I know."

14

Georgie's diary

I run up the stairs two at a time. I can still feel the warmth of Raúl's hands around my waist, our legs pressed together between the horses. I want to lie down on my bed, pull the memory tight inside myself. But when I arrive at my room, the door is ajar. I pause, holding my breath. The relentless wind seeps through every crack, blowing icy draughts along the corridors. Yet another rule: all doors, inside and out, are to be kept closed. Windows, too, unless secured by their hooks. A sudden gust can shatter glass. I give a little push and the door swings away from my fingers. I stand for a moment on the threshold, not quite daring to step inside. Everything is as I have left it: my dress flung over the arm of my little wicker chair, my meagre possessions – hairbrushes and combs, a few books – scattered across the dressing table. Nonetheless, there is a prickling sensation at the back of my neck, as though someone has been here just before I arrived.

My journal lies open on the bed. I flick past my arrival – hasty accounts of the demonstration, the mad girl at the port, long descriptions of the wagon and the plain – to sketches made from the nursery window. Paper filled with blue-grey hummocks of snow. Empty white skies and distant hills in palest lavender. When I look up, the plain stretches away in front of me. When I look down, I am holding it in my hands.

Apart from the sketches, my scrawlings consist mainly of lists.

Animals I have seen: Patagonian hare, Guanaco, Ostrich, Caiquén, Flamingo

Bandurria – its beak as long as a straw for sucking worms out of the ground

Queltehue – southern lapwing (according to Mr. Chambers), armed with sharp feathers for attacking its prey

Caranchos – crow vultures, brooding and vile, harbingers of death

Condors – the males have a white collar around their necks, the females are plain black. The tips of their wings are jointed, so they can steer better when gliding on the wind

Still to see:

Armadillo. Ian tells me they are hibernating. The men call them Pichi, and bake them in their armour

Puma, Sloth – a Milodon, perhaps

How naïve I sound, how childish. The Creeds were among the first to visit the Milodon caves after their discovery. They entertained Captain Eberhardt himself, back when Germans were still acceptable. They dined with Shackleton in Punta Arenas and attended service with him at the English Church. The Creeds were true pioneers.

I flick over a couple more pages.

Mrs Creed never goes beyond the sticky gate. She doesn't speak a word of Spanish, and makes everyone speak to her in English, but sometimes she uses Spanish words as if they were English, like The Camp when she's referring to the land – the campo. And it works the other way round, too. My favourite is reque – the practice of salvaging building materials from a wreck. What a strange place this is, where everything, even language, can be invented out of everything else.

I wonder what happened to Stephen Creed. I wonder how he died.

The words shiver, as if someone has opened the pages and

read my questions aloud. I toss the journal back onto the bed. Don't be ridiculous, I forgot to close the door behind me, nothing more. As the leaves flutter and settle, a dog-eared photograph falls loose onto the coverlet. I touch each of my brothers to my lips, then tuck the photograph back inside the cover, where it lives alongside a postcard from Eddie. Brief as it is – how typical of Eddie – it is the only thing I have left of him now. I know the words by heart.

My darling Georgie. I've just received your magnificent letter, and I'm smiling out loud at your stories. Here, there is nothing but waiting. Mud, of course, and weather, but that's about it. Leave coming up soon. Not long now, my dearest, not long. Your own Eddie.

Not long now, my dearest. Back then, Eddie had been my first and last, my every thought. Since my arrival in Patagonia, without my even noticing, the memories have become more infrequent. Now, when I think of him, it is more with relief than with regret.

Today, though, memory catches me unawares. Despite myself, I long to see his handwriting on the little card. That faded ink holds something of Eddie himself. A sob catches in my throat at the thought of him in his uniform, the courage in his smile.

But behind the photograph of my brothers, where the postcard should be, lies only the flat, empty cover of the journal. I pick up the book again and shake it. Nothing. I smooth my hands across the bedcover, bend down to look beneath the bed. I open drawers, toss clothes aside, pull my bag from the wardrobe, unlock my trunk and feel around all the pockets and corners, even though I know perfectly well that I have seen the postcard tucked inside the jour-nal countless times since I unpacked. I stand, trembling, in the middle of the room, surveying the chaos around me. The postcard is gone. Someone has taken it from my diary, pausing perhaps to read my stupid, judgmental little observations.

A small figure appears in the doorway.

"Georgie," Leo says, rubbing his eyes. "I'm hungry."

"Oh, darling. Yes, of course." I stuff clothes back into the wardrobe. "Leo – have you been looking at my journal?" He stares at me, uncomprehending. Of course he hasn't. "It's just – I've lost a postcard."

He is surveying the chaos. "Your bedroom looks like a carancho's nest."

"I've been having a search. Will you help me?"

"Grandmama is looking at her letters today too."

"Is she? Really?"

"Come and see." He tugs at my hand.

"No… wait Leo, no. I don't want to speak to your Grandmama." But he has let go of my hand and disappeared. I run after him, too late. Already he has burst into Mrs Creed's bedroom. I pull up short behind him in the doorway.

His grandmother is sitting by her dressing table. Her wardrobe is open, a drawer at the back pulled out, a wooden box on the floor. All around her are letters, some folded and tied with ribbon, others opened as if she has spread them out to read.

"Georgie. Do you want something?" She looks startled. Leo must have taken her by surprise.

"My diary." I say, helplessly. "Someone's been reading my diary."

"Are you sure?" Her hand moves over her letters, covering them. "How do you know?"

"Something is missing. A postcard…"

"Really? I'm sure it's there somewhere. You're not very organised, are you?"

"Her room is a carancho's nest," Leo says.

"There. You see. Honestly, Georgie, what on earth will you do when you're married? How will you manage a house of your own?"

I feel my face glowing. I want to say, how dare you talk to me about getting married? This has nothing to do with me being disorganised, I've looked everywhere, and I know you've taken it because you have been watching me and you have read my diary.

"Sit down," she says. "I've been reading some old correspondence." She waves her hand over the pile of letters. "Do you know, it's made me feel terribly nostalgic." She isn't trying to conceal anything. I begin to feel foolish.

I perch on a low wooden chair, hands folded in my lap. The dressing table is lined with photographs: Stephen Creed, playing billiards, careless and handsome as he leans across the table; Ian as a little boy astride a donkey, wearing a straw hat; a young woman in a wedding dress gazing out from beneath her veil with huge, dead eyes. A family history. Faded sepia images turning their subjects into ghosts. Perhaps, at last, I will learn something about the lost Creeds.

Sure enough, she points to one of the photographs. Three stiff little girls in lace collars. "My sisters," she says. "I'm the only one left. That one..." the dark-haired girl on the right side of the frame "...died not long after this picture was taken. Typhoid. The other one..." she indicates the smallest of the three "...just recently. The Spanish flu."

So the girl in the middle, relentless black hair, straight back and piercing stare, is Maud Creed herself.

"Do you miss them?" I ask, without thinking.

"I do now," she says, without a trace of sadness in her voice. "When Ian's father was alive, I didn't miss anybody. He was all I ever wanted." She points to another photograph: Stephen Creed, dressed for riding this time, standing in front of the house. "Stephen was a wonderful man. We grew up together. He built this house." She sounds dreamy, as though her thoughts are very far away. "There was nothing when he came here. Nothing at all. The camp was a wilderness. But Stephen wasn't afraid of anything. He built this house for me."

"Were you afraid?"

"Oh no, I don't think so. Not with Stephen. Of course,

there were terrible dangers at the beginning. Pumas, bandits, he saw them all off. He traded with the Indians. We were all safe when he was here. This was the most perfect home anyone could ever dream of."

She looks straight into my eyes. "It was a riding accident, you know."

"I'm sorry?" I am lost, dreaming of the Creeds' perfect home.

"Stephen. In case you were wondering. That's how he died. It was wintertime. He was crossing the river and his horse slipped on the ice. It fell backwards and Stephen fell underneath it, onto the rocks. He broke his back."

So she has read my diary, my stupid, humiliating questions. "I'm sorry. I'm so sorry."

"Yes," she says. "Well. It was a long time ago. Accidents happen here. They happen and they can't be helped." She stops abruptly. "Everything's different now."

"Now?" I prompt.

"It's different," she repeats. "The danger's on the inside." The intensity in her voice makes me shiver. Her eyes flicker over my shoulder to Leo, sitting on the floor beside the fire. She leans forward and grips my wrist, pulling me closer. "They say things about Ian. Cruel, terrible things. Remember, dear, whatever you hear, it's all lies." The words hang in the air between us. No wonder she refuses to go beyond the sticky gate, or to speak to anyone in Spanish. "I won't hear of it," she says, as if she has read my thoughts. "Ian's a dear, good boy, and this is his home. His father built it, we made it what it is and God knows, we have earned our right to this place. Anyway..." She seems to want to say more. I wait, but she adds only, "Go. Leo will help you look for your postcard. It's bound to be in your room somewhere."

As we leave, Leo tucks his hand inside mine and whispers, "I think it was the ghost who took your card, Georgie. Grandmama doesn't know about the ghost."

A week later, I find the postcard where it had slipped through a crack in the wardrobe floor. I sit on the bed, turning it between my hands, feeling Eddie's words beneath my fingers. Am I really so disorganised? I am too embarrassed to tell Mrs Creed: my stupid accusation hangs unresolved between us. I'm not sure I will ever be able to look at the card again.

15.

The girl who was let go

The girl who was let go turned up at the house in Río Gallegos about a month after she disappeared from the estancia. Raúl walked inside stamping snow from his boots, feeling in his pocket for coins, and there she was, crouched beside the fire, arms wrapped tight around her knees. He didn't recognise her at first. Her hair fell in rats' tails across her eyes, her face was scarred and pinched with fear. He had forgotten how young she was. His first reaction was one of relief: she wasn't dead. Everyone said she must have died, her boot prints disappearing into falling snow. He would have helped her, they all would, but she left in the night and no one knew she was gone until it was too late and she was dead.

Now that she was alive, and safe enough, his relief turned to anger: what kind of stupid girl would tell such stupid lies? She deserved to be let go. Though not like that. If Lali had known, he would not have let it happen. When the men found out what the Creeds had done, letting her go in the night like that, anger rippled across the farm. The rumour she'd spread about the young Señora's death took strength and held. There were other revenges too: since that time, Ian Creed's reputation has been hanging by the slashed wires of his own fences.

Raúl pretended not to see her, but it was too late. The sight of him had set her shaking and she buried her head in her arms, like a child trying to make itself invisible. Teresa, the gentlest of the women, caught his eye and tapped her forefinger against her temple: she's crazy. But he knew that already, from the lies she'd spread.

"She's never told us anything," Teresa whispered, "except she's sorry for something she said that wasn't true. She had a man, he was with the union, she thinks he's dead now. Some gauchos found her and kept her for a while, then she ended up here, with us. She was alright until she saw you."

She was alright until she saw you. He was repelled, both by the story and by the implication. The faces of the women were more than he could bear, he wanted to leave, but that would look like fear. Instead he crossed the room and sat beside the fire, not too close. She bared her teeth, but he stayed still, said nothing, until her breathing slowed.

"I didn't tell," she whispered. "Only one, and I told him it was a secret. On my life, I swear it."

On her life. It had cost her almost that. "But you lied. You didn't see anything. Did you?"

"I lied. I didn't see anything."

She was a stupid girl who made up lies. Nothing more.

*

Since that first time, he got used to seeing her crouched by the fire, her eyes glazed with laudanum or whatever they gave her so she could do her work. Most visitors avoided her haunted face, looking instead for softer, more tender bodies; she was left with men who wanted something the other women wouldn't do. They were not unkind to her, the women: Teresa, motherly and soft, Verónica, tall and black-browed and decent enough. Sometimes Raúl took pity and gave the girl a few coins. He told no one, not even Lali, though there must have been others from the estancia who visited the house and saw her there. He noticed how she gathered shiny objects, hoarding them like a carancho, how she played with them when nobody was watching. She hardly ever laughed, but when she did, she covered her mouth with her hand.

She might have been from Uruguay, or some place far away in the north. She talked of sunlight, of returning home. Once he told her of his own dream, how he was saving money to buy horses, a plot of land. As he spoke, her face softened and her eyes grew hazy.

"What will you do?" she asked him.

"Have you heard of Héctor Torres, the famous horse breaker?" he asked her. "I saw him once, and he told me when I was ready, he would help me."

She nodded. "If he helps you, you will have good fortune."

He felt a swelling in his chest, the excitement of knowing he would have good fortune.

She turned to him with a smile on her face. "It's a beautiful dream, Horsebreaker." She ran a finger lightly down his arm. "I could stay with you, on your farm." She leaned closer. "You'd like that, wouldn't you?"

He could feel the pulse of her, the pressure of her fingertip against his skin. It was true, he could take her to live with him among his horses. But there was no place in his dream for a woman like her.

If she had dreams of her own, he did not think to ask.

*

Half a year later, soon after the trouble had started again, Raúl came to the house, and she was gone. It wasn't in his nature to be curious, all his life, men and women had come and gone without a backward glance, but something in the faces of the other women troubled him. They curled their arms around his neck, Teresa whispered into his ear that the girl had offended a client, a man with a monstrous ego. She was at the police station; the police had threatened to close the house. Raúl stood up to leave. He was sorry, but her mistakes were none of his business. Living in this house had always been borrowed time for such a girl, one who made trouble, or let trouble find its way to her. But the women tightened their arms around him. She's done nothing, Verónica told him in her fierce, proud voice. Maybe the man had demanded something unusual and she had angered him by asking for more money. Or maybe he couldn't get it to work, he had tried, she had tried, his masculinity had been exposed and he was enraged. It happened. Most men were content to give a girl a black eye and leave without paying, but the one she had offended, he was spiteful, he told the police she stole from him. Now she was in the prison, which was bad enough, but if the police knew she had been connected to a striker, they would make it worse for her, for everybody. They would close the house and everyone would lose their living. The women begged, the injustice gnawed at Raúl's mind, until, against his better judgement, he found himself agreeing to carry their money to the prison to get her out.

He had never seen the prison. He never had business on that side of the town. The silence of the compound made his chest tighten and his heart beat wildly. Wire fences and low windowless buildings. Slouching men in uniform, hats pulled low across their eyes, hands resting casually on the batons that hung from their hips. A spidery sickness crawled across his skin, a fear that once inside they might never let him out.

The guard held out his hand without a word. In an airless little office, more police took more money. When he asked for the girl, their eyes glittered, and their mouths curled. He flinched from the knowingness in their stares. They made him hand over all the money he had, then pushed him away: there will be paperwork, she'll be out this afternoon. He stood his ground, insisting he would wait, and their hands closed around their batons. Wait then, if you want, but outside the gate. And don't expect us to hurry. He felt the blood drain from his face as he understood what they would do before they let her go.

Two of them walked him outside and locked the gate behind him. He was so grateful to be free that he sighed aloud, and they burst out laughing. He turned and walked away, back to the yard where he had left Hero. He had lain his head for a long time against the horse's flank, breathing his warmth and strength, then ridden out of the town, leaning into the wind, gulping air, trying to clean the memory of laughter from his body.

*

Since that time, he avoided the house. Being in the town unsettled him, even when he returned on his regular errands. One late summer morning, he came out of the general store, laden with sacks of grain and tools and saddlery and saw her standing in the road. His stomach lurched, remembering the prison, the police, the gleam on sweaty faces. And on top of the sickness, a shameful tightening in his groin.

He hesitated, ready to run back inside. She must have sensed his indecision, because she lifted her head and looked directly at him. Carefully, deliberately, he carried the supplies to his wagon, then turned back, brittle with self-consciousness. Her face was thinner than he remembered. Her eyes were red, her shoulders drooped. She didn't bother with a greeting, simply gave him a weary nod of acknowledgement. All the intensity of feeling drained from him.

"We have to leave," she said. He followed her gaze along the road to a battered wagon. Verónica stood beside a shabby suitcase. Teresa held a child hitched on her hip. "All of us. They don't leave us alone. Because of me."

Always walking into trouble, like it was a hole in the ground.

He dug deep into his pocket and pushed coins into her hand. She managed a half smile, shoving the coins inside her blouse, then ran her finger lightly down his arm.

"I could come with you, Horsebreaker, to your farm."

He stared at her. It was true, on his farm she would be safe, no one would touch her. But his dreams were of himself, of Lali, and of Hero. When he didn't move, she gave him an odd little salute, picked up her bag and turned away.

The prison

They said I was lucky to go to prison in the summer: in winter, the walls froze on the inside. I believed them, even though it was ice-cold in summer too, the wind so strong the whole building shivered. The days were long, though, and when sunshine slipped through doors and windows, we closed our eyes and held our faces to the light.

An old woman came to the prison with a basket, handing out food. She was so old and polite to everyone, the police thought she was harmless, but we all knew she was passing messages for the strikers. My own dear gaucho was with the strikers and if the police had put him into prison instead of shooting him dead, she would have brought messages for him. I never found out why they shot him, except that he was with the strikers, and that, it seemed, was enough.

The woman told us stories about a prison angel, Simon Radowitsky his name was, a true revolutionary. She wasn't religious but she prayed for him, an anarchist's prayer, that he be set free to save us all. I said the anarchist's prayer with her and it worked, because somebody did get me out of there in the end. I don't think it was the old lady, or the angel Radowitsky that she talked about, because he was still locked up in another prison in far-away Ushuaia. I liked to think I had my own angel watching over me. I wanted it to be my mother.

Even after they let me out, the police wouldn't leave me alone. Verónica complained and they closed the house and took away our permits. I didn't care because I hated that place. I was carried there like a leaf on the wind and I stayed only because I did not know where else to go. As summer slipped towards autumn, a wagon carried us all out of the town, west toward the snowy caps of the Cordillera, over the border to Punta Arenas. Teresa brought her little boy. He had a lazy eye. Verónica wasn't happy – Why did you bring him? You should have left him behind – but Teresa's eyes were full of tears and she said Who should I leave him with? Her husband went with the strikers, like my gaucho. She doesn't know if he's alive or dead.

I always believed I would find my mother. I spent all autumn searching the city, but there was no sign, no message. By the time winter came, Verónica said we should move back to Argentina, and I went with them because nothing was left to hold me to the life that I had lost.

My mother took me from the north when my father died. We were carried south and further south, following a promise of beautiful things – gold and fur and wool – until we reached the end of the world itself, where it was winter all year round and the wind blew strong enough to knock you from your feet. My mother never found gold, or if she did, she never told me. Instead, she found work for me in a house across the border in Argentina, a house filled with attic bedrooms and English voices, a house so big it made me cry. When I understood that I was to go alone, I couldn't move. Her hands pressed against my back, pushing me into the wagon. All the time I lived in the English house, I told myself every day that she would find gold and come for me, and we would drive together in a golden motor car, far, far towards the bright yellow sunlight of the north.

I never saw gold, but I saw some golden paper once, wrapped around a gift my mistress, the young Señora, gave to my little man at Christmas time. When she saw how I looked at it, she let me play with the wrapper and it nearly burst my heart.

In that big English house, I hung my dress beside the fire to dry. The fire was lit all day and most of the night. The old Señora used the golden wrapper to light the fire. She said it was only paper.

I had my own room at the top of the house, but I didn't like it next to the attic with the cold and the house creaking at night. My master used to come up the stairs and stand on the landing, smoking and looking out over his farm. He never said anything, but it frightened me, him standing there like that. I preferred to sleep beside the fire in the nursery so I could listen for my little man. Sometimes I'd pick him up and hold him to be sure he was warm. He was a wriggler, my little rabbit. I loved him so much and played with him and bathed him and hung his clothes with mine beside the fire. Sometimes he wept at night for his mama, and I wept too, for mine.

His mama's skin was so white and thin, you could see the veins beneath. Blue blood, she told me. She was not made for so much winter: she was cold all the time, her hands chapped, no matter what she did. I heard her say she wanted to live in the north. The Señor was always outside, with his dog and his horse. Sometimes she went outside with him, but when she came back, she was so cold she could hardly move. I rubbed her hands to get the blood going, and when she cried out at the pain, I held her in my arms. Her hair was soft, like her voice. She smelled so sweet I wanted to stay wrapped around her forever. I held her and kissed the top of her head, but she wiped her eyes and pushed me away.

After that Christmas, my mistress gave me a dress to thank me for working so hard and caring for my little man. She said it was old and she didn't need it. I knew it was because of the gold paper. She used to argue with the old Señora, though it never did her any good. The old woman would go to her own room, leaving my mistress even more lonely. Her own mother was far away like mine. Sometimes I saw her looking at photographs that made her cry. She said I mustn't tell the old Señora about the dress. I could never wear it as long as I lived in the house, because it was too fine for a servant and I might get into trouble, so I hid it under my bed. It smelled of my mistress's skin.

At night, when the cold crept through my legs and arms and ran along my spine, I tried to remember the touch of my mother's hands as they pressed against my back. I tried to feel the warm city that we had left behind and sunlight on the sea.

16.

Lady Mary and Mr Fox

*Lady Mary was young, and Lady Mary was fair. Of all her
many lovers, her favourite was Mr Fox. Mr Fox was gallant
and handsome, and soon it was agreed between them that
Lady Mary would marry him.*

*One day, when Mr Fox went away on business, or so he
said, Lady Mary decided she would like to see his castle,
so she set out by herself to find it. After she had travelled
some way, she discovered the castle, and very fine it was,
with a great, high wall around it. And over the gateway
was written:*

Be Bold, Be Very Bold.

*Now, Lady Mary was bold, so she went through the gate
and across the courtyard, to the door of the castle. And
over the door was written:*

Be Bold, Be Bold, But Not Too Bold.

*Now, Lady Mary, as we know, was bold, so she did not
hesitate. She opened the door and went inside. Finding
herself in a great hall, with stairs to a gallery, she went
straightway up the stairs and along the gallery until she
reached the furthest room. And over the door was written:*

*Be Bold, Be Bold, But Not Too Bold, Lest That Your
Heart's Blood Should Run Cold.*

*But Lady Mary, as we know, was bold indeed, so she
opened the door. And what do you think she saw?*

"What? What?" Leo's little eyes are perfect round circles.

I snap the book shut. "No more, Leo. I'm not reading this to you."

"My papa likes this one." He pouts and I try not to laugh.

"It isn't suitable. Let's do something else."

I distract him with maps. We have made sketches of the farm to hang on the nursery walls, and now I show him how to stain our drawings with tea and singe the edges with a candle flame. In the corners we draw guanacos, pumas and a condor. Leo adds a wobbly compass.

I, too, am horribly compelled to find out what happens in the story. While Leo plays with his treasure chest, I open the book again.

And what do you think she saw? Why, the bodies of beautiful young brides, all piled up and stained with blood! Lady Mary thought it high time to get out of that horrid place, she closed the door and turned to leave, when who should she see through the window, but Mr Fox, dragging a beautiful young lady. Lady Mary rushed downstairs, and hid herself behind a cask, just in time, as Mr Fox came in with the poor young lady, who seemed to have fainted. Just as he got near Lady Mary, Mr Fox seized a diamond ring glittering on the finger of the young lady and tried to pull it off. But it was tightly fixed, and would not come off. Mr Fox cursed and swore, drew his sword, raised it, and brought it down upon the hand of the poor lady. The sword cut off the hand which jumped up into the air and fell, of all places in the world, into Lady Mary's lap. Mr Fox looked about a bit, but did not think of looking behind the cask, so at last he went on dragging the young lady up the stairs and into the Bloody Chamber. As soon as she heard him pass through the gallery, Lady Mary crept out of the door, and ran home as fast as she could.

Leo looks up from his game and I pretend to be tidying the bookshelf. At least I know Lady Mary escaped. Later, while he takes his nap, I finish the story, and hide the book at the back of the shelf where I know he will not find it.

Alice's ruined dress hangs like a reproachful spirit in my wardrobe. When I open the door, I think of brides piled in the bloody chamber. I am afraid I will find Alice herself in there, waiting for me.

I can't return the dress to Mrs Creed. The only way I can get it out of my room is to put it back in the attic and now I've had the thought, there's no going back. Leo is asleep: if he wakes, Pilar will take him for his bath. The servants are busy in the kitchen, the Creeds will be dressing for dinner. I fold the dress carefully to conceal the damaged hem. The house holds its breath as I tiptoe up the attic stairs.

The attic door swings open with a sigh. There are more boxes and piles of furniture than I remember, and I am afraid I will get lost. I pick my way between formless shapes, fighting an absurd urge to look back, in case they truly are ghosts and have moved to block my escape. But there is the trunk, shadowy in the darkness. I open the lid, trying not to think of Alice.

My eye is at once caught by a small box, elaborately collaged with flower arrangements, pieces of furniture, tiny figures posing in party dresses. So, this is what happened to Alice's chopped-up magazines. I run my fingertips over the smooth, varnished surface. When I lift the lid, tissue paper glimmers. I ease open the first package, careful not to tear the edges: nestled inside is a heart-shaped wooden frame, not much bigger than a locket, containing a tiny, perfect paper rose rising in three dimensions towards the glass. In the next, a small butterfly, jewelled wings spread wide, poised on a miniature branch. I've never seen anything so delicate, so meticulous. I imagine Alice sitting at the green baize table in the sewing room, leafing through the magazines for illustrations, painting with the finest of brushes, cutting and crafting with neat and careful fingers.

At the bottom of the box lies a curl of thin red ribbon and a single folded sheet of paper. I pick it up and hold my candle close. A letter. Tiny, elegant writing – the perfect partner for the decoupages. The letter is unfinished: Alice must have put it away in the box and never returned to it.

There is a sound outside the attic door. Someone is coming up the stairs. I freeze, letter in hand, holding my breath. The footsteps stop on the landing. I hear the strike of a match, and a moment later, faint hints of sulphur and cigarette smoke drift into the attic. Ian.

He can't find me here. I shrink deeper into the darkness, waiting for him to leave. But then another, more terrifying thought occurs: what if he notices the attic door ajar? He might close and bolt it, leaving me trapped inside. There is nothing for it. I slip the letter into my pocket, put the box back inside the trunk and smooth the dress on top. The tissue paper rustles.

There is an intake of breath on the landing. Ian's voice calls out, "Who's there?"

I close the trunk and walk towards the door, letting my footsteps land heavily. "It's me. Georgie. I was returning your mother's dress." The letter burns in my pocket.

"God, Georgie, you gave me a fright." He is laughing, but his eyes are very wide. It's true, I have startled him. "So that's why the door was open," he continues. "I couldn't imagine what anyone would be doing up here."

And what about you, I think. What are you doing up here? Though who am I to say where Ian Creed should go in his own house? There is not quite enough space for both of us on the landing. I shift uncomfortably, trying to put a little more distance between us, feeling myself at the edge of the stairs.

Perhaps he has read my mind. "I come up here some-times for a smoke," he says, waving his hands at the view. "My mother hates it, she thinks it's morbid, with all the old furniture and whatnot." He laughs. "It's like being in an eyrie. I think about things differently up here."

Nothing unreasonable about that, I suppose. From the window I can see the farm, the empty plain, the snow-capped hills. A peon is sitting outside the bunkhouse, washing something in a bucket.

"Are you alright?" Ian asks. "You look a bit... I don't know. You're frowning."

"Oh, it's nothing," I try to compose a smile. "It was dark in there, that's all, and I got a bit spooked. It's my own fault, I read a stupid ghost story. Don't worry," I add hastily, "I didn't read it to Leo. He'd have the most awful nightmares."

He grins. "Well, that's something. But I'm sorry you were scared." A pause. "Thanks for putting the dress away. That was brave of you." He glances at the stairs as if to go back down, then pauses. "By the way," he says, and his careful, casual tone is enough to make me lean my hand against the wall for support. "My mother told me about your fiancé." So the Creeds have been talking behind my back. "It must have been dreadful," he says, gently. His eyes are very kind.

"It was impossible." I hear the words as if from a great distance. "It would have meant no life... for either of us." At least not the life I'd expected. No intimacy. No children. My heart contracts to think of the way Eddie's beautiful, laughing mouth had once met mine. "We might have found a way to live together, even without..." I stop. I can't tell him everything. But something has loosened inside me now, memories are welling, spilling over. "The worst thing was... he changed. He was so beautiful, but all the love, the joy, got locked up somewhere out of reach and there was nothing I could do. He was scared, and it made him angry all the time. I was scared too. I..." For the first time, someone is listening to my side of the story, and for the first time I am going to admit what everyone else knew. "He wanted me to stay and look after him. But I couldn't do it. They all blamed me. Everyone. They all loved him, and they

94

knew he wanted me to stay. My mother..." When have I ever talked to anyone about my mother? "She couldn't believe that I... you see, my brothers both died, and as it turned out, they were all she really lived for. And if they had lived, like that, she would have nursed them. Anyone would, who had lost a loved one. Except me." My voice is cracking. "I abandoned him. My father was the only one who understood that I couldn't... that it wasn't possible. That's why he sent me here."

"He sent you away?" Ian sounds incredulous. "But it wasn't your fault. It was the war. The war changed people." He's right. The war changed people. "You did nothing wrong," he says firmly.

Is that it? I confess and he absolves me. Can it really be so simple?

"Would it help if I told you I know how you feel?" He continues. "At least, I know how it feels to be blamed for something you couldn't help."

"Do you mean... in the war?" I have understood enough about the war to know that those who came home have to live with the price of their survival.

He gives a little laugh, as if I have taken him by surprise. "Oh God, yes. The war. Of course. Every day. If I stopped to think about everything I couldn't help – or some of the things I could help, but did anyway – I'd go mad."

He's right. The war didn't just change people, it broke them. Everyone was broken – into parts and bits and pieces – and if we stopped to think about it, we would all go mad. I hug my arms around myself, trying to hold the broken parts together.

"Actually," he says. "I wasn't really talking about the war. For me, it's something different."

"Oh. I see. I'm sorry."

"There was this girl, working here. She adored Alice, but she was a bit simple, and after Alice died, she started saying the most awful things – how it was my fault, I could have done more to save her. It shouldn't matter, she was only a servant, but somehow it got around the men at just the wrong time." There is a tautness in him, a fixed expression, as if looking at something I can't see. "It was horrible. So, you see, I understand what it's like. Really, I do." He stops and leans against the wall as if the story has exhausted him. Silence hangs like glass between us. He turns away, taps another cigarette from the packet. "Sorry. You didn't need to hear all that. You go on down. I'll be there in a minute." A pause. "No need to tell my mother we've been up here. She wouldn't like it, you know."

I can feel his eyes on my back as I walk down the stairs. I hold my hand over my pocket and hurry away to my room without looking back.

August 1920

Dearest Claire,

Thank you so very much for the beautiful parcel. It's the most cheering thing that has happened here in ages – I can't tell you how much your magazines have improved my days. I promise to make you something beautiful with the illustrations.

The baby is kicking already, it's quite the little demon. I can't wait until it is out so someone else can take care of it for a while. I have quarrelled with Ian and Maud a few times about Marta, they say she's a bad influence, but I won't let them get rid of her. I'm going to need her more than ever once the baby arrives.

Ian is endlessly preoccupied. He came back from the war full of ideas, but it seems he has overestimated the costs of all this new investment, and now he worries all the time, and it makes him miserable. Sleep only makes things worse because he suffers dreadfully from nightmares. Maud and I try to quiet him, but he is so frightened, sometimes he mistakes us for the enemy. Fires light behind his eyes, bayonets grow at the ends of his fingers, he truly believes he is back in France. In the day he is all contrition, and I feel terrible for him.

Please don't breathe a word to Robert. Ian would hate that I have told you, and he has enough to worry about without feeling that I am not on his side.

We are all so tired. This place is a tomb in winter, no glimmer of light for a thousand miles. But I am packed and ready, and as soon as the snow thaws, we will set off.

17.

Ian dreams

I kneel in prayer beside the bed, but God is nowhere to be found. Only brides in the bloody chamber and Alice, somewhere among the shadows, watching. Is Marta, the bad influence, the girl who spread the rumours after Alice's death?

The wind rattles at the windows. Above the sound rises a high, unmistakable wail: Leo. I listen, shivering, hoping he will fall back to sleep, but the sound persists. I don't care what Mrs Creed says, I can't leave him crying. I pull my shawl over my shoulders and slip out onto the landing.

A shadow wavers at the end of the corridor. As I creep toward the nursery, I hear a thud and a stifled cry from one of the rooms beyond, a lower-pitched sound that cannot possibly come from a child. And at once, I understand. The letter has explained everything. No wonder Mrs Creed forbade me to investigate the house at night, no wonder she herself is up and fully dressed. It is not Leo who is weeping. This must be Ian, having one of his dreams.

A sudden howl makes me cry out and almost drop the candle. Wild shadows bounce across the walls. When the light steadies and the pounding of my heart subsides, I see Ian's dog, Loca, tail between her legs, face pressed against Ian's door. I hurry back along the corridor and lean down to snatch her by the collar.

"Come on, you," I whisper. "You can't stay here. You'll

wake everyone up." The dog raises her hackles and bares her teeth.

There is another thud inside Ian's room. Loca lifts her head and howls. From behind the door, I hear shuffling sounds, as if Ian is running his hands along the walls.

I must get back to bed. Mrs Creed can't find me outside her son's bedroom in my nightdress. I reach to pick up my candle and in the same moment, Ian's door flies open. I cry out, the sound lost beneath the moaning of the wind. The dog slinks past, vanishing into the darkness.

Ian stares into the corridor through unblinking eyes.

"Ian," I whisper. "Please. Go back in your room."

He cocks his head and rubs his fists hard into his eyes, a gesture so childlike it could be Leo. I can't leave him here. Breathing as quietly as I can, I lead him back inside his room and close the door.

"Ian, listen. You have to go back to bed." He nods, and pulls back the covers, then lays one hand on the mattress, patting it a few times, as if feeling for something, sniffing at his fingers. When he seems satisfied that nothing is there, he allows me to lower him gently into the bed. As he lies down, his knee judders and he pushes at it with the palm of his hand, an automatic gesture. His eyes open very wide.

"Did I wake you?" he asks, and I tremble at the sound of his voice.

"No, no," I whisper. Don't be afraid. He is asleep. Just keep him quiet so his mother doesn't come.

He grips my wrist and holds it tight, muttering again, incoherent phrases I can't understand. I try to slide my hand out of his grasp, but he pulls me close, puts his mouth to my ear and whispers, "Alice."

I feel my hair stand on end.

He is twitching now, trying to push past me out of the bed. I hold him as tightly as I dare. "I mustn't fall. I mustn't fall."

"You won't fall. Please lie down. Then you won't fall."

"Alice is lying down." His hands tighten into fists. "Her hair's in her mouth."

So this is where he keeps his memories. It is as if he has handed me the key to his soul.

I dare not move. I am afraid I will see Alice, here with us in the room.

Tears are pouring down his cheeks. I wipe his face with my fingers and push his shoulders down towards the bed. For a moment he resists, then he allows me to lower his head onto the pillows. I sit beside him, holding my breath, until he closes his eyes and subsides back into sleep.

18.

Revolutionaries

Leo and I play chase between the outbuildings. We run all the way to the outer edges of the farm where old, corrugated-iron sheds sit facing the bunkhouse, their backs to the open plain. The wind has dropped, the afternoon lies still as a frozen lake. Nobody is about. When we pause to catch our breath, the blackened windows of the bunkhouse watch like eyes. The empty building tugs at me with an invisible undertow.

"No, Georgie," Leo pulls at my hand. "You're not allowed."

"Oh, darling, don't worry, I'm not going inside."

But his eyes are huge and anxious. I feel a little skip of fear. "Marta went in the bunkhouse," he whispers.

"Marta?" I am whispering in return. "Who was she, Leo?" *They say she's a bad influence.*

"She played with me, before my Mama died."

"You mean she was your nurserymaid? Like Pilar? Why did she go into the bunkhouse?"

But the little boy shakes his head, pulls harder on my hand.

"Leo, please. It's fine. I only want to look…" I tiptoe closer to the metal door, and ease it open, just a crack. When my eyes have adjusted to the gloomy interior, I make out lines of bunks stretched along both walls, covered in what look like old guanaco hides and greying sheepskins. From what I can see, it isn't much of a home.

I am about to close the door when there is a movement inside and a shadow looms in the darkness. An old peon emerges, blinking at me through red-rimmed eyes. He looks me up and down, not insolently, but without haste, and asks in Spanish "What do you want, Miss?"

I shake my head. "Nothing, I…" What can I say? That I wanted to see how he lived and where he slept? That I would like to be useful, if only I knew how. "I was wondering if I could…" What? His head is tilted slightly to one side, waiting to hear. "I'm sorry. I didn't mean to disturb you. I thought, perhaps if I introduce myself, I can be useful, somehow."

He laughs. The sound is not unkind, but it is obvious I have amused him. "You want to be useful? Don't let the men hear you say that, Miss."

His mockery is an affront. "I have to go," I say in English, firmly.

The old peon raises an eyebrow, his demeanour both humble and challenging. I snatch Leo by the hand and pull him away across the yard.

*

Later, I curl up in my bedroom, chin on my knees, staring at nothing. The old man has awakened a memory of another time. A different doorway, another humiliation.

When Sarah Gerard's husband went to war, the stranger known to the village only as Uncle moved into her cottage. Despite the impropriety of this arrangement, my conscience pricked. Most of our parishioners preferred to save their charity for a more deserving cause, but remembering the little girl in callipers, I knocked at Sarah Gerard's cottage with a basket of provisions. I felt modern, bold and selfless. My father would be proud of me.

The door opened and Sarah Gerard looked out. When she saw me, she stood with her arms folded, blocking the entrance. A man's voice called out behind her, "What is it?"

and I almost took flight at the prospect of Uncle appearing in front of me.

Sarah Gerard shouted back over her shoulder. "Nothing. Just the vicar's girl."

"What does she want?"

"I don't know."

"I brought you these," I said, as warmly as I could. "For the children. For your daughter. I thought she might..." I trailed off, holding out my gifts: rhubarb and parsley from the garden, a pot of apple sauce, a threadbare teddy with one torn ear, some used crayons. Sarah Gerard took the basket and glanced through the contents. She picked up the old teddy and dropped it again.

"Do you want the basket back?" she asked, through gritted teeth.

"What? Oh... no, no of course not," I lied.

Sarah Gerard nodded and shut the door in my face.

The entire interview had lasted less than a minute. I stared at the door as if expecting her to reappear. "Well..." I said aloud, blinking my surprise. What kind of woman took gifts and showed no gratitude? My face burned with embarrassment. I had tried to be useful, and Mrs Gerard had scorned my offerings. So much for good intentions.

*

At dinner, Mrs Creed says, "You may visit the farm, Georgie, but you are not to take Leo to the bunkhouse." With each chilly emphasis, a new ripple of anxiety. How does she know about the bunkhouse? I had thought, in this place, to have escaped from eyes and whispers. "You grew up in a vicarage. Surely your parents taught you how to behave?"

My cheeks burn. "I'm sorry." At least she doesn't know I was in Ian's room last night.

"I'm thinking only of your safety." Her voice drops to a whisper. "There are revolutionaries in Santa Cruz."

A prickle of fear. How quick the Creeds had been when

I arrived to tell me there was no danger here. I remember the newspaper announcement on Ian's desk – an attack on an estancia, shots fired – how Mrs Creed had folded the newspaper and hurried me away. I had hoped she was being kind by giving me Alice's magazines. Was she just trying to distract me?

"Mother's exaggerating," Ian's face is dark with fury.

She flashes him a sharp frown. "If any revolutionaries show their faces here, we will have to inform the League."

"Rubbish, Mother."

"What's the League?" The words are out of my mouth before I can stop myself. Mrs Creed clicks her tongue with irritation.

"Just a group of local landowners," Ian cuts in. "An… affiliation. We all stick together and help each other out. Supposedly."

There's a bitterness in his voice which I don't understand, and I sense I'm caught in the middle of an old argument. I wonder how the Creeds speak to each other when I am not here. It occurs to me, from Ian's description, that the League could also call itself a union, but this time I manage to bite my tongue. "That sounds like a good thing."

"In the main. Most of them are decent enough. The big ones are caranchos, waiting for us to fail so they can swoop in and pick over the pieces."

"Georgie doesn't need to hear about that," Mrs Creed's cup rattles as she sets it down. "What you do need to know, Miss, is that it is not acceptable for a young lady to go anywhere near the bunkhouse."

I hear my mother's voice: There, Georgie, see what you've done. You've made everybody unhappy.

"I'm so sorry, Mrs Creed. I didn't mean to upset you."

Now Ian is laughing. "Don't look like that. You haven't upset anyone. You do like to shoulder the world's responsibilities, don't you?"

"Oh, for goodness' sake!" Mrs Creed snaps.

Ian catches my eye and winks. I feel the tension melt away. As long as I know he is not angry with me, I can cope with his mother's ill humour. Things have changed since the conversation in his eyrie; somehow our confessions have made us freer, lighter with one another. I try not to smile too obviously as we all lapse back into silence, watching the snow.

19.

Álvaro

A rider appears through the snow with a sheaf of letters bearing the stamp of the Patriotic League. Ian carries them into his study and closes the door. His mother follows him inside, only to retreat to her room a few minutes later. Tension crackles between them.

Ian is absent minded, his eyes red-rimmed with weariness. "Sorry," he says apologetically, when I ask a question about Leo, "I'm a bit strapped for time today. Got some complicated business to attend to." He leaves instructions for the farm boy, Álvaro, to accompany me on a ride.

Whippet thin and rangy as the dogs, Álvaro slinks between the kitchen and the yards, a servant to all masters. He breaks ice in the water troughs beneath the windmills where the mares gather, carries buckets to the kitchen, scrubs the steps, cleans the leathers, sweeps the yards and the sheep pens. He hauls pallets and stakes, drags sacks of feed and bales of hay, forks the straw in the stables, spreads manure on the gardens and pushes the wheelbarrows back and forth. And, young as he is, the peoncito is an accomplished horseman.

Álvaro takes it upon himself to become my teacher. He and Old Aquiles, the gentlest and oldest of the farm horses, show me how to open gates and turn Ángel to close them again behind us, how to ride along the fences so I don't get lost, how to follow the invisible grid of trails and paths that criss-crosses the estancia, and how to master the jogging gait of the gauchos.

"Do the gauchos have maps?" I ask, and he laughs. The gauchos carry the landscape here, he tells me, tapping a finger against his forehead. He tells me about the baqueanos, pathfinders who watch the sun and stars, the moon and the mountains, listening to the direction of the wind. They understand the earth beneath their horses' hooves, the movement of trees and plants. They can follow a trail, find water or shelter, track an animal. A leaf, a handful of dirt, the shape of a bush or the remains of a footprint is enough to lead them across hundreds of miles of uncharted land, even in the pitch darkness of the Patagonian night. They have no need of maps.

I don't know what to say. I wonder whether one day I too will be able to find my way across this land using just my instincts, like a gaucho.

As I ponder this new magic, Álvaro chats away about the colours of horses, the layers of a gaucho's saddle, the tribal origins of the peons. Later, I write in my diary:

Horse colours – too many to mention and frighteningly specific. My favourite is Tostado Retacón – a dark brown horse with short legs

Pingo – a horse

Potro – a colt

Che – man, from the Mapuche, used in a friendly way among the gauchos

Peoncito – a young worker, diminutive of peon

Guachito – an orphan child, used on the farm as an insult for boys like Álvaro who never knew their fathers

Campo – countryside

China – indigenous word for a gaucho's wife, a woman of the countryside

Aike – Aonikenk for "place"

Querencia – home. But more than that. From the word querer, to love, it is the place you long for. The place an animal will always return to. Your roots.

I try not to shudder when Álvaro describes the gauchos' polainas – long goatskin chaps – and rawhide boots, botas de potro, cut from the skin of a dead colt and worn fresh until they take the shape of a human leg. Álvaro's own filthy shoes are stuffed with straw against the cold and his thin body shivers in the wind. I wonder why Ian has not provided him with boots.

The bones of the dead – sheep, guanacos, cattle – poke through the snow. We stumble upon the carcass of a horse, stiff and frozen, dead from the mal secco, and I gaze in horror at its blackened eye sockets, pecked empty by the caranchos. "Doesn't it give you the creeps?" I ask Álvaro, and he stares at me, puzzled. To him, these scattered corpses are as much a part of the landscape as the earth itself. He shows me how to throw the boleadoras and brings down a guanaco we surprise by the stream, dragging it proudly home across the ice.

As his shyness falls away, he is willing to answer questions I can't ask the Creeds. I learn the names of the peons in the bunkhouse, who manages the corrals and cowsheds, the gauchos and the ovejeros scattered across the hills, who rides the strongest horses and keeps the best hunting dogs, who can roll and light a cigarette while cantering into the wind, who has the most silver coins studded onto his belt, who is fastest with the boleadoras and quickest with a knife. I delight in the improvement in my Spanish, compare myself to Mrs Creed, and immediately feel guilty.

I ask: "Who was Marta? Did you know her?"

Silence. When I had asked Pilar how long she had been at the estancia, and who her predecessor might have been, she made a little curtsey and hurried away, muttering about her work. Nobody, it seems, wants to talk about the girl who went into the bunkhouse.

"You did know her, didn't you?" I prompt. "What happened to her?"

"They sent her away."

Perhaps if I pretend to know the story, he will say more. "For visiting the bunkhouse?" A tiny shake of his head. "So what happened to her?"

But Álvaro clamps his lips shut. I have gone too far.

*

One quiet afternoon, when Leo is curled in his father's lap, I say, "Ian. I was just wondering… you know Álvaro, the peoncito?"

The farm office smells of hay and woodsmoke. Ian smiles. "Yes. I know Álvaro."

"He doesn't have boots."

"Doesn't he?" Ian looks tired. "We've had to tighten our belts a bit recently. Lali will see to it."

"Does Lali look after him?"

"We all do. It's how we do things here. If someone turns up, like Álvaro, we look after them."

I think about the immensity of the plain and this house, a tiny pinprick on its vast surface. How could anyone just turn up? "Where did he come from?"

He sighs. "You and your questions, Georgie. You don't let up, do you?"

"Oh, I'm sorry. I didn't mean to pry." I feel myself contract like a snail hiding its head. My mother would have been appalled. Curiosity killed the cat, Georgie. Control yourself. When will you learn to hold your tongue? Then an hour on my knees, perhaps two, before my father rescued me. Mama's not herself today. Let's not trouble her. Come.

"No, it's fine. You know I like it when you ask questions. Really, I do." Ian is smiling, the warmth in his eyes is genuine. He wants me to care about his farm. "I have no idea where Álvaro came from," he continues. "Sometimes lads just… arrive. Off a boat, looking for work. Or thrown off one of the other farms."

I remember the drive from Punta Arenas, nothing but

scrub and wild animals as far as the horizon. To be thrown out into this wilderness would be a death sentence.

He notes the horror on my face. "Oh, don't worry, it doesn't happen often." But I am lost, imagining a child alone on the plain. Ian lays his hand on mine and I feel the warmth of his fingers closing over my own. "Don't be upset. Nothing like that would ever happen here. And remember, these are tough lads, they fend for themselves pretty well. Lali sees to it that Álvaro has what he needs and gets paid fairly. They all do." A hint of warning lies behind the words. "Some of the lads arrive when they're very young and stay with us for years," he continues. "Like Álvaro. They care about the place as much as we do. Our Horsebreaker is another one."

Horsebreaker. At his name, unexpected interest ripples through my body and out into the space beyond. Ian is still holding my hand and must surely feel it. I compose my face into indifference.

He has not noticed. "Lali took Horsebreaker in when he was just a boy. Taught him English – Russian too, for all I know. I don't know why, he must have seen something in the lad, some natural intelligence. And Horsebreaker's proved him right every step of the way, he's a clever chap. The two of them are like father and son."

What an odd assortment of strays, washed up at this house built of the remains of old boats, a Noah's Ark on the plain's vast, empty sea. What a population of human wreckage has found its way here. Sometimes at night, when I can't sleep for homesickness, the wind really does sound like waves crashing against the walls.

"Raúl must be rather special," I say, in the tone my mother would use to speak about a servant.

"I'll say. We have the finest horses in Southern Patagonia." There is something touching in that glint of pride. "Anyway," he continues, "you wanted to ask me about Álvaro?"

"Oh." I had forgotten Álvaro. "It's nothing. I just wondered, that's all."

I am turning over a new project. I think of Leo, snug in his nursery, surrounded by toys and books, and am spurred by a longing to do something good. If Lali taught Raúl English, I could do the same for Álvaro. With my help, the boy can learn to read and write and perhaps grow up to be more than just a farm worker. Perhaps, at last, I have found something I can do.

I write in my diary:

IR AL HUMO – literally, to go towards the smoke. I learned this from Mr Henry O. Chambers' book. It is an Indian expression. A column of smoke means an encampment so to go towards the smoke means to confront whoever has lit the fire.

I know I must stay away from the men. I have no desire to go toward the smoke, but I would like to do something for Álvaro. Lali has not yet provided him with boots.

20

Old Aquiles

August: the very depths of winter. The wind drops, ice thickens on the water troughs, snow continues to fall. I keep away from the men. They have never warmed to me, perhaps because they associate me with Ian. But Álvaro is different and I haven't forgotten my plan to teach him to read. With my help, he can grow up to be more than just a farm boy.

The day Álvaro dies, he is repairing fences. As the afternoon fades, the news finds its way to the house. I become aware of servants gathering, a shuffle of footsteps, a familiar, prickling dread. I've felt it all too often, in a patient's folded belongings beside an empty hospital bed, or the sick, electric moment before opening a telegram. I follow the sounds, and find Pilar standing at the kitchen door, crossing herself.

Something spooked Old Aquiles. The horse leapt like a wild thing, Álvaro's foot caught in the stirrup as he fell, and Old Aquiles bolted, dragging Álvaro over the rocks like a bundle of firewood. They say that in the civil wars, the army executed criminals in this way. It's a common enough accident, but Old Aquiles was the calmest horse on the estancia, nothing less than a ghost would make him tremble and leap like that. The servants mutter about dark angels and ill fortune, the curse of a child left unburied during the winter months.

I am not allowed near the bunkhouse. But I am a nurse and Álvaro is a child and he was my friend.

The door is open. Icicles have formed at the open corners of the corrugated roof. The air is musky, thick with the smell of straw and unwashed bodies. Men sprawl on bunks, dark shadows in the gloom. Two or three candles flicker on the floor.

The Talker bends over a pallet, muttering. Beside him, his efforts to save a life: a knife, a chipped enamel bowl, some bloody cloths. When he sees me, his eyes open very wide, his mouth sets in a thin, hard line. For once, he says nothing.

I should go back. This is a terrible mistake. But the body on the pallet makes a gurgling sound and I remember why I have come. "I'm a nurse."

The Talker shakes his head. "I have done everything it is possible to do."

It is true. I can see he knows how to debride the wounds, to wash them with iodine. He knows how to splint and stitch. In the candlelight, Álvaro's face is black with bruises. A dark trail slides from the corner of his mouth.

An empty bottle glitters on the floor and The Talker kicks it aside. I snatch it up, searching for clues.

Compound tincture of chloroform and morphine. DIRECTION – For an adult ten minims may be taken in a wineglass with water, and repeated in three or four hours as necessary. In severe cases, the dose may be increased to fifteen minims. As this preparation contains potent poisons, it should be used with caution.

"How much did you give him?"

The Talker shrugs.

"How much?" How do I find the courage to speak like this?

His eyes meet mine. "He was in pain. All of it."

"All of it? But it says…" the words wither in my mouth. The Talker speaks no English. How would he know?

The peons close tighter around the pallet, shuffling their feet and muttering amongst themselves. I should tell them

to raise Álvaro's head, fetch black coffee, something, anything to make him vomit up the drug, but it is pointless,
they won't listen and, in any case, it is too late. There is
a sigh from the pallet, a massive heave. The Talker turns,
and Álvaro is gone.

The glass vial is still in my hand. I want to smash it
beneath my feet and grind it into dust. Instead, I turn and
hurl it with all my strength into the snow.

Ian is waiting at the kitchen door. The effort of meeting
his eyes is more than I can bear.

"Oh Georgie." His voice is very gentle. "I'm so sorry
you had to see this." He takes both my hands, presses them
tightly between his own. "It was an accident. Accidents
happen here. There's nothing we could do." He shakes his
head as if trying to convince himself. "There's nothing we
could do."

"I could have helped, Ian, if they'd let me."

"They'd never let you. This is a wild place and the men
do things their own way. They don't want my help either."
A rueful half-laugh. "Some of them think I'm the Grim
Reaper, remember?"

There is anguish beneath the words. I long to take him
in my arms and comfort him. We stand together in the
darkness, his face unreadable in the gloom.

"There's trouble coming," he says at last. "They won't
care that it was an accident."

"They? Who? What do you mean?"

"The unions. They'll be back, making trouble. I know
it."

*

The following morning, icy winter sun casts its pale glow
through the window, and Leo drives a wooden truck across
the nursery floor. When we wander through the yard with a
cache of sugar lumps for the horses, I hug Leo close, feeling
Álvaro's absence like a great weight against my heart.

"Penny for them, Georgie," Ian says, coming upon me so suddenly I leap and let out a little cry.

"Goodness, you startled me. I was just thinking…" I stop.

His face falls. "I'm sorry, it was stupid of me to ask. I feel the same. It's awful." He hesitates. "Do you want to walk with me?"

Leo is absorbed in his own conversation with the horses nosing greedily at his pockets. I tuck my arm through Ian's, feeling the warmth of his body at my side. I am shivering, not just from cold, but from the unaccustomed closeness. He gives my hand a little squeeze and I tremble at everything that lies unspoken between us.

"This is a wild place," Ian says. "Sometimes terrible things happen. It can't be helped."

I shake my head, unable to answer. But I understand that he wants to comfort me.

"By the way," he continues. "Do you have that wretched chlorodyne bottle?"

"I threw it away. Why?"

"Oh, I don't know. No reason. I suppose I just wanted to see it for myself."

We have reached the barn. An old man in a crumpled jacket and shapeless felt hat stands with his back to us, reading a poster. I recognize him at once. It is the peon who caught me peeking into the bunkhouse.

"Hey!" Ian calls out. "What's this?" The old man hurries away, slipping on silvered ice-puddles. "God damn it," Ian curses as he lets go of my arm and strides ahead to rip the poster from the wall. "God damn it to hell."

I see the word *Asesinado* printed at the top of the page above two crudely drawn faces, before he crumples the paper between his hands. "Ian… what is it?"

"Some rubbish from the union men." His mouth is twitching. "I knew this was coming, only I didn't expect them here so soon. Will you be alright? I'd better go and deal with it."

"What will you do?"

"Find out who put that fellow up to it. Make sure there aren't any more of these things littering up the place."

I feel a shock of cold air where the warmth of his body has been: his anger has severed us as brutally as a surgeon's knife. He trips over the dog, Loca, kicking her in the ribs so she yelps, cringing away behind the barn. At the corner, he breaks his stride and his shoulders slump. Perhaps he thinks I can no longer see. Lali appears from the other direction, Ian stuffs the paper into Lali's hands, and turns his head away. So much hurt in that small gesture. I remember his words from last night: the trouble, it seems, has already begun.

21.

Lali will kill them all

Raúl and Lali cover the pallet and carry Álvaro's body to the farthest of the outbuildings, to wait for the snow to melt and the earth to soften. Until then, all but the most unsentimental of the men will avoid passing too close to this temporary resting place.

The dogs are quiet in the kennels by the time Raúl has unhitched the horses, hung the harnesses in the saddle room, fetched buckets of feed. Steady, familiar tasks. He breathes in the rich smells of the farmyard, straw and bran and sweat, as he leads the horses round to the corrals and leans against the fence, watching their shadow shapes blow ripples over the dark surface of the water trough. A soft whicker from his own Hero, who trots across the corral to nose his hand for treats.

Raúl puts his arm around the horse's neck, pulling him close as if he were a lover. He is sorry about Álvaro. When he closes his eyes, the boy's body is printed on the inside of his mind. He is sorry too that Old Aquiles is part of the story. Raúl doesn't believe in ghosts, but he believes in horses. Some invisible danger spooked that placid old animal, and Raúl is certain it was a danger Old Aquiles sensed among the men.

A footfall at his back startles him. "The strike leaders will come here." Juan Sant is at his side. "This place has a reputation for trouble. They will want to know what happened."

"Accidents happen."

"True. But this wasn't an accident. The labels were supposed to be in Spanish. If the medicine had been labelled properly like the Señor promised, the boy might have lived."

Álvaro would not have lived, Raúl is sure of it. But Sant is right, something is coming. He can feel it as surely as if a horse has walked over his grave.

"Sooner or later," Sant says, watching him, "the strikers will come and then you will have to decide."

"I can't leave Lali. I will never leave him. Anyway, I've got plans."

Sant smiles. "I had dreams in my head once too, remember. That little strip of land. Green grass. Fish in the stream. But you know what they told me? They said: Forget it, chilote."

Raúl's fists clench. He has to breathe deep to stop himself from punching the wall. Or Juan Sant. "I don't care. Anyway, you made an enemy. I don't plan to do that." Sant raises an eyebrow. "The Señor's already promised to help me. When I've saved enough to get started."

"I see. No wonder you don't want to strike against him. In that case," Juan Sant holds out his hand, "I wish you luck."

*

The poster curls, the faces blacken in the flames. The boy who died and the girl who was let go, tiny flakes of ash that float up and disappear toward the sky. Lali spits into the fire and lights another cigarette, then kicks his toe against the charred remains. "If they try that again here, I'll kill those bastards myself."

He passes Raúl a cigarette and they stand together in silence, enjoying the momentary warmth of the dying embers.

"What did it say?" Raúl asks.

"I don't know. He'd already ripped it up by the time I got my hands on it. I don't care."

Last year's rumours back again. Raúl feels a quiver of anxiety, like a horse's shoulder shivering a fly.

"What matters," Lali continues, "is that those bastard unions think they can come here and spread their filthy propaganda."

"I heard they want to know about the medicines." Raúl keeps his voice casual. "You must have seen the agreement." Of course Lali has seen the agreement. Raúl feels a tiny flicker of triumph. If Lali doesn't answer, it'll look like he doesn't know.

"What they want is money," Lali says evenly. "Better wages. And there's nothing we can do about that. Not right now." Raúl nods. He knows the Señor has bought new land, new flocks. Nothing wrong with that. "But it's true," Lali is saying, "there are other things they want too."

Other things. In his mind, Raúl can hear Juan Sant: things that make us human. "What do they want?"

"You're right about the medicines. They want them labelled in Spanish."

A pause. The shadow of the boy Álvaro hangs in the air between them. Raúl breaks the silence. "What else?"

Lali's hands are fists, the knuckles white. "Candles for the bunkhouse. Water for washing. We do all that."

"I know we do." Once a week, the men wash away the stink of blood and mud and shit that comes with farm work. There is talk of a washroom, even a boiler, like the one in Ian Creed's office. Without water, how are they different from the animals? Juan Sant has said that as well. Both men sit silent for a moment, watching the flicker of the fire.

"What else?"

"The right to be returned." Lali's face is half-shadowed in the firelight.

Raúl knows about this too. Casual workers must be taken back to the place where they were first hired – the town, or at least the roadside. Not left standing in the middle of the open plain, no horse, no food, no money. He shakes his head, trying not to think about the girl who was let go. An unexpected surge of anger in his chest. Twice, then, the Señor has broken the agreement. "What's wrong with that?"

"Nothing's wrong with it." Lali's face is tight with anger. Even he didn't know about the girl until it was too late. "Stop talking like a revolutionary. We don't make trouble and we don't want any. If they come back here, I'll shoot them."

It's true that Lali would shoot the strikers. All he wants is to be left alone. But Ian Creed has broken the agreement twice now and Raúl sees how the peons look at him.

"What are you going to do?"

"I'm going to give that bastard Juan Sant a kicking."

"What for?"

"For reading it. In the old days we'd have stuck his head on the gate as a warning."

Raúl looks sideways at Lali and says nothing. Whatever is on the posters, if it is about Ian Creed, Lali will not forgive.

"What?" Lali has seen the look.

"Nothing."

"You want to say something, say it."

"It's not my business."

"Don't give me that shit. You think I don't know when you have an opinion?"

"It's not important." Raúl flicks his cigarette into the fire. "Sant's an old man, is all. It's not his fault what they write." He pauses, trying to find the right words. "Not much goes his way."

"What's not gone his way that's different from the rest of us?" Lali's voice is like fingers scratching an old wound.

Raúl watches tiny feathers of ash float onto the snow. Lali's mother and father, brothers, sisters, grandparents, aunts and uncles, cousins and second cousins, and cousins many times removed, all caught in the pogroms, somewhere in Russia. All ashes on the snow. "Seems like he was only reading."

Lali narrows his eyes. Raúl stays very still. If he says the wrong thing now, Lali will knock out the old man's teeth and spend the evening with a bottle of whisky. Raúl wonders if he has time to find Juan Sant first. And if he does, whether Lali will feel it as a betrayal.

"You trust him?" Lali asks.

"Sure, I trust him. But I'm not the one who owns an estancia."

Lali laughs. A hearty, bear-like laugh, from the very centre of his body. He kicks snow over the burnt remains of the poster and claps Raúl on the shoulder. For now, the argument is over. But something is coming. Just as he has learned to spot danger in the flicker of a horse's ear or the stillness of a dog when it drops to its belly, Raúl can feel it among the ashes smouldering in the snow. And when it comes, not even Lali will have the strength to protect them all.

*

A week later, Raúl wipes his face with the corner of a towel. His neck cloth is clean, his hands are washed. As he crosses the yard towards the farm office, he rehearses words he has been saving for the best part of a year, practicing them in English inside his head. Now, more than ever, it is time to get free of the Creeds, the agreement, the trouble everyone knows is coming. It is time to make his own way.

He has waited until Lali has calmed down after the poster incident, hoping that if it's long enough for Lali, it will be long enough for Señor Creed as well.

"We talked, Señor, a while back, about you helping me. To set up on my own." A little plot of land. Green grass. A stream with trout in it. Horses. When he pictures it, his whole body aches with yearning.

Two deep lines appear between Don Ian's brows. He

leans back in his chair and passes his hand across his forehead. Raúl has seen him do this before; it reminds him of the way a horse shakes its head when it's more tired than angry. "Now is not the time," he says. "You know how things stand. I need people I can count on."

There is a tiny hint of threat in the Señor's voice. Raúl feels his face fall, but gathers himself and stands still and upright in front of the desk, gripping his hat in his hands. He is not used to the office, the desk a barrier between them. What would Lali say?

"You can count on me, Señor."

"I'm glad to hear it. So you'd better show it. If you leave now, people will think you don't trust me."

Lali has said the same thing, in his own, more colourful, way. But he couldn't bear to believe it. "If they know you've helped me, Señor, how can they think badly of my trust?"

Silence. What is in the Señor's mind? Does he think he can't give something to one of his men without stirring up unrest among the others? It makes no sense. The peons want their master to be generous: it gives them hope. In any case, one man is always paid more than another. The poorest of the shepherds earns less than the shearers, less than Raúl himself, far less than Lali. Sometimes his boss's logic is more than he can fathom.

Don Ian sighs. "Be patient. It's not a good time."

Be patient. When he has waited so long already. "But Señor," he says, hesitantly. "You know I'll pay you back."

"Yes, yes. Of course." The Señor meets Raúl's eyes. "Look. Wait six months and ask me again. We'll see." Raúl grips his hat tighter, tries not to look away. "When the time is right, I'll give you two or three more of the colts to bring on, how about that? Think about it – it's a better offer. You'll be making money hand over fist before you know it."

Three more horses from the Creed stock? In six months? This is more than he could have hoped for. Raúl leans forward to shake the Señor's hand, trying to conduct himself properly, like a businessman.

"Thank you Señor. I can wait six months. I will go to Héctor Torres, the greatest horse breaker in Santa Cruz. He has promised to teach me everything he knows. And in return, you know I'll break all your horses for you. The Creed estate will still have the best horses in Patagonia."

The Señor laughs. "Be careful. Don't promise more than you can afford to give. You're a businessman now, you should start striking better deals."

"Not with you, Señor. I owe all this to you. I owe you everything." It is the most effusive speech he has ever made. He can feel the heat rising in his chest, his throat tight beneath the knot of his neckcloth.

Outside the office, it is all he can do not to give a little skip of excitement. He feels light, skittish even, like a colt. As he passes the corral, Hero lifts his head and calls out. Raúl ducks under the fence and puts his arms around Hero's neck, whispering, "We did it. In six months' time you'll be living on our land and eating our grass," and the horse, sensing the excitement, throws up his head, making Raúl laugh out loud. "My boy. I'll give you the best oats in Santa Cruz. And you know what else, I'll build the stables first, I promise you. Then, a house. I'm going to build a house. Two rooms, one for Lali, a stove, and a table, and I'll sit there and talk about horses with Lali and with Héctor Torres, and some day I'll be a legend like he is. I'll have a water boiler like the Señor has in his office. And one day, who knows, even a girl. With shiny eyes like yours and curly hair." He stops abruptly, struck by the precision of the image. Hero throws up his head and Raúl blows softly onto the horse's nose to calm him. Hero's liquid eyes look straight into his, trusting and kind. "Look at you, Hero. You'll be king, you know that?"

When he turns, Lali is lounging against the fence, smoking, watching him.

"Well, Horse-Boy? How did it go?"

"He promised me. In six months."

"So soon?" Lali sounds surprised, but Raúl is too excited to care.

"He's going to give me extra horses. I'm going to go to Héctor Torres. He'll teach me everything he knows."

"Well then. You're all set. One day you'll be the most famous horse breaker in Santa Cruz, I know you will. More famous than Torres himself."

Their eyes meet and both fall silent. Lali's old gaze is uncharacteristically soft. Raúl is flooded with unexpected warmth. He wants to reach out and pull Lali towards him, put his arms around Lali's neck like Hero's, and he can't help thinking that if he were to do this, Lali would be not grey and grizzled and scratchy with age and ill temper, but soft, like the horse, and warm and gentle and kind.

Marta, Part III
Spring, September 1920

A house in Río Gallegos

I close my eyes and pretend I'm back beside the fire in my English nursery. It's still so cold, even though the snow is melting. Ice is dripping down the walls.

I dream my little man is in my arms. I whisper songs to him in case he's afraid of the dark. I'm rocking him to sleep.

Voices come and give me drink. They pick me up by my arms. I am heavy, I can't stand by myself. The women's hands are soft, their voices soft, as they carry me up the stairs. I want to tell them I'm afraid of stairs.

The men are hard. Boots and belts. Push and pull and heave. My eyes are shut.

When my gaucho was alive, he held me to the world. Without him, I am afraid of being gone. At least he has me to remember him. I have nobody. I am a rabbit, skinned and hanging on a stick.

Snow melts, ice drips. Winter, slipping into spring. Customers come and go. The women carry me up the stairs and down again and I sleep between their arms. They have names. Teresa. Verónica. Sometimes I don't remember their names as I don't remember my own. Pain is sharp and deep inside, or the crack of a hand against my face. When I wake up, I want to kill someone but I have nothing except my own bare hands. I hit my head and the jolt of it tells me I am still alive. It reminds me of the rattle of shaken bones, the thud of my mistress, falling on the ground.

When Horsebreaker came to this house I didn't recognise him. I thought he was my own beloved gaucho come to find me, and then I was sad, remembering my gaucho was dead. It was wrong of me to forget. I was afraid my old master had found out I was only half dead and sent Horsebreaker to kill me properly, but he didn't kill me, he took the thread that stopped me disappearing, that had been stretching thinner and thinner ever since my gaucho died. As long as Horsebreaker was there, I knew I was alive.

He reminded me of the English house, my mistress and my little man, my own dear, dead gaucho, and our dreams of the home we'd have together. The last time I saw my gaucho was in the days after my mistress died, when I slipped out of the house at night to meet him on the farm. Nobody noticed; they were all too sad. But when I crept back to my room like a tiny animal in the dark, my master was standing in the shadows at the top of the stairs. All those times I was so quiet, not getting caught, I never imagined he was up there, watching from the window.

He said, "You're a wicked girl. A wicked girl who lies. You spread rumours that are untrue, you've made trouble all over this farm. And you go out at night with men. You're lucky I won't say anything. If I tell the police you go with men at night, you'll be in worse trouble."

I never went with any other man, only my gaucho. He was mine and I his, and I tried to say so to my master. I tried to tell him that I hadn't spread rumours after my mistress died. I was crying. My gaucho had asked me what was wrong and I told him I saw nothing. That's all. But the Señor wouldn't listen. He held the candle close to my eyes so I couldn't see his face. He gave me some coins and told me to leave the house. I was still wearing my cape and boots. I wanted my second dress, the one my mistress gave me that I hid under the bed, but I dared not ask for it.

He put me out of the door and I heard him pull the bolt across. Still I stood there for a long time. I couldn't move. You know when you lose something, like a hairbrush or a pin, and you keep looking where you think it ought to be? Well, I just kept staring at that door, expecting it to open. I couldn't believe I had been put outside into the darkness, in the snow. I couldn't believe he wouldn't let me back in to sleep with my little man beside the nursery fire.

When the snow had covered my hair and my shoulders, and it was too cold to stand there any longer, I went looking for my gaucho, but he was gone. The only place I could think to hide was in the barn where the coffins lay, my mistress and her tiny baby, waiting for the ground to thaw. Nobody went near that barn, I knew I would be safe in there. I sat in the corner, covered in straw to keep warm, my back pushed against the wall, watching all night in case the coffins moved. I wish I had stayed outside and died of the frost.

My gaucho told me, after my mistress died, that if ever I felt in danger, I should run to a secret place, a faraway field on the edge of a clump of trees, and he would come to find me. I laughed when he said it, I thought he was joking. But that night I remembered what he said, and when the coldest hours had passed, I waded through the snow, the map he made for me clear inside my mind. Over the far side of the ridge, follow the fence all the way to the field shaped like a saucepan, past the clump of ñira trees where the sheep gather in springtime waiting for the sun to find the hill. It took me most of the day to get there. My hands and feet hurt, I was sick with cold, so cold I couldn't feel myself, but once the daylight came, I wasn't afraid. I knew he would come. When I saw a rider coming up the hill, I was flooded with joy. I wanted to fall down in the snow and weep with relief. But more horses followed, three, or four, and all of them were strangers.

The strangers wanted to know what I was doing, waiting in the snow. When I asked them where my own gaucho was, they said, "That man? He's a trouble-maker, now trouble has come for him." They meant he had been shot. I wanted to punch the one that said so, but he just laughed and said, "Believe me, you'll die out here of cold before he comes." He had folds of loose skin around his cheeks, and small, sharp eyes, like a carancho. He lifted me up onto his horse and put me inside his cape. A carancho, carrying me away. Through the cold I could feel him against me, and I couldn't breathe, I was shivering so hard I thought I might fall off the horse. I wanted to go back to the nursery and lie by the fire. I thought of my little man, how he would cry without me. When the gauchos stopped to make their camp, the carancho shot a rabbit and hung it over the fire. I was like that rabbit, skinned and hanging on a stick. I felt nothing.

During the day, one of the gauchos took me on his horse. At night they lit fires in puestos or caves, anywhere they could find shelter. We travelled at a trot, hours and hours together, wandering into snow so deep it reached the horses' shoulders, searching for ways to cross the frozen rivers, slipping on the ice. One of them shot a guanaco. I saw its frozen eyes, little runnels like tears in the corners darkening the fur. I shut my own eyes and remembered my gaucho, how he held me to the world.

All day I slept against the body of one rider or another, and at night one or other of them slept against mine.

When we reached the town, the gauchos took me to a house. At the sight of chairs around the fire, my knees buckled and I almost fell. The warmth of it loosened me. For a moment I thought I was back again in the English house with its fires and its furniture, safe at home with my little man, and my mistress still alive.

One of the women carried me inside and washed me. She dressed me like a doll in clothes too thin, too bright, too dirty. She tried to touch my face, but the cold had split my lips and the corners of my eyes where the wind made tears like the guanaco, and it hurt too much, so she stopped and gave me something to drink. That drink took away the pain and made the edges of me vanish like smoke into the sky. I slept. I dreamed my mother found gold at last and came to set me free.

A man came and lay beside me. I didn't feel him, but I knew he was there. He told me the woman had paid money for me to the gauchos. I don't know how much money. I wanted it to be gold, piles of gold, as if I were a princess. Other men came and went. The women gave me drink. Sometimes I woke up and remembered my gaucho shot by the police for being a striker, and my mistress, broken at the bottom of the stairs. When I remembered everything that happened, I wanted to kill them all.

22

Ian and Georgie

I am sitting with Ian in his study after dinner, watching the fire crackle and dance. Outside, snow whirls against the windowpanes.

"I want to thank you, Georgie."

"Really? What for?"

"You've survived almost a whole winter. It can be stifling here when you can't get away, but you've never once complained. You've worked wonders with Leo, and you've brightened up this sad old house." He smiles. "My mother is impressed, I can tell you."

"High praise indeed."

"It is. You know it is."

It's been so long since I've managed to impress anyone. For a brief, happy moment, I bask in the unfamiliar deliciousness of approval, like a cat arching its back beneath the hand that strokes it. We listen in silence to the flames, until he gives a shiver and sits upright. Like a horse, I think, when a fly lands on its shoulder.

"What is it, Ian?"

"Oh," his face looks hot in the firelight. "Nothing. Nothing, really."

"You can tell me. I won't mind."

"Really? Well... it's just, here we are, the two of us sitting side by side, looking into the fire and I thought, this is the picture I'd always imagined. Of how my life would be."

How his life would be? A widower in his twenties, alone at the end of the world? "I'm not sure what you mean."

"I don't quite know myself. Something to do with companionship."

Companionship? With me? I curse myself for being over-eager.

"Being able to sit in silence with someone," he continues and his voice is very soft. "Not being lonely." A wry twist of his mouth, an almost-smile. He has no idea how obvious his loneliness is.

"It must have been so hard for you." He blinks as though I have introduced something harsh. "I'm sorry," I add hastily. "I didn't mean…"

"No. It's fine. It never quite goes away, does it?"

He's right. It never quite goes away.

"Did anyone ever talk to you about the war?" he asks abruptly. "I mean, really talk about it?"

"Not at the beginning. They didn't want us to know. But some of the patients did, in the hospital. The ones who couldn't help it."

"Men wore out, you know, in the war. They simply… wore out."

"Yes. It's true. I've never heard anyone say it like that, but it's true."

"I dream about the war," he says, then shakes his head as if to clear a thought. "Sorry. I don't want to talk about that." His laugh is thin and mirthless. "My mistake, bringing up dreams. I dream all the time."

I want to tell him that I know about his dreams, that they are where he keeps his memories. Instead, I imagine my own memories, how I circle above them, diving in and out of the past. A remembering of the mind. Like flicking through the pages of a book. With practice, this kind of memory can be stowed, like luggage, beneath other thoughts. Beyond that, though, lies another kind, a wordless sorrow, carried always, a great weight inside my chest. I think of it as a remembering of the heart. With enough determination, or distraction, I could bear this weight, were it not for yet another, deeper remembering, the one that lies hidden and in wait inside the vessels and pathways of my body until a certain catch of light, a sound, or turn of phrase, skewers me, defenceless, to the past – to my brothers' laughter, the flicker of Eddie's smile. From this kind of remembering, there is no escape.

"Sometimes I dream about Alice," he says, sharply, putting out a hand as if I have interrupted him. My mouth goes dry at the thought that he might confide in me.

"How did you meet her?"

"At Cambridge." He seems unperturbed by the question. "I was invited for tea with my tutor in Grantchester. He had this old house by the river, a dusty, bookish sort of place, and there she was in the middle of it all, in a white dress, handing round the Battenberg. Who would have thought that old fart could father such a creature?" I wince at the unaccustomed coarseness, but Ian does not notice. His eyes are vague, as if looking at something I can't see. His fingers pluck at the tablecloth. "She thought I was exotic. All the English boys were so bloody predictable. Cricket, rugger, punting. Rugger, punting, cricket. I used to take her to the river and tell her stories. How my mother and father built a house out of old boats. How they saw off Indians and bandits. I was so homesick, all the time I was in England, but being with her made it bearable. We used to sit on the riverbank and I'd tell her about mountains and lakes and glaciers. She couldn't believe I had seen real whales and albatrosses, and pumas and condors and wild horses. She wanted to see it all too. She let me kiss her when I told her stories."

He breaks off and his eyes mist. Somewhere in his mind he is tasting Alice's white skin with his tongue, feeling the soft lash of her silky hair against his face. He is whispering stories in her ear, cupping in his hands her calf, her thigh, her tiny waist, gasping aloud at her perfection. I sit mesmerised, lost alongside him in his dream.

"It's been awful," he says softly. "Leo misses her, and honestly, I don't know what to say to him."

"I'm sorry."

"You understand, I know you do. But there were people round here who wanted to make it worse." A bitter laugh. "Talk about kicking a man when he's down. Do you know, after that dreadful girl started spreading rumours, the strikers even invented a story that I did away with Alice myself."

"What? That's ridiculous." I have read Mrs Creed's letters. The scene is clear enough: anxious midwives, grim-faced doctors, Ian distraught at the bedside, weeping over the loss of his wife and child.

"Obviously. There was some fairly incontrovertible evidence. You can't invent a dead baby." His tone is flat as a death certificate and I recoil from the unexpected brutality. But he's right: you can't invent a dead baby. He reaches over, gives my hand a little squeeze. "Don't look so upset. It's all nonsense. They were just trying to frighten me. But it meant I couldn't be quiet and think about her the way I wanted to, because there was all this other stupid mess to clear up first." A pause. "It still makes me angry."

"I can imagine." He had tried to warn his wife – *they say she's a bad influence* – but Alice had refused to listen.

His leg is twitching and he presses his knee into the floor to make it stop. "Sorry. Sometimes, when I think too much…" A rueful smile. "That definitely is a hangover from the war."

"Please don't apologise. Remember, where I've come from, I'm quite used to it."

He nods. "Of course. You were a nurse."

"Oh, I didn't mean…"

"That I'm an invalid? Thanks very much."

We both laugh. Ian leans over and pats my shoulder. Like a brother, I think, like one of my brothers might have comforted me, back in the days before they became part of my sorrow. I lean towards him, appreciating the gesture.

Snow swirls against the window. His hand lingers a moment longer on my shoulder, then I feel his fingers slide beneath my hair, brushing the nape of my neck, tracing the little knot of bone at the top of my spine. No longer a sibling's touch. No one but Eddie has ever touched me like this. I try not to quiver as his fingers scorch my skin. I am longing for him to comfort me; I am melting beneath his hand.

How stupid of me not to have seen it coming. I have felt it: small touches, the warmth of him through his coat as he walked at my side, but I didn't understand it then. No, that's not true. Of course I understood it. I did not dare to believe it. If I had, I would have been more careful. I must stop him. He is my employer. I must stop him before I lose control.

"Oh look. The fire needs a bit of help." I spring away from his touch, snatch up a log and thrust it into the flames, dislodging the wood already burning in the grate. Red hot sticks tumble onto the floor in a flurry of sparks. Ian crouches beside me. I can feel the tension in him. I try to smile, without looking up, busying myself with the embers. He takes my hands, forcing me to stop and look into his face. His eyes are kind, his face hopeful. He is so lost. And with a rush of panic, I realise – his mother knows about this. This is why she's been watching me. She thinks it's me, doing this.

He brushes a strand of hair from my cheek and I hold my breath. "Georgie, please. Whatever happens, don't leave us. We can't manage without you."

"Of course I won't leave." I must be careful, or I will ruin everything. The thought of leaving is as terrifying as the empty plain itself. I reach away to pull another log from the basket, making space between us. He waits for a moment, to see what I'll do, then straightens up and busies himself lighting a cigarette. I feel his hurt at my rejection, all the more painful when my skin is yearning for his touch. He is not the only one who is lonely. "Ian. I..."

He holds up a hand to stop me and turns away to stare out of the window into the darkness. The tip of his cigarette glows, mirrored, in the glass. I wait, but he does not turn back. Silence lies between us heavy as stone, the weight of it more than I can bear. I creep out of the room and softly close the door.

*

Tonight, the house feels more haunted than ever. I lie rigid in the darkness listening to nothing. What if his mother sends me away? I imagine my father's disappointment, the whispers of the village. I am too afraid to think about my mother. I want to creep into the nursery, curl up next to Leo's warm little body, but I daren't leave my room. After a while I give up trying to sleep, light my candle and slip onto my knees beside the bed.

All through the tiny crises of my childhood – homework left undone, petty thefts from the pantry, the accidental breaking of a vase – I have prayed. During the war, everybody prayed, even if they didn't mean it. I prayed before breaking off my engagement with Eddie, and afterwards, blinded by tears. I prayed when my father showed me the Creeds' letter: Look, Georgie. God has found you a home. I prayed when I caught the train to Southampton, and every night on the boat. After all those prayers, my mind is empty. I am conscious only of my body, the longing I felt when Ian's fingers touched my skin. My knees ache on the wooden floor. My father preached forgiveness: There is no condemnation for those who are in union with Jesus. Of course not. But what if I want the very thing I should be confessing? The union I yearn for is not with Jesus. The prayer is all wrong. And through me, like a wave, sweeps the prayer I have not dared to speak, the prayer I long for God to answer: Please, let him marry me.

PART TWO

23.

Horsebreaker

Dark days of winter lengthen into spring. The earth softens and Álvaro's body is laid into the ground. Lali scratches the child's name into a rough stone, somebody lays foliage and pebbles around the edges of the grave. The Talker sits on the ground outside the bunkhouse, drinking whisky through the night, muttering curses under his breath. In the mornings, his eyes are bloodshot and his hands shake. One day, he and Lali saddle their horses and ride over the ridge. Lali returns at nightfall with both horses. The Talker is not seen again.

Light begins to dance on the windows, early leaves on the silver birches throw patchwork patterns against the back of the house. Puddles and troughs still freeze in the hours of darkness, but water runs in the brook and white sky breaks into scudding clouds that cast shadows like moving inkblots, revealing behind them patches of brilliant blue. Men lift their faces to the sun, push their hats back from their foreheads and loosen scarves and collars closed tight against the winter cold.

It is time to bring in the colts from the winter grazings. Raúl likes to work in a paddock far from the corrals, where there will be no distractions for the horses, no gauchos leaning over fences offering advice: Why're you so slow? I can break a horse in an hour. Tie a rope around his legs, pull him down. Show him, if he doesn't look at you, he's in trouble. Give me the whip. Raúl has observed their methods and reached his own conclusions: el que se apura en la Patagonia pierde el tiempo. He who hurries in Patagonia, wastes his time.

The Englishwoman walks beside him. The air tingles with her presence. He has hugged each encounter with her tight against his chest: the way her expressions change as she looks at him, how each unintended touch stirs and unsettles him, as if she is both cause and relief of his disquiet. Sometimes he lies on his bed and examines these unfamiliar feelings, cautiously, as if tracking some timid creature burrowed deep inside himself.

But he must concentrate. He is afraid she will distract him. She will probably get bored and disturb the horse, and the work will be wasted.

"Siéntese y quédese quieta," he tells her.

This colt should not be too difficult. It is redomón – already part tame – though over the winter it will have forgotten what it learned. Now it stands at the far side of the meadow, rolling its eyes, snorting breath through flared nostrils. To win this horse's trust, Raúl will need to forget the nagging irritation of being observed.

As he approaches, the colt flattens its ears against its skull. Before he can get near, it is off, lunging to the end of the rope. Raúl holds the bridle behind his back until it settles and he can get close enough to stroke its neck. When he takes the halter, it jerks its head, throwing his arm backwards, but he hangs on, smoothing its nerves with words. The rope is taut between them as it drags itself away.

Slowly, slowly, he approaches once again. Eyes soft, but steady. This is the moment he must watch. If he lets the horse get away now, at best it will tear the rope through his hands. Worse, if it rears up, its hooves will flail above his face, and if it chooses, come down on his shoulders. Slowly. Slowly. The colt's ears flicker and relax. It lowers its head and the rope slackens. He never knows how it happens. Each time a miracle.

He could not tell how long he stays in the paddock, walking and stopping, walking and stopping, first in circles, then at the horse's side, showing him how the reins move, how to turn, to start, to stop. The sun has crossed the sky by the time he leads the colt towards the fence where he has left the saddle. He will start with just the sheepskin, laying it across the withers, then the saddle itself, slowly, slowly, until he can lean his whole weight on it without the animal objecting. When the colt stands still, he will know it is safe to put one foot in the stirrup, then up and over, onto its back. If it won't stand, he will use the maneas to hobble its front legs.

As he reaches for the sheepskin, he notices the Englishwoman sitting beneath a tree. Has she been here all this time? She must be frozen. He busies himself again with the horse. Now the hardest part is over, he does not care that she is watching.

The colt's flank twitches at the sheepskin, as if shuddering a fly. Raúl presses down a little and it lowers its head in acceptance. Harder will be the saddle itself, and then the girth around its belly. When he pulls on the buckle, the animal bares its teeth and flashes the whites of its eyes. Raúl keeps talking, very slowly leaning more and more weight against its back, and, although it stamps and shakes its neck, the colt does not fight him. But when he finally lowers himself into the saddle, it barrels its spine and leaps off all four legs, bucking and spinning. He clings on as it fights to be free, but his grip loosens until he is at a right angle to its flank. The next minute he is sitting in the grass, still holding the reins, the colt snorting and heaving at the other end of the rope. He had forgotten the Englishwoman again, now he sees that she has rushed to the fence and is watching him with fear in her eyes. She has no idea. This is how it works, a necessary part of the job. As the rodeo riders say, he can only fall as far as the ground. Nonetheless, it is humiliating to see the concern in her face, as if he has made a mistake. He dusts

himself down and pulls the maneas from his pocket. This time
he will take no chances. This time he will mount the horse.

Once its forelegs are hobbled, Raúl begins again. The
colt quivers, all nerves and flattened ears, but allows him
to lower his weight into the saddle, then lean down and
release the maneas. Slowly, they walk around the paddock,
Raúl reminding the horse how to turn, until he is ready to
guide it along the path, back into the yard. He glances at
the sky; he must have been working another three, maybe
four hours. Occasionally the horse turns its head to stare
at the Englishwoman, who walks beside them without a
word. Sometimes she is distracted by the flutter of a bird
or the passing of a shadow across the grass. If she is cold
or tired, she doesn't show it: when she catches him watching, she smiles. Her eyes are very bright. She is probably
the same age as himself, though she seems much younger,
with a childlike manner he does not recognise. If she were
a horse, she would be brave and unusual, like Hero, with
his bright eyes and flying mane.

In the corral, he takes off the horse's saddle, brushes
sweat from its back. This one, he will counsel Lali to sell.
The horse is good, better than good. But only the very best
horses in Santa Cruz are good enough.

When he has finished, she is waiting. "That was wonderful," she says in English. He feels the warmth of her words
and wishes he had been less impatient with her.

"You stayed all the time?"

"Was it very long? I didn't notice."

Now he is free of the horse, she asks questions. How,
and how, and how? Her questions are like water, sliding
away before he can grasp them. He cannot find words in
English, or in any language, to explain what happens with
the horse, the trust and the tenderness.

"At the shearing, I will show you," he tells her.

"It's a kind of magic," she says, but her eyes are serious.
"I want to understand what you do."

For a moment he considers telling her about Ian Creed's promise, about Héctor Torres, about what it would mean to become the greatest horse breaker in Santa Cruz. He has no idea how to talk about these things. Instead, he will show her Hero. How it is possible to work with a truly fine horse. How he crawls between Hero's legs to shelter from the weather, or stands on the saddle like an Indian to look across the plain. How he puts a hand on Hero's neck and lays him down, stretched out on the grass, and from there, rolls Hero onto his back and holds his forelegs and lies flat along the horse's belly, like a lover. As he imagines showing her, he wonders why it matters to him that she should understand.

Georgie's Diary

It's been some time since I've written, and there is so much to say. Every day I see things for the first time, as if the world itself is in the very process of creation.

Today I observed an episode that reminded me that nature is indeed red in tooth and claw, that this land may be innocent, but it is also brutal. I am not naïve, I know there are times when we cannot save those we love. But surely, when given the opportunity, we have to try.

Riding with Ian beside the river, my eye was caught by a carancho struggling in the grass, clutching a gosling in its claws. Each time the carancho tried to fly off with its prey, it could get only a few inches off the ground before it dropped the gosling, which then picked itself up and hurried on its little legs in the direction of the river.

The baby must have been exhausted, perhaps even injured from its repeated falls. If we did not intervene, the carancho would certainly win in the end. Of course this is nature's work, but I couldn't bear it. I jumped down, ran towards the battle, and shouted. The carancho took flight and hovered out of reach, and this time, the gosling managed to reach the water. It struck out for the other side where the mother was fluttering anxiously, calling to it. I was sure it would be safe, but there was the carancho again, swooping down, the gosling, quite literally, a sitting duck in the middle of the river.

My heart was in my mouth. But at the last minute, just when I was sure that all was lost, the gosling dived beneath the surface and disappeared. What a trick! The carancho swept over the empty spot, flew up and away. The gosling resurfaced. Twice more the carancho dived, twice more the baby ducked, confounding its attacker. Each time, I cheered.

After the third time, the frustrated carancho gave up and flew away in disgust. I was ecstatic. It felt so grand to stand up for such a tiny, defenceless little thing. Ian laughed at me. Look, he said, now the carancho has to go hungry. But why should it eat the gosling? I asked. It's a scavenger. It can eat all the dead things and do no harm. Why must it insist on taking a vulnerable little gosling? And why do we not have the right to intervene, to help when we have the power to do so?

And to this, Ian had no answer, because he knew that I was right.

24

Mr Green and Mrs Foster

As Pig Day defines the winter, so the first shearing is the mark of spring. Passengers and puesteros fill the bungalows and barns, new peons move into the bunkhouse. Local farmers add their flocks to the Creeds' vast herds to be shorn in exchange for helping hands.

The estancia's closest neighbour, Thomas Green, arrives with his wagon. His tiny farm carries just a few hundred sheep.

"I'm a shabby little outfit," he tells me in his soft Scots accent. "A one-man show. Nothing like your Creeds. I'm lucky they tolerate me." He quizzes me about Suffolk farming practices and regales me with stories of his Falklands childhood. "Full of Scots it was, a home from home." When I ask how he came to Patagonia he laughs gently. "That's a story for another time. Come and visit, Miss. You'd be most welcome and then we would have plenty of time for stories."

His quiet civility infects me with a little flutter of homesickness: he reminds me of my father.

"How is it that he's all alone out here?" I ask Ian.

"I've no idea, though there are plenty of rumours. I don't know what the truth is, and I don't care to pry, but apparently he fell foul of his family when he was a young man and was packed off without much more than the coat on his back. Had to fend for himself ever since. So he has his little farm and minds his own business. Keeps his head down."

"Whatever can have happened?" I wonder. "He seems so kind."

Ian shrugs. "Something to do with an unsuitable woman, I believe." He laughs. "It usually is."

The Creeds and Mr Green shut themselves in the study for hours. I hear raised voices. When they emerge, Ian looks exhausted. Mr Green's face is hot and flushed, but he lays a hand on Ian's arm in a gesture that seems like friendship.

Next to arrive are the Fosters, in a motor car from Punta Arenas. They are to stay in the guest bungalow. Robert Foster is Ian's accountant. He joins us for lunch, but his wife sends regrets: she is not well enough. "She's terribly tired from travelling," he tells me apologetically. Behind his back, Mrs Creed rolls her eyes and taps her finger against her forehead.

"Might she like a visit?" I ask, trying not to look at Mrs Creed. "When she has settled in?" Mr Foster gives a vague smile, which I take as permission.

*

The visit is brief. Expecting an invalid, I am taken aback by Mrs Foster's neatly pinned hair and smart city dress. "Forgive me," I say, suddenly self-conscious in my muddy boots, "I'm such a fright."

Mrs Foster scans me up and down and nods before extending a bony hand, limp and cold in my palm. She is young – the Fosters can't have been married long – and very pale, with a mouth that turns down at the corners, as if in a state of permanent dissatisfaction.

We stand on either side of the doorstep. "Might I come in?" I ask.

"Oh, yes. Of course." Mrs Foster sounds distracted. "You must forgive us. We haven't unpacked. I can't offer you any-thing." The dark little hall is full of luggage. Mrs Foster steers me through to a small sitting room and throws some cushions on the armchair. On the desk a small picture frame holds a decoupage rose, sister to the one I found in the attic.

"It's lovely to meet you," I venture, trying not to stare. "I've hardly met a soul since I arrived. Especially not other ladies." Next to this languid woman, I sound ridiculously over-eager.

Mrs Foster gazes at the grey sky outside the window.

"Yes. You must find it pretty dreary."

"Oh no. Not at all. I'm busy all the time. But…" I glance at Mrs Foster's expensive dress, "I'm only the governess. I suppose it's a bit different."

Mrs Foster nods and I stifle a quiver of irritation. I was not expecting her to agree. Now I am cross with myself for allowing her to patronise me.

"And you're surrounded by all those awful farmers. That's why I have to hide out here. Most of them can't stand each other. Green's a frightful communist." I gasp. "Anyway," she continues before I can protest, "I expect you have your work cut out with that poor child." Her thin fingers pick at a loose thread on her sleeve. "Alice was my best friend."

"Oh, I'm so sorry." No wonder Mrs Foster's manner is so strained.

"Didn't Ian tell you?"

"No… No, he didn't." I shift in my chair to avoid looking at the rose. "Did you and Alice come out here together?"

"I came to visit. We knew each other at school."

"And… you stayed?"

"Yes. I met Robert." A short laugh. "It seemed a good idea at the time."

"What was she like, Alice? I mean, I've seen photographs, but Ian doesn't say much. Obviously."

"Obviously," Mrs Foster looks me up and down. "As you say, you are only the governess."

I try not to flinch. "She was very pretty."

"Pretty? She was an angel. Maud was terribly jealous. I'm sure Maud was the toast of Río Gallegos." Mrs Foster's tone is scornful. "But Alice… the whole of Buenos Aires would have gone mad for her if she hadn't been stuck here. I stayed with her, of course, as often as I could."

The statement feels coded, as if Mrs Foster is hinting at something, and would say more if only I could find the right question. But I have no idea what is expected, so I resort to simplicity. "Were you here when it happened?"

"No. I was in Punta Arenas, waiting for her. She was supposed to come, to have the baby. As soon as the snow thawed."

Alice's letter. *I am packed and ready.* I leap in my seat as if she has spoken the words aloud. This woman must be Claire, Alice's correspondent, the keeper of her secrets. She knows about Ian's nightmares, and about Marta. When I read Alice's letter, I was so fixed on Ian's dead wife that I heard only the voice of a ghost. But of course the letter was intended for a reader, someone still living. I have intruded on a real conversation.

Mrs Foster hasn't noticed. "I can't stop thinking that if I'd been here I might have been able to… oh, I don't know. Robert says it's stupid, there's nothing I could have done, but still, I still think…" She breaks off, stabbing at the braiding with her fingernails. "Do you know, the ground was so hard, he couldn't even bury them." Behind her words, a shutter bangs somewhere in the wind. The chilly room seems to whisper before it settles back into stillness. Mrs Foster's restless fingers twitch. No wonder the servants believe in ghosts.

"I'm sorry." She rouses herself a little. "It's just… it's been a year now. I should be getting over it, but I can't seem to. Robert's worried about me. He says it's making me ill. But I'm not ill, really, I'm just terribly, terribly sad."

"Oh…" A rush of sympathy. "It must have been terrible. No wonder you're cut up. But I can help. I'll think of ways to cheer you up." The prospect of having a friend, someone other than the Creeds to talk to, is suddenly overwhelming.

Mrs Foster smooths her skirt. Her back is very straight. "I'm not staying. Robert's taking me away, right after the shearing." She glances around the room, then leans forward and lays her cold hand on mine. "Take my advice, dear. Don't stay here too long. It really isn't safe."

*

Mr Green takes my arm and we walk together into the garden. The late afternoon light is grey and soft.

He gazes out towards the hills with a sigh. "Such a magical moment. Time caught between day and evening." A pause. "I do envy you, Miss. This is a magical moment for you too. Your whole future is waiting for you. You should treasure it."

"And leave the past behind," I say, without thinking.

He looks at me in surprise. "Yes. Quite right. You can choose what to take and what to leave behind." There is a hint of sadness in his voice. "I wish you only joy, Miss Georgie."

I want to ask questions, but I don't know where to start. Mr Green gives my hand a little squeeze. "Come, my dear. It's cold. Let's get you home. One day, we will sit together, you and I, we will drink maté and laugh and tell stories. I have a feeling we will always be friends."

25.

A proposal

Leo and I sit side by side in the nursery, chanting numbers. Two twos are four, two threes are six. Milky sunshine streams through the windows and the fire crackles warmth. I am still thinking of Mrs Foster. Don't stay too long. It isn't safe.

A swishing of skirts in the doorway. "Georgie!"

"Mrs Creed. Can I help you?" I jump to my feet, trying not to look guilty. "We've been doing times tables," I add pointlessly.

"Yes, Georgie, I see. Perhaps Leo can play by himself for a few minutes."

Before I can reply, Leo has hopped down from his chair. Mrs Creed watches him go, her hands clasped together. The knuckles gleam white.

"Mrs Creed… is something wrong?"

"On the contrary." The words are clipped, unusually high-pitched. I feel my own mouth tightening. I am catching her anxiety like a disease.

"Georgie, dear, I wanted to speak to you about something very… particular." We both hear the tiny pause, the slight inflection. I hold my breath.

"My son has expressed to me his affection for you."

My mouth drops open. "No, please." She puts out her hand. "Let me go on. This is not easy." Another pause. "You must know that Ian is very – charmed – by you, Georgie.

It's impossible not to notice that he is…" She clears her throat. "That you have attracted his attention."

I feel a slow flush rising from my neck.

"I understand why he has fallen for you. You have been more than a governess, Georgie, much more. We love our home, but for newcomers it can be… difficult." I open my mouth to protest, and she holds up her hand again. "Let's not pretend," she says. "When I came here to marry Stephen, I knew what to expect. But Alice, if she had lived, who knows? Perhaps she would have stayed, perhaps not. She was rather… self-important." A little shake of her head, as if clearing a memory. It is the most she has ever said about Alice. "Anyway. I have been watching you."

Yes, I think. You have been watching me. And now I know why. I have been on trial, but not as a governess.

"You are young," she continues, "but I believe you have the right qualities to be happy here. I believe you would make Ian a good wife."

I bite down hard on my lip and taste blood in my mouth. I want to laugh aloud at the absurdity of Maud Creed making a declaration. "I had no idea." I can't think of anything else to say. She must surely know I am lying. Although I have hardly dared to hope. "He still seems so…" I remember my words to Mrs Foster. "So cut up."

"Be that as it may." Her eyes are almost closed, her face shuttered like a pair of blinds. Her blue-veined eyelids tremble slightly. "Ian is a young man, a father. It is wholly desirable that he should…" She opens her eyes again and takes a deep breath before continuing. "Georgie. It has always been Ian's intention to marry again one day. He has told me he would like to marry you. I believe he wishes to speak to you after the shearing."

"Why hasn't Ian spoken to me himself?" And why has his mother chosen to tell me now? Mrs Foster's words whisper in my mind: Don't stay here too long. An image arises, unbidden, of Raúl leading Ángel down an icy slope, back braced, his whole body intent on keeping me safe. But this is no time for childish fantasies.

"I am telling you, Georgie, because Ian is all I have." I open my mouth to interrupt, but she silences me again with her hand. "I was seventeen years old when I married Stephen. I believed I could do anything. We expected to have many sons." What happened? Babies lost, or never born at all? Does Mrs Creed lie awake at night, listening to the tapping of other tiny fingers? With an effort, I drag my attention away from the wind in the trees, the creak of branches outside the window. Her voice drops. "He has no idea that I am speaking to you, Georgie. I am trusting you to keep confidence for his sake. He has suffered – greatly – and I would not wish you to make an ill-considered response to his proposal. Please, Georgie, remember, he has suffered."

So this is why she has been watching. For the sake of her son. And I, so foolish, so quick in jumping to conclusions, have misunderstood everything. A rush of reluctant admiration, jealousy almost. Isn't this true motherhood, this fierce protection?

I think of my own mother, rendered incapable by grief, retreating into indifference. The day I came back from Eddie's house, she looked, unblinking, at the tears tracking my cheeks. "I'm not getting married anymore," I told her, and she narrowed her eyes and pulled back her head as if smelling something unpleasant. "Aren't you going to say anything?" The words were a plea.

My mother sighed. "What do you want me to say?"

If she had stood up for me, I might still be living in my home, not thousands of miles away on the other side of the world.

But it's too late for that now. Here I am, in Patagonia. And, at last, the path is clear. "I understand," I whisper.

Mrs Creed lays her hand on my sleeve. "I wouldn't like Ian to think we have been talking about him. This must be our secret. Let us not speak of it again, at least until after the shearing."

She holds out her arms, and I step clumsily into her embrace. My heart is bursting. If what she says is true, I am to have a husband. I will care for Ian and Leo, Mrs Creed too, if she will let me. I will have a family. And I can make amends.

26

The gauchos

Icicles hanging from the eaves drip into puddles. The brook roars. Through the damp haze the scrub glows with wild-flowers, and October sun streaks across the green tips of new grass which flows like water in the wind. Patches of brown and purple earth appear across the plain. Sometimes I run onto the ridge, leaning forward, letting the wind hold me in its invisible arms, or sprint across the plain, pulling Leo behind me, guanacos galloping before us and disappearing against the horizon. Upland geese rise from the stream with the cry that sounds like their name – caiquén, caiquén – leaving their eggs hidden in the grass in nests of warmest feather down.

We find a collection of bones under a bank of trees: a lamb, ribs and jaws picked clean, neat leg and hoof still covered in fur. "A carancho lives up there," says Leo wisely, and sure enough, when we sit on the grass and wait, the bird appears, its absurd cockerel strut and puffed-out chest belying the cruel beak and glinting eye.

There has been no further hint that the conversation with Mrs Creed ever happened, and I am beginning to wonder if I misunderstood, or even imagined, the whole thing. A land for people who aren't interested in talking, Ian once told me, and the Creeds more than anybody seem content to fold themselves into silence. I try to contain my impatience, telling myself to wait for the shearing. I busy myself as best I can with Leo and the rest of the household. How very English we all are.

*

More travellers arrive at the estancia. I gather food from the kitchen garden with soil-blackened fingers. When I was little, I used to follow behind my mother as she cared for her roses; eager to please, I marvelled at every shoot and bud, stroked velvet petals with my fingertips. On good days, she allowed me to hold her gloves or carry the basket. Once, when she lost patience with my chatter, she pulled my hand into the rosebushes and crushed my palm around the thorny stems. Now will you learn to keep quiet?

Cook teaches me how to tend the flowers that grow along the beds, encouraging bees for honey and wasps to kill pests that might otherwise eat the lettuce and spinach leaves. She shows me the rye, cropped in autumn by the cows so it grows back stronger after the winter freeze. While Leo chases the dogs in circles, I make a list of seeds and bulbs to order from Punta Arenas, and imagine experimenting with fruit trees. When the calafate is ripe we will gather the berries to bottle and preserve, saving some for medicines to treat colics and fevers. If The Talker had used calafate instead of morphine, perhaps Álvaro might still be alive.

One morning, I find two unfamiliar gauchos lingering in the shadows between the outbuildings, blocking the narrow path. There is an oppressive heft to their stillness, concrete as a boundary drawn in dirt. Their eyes flick over me and back to each other, the taller gaucho raises his hat. He has blue eyes that chisel into mine. I shift uncomfortably beneath his gaze. Mrs Foster's words whirl inside my mind: it isn't safe.

"Do you want something?" I ask in Spanish. "Shall I fetch Señor Creed or Lali?"

"Fetch Señor Creed and Lali." The shorter man speaks Spanish with an unfamiliar accent. He has the bowed legs of a horseman and snakes of filthy hair beneath an unusual

156

black-and-white hat. Beneath the discomfort, he seems oddly familiar. His mouth twists into a sneer. "Maybe Señor Creed would like to tell us what is happening here. First, the girl, and next the little boy." He is holding something in his fist. Now he opens his palm to show me. The label is illegible, but I know what it is: the empty vial of chlorodyne I threw into the snow.

He taps the knife at his belt, then slides his thumb across his throat. The blue-eyed gaucho makes a mocking bow and gestures for me to pass. Neither of them moves aside. I know now where I have seen the shorter man before: at the demonstration in Punta Arenas. The revolutionaries have found their way here to the estancia. My eyes are fixed on the knife. I edge past the two of them, holding my breath, and hear their laughter behind me as I break into a run and bolt for safety.

When I look back across the yard, nothing remains but the shadows cast by the outbuildings. The horses rest slack-mouthed, their backs turned against the weather. Scurries of dust blow across the corrals. I hurry on, head-down, until I collide with a figure coming from the stables.

"Miss? What's the matter?"

It is the horse breaker. He takes my arms, steadying me.

"Oh, Raúl. That man from Punta Arenas is here, the one with the knife." I am gulping for breath like a child, willing myself not to cry.

The horse breaker's eyes flicker across the yard. He is still holding me, and I am afraid he will let go. "Did he hurt you, Miss?"

I pull myself together. "No."

"I will take you back to the house."

"No, wait. I'm alright now. Raúl... what is happening? Why did those men come here?"

"They have come to find out about Álvaro, how he died."

I picture the empty chlorodyne bottle.

He does not look at me, but picks at green moss growing along the top of the fence. I stare at his broad fingers, jagged nails blackened with dirt, knuckles lined and dusty. A working man's hands. I have seen those hands tousle Leo's hair and steady a wayward colt. I have felt them beneath my foot, and warm around my waist.

When I look up, he does not move. His face is alive, even in stillness. With my eyes I trace the arc of his cheekbone, the dip of his temple, the hairline, strong and square, and back down to the nape of his neck, disappearing into the cloth he wears at his collar, the thick flannel shirt below.

Never before have I looked so closely at a man's face. Not Ian's, with its weary pattern of lines and shadows. Not Eddie's. Eddie was quicksilver, always moving: when I looked into his face, it was straight through his eyes to the bright flicker of his soul. The horse breaker stands motionless before me. A hundred years pass. Time to wonder what he might think of me, staring as if I have never seen a man before. A movement takes seed beneath my skin, a melting and a tightening.

A shout from across the yard. "Georgie!" It is Ian. I jump as though I have been caught doing something wrong. Perhaps I have. I had forgotten him. "Horsebreaker?" Ian's voice is assertive. An estanciero speaking to his shepherd.

"The Señorita was concerned, Señor, about a gaucho she has seen here today."

"And what has that to do with you?" I try not to flinch at the sharpness in his tone.

"I startled her, Señor, as she crossed the yard."

"Georgie? Are you alright? Did someone harm you?" Now Ian is all solicitude, Raúl forgotten.

"I'm fine. It's true, Raúl made me jump, but I'm fine now."

The horse breaker touches his hat. The gesture reminds me of home, of every countryman I have ever passed out walking in the Suffolk lanes. It makes me want to fling my arms around his neck.

"We should get you inside," Ian says, and something in his voice compels me to disagree.

158

"There's no need. I'm fine, honestly."

But he takes my arm in his. I feel no excitement at his touch, rather an unfamiliar resistance. I dare not protest: an argument in front of the horse breaker would humiliate us all. Instead, I allow him to lead me through the sticky gate, across the garden and back inside the house.

*

In my bedroom, I take my little Bible with its well-thumbed leaves, my father's beautiful copperplate inscription unwavering across the frontispiece. I push my face between the pages, breathing in the history of my life. The book smells damply of salt and sea air. Behind the sea voyage, I can still smell the comforting leather-and-tobacco of my father's study and, more distant, Suffolk clover and cow parsley, the faint country church echo of incense and dust, even the trace of sweet peas in my attic bedroom. When my father gave me this Bible, my love of God was as simple as a summer walk to church. In Patagonia, I have no experience of summer, only the vast snow-laden weight of winter, and scudding clouds flying before the spring wind. I can't pray. Instead of God, or Ian, I see only the horse breaker's blackened hands, the lines around his eyes, the shadow where his neck disappears beneath the collar of his shirt.

I have forgotten the world. I have forgotten everybody. When Leo tiptoes through the door and climbs onto the bed beside me, I roll over and hug him tight. He squirms and pulls against my arms.

"Ow, ow... Georgie, what are you doing?"

"I'm sorry, darling. You woke me, that's all. For a minute, I couldn't remember where I was."

"I came to get you for dinner. Will you get ready now?"

"In a moment, Leo, of course. I just need to wake myself up first." I kiss the little tousled head.

He wriggles himself free. "Don't be late, Georgie. Dinner's almost ready."

At dinner, I remember the gauchos.

"What gauchos?" Mrs Creed asks. "What are you talking about?"

A throb of anxiety passes across the table. Ian widens his eyes, just a fraction, silencing me. "Nothing," he says. "Right, Georgie?"

Mrs Creed pushes back her chair and stands at the window, staring into shadows. The wind blows across the plain, loose fingers of brush scraping new patterns into the dirt.

"There's no one there, Mother," Ian says, and I look at him, questioning. He lays down his napkin and sighs. "Mother's got the wind up. Damn union men poking around again." She closes her eyes, as if to shut out his words. "We had some nasty problems here last winter, after…" He breaks off, and I see the pain in his eyes. "After Alice died. I told you. But it wasn't just talk… they cut some fences, damaged a bridge. Pretty awful stuff."

Cut fences? I remember, on our ride, Raúl frowning, turning a broken wire in his hands. A lurch of fear at the gaucho's thumb, drawn viciously across his throat. If they cut fences, would they cut throats too?

"Can you go to the police?"

"Nonsense," Mrs Creed snaps. "We don't want anything to do with the police. When will you learn to stop talking, Georgie?"

The rebuke stings. I bite back tears.

"Oh, for goodness' sake." Ian's eyes dart between us. I can't tell whether it is me or Mrs Creed who has made him angry. His gaze rests on me and his voice softens. "Can we please drop this? It's not Georgie's fault. Mother, you're behaving as if we've got the Russian Revolution here. It's just a pair of stupid gauchos."

Mrs Creed draws her face in towards her neck as if she

has been struck. "Well," she says. "Let's hope for all our sakes that you are right."

"Of course I'm right. Let's talk about something else, shall we?" He turns to me, spreads his arms wide in apology.

Mrs Creed puts her head in her hands. Suddenly she looks tiny, and very lost.

"Come, mother," Ian says. "It'll all work out." A short laugh. "We can fend off these gauchos and anybody else who's coming our way. Just like we've always done."

After she has left the room, he lingers for a moment at my side.

"I'm sorry, Georgie."

"No, please. Don't be." I have seen the gauchos. I understand his mother's fear.

"Is there..." he falters for a moment, bites his lip. "Is there anything else they said? That I should know?"

I don't want to look at his throat. "They said..."

"What? What did they say?"

"They said, 'First the girl, and next the little boy.'"

"Oh, God, did they?" He wipes his hand across his forehead. "That's the girl I told you about, the one who worked in the house. For goodness' sake, it was a whole year ago. I can't even remember her name."

But I can. *They say she is a bad influence.* "The gauchos made it sound as if both of them were dead."

"Did they?" He sounds so tired. "I don't know what happened to her. How could I? She's not here anymore. But if she is dead, I suppose they'll make it my fault for letting her go. Not that I wanted to, it was my mother's idea, she was trying to protect me." He shakes his head and rubs his fists against his temples. "God, how awful. I can't bear to think about it. Let's have a drink in the study, why don't we? Talk about something more cheerful." He holds out his hand and for a moment, I panic, thinking this is it, he is going to propose. Instead he says merely, "Come with me, Georgie," and I feel my shoulders fall as I breathe out in relief.

27

Union meeting

Some days before the shearing, Horsebreaker and Juan Sant ride into town with errands to run. It's an uninspiring raggle of a place, but where else are the peons to spend their hard-earned wages? Raúl expects to part company, but Juan Sant takes his sleeve and pulls him back.

"Come with me. I'm going to a meeting. You might find it interesting."

*

Raúl lounges against the far wall of the union building, breathing in sweat and sawdust, watching the backs of men crowded into the hall. He can tell a lot from men's shoulders. Like horses. Broad shoulders mean the horse is strong and true. Narrow shoulders, blades sharpened with hunger – think twice before you trust.

It was stupid to come. Too many people, too many words. He doesn't want to think about what would happen if Lali discovers he has been here. Lali wouldn't understand his curiosity, the need to find out for himself. He would slit Juan Sant's throat.

Sant pulls at his arm. "Look, there's Soto."

The crowd falls silent as Antonio Soto walks to the front of the room, shaking hands and slapping backs. The gestures are jovial and open-hearted, but with each greeting Raúl sees anxious eyes, muscles held tight around smiling mouths. He feels an unexpected lurch of fear.

Soto seems absurdly young. His eyes are shining, his face is bright as a child's. Unlike the others, he seems utterly unafraid. Despite himself, Raúl leans forward to listen.

"Comrades." Soto's voice rises and falls. "The government of Santa Cruz has turned its back on us. The estancieros have betrayed our trust."

There is a low rumble of assent and disapproval.

"Not our estanciero," Raúl mutters to Juan Sant.

"Our demands are not great," continues Soto, his words quivering with emotion. "We ask only for the most basic of conditions. What man can live like an animal, working without pause, beaten by his master when he wearies at his labours, valued less than the mules and oxen? Are we serfs, or slaves?"

Again, the assembly murmurs. Raúl stands up. "Me voy. I'm going. I don't belong here." A couple of listeners gesture for him to keep quiet and he shoves past them towards the doorway. Juan Sant follows him through the crowd to the edge of the room. "Our estanciero has nothing to do with any of this," Raúl hisses. "He is keeping to the agreement. He's a good man."

Juan Sant laughs softly. "Lucky him. Wouldn't we all be good men if we had the chance?" He lays a hand on Raúl's arm. "Anyway… you think he's doing it for love?" His voice is heavy with sarcasm.

"Why shouldn't he be?" Now they are daring each other with their eyes.

"Oh, come on." Sant is still half-smiling. "We both know what his men would tell the police if they thought it would do any good."

"Shut up. There's nothing to tell. Only rumours."

Sant shrugs. "You're right. Only rumours. I heard there was a wife and now she's dead. I heard there was a witness and now she's missing." Raúl opens his mouth to speak, but Sant hushes him. "It doesn't matter. The police aren't going to listen, they'll say it's revolutionary talk." He laughs. "Your estanciero had better stick to the agreement. The law won't touch him, but sometimes justice comes in other ways. Somebody cut his fences. And the bridge. That could kill a man."

"I'm telling you, che, it's all nothing. Shit. Mierda." Raúl's fists are clenched.

Juan speaks soothingly. "So it doesn't matter, even if he is a murderer..."

"He's not a murderer!" The missing witness is another story, not one he's willing to share with Juan Sant. Right now, he hates the old man and his union and his stupid revolution.

"At least if he sticks to the agreement, some good has come from it. You know Green is sticking to it as well."

"Green? Who cares about Green? He's nobody."

Juan Sant smiles his mocking smile. "You're right. But he's an honest man. He's sticking to the agreement. Not because he's afraid like Creed, but because he knows it's right. That makes him important."

"But don't you think it's this man..." Raúl gestures towards Soto "...who creates the problems? We're not slaves."

"You're right. Creed treats us well enough. But I've seen places where the workers live among the animals and don't get as much to eat."

Raúl sighs. The man's conviction is like a pebble in his boot. It will not let him walk free. "I wish you luck, friend."

Sant holds out his hand. Before Raúl can take it, there is a whistle, a soft knock at the door.

Raúl jumps. "What's that?"

"Police..." The warning ripples through the crowd. At once, someone is turning a key. Those nearest the lamps lean over, with a soft breath, the room is plunged into darkness. Juan Sant grabs Raúl's sleeve. On the other side of the building another door is swiftly, silently unbolted. The men gather around the narrow doorway, then part once more to let Soto pass between them. Raúl can feel the hammering of hearts as he waits his turn with the rest: one at a time, or they'll jam the only safe exit, but quick, quick, before it is too late. The smell of sweat rises. Behind them, there is a pounding on the front door. Someone is shouting. Wood cracks, the lock splinters, the police are inside as the last of the crowd pours onto the street, soft as water, slipping away into darkness. Nothing remains but a whispered presence, vanishing over the crossroads and scattering along the streets of the darkening town.

Heads down, collars turned up against the wind, Raúl and Juan Sant stand at the corner of the square watching shadows disappear into the gloomy night.

"Now what?" Raúl's heart is still pounding.

"I'm going to see a friend." Sant seems unperturbed by the narrowness of their escape. A conspiratorial wink. "You want to come?"

"What? No, I..."

"Ah, come with me. I'll treat you. We're almost there. Don't pretend you have anything better to do."

Raúl follows Juan Sant along a muddy back street to a dark little house close to the port. No light escapes the windows, but when Juan taps at the door it opens almost immediately, just a crack, as if the proprietor has been waiting. A pair of black eyes peers round, a long white arm in a black glove reaches out and takes hold of Sant's jacket – that crumpled, inadequate coat – and pulls him inside. Raúl slips in behind, blinking in the light.

He has not been in this house before. It has a pungent smell he recognises, at once sweet and acrid, of talcum and soap and cheap scent, over a headier mix of cigar smoke and ripe, unwashed bodies. The woman with the black glove wraps herself around Sant, twining her fingers into his hair. She pulls his head back and puts her mouth to his neck. Sant groans. Raúl looks away, stuffing his hands in his pockets.

When he looks back, he is alone. Across the doorframe, a curtain ripples. Pushing it aside, Raúl finds himself in a dimly lit hall, Sant and the woman a single shadow beside the stairs. He sits in an armchair, listening to the whispered slur of voices, breathing in the warm scent of women.

Whatever Raúl knows about women, he has learned in houses like this. He has no memory of his mother. He knows nothing of sisters or grandmothers or aunts. Sometimes a curious passenger asks about his family, but he can only shake his head and shrug. Perhaps he carries somewhere in his mind a vague picture of long hair and soft arms, but he has no idea if the picture is real. Memory begins with a gaunt man calling himself Uncle, who carried Raúl from Chiloé with whispered stories of sheep and gold, and untold riches at the end of the world. Uncle lay down in the snow one night and never got up, taking with him anything that might have remained of Raúl's past.

Lali is the nearest thing Raúl has to family now, and he never speaks of women. Just as Raúl's past was lost somewhere on Chiloé, so Lali's was left behind in Russia. At some unspeakable time in a long-ago life, a part of Lali burned and died along with his family. The body that remains is dried like a calabaza, husked and impervious to the softness of women or the liquid sensations of desire.

From childhood, Raúl listened to the talk of peons seeking relief from the solitude of the plain and the brutality of the bunkhouse. These are the lucky ones. Those who live alone in the huts, or work along the remote shores of the islands have no such recourse, they find other ways to satisfy their needs: an occasional stranger who rides too close, or one of the unfortunate animals in their care. One winter, when Raúl was eight or nine years old, an emaciated shepherd with empty eyes and a face covered in scars trapped him against the back wall of the empty shearing shed and fumbled between his legs. Raúl bit and kicked, but the struggle lit fire in the man's dead eyes. He held a hand over Raúl's mouth, turned him over and tore off his belt. By chance, Lali was passing. He hauled the peon off, beat him senseless and sent him away. To Raúl, this house and its women seem wholesome in comparison.

He had always understood that one day he would follow the other men into town, and they would induct him into the mysteries of their experience. Privately he wished it could be Lali who would show him what was expected, but Lali never spoke of such things and Raúl could not bring himself to ask. Publicly he smiled and shook his head when men slapped him on the back, telling him he'd be in there soon enough. In the end it was El Gordo, an ugly old gaucho named for his great belly, who plied him with drink and shoved him through the crack in a door much like this one, roaring with laughter at his discomfort.

"Here," El Gordo shouted, digging his hands into his pockets and throwing a pile of coins onto the table. "This one's on me. It's your birthday, Horsebreaker."

He pushed Raúl down onto a filthy chaise. Raúl, who had never sat on anything other than a wooden bench or a horse's leather saddle, perched on heavy velvet, trying not to touch the tassel that swung beside his boot. El Gordo disappeared behind a curtain on the other side of the hall, Raúl heard whispers and giggles before the curtain rustled again and a woman appeared.

She stood back, appraising him, mocking him with her smile, then tucked El Gordo's money into the front of her dress, and climbed onto his lap, pushing him backwards into the chaise, threading her arms around his neck. Her face was so close that even in the dimness of the lamplight he could see flakes of dry skin underneath the powder on her cheeks, the fine spider of lines around her mouth and eyes.

"First time, my darling?" When he was unable to speak or even nod his head, she hitched up her skirt, took his hand and slid it along her leg, flattening his palm against the bare inside of her thigh. Her skin was softer than the softest thing he had ever touched, softer than the velvet nose of a horse, the silky fur of a puppy. Despite his fear, he wanted to keep his hand pressed there, to lay his cheek against that skin, to touch it with his mouth. The heavy sweetness of her perfume made the room swim. He felt an unfamiliar tightening, a flood of heat to his groin, and seated as he was, he had to grip her hard to stop himself from falling. She gave a whimper and slipped out of his grasp, then took him by both hands and pulled him up the stairs.

The bedroom was dark with heavy curtains at the windows and across the door. He could not see her face and understood that it must be so: if there was light enough to show the stains on the bedclothes, the tired lines around her eyes, the sagging skin, he would be disgusted with her and with himself.

Spreadeagled beneath her, he felt the lumps of the mattress under his back. Her fingers unbuckled his belt, she nuzzled at his belly and for a second her tongue flickered over the tip of his cock. He could not breathe. She clambered onto him, pulling her knees up each side of his chest, clamping herself around him. The soft warmth of her took him by surprise. He arched his hips and shuddered in her arms, emptying himself in wave after wave of heat and wet and salt and spray, then pushed her aside and rolled away, brushing back tears that welled unexpectedly in his eyes.

He had wanted to go home.

He never saw the woman again, or learned her name. Since that first time, his irregular visits became as routine and mechanical as a stop at the general store. No more tears. Neither anticipation nor regret. Despite the briskness of the business, he learned to appreciate the uncritical good humour of the women who ebb and flow through houses such as these. They seem happy enough to see him. Watching their bodies draped across one another, stroking each others' hair, they remind him of kittens rolling together in sunshine. In those moments he has felt the faintest echo of longing, not for their sex but for their softness, the tactile warmth of their companionship.

This time, he remains downstairs, listening to the music and murmurs of the house. He has no money to spend and everyone seems to have forgotten about him, so he waits among the rich, heady smells for Sant to return. It seems that against all his better judgement he is willing to follow this old man's lead into unexpected places, and into memories he would rather leave undisturbed. The girl who was let go scratches at the back of his mind; most likely she will have found her way into another, similar house. It is easier not to remember her. His thoughts turn instead to the estancia, to the colts he will break this spring. As his mind drifts home, it rests again on the English governess. Another kind of woman. The women of these houses are thick-limbed and broad-shouldered, strong as oxen. They think nothing of working in a laundry all day, servicing their customers at night. The Englishwoman is different: fragile, with her wisps of pale hair, her transparent skin and slender limbs. Now he is caught, thinking of her waist, the curve of her hips when he held her between his hands. The way she leaned against him, how the warmth of her took the breath from his body. How she looked at him so closely he was afraid of her, and of himself. As he conjures her in his imagination, he realises how much he does not know. He is overwhelmed with longing for the familiarity of Lali and the safety of his home.

Marta, Part II:
First winter, August 1920

The estancia

Snow fell. My first winter in the South, I had no idea such cold was possible. I missed my mother. My mistress was tired all the time, even before she was carrying the baby. We all heard the Señor at night, came to know the low rumble of his dreams, the screams that followed, the crash of fists against walls. The first time, I hid my head and stuffed my fingers in my ears, but the other servants explained to me that terrible things had happened to him in a far-off land called Europe, in a war, and once I understood it was not some ghost or monster in the house, I wasn't afraid. I was sorry for my mistress though, sharing her nights with those dreams. I used to creep along the corridor to help her as she leaned over him, stroking his hair. I knew she preferred me to the old Señora. Sometimes, when she could hardly lift her head for tiredness, she would let me take her place at his side so she could rest. In the mornings, her face was grey, her eyes red-rimmed. I was so worried for her, especially once she was carrying. When she told me she would go to Punta Arenas, to have the baby there, I was happy, knowing her friends would take care of her. We just had to wait for the snow to melt and then she would be safe.

The day I met my gaucho, I was walking on the ridge as he rode by. It was still winter, but the sky was clear, the snow sparkled and I wanted to be outside. He asked my name and I couldn't speak, his belt and his silver spurs shone so bright my heart was bursting. I thought I might die at the sight of him. He laughed and his voice was full of brightness too. He said it was too cold for me to be out on the ridge, but not to worry, he knew how to warm me. He took me in his arms and stroked my hair. I was grateful for his warmth, the way his body covered the empty spaces on my skin. He made me forget about my mother. In the days and weeks that followed, he taught me how to creep out of the house at night and wait under the straw in the furthest of the barns until he came to meet me. I was his china, his woman, and the day was coming when we would have a place of our own and always be warm together. All day I waited for the night to come.

He taught me about politics. I wasn't to tell anyone that he touched me. They would say it was wrong, even though it wasn't. He said the estancieros told lies because they wanted to control me. He told me how the workers had tried to be honest, they made an agreement asking for small and simple things, but the estancieros always lied, they said one thing and did another. I know some of what the workers asked for, though I don't remember everything. They wanted money, of course, and candles. I shivered to think of that bunkhouse in the night-time, without a single lick of flame to light the dark. They wanted water too, to wash themselves better, their clothes all smeared with mud and shit and worse from the animals and the weather. When I told him we had candles and water in the house, how I washed my dress and dried it by the nursery fire, he laughed and said I was so grand, he was a lucky man to know me.

I told him how beautiful my mistress was, how much I loved her, and my little man. My gaucho warned me to be careful because any child born in that house would grow up to tell lies like the rest of them. I cried to think of it, but he said I would find out soon enough. Sometimes I dreamed my gaucho and I would carry my little man away with us, so he could grow up fine and honest.

That winter was the worst anyone could remember, even the old men said so. It broke my heart to think of my poor mistress after she died, how she and her poor little baby had to lie outside in the barn with nothing to cover them but the wooden lid of a box. No wonder my little man heard the baby knocking and woke up crying in the night.

After my mistress died, the old Señora kept my little man close. Nobody noticed me. I crept out to meet my gaucho because I wanted his comfort, but when he tried to touch me, I was stiff and cold as a corpse myself. I couldn't feel anything. When he asked me what was wrong, I couldn't tell him about my mistress. I just told him the baby came and she was dead. He said, we all know that, but what has happened to you? Why are you so frightened? I was too afraid to say anything different from my master, I told him only that I didn't see anything. He asked, what do you mean, you didn't see anything? But I could not say anything else, I just kept telling him I didn't see anything, I didn't see anything, until he shook me, saying, Stop, I understand you. Stop. You don't have to say this any more.

I don't know what he understood, but he held me in his arms and whispered, Now is the time, and I had no idea what he meant.

The truth is, I've never told anybody what I saw, but the next morning, rumours started. Posters in the yard with writing. Whispers at the kitchen door. I didn't know what a witness was, but my gaucho said I was one. I tried to tell him it was dark, the candle fell, I saw nothing, but he said it was too late for that. He said the Señor had promised to take care of me properly, it was part of the agreement. If he wanted to let me go, the agreement said he must take me to the town because I couldn't get there by myself.

I laughed at him. I couldn't believe what he was saying.

What was he talking about, take me to the town? The Señor would never let me go. Who else would look after my little man? Who would care for my little rabbit now his mama was dead?

My gaucho shook his head at me as if I was stupid. Weren't you listening? I've told you, you can't trust them. Listen. If something bad happens, you must run to the field – the one shaped like a saucepan – and wait for me at the crest of the hill, beyond the ñire trees.

That field is far away, I didn't want to run there, but his voice frightened me, so I held his words and whispered them at night to keep me safe.

Soon after came the night I ran upstairs and found my master waiting for me in the attic. He was watching for me from the window. He wanted to catch me. I thought he would kill me there, but instead he took my wrist in his hand and led me down the stairs. Right up until he opened the door, I didn't understand what he was doing. I didn't believe it. He put me out of the house to die in the darkness and the snow and save him the trouble of killing me himself.

I knew from my gaucho that the Señor was supposed to take me to the town. That was part of the agreement and he had signed a paper with the unions to say so. I didn't know how to tell him though. How could I tell my own master what he was supposed to do? So he put me out of the house. When I heard the bolts drawn against me, I knew my gaucho was right, my master was a liar after all. My mistress was good but she was dead, and my little man would grow up without her and they would teach him how to lie. I wept and hammered at the door. I didn't want to leave my little man to grow up among such terrible people.

I stood outside in the darkness, knocking and crying, but nobody came. If anyone heard me, they might have thought it was the Señor having one of his dreams, grieving his lost wife. Or a ghost, asking to be let in.

I didn't believe I would die. Even when I was outside in the dark, hiding in the barn with the coffins, so scared fear froze me more than cold, I knew I had my gaucho and I knew he would save me. He was the thread that held me to the world. I didn't have a candle, but as soon as there was light, I ran like he told me towards the field where I should wait. I knew that he would come.

28.

The shearing

For days, a roiling ocean of sheep has gathered in anticipation of the shearing. When the work at last begins, a
tremor spreads across the farm like the echo of a distant
earthquake. Leo is shaking with excitement as he and I
race across the garden and through the sticky gate. Outside
the shearing shed, peons whoop and whistle over hectic
high-pitched bleating. Gauchos loop their horses back and
forth, herding the sheep between the mata negra bushes,
their dogs running at the fringes of the herd, barking strays
toward the pens. The sheep are funnelled through wooden
runs into the barn. Boys wait inside to drive them forward,
shouting and whipping the air with rags.

The team of shearers stands in front of the gates. At the
clang of a bell, each man drags a sheep out of the pen and
hoists it onto its haunches, clamped between his knees. A
few deft cuts, twisting the sheep from one side to the other,
and the fleece is removed in a single piece. The boys run back
and forth along the line, snatching up each fleece, clearing
the way for the next animal, while the newly naked creature
staggers away, dogs snapping at its heels. Each shearing
takes only minutes. Lambs shrill beside ewes, springing in
vertical leaps and bounds. The stink of lanolin rises above
the dust as the boys snatch brooms and sweep up cast-off
lumps of wool, tossing them into huge sacks, climbing inside
to trample down the contents in a wild, high-kneed dance.

Others carry great armfuls of fleece to be picked clean of the filthiest scraps and loaded into the baler, the finished stacks trundled along metal rails to wagons waiting outside.

I stand against the wall, gripping Leo's hand, absorbing the pungency of leather and lanolin, the cacophony of sound, the ceaseless flow of horses, dogs, and sheep. Ian's eyes are shining, his cheeks flushed. Excitement pulses in him, quickening my own blood.

"What do you think, Georgie? Quite something, isn't it?" He has to shout above the noise.

"It's extraordinary," I shout back at him. "But isn't it cruel, Ian? Look how the shepherds are holding them."

He leans down, his mouth close to my ear. "Oh, they're alright. It's only the yearlings who panic. Next time they'll know the drill. It would be crueller not to do it."

"How so?"

"The fleece would be too hot in the summer. And the wool grows so fast, we have to shear around their faces, otherwise it grows over their eyes. If it freezes, the shards of ice can blind them."

I observe the skill of the men. The work is backbreaking, the clippers shave perilously close. Sinews strain and muscles bulge as the shepherds turn the sheep between their legs. I begin to see a kind of magic in the way they hold each animal perfectly still, mesmerised almost, until the work is done.

After an hour, the bell rings again. The shearers stop to rest their backs and wipe sweat and grease from their faces. During the break, one or two of the older boys take up the clippers for practice. I watch as they wrestle with a struggling sheep, trying to control its scrabbling legs, while the shearer explains how to hold and where to cut. These lads don't yet have the magical powers I have observed in their elders, but they will learn. Year on year, they will practice and become skilled. A little sob catches the back of my throat: Álvaro should have been here, running and laughing, his arms full of wool, trampling in the sacks like the other boys. Learning his trade.

Leo tugs on my hand, pulling me into the yard. Thomas Green waves as he circles his little flock. At the far end of the track, Lali sits tall on his horse. I put a hand over my eyes against the sunlight and watch him flick the end of his reins across the horse's shoulders and canter to the back of the herd, a dark silhouette against the bright sky. He draws alongside Raúl, on his Hero, and leans over to say something as he passes, touching the younger man lightly on the face. The gesture is one of such shocking intimacy in the middle of the teeming mass of sheep and shepherds that I lower my head, as if I have intruded.

When I lift my eyes, the horse breaker is looking in my direction. He could not have seen me watching, yet I flush beneath his gaze and turn away. When I look back, he is gone.

I find Leo sitting high on one of the wagons, bouncing up and down on the bench beside Mr Green, helping to count the old gentleman's tiny flock.

"Georgie, Georgie. Mr Green has a baby ostrich. It lives in his house."

"Really?" I am as delighted as Leo.

Mr Green smiles. "My ostrich and I would be honoured if you would pay us a visit."

"We would love to." It would be a relief to do something so ordinary. Soon the shearing will be over. I have not dared imagine what might happen next. "I look forward to it," I say, firmly, as I reach my arms up for Leo, and the little boy jumps down, nestling against me like a baby. "Oh, Leo, you're too heavy for me," I tell him as I hug him close, feeling the warmth of his breath on my cheek, his little heart beating against my chest. Did Alice grieve as she felt herself leaving him behind? When my brothers died, my mother would have gone with them if she could; two sons dead left her indifferent to the living. The hurt of knowing she loved them more still splits me in pieces. I bury my face in Leo's soft cheek, kissing him until he squirms, giggling in my arms. Perhaps one day I will truly be his mother.

On the last night of the shearing, when the barns are still and the exhausted dogs stretch flat across the grass, the shepherds sluice themselves clean of sweat and filth, and build a bonfire behind the outhouses. I hear their music rising with the smoke and slip outside the kitchen door to listen. Soft notes mingle with grey sky. I had not realised until now how much I have missed music, the plangent tone of an organ, the soaring voices of a choir.

Ian finds me sitting on the step, eyes closed, leaning my head against the wall. "So this is where you are. Do you want to go and see?"

"May I?"

"I would have walked over later anyway. I ought to show my face. I'll take you now, if you like."

The night is cool but clear, and for once it will not rain. Stars are beginning to prick through the dusk. I have no idea what time it is: these long southern evenings, sky pale almost until midnight, still confound me. At home, villagers are waking in darkness, stamping frozen feet in the lanes. Soon they will be preparing for advent, lighting candles, gathering holly to hang in the churches. Somehow it is a relief not to recognise the season: the strangeness keeps my homesickness at bay, protects me from tiny moments of familiarity that pierce my heart. In any case, Advent, and Christmas, have meant nothing since my brothers died.

"I wanted to talk to you." Ian's voice is tender.

I am shaking so hard I might fall. I have prayed for this, now I can't bear to hear him speak. What if it is nothing – a horrible mistake? Or worse, some other dreadful trick of Mrs Creed's? I push open the sticky gate and run ahead of him into the yard. "But we're almost there."

"Hold up, Georgie. Give a man a chance." When I look back, his eyes are fixed on me, shining in the grey light.

From behind the bunkhouse rises the sweet smell of

woodsmoke and roasting lamb. A metal tripod straddles the fire, flattened carcasses hang across the frame like crucifixions. Fat sizzles in the flames, shooting blue sparks into the sky. Men are draped across the ground, or lean against the fences, smoking and passing the maté. Some of the Europeans pick at guitars or mouth organs. The Chileans play small flutes, breathy threads of sound that disappear like smoke into the night.

Thomas Green lies on the grass among the shepherds, next to Juan Sant. Sant's haunted expression unnerves me and I look around for other familiar faces. A tiny handful of women sit with their men – puesteros who have brought their sheep to the shearing. I don't recognise any of them. Robert Foster, perched on the edge of a stool, waves in my direction. I avoid his gaze, scanning the crowd for somewhere else to sit. There is no sign of Mrs Foster.

Mr Green spots me hesitating. "Over here, Miss," he calls. The gathering parts to receive me, someone lays a scarf across the grass. Lali, presiding over the bonfire, hands me a hunk of meat, still spitting and steaming. Green passes a maté bowl and I lean forward to sip through the straw, the sharp jolt of bitter herbs burning the back of my throat.

The music swells. Ian has caught up, now he lowers himself onto the grass behind me, too close, all limbs and angles, so I have to shift to make space between the two of us. The peons narrow their eyes and edge away. It hurts to see them make their dislike of him so obvious, but for once he doesn't seem to notice. His hand shakes slightly as he leans forward and lays it over my own.

"Eat, eat," Lali exhorts me, digging me in the ribs and pointing to the lamb. I pull my hand free from Ian's, hoping no one has seen, and bite into the tender meat, juices running from my mouth and through my fingers.

When the bones are licked clean and thrown to the waiting dogs, the musicians sit up and their tunes grow faster. Some of the men dance little jigs, feet tapping in double time until the whole crowd is clapping and chanting. Juan Sant sways from side to side, his old eyes rheumy and vague, as if remembering some distant past. A couple dance a polka, the woman's skirts whirling in the firelight.

Thomas Green jumps to his feet. "Come, Miss Georgie, dance with me." He holds out his hand. Ian smiles – go ahead, it's fine – so I allow Mr Green to swirl me around the flat grass beside the fire. More couples join the dance, flying in circles, spinning past me in the firelight.

The song changes and the dance grows faster. Thomas Green makes a little bow and hands me to Lali. Lali's long grey hair flies as he swings me around in an increasing frenzy of whoops and turns before tossing me back across the circle towards Ian. But Ian is not ready – or perhaps he is afraid to dance with me in front of them all. For a second, he hesitates. And it is Raúl who jumps in front of me, opening his arms. I fall against his chest and we swirl together into the dance.

The breathless notes of the pipes and the racing fingers on the guitar strings fly us round, faster and faster. Raúl's hands are strong around my waist. I laugh up into his face and see the reflection of my own eyes shining in his, or perhaps it is just the glint of firelight. Somebody trips, pushes against a neighbour, and the dancers topple, falling one over another into the grass. Raúl's arm tightens around me. I feel the rise and fall of his chest as he takes the weight of our tumble and we are sprawled together on the ground.

At once he has righted himself, and is crouching at my side. "Are you all right, Miss?"

I can scarcely speak. The crowd has disappeared, the music has receded into silence. I dare not move in case the spell is broken.

Now Ian is here and leaning over, taking my hands, lifting me.

"Are you alright, Georgie? Let me help you." His voice is tender, anxious. I nod and smile as Raúl jumps to his feet and disappears into the crowd.

29.

I am on your side

After the shepherds' party, Ian and I walk side by side back to the house. Somehow I am still breathless from the dance. The juices of the lamb have dried stickily between my fingers, the echo of a bruise throbs at my hip, and I feel the imprint of Raúl's hand on my waist as clearly as if he is still holding me. I stumble against the kitchen step and pause inside the door to light the lamp.

When I look up, Ian is on one knee, gazing at me with huge, hopeful eyes, his folded limbs vulnerable as a child's, all pointed joints and elongated shadows. I suppress a sudden, vivid wish that he had proposed on horseback. But when he takes my hand and holds it to his mouth, the pressure of his fingers, his lips, the intensity of the gesture is overwhelming. A flush of excitement rises in my cheeks. I can feel the heat of his palm as his hand grips mine: he is more nervous than I am.

"You know what I'm going to say. And I mean it, Georgie. I swear I mean it. It's what I'd like more than anything. I want you to stay here forever, and this to be your home. But…" He hesitates, biting his lip.

"What are you doing?" I ask, trying not to pull away.

"All I want is to ask, and for you to say yes," he says, urgently. "But I love you for your honesty. You've levelled with me about Eddie, so it's only fair for me to do the same. There's one more thing I want to tell you. Then you'll know everything about me." I wait. Something about the war, probably. I heard confessions in the hospital, too many. I know the shame and horror soldiers brought home. Or perhaps he wants to tell me about the sleepwalking. It feels oddly satisfying to think I already know him far better than he realises. "It's about Alice." I think of Alice, how she follows me around the house, and pull my hand from his. Immediately, I feel guilty. "I haven't told you," he continues, "because, well, I just couldn't bring myself to say it." A pause. "But you're so honest and fine and truthful. I can't go down on one knee and ask you for what I want – what I want with all my heart – until I've told you everything."

My throat is dry, my heart beating so hard he must hear it.

"You know what it's like," he says, "when something bad happens and you feel dreadful, even if it's not your fault, and then everyone tells you it actually is your fault, so often that you start to believe it yourself." He's right. I know better than anyone. I take his hands again. "They've tried to turn me into a monster," he says. "But I'm not. I swear I'm not."

All his sad little jokes, trying to pretend it doesn't matter. "Of course you're not."

"The thing is, everything I've told you about Alice, about what happened to her, it's all true. What you don't know is that the baby came early. We were waiting for the snow to thaw, to take her to Punta Arenas. There was plenty of time. She wasn't supposed to have the baby here, she should have been in town, with doctors and nurses, with her friends around her."

I say nothing. He can't know that Claire Foster has already told me. And Alice herself, in a letter I never should have read.

He presses the heel of his hand against his forehead as if trying to awaken a memory. He looks so much like Leo, I want to put my arms around him. "She had an accident. I want to tell you what happened," he says, "but the damnable thing is, I don't know. I honestly don't. It was at night. I had this terrible dream. I have nightmares, since the war." I nod, but he doesn't seem to notice. His voice is barely audible now. "All I know," he continues, "is that I woke up, and there was a god-almighty thud. You know what it's like here, the wind, it's always crashing around, but for some reason it scared me half out of my wits. Alice wasn't there, so I went out to the hallway, and she was at the stairs. Running. And then she tripped."

I sit down, abruptly, as if the air has been punched out. Of course. He has already told me. Alice is lying down. Her hair is in her mouth.

He doesn't notice. "Dying in childbirth is irrefutable, but falling downstairs isn't. Not when there was a witness."

"A witness?"

"The girl. The servant I told you about."

Marta.

"She was already causing trouble," Ian continues. "She'd got all caught up with this union fellow and it was obvious we had to let her go. I was even afraid she might do harm to Leo. I overheard her once telling him she wanted to take him away. Can you imagine? But Alice felt sorry for her, so she was still in the house. Anyway, she told her fellow she'd seen me there when Alice fell. She couldn't say more, I wasn't on the stairs, I was nowhere near, and she knew that, but the whispers got around, and once they took hold..."

He takes a long breath. "That's the whole story. I swear it. It's politics, Georgie. We all know the peons don't care about Alice, and any other time they'd just be sorry for me and forget about it. But Marta gave the strikers something to hold against me, to justify their grievances. My mother let her go, of course, but that just made it worse. One more thing for the unions to complain about. And now there's..." He stops abruptly, but I know what he can't bring himself to say. Álvaro. One more thing for the unions to complain about.

"No matter what I do," Ian continues, "however hard I try to help my men, there's always someone who'll start the rumours up again." He shakes his head. "Talk to Lali, to Horsebreaker. The people who know me. They know how much I loved her."

Talk to Raúl. Raúl is everything that is trustworthy and good in this place. And I too know what is true. Ian doesn't lie. Look at his face, everything he's been through etched into the shadows beneath his eyes.

It is I who have been sleepwalking, too preoccupied with my own grief to notice what is happening around me. Too complacent, thinking I knew everything. "It's all nonsense," I say, trying to sound calm. "How can they possibly blame you? Who listens to a disgraced servant?"

"I know." Now he is looking directly into my eyes. "Nobody who matters believes any of this. But here's the thing, Georgie. I don't know what Alice was doing in the hallway and I'll never know."

I resist an urge to look back at the stairs. "But – if you don't know – I mean, Marta was there too…"

"I know," he says quickly. "I've had the same thought. If she could spread those rumours, what else was she capable of? Maybe she…" He breaks off. "I've hated myself ever since, for not knowing. For not waking up sooner or getting to her quicker. For not protecting her. None of us will ever know what happened. But the men, they're so bloody superstitious. They need an answer for everything."

I think of Pilar, the baby knocking at the window. They need an answer for everything. "But they mustn't matter. Your mother knows the truth. And your friends."

"And you? What about you, Georgie?"

No hesitation. "I'm on your side." I feel him willing me to tell him the truth. After such a confession, it is the least I can do. I nod my head fiercely in affirmation. I am shaking, not from fear, but from the injustice of it. I would run through fire to defend him.

"I can't tell you what that means to me. Please, Georgie – tell me you don't hate me."

"No. No, of course I don't hate you."

"My mother, she fights for me like a puma. And Lali too. He's on my side. Apart from that – who else have I got?"

He is on his knees again. My heart is in my mouth.

"Please," he says. "I don't want to be on my own anymore. You said it yourself: each time it's like a little bit more gets scraped away. We've both had to put ourselves back together as best we can, and we live with what's left – this patched up, broken version of ourselves. Someone has to forgive us. Don't we both deserve a second chance?"

There are tears in his eyes. I think of his men, their bitter, hostile faces. He was going to build a water boiler for them in the bunkhouse. I picture Raúl, the vivid warmth of him as we danced. With Raúl I am like a foolish village girl with a childhood crush. But Ian is offering me the chance to grow up, to help this poor, broken family heal its wounds. I am needed, I am loved. How could I ask for more?

30.

Eddie

In the days after the shepherds' party, I stand on the ridge, watching the wagons lumber across the plain towards the great ships that will carry the wool to Europe, then sit alone under the carancho's tree, thinking about Eddie.

The night Eddie was brought in, the other nurses tried to stop me from seeing him. It was a miracle he made it back to England; by rights, he should have spent his last hours in a field hospital in France. But there he lay, a wretched heap of bandages piled haphazardly onto a stretcher, carried home to die by fellow officers who loved him. How like Eddie – right up to the end inspiring acts of devotion in friends and strangers alike.

I held his hands, whispering words he couldn't hear. "Eddie, darling, I'm here. I love you. God is coming for you, Eddie. Soon it will be over."

Except it wasn't over, because God, working in one of his more mysterious ways, performed an unexpected miracle. Slowly, slowly, the doctors pieced Eddie back together. We all thanked God, the hospital, anyone who would listen. But the Eddie who survived did not share our gratitude.

I accepted his bitterness when he railed against his own survival, the curt responses, the long, painful days when he withdrew into himself and turned his face towards the wall. I was sure his spirit would heal along with his body, and all would be well. I told myself that one day we would hold each other and laugh to think that we had ever been afraid. I searched for the brightness in his soul, and pretended to myself and everyone else that I could still feel it. I pushed aside tiny cracks in my patience and regaled anyone who would listen with stories of Eddie's courage and resilience, refusing to believe that all I had left for him was pity. But whispers of doubt played havoc with my dreams. I prayed the doubt away and it pushed against my prayers. In time, I began to fear that the unthinkable had happened: Eddie's brightness had been extinguished and only its shadow remained. Still, I smiled through the gradual scraping away of hope and spirit, reminding myself that I was one of the lucky ones. My fiancé was alive. I was not the one who had suffered. How dare I imagine myself unhappy, how dare I talk of wants and needs, when Eddie had lost everything and I still had so much?

The end, when it happened, was quick.

It was a grey autumn afternoon, still warm but muggy, heavy with the expectation of colder weather. The leaden atmosphere inside the big house was more than I could bear. Full of manufactured enthusiasm, I offered to take Eddie to the village. It was the first time I had suggested we go further than the big house gardens.

"Let's try it," I said brightly, as if to a child. "I promise I'll bring you straight home if you don't like it. You'll love it once you're out there." I could hear the pleading note in my voice.

"I don't see – why you want to," Eddie had answered hoarsely. Each word cost so much. "If you're bored – you might as well go home."

"Of course I'm not bored." Now I was indignant. "I thought you'd like it." I pressed my hands against my forehead, trying to relieve the frustration.

"I don't want – to see the bloody village." His voice was jagged as a broken knife. "People – staring." He stopped to draw breath, hands twisting in his lap. "Oh look, another bloody cripple. What the hell – is wrong with that one?"

"Oh, Eddie." A rush of sympathy. Once, he had been the most beautiful creature in the whole county. "Nobody thinks that. Everybody loves you. They're grateful, and respectful. They'd never..." Did he really hate himself so much? "Honestly, is that what you'd say if it was you looking at somebody else?"

"No – of course not – I... It doesn't matter." His voice was small. I felt a tiny moment of triumph at the admission.

"You see." Now I could be brisk, encouraging. "So why would anyone think that way about you? Let's go out, Eddie. Please."

He shrugged, defeated. I wrapped him in his blankets and called his man to carry him down the steps and wheel him along the gravel path. At the gate I said, "Let me take him from here." The man had raised an eyebrow, glanced toward the house – what would Eddie's parents say? I insisted: the road was flat and smooth. And besides, I wanted to show the world what I was prepared to do.

I took a deep breath and set my strength against the chair. As we rolled forward along the lane, my confidence grew, and I began to chatter freely, pointing out sparrows and blackbirds, old man's beard in the hedgerows, rabbit holes along the verge. Tiny things, simple and familiar. Eddie was quiet, but I could tell by the steadiness of his breath that he was not agitated. My spirits lifted to feel the softness in the air, the gentle green of the countryside weaving its magic, perhaps drawing Eddie back from the barren landscapes of his nightmares. Bringing him home.

We came to the crossroads at the end of the big house lane. Earlier in the week it had rained, and the road was in poor shape. Across the path lay two deep and rutted tracks.

"Stop," said Eddie.

But I was full of optimism. "Come on, Eddie... we've only just got going. Let's try it."

"Georgie." His voice was raised as far as he could lift it. There was a rattle in his throat as he gasped for breath. "Stop. Go back."

He was at my mercy. We both knew it. But I was convinced the walk was doing him good.

"Just one try. If I can't get across, we'll turn back, I promise. But I think I can do it." Without waiting for an answer, I braced myself, hauled on the handles to tip the chair back, and gave a decisive shove.

The chair moved forward a few inches, then jerked to a sickening halt as one wheel caught and stuck in a deep furrow. Eddie shot forward, then fell back again with a cry. I threw my shoulder against the handle, pushing with all my strength to keep the chair from tilting further, terrified it would tip him into the mud. He was grunting with pain, jamming his weight as best he could against the awful angle of the chair. At last, between both our efforts, I managed to set it more or less upright, but by now it was caught fast, heavier than ever and listing horribly, with Eddie pushed painfully against one side, swearing under his breath.

Once I was sure the chair would not topple, I threw myself down at his side.

"Oh God, Eddie, are you alright? I'm so sorry." And with the words, tears coursed down my cheeks.

"Shut up." Eddie hissed. "Shut up. Stop it." His voice cracked with pain. Beads of sweat glistened on his forehead, the pressure of leaning against the metal arm almost unbearable. Fear rose in my chest, and I held my breath to stop myself from screaming. I could never lift him on my own, nor could I leave him while I ran for help.

As I crouched, useless, at his side, Eddie lifted his head and jerked his neck forward, to something on the other side of the lane. I followed his gaze. Someone was watching from the shadows beneath the trees. Of all the people in the village, it was Sarah Gerard – *that* woman. Before I had time to call out, she was running across the lane, wading through the mud and bending down over the chair. Her arms were under Eddie's shoulders.

"Lift," she said curtly, hoisting him up, and I yanked the stuck wheel free, back onto firm ground. Sarah Gerard, blowing from the effort, twisted Eddie's body round so it was level with the chair, and dropped him into the seat. He gave another grunt of pain. She stepped back, panting, and stared, not at Eddie, but at me. Through the terror I saw her, as if for the first time, lifting her crippled child, shouldering her drunken husband, carrying an entire family on her exhausted back. I tried to mutter thanks, but already she had turned and was hurrying back along the lane, her head down.

The sky had darkened. Trees and hedges loomed over us, ragged fingers pointing at my failure. The churned-up mud and dead leaves smothering the ditches smelt thickly of decay. I pushed the chair back along the lane toward the house muttering prayers and apologies, swearing promises to myself and Eddie, who sat in silence, curled with pain, while my knuckles gripped white against the handles, and my shoulders, rigid with effort, bent over his crumpled back. I wanted to rip open my heart and wrap him inside. The war had destroyed us both, my future husband a mockery of the child we would never have. I was not meant to push this chair. And I knew what Sarah Gerard's eyes had said to me across the mud: Get out. Go. Get out of here.

At the big house, I left him at the bottom of the steps and flew inside, shouting for his man and for his mother. Servants ran in all directions. Eddie's parents hurried across the hall. I watched them carry him into the house, then I turned and fled, back out of the gate, down the lane, past the dreadful place where I had almost turned the chair, through the tunnel of trees that led towards the vicarage. Blinded by tears, I did not see if Sarah Gerard was still there, standing at the roadside. Back in my own little room, I tore off my boots and hurled them against the wall, pounded my fists against my temples, sobbed into my pillow. Even the old familiar lane that I had walked every day of my life was treacherous. I was slipping on sodden winter leaves and greasy mud, the ground beneath my feet perilous as a frozen lake, so deep and dark that if I fell, I would disappear below the surface and nothing would remain but my wide dead eyes and open mouth calling uselessly for help.

When I went back to see Eddie, I was resolved. I had listened to the lectures from my mother – stupid, selfish, thoughtless girl – without a word. She could not be allowed to guess at my intention or she would have refused to let me go. She thought only of Eddie.

At the big house, I heard the same lecture from Eddie's mother, furious on the doorstep, berating me for doing too much, not enough, getting everything wrong. At the end, she stood back and said, "You'll learn," and that, apparently, was a kind of forgiveness. But I knew that what I had to learn was more than I could bear.

"I'm sorry," I said to Eddie's mother, not bothering to explain.

I was afraid Eddie would beg, but of course he was too proud. Instead, he mocked me with the vows I had been ready to make.

"You don't have to – lie," he told me, each breath a torment. "I know you can't – stand the sight of me." I shook my head, too miserable to defend myself. "Before you go…" he continued, his voice shaking with effort and with rage, "I want you to tell me. Which of us – Georgie – tell me, honestly – which of us is the monster now?"

Without Eddie, what is there to stop me from marrying Ian? After so many losses, so many judgements and accusations, he deserves to be loved. My father would regard this engagement as an act of redemption, a chance to make amends. Surely, he must be right.

*

Ian announces the engagement to anyone who cares to listen. The Creeds have a house over the border in Punta Arenas. We will be married at the end of summer in the English Church. In the absence of my father, I ask Thomas Green to give me away.

He smiles and squeezes my hand. "It would be an honour."

"I'm so grateful you are here," I tell him. His warmth touches my heart.

"Oh, my dear," he says. "My dear Miss Georgie. The gratitude is all mine."

I have made him a present: a pictorial map, drawn in ink and watercolour, imagining the route from the estancia to his farm. I present it to him, feeling slightly foolish, but he takes it with a bow and studies it with delight.

"It's been a very long time since someone gave me such a beautiful gift. You have created the path between our hearts." His eyes are wet with tears, and he dashes them away with a laugh. "Now you have handed me a challenge. I must think of a wedding present for you that comes close to bringing as much delight." A glint of amusement. "I don't suppose you'd like an ostrich?"

The wind is stronger than ever, I feel it might lift me off my feet. "It's even worse in high summer," Ian says when I shiver, putting his arms around me and pulling me close. He wants to touch me all the time, to run his fingertips over my cheekbones, lay his hand against the curve of my hips, smooth my unruly hair. The hunger in him is consuming. "I want to kiss every inch of you," he whispers, catching me as we pass each other in the house, while I smile and slip from his grasp, afraid his mother will see. Sometimes I imagine Raúl's hands holding me at the dance, and shiver the memory away, remembering my delight in Ian's newfound happiness. When he smiles, the tension in his face dissolves, the shadows disappear into a crinkle of lines around his eyes. Already, he is making plans. A dinner in

Punta Arenas. A new governess. He has arranged for an advertisement to be placed in the Magellan Times. I put my hands over my ears, unable to bear the thought of anyone else looking after Leo, and he agrees to change the subject, painting pictures instead of our honeymoon: sailing north through the Chilean fjords towards the sunlight, a hotel overlooking the cliffs in Valparaíso among bougainvillea and brightly coloured wooden houses that tumble down towards the sea. I fold my hand into the crook of his arm, feeling the warmth of him through my coat. Soon, we will be Mr and Mrs Creed.

When the last of the wagons is gone, and the naked-bellied sheep are driven back across the plain towards the summer grazings, the passengers and puesteros take their leave. Mr Green shakes me warmly by the hand.

"Goodbye, Miss Georgie. I'm so very happy for you. Ian Creed is a fine young man." Perhaps he has not heard the rumours. But he grips my shoulders and looks hard into my eyes. "Remember, in these troubled times, your fiancé is the best of men." So he does know. He gives my shoulders a little squeeze. "And what's more, my dear, he's the luckiest of men. He should count his blessings every day that he has you."

Tears well, in a sudden rush of homesickness. His gentle kindness, the leather-and-tobacco smell of him, remind me of my father.

He pats my back and passes me his handkerchief. "Ah, this wretched wind. Never mind, my dear. The ostrich and I do hope you will come and see us very soon. You can be sure of a welcome any time."

I watch him drive away with an unexpected heaviness in my heart.

The Fosters drive round from the bungalow in their motor car. I try not to feel guilty that I have neglected them, reminding myself that Mrs Foster has neither returned my visit nor congratulated me on my engagement.

She stands behind her husband, watching his exuberant farewells without expression, scarcely touching my extended hand with her gloved fingertips, though she can hardly be haughty with me now. Perhaps she hates me for taking Alice's place. When Mrs Creed reaches to shake her hand, Mrs Foster leans forward to whisper something into her ear. For a second Mrs Creed freezes, before drawing her hand away, a long exhalation of breath, as she adjusts her hair in the wind.

"Nonsense." I hear her say. "You shouldn't listen to gossip, dear. It will only upset you."

Why does Mrs Foster insist on bringing up these dreadful stories? Her husband is right: grief has made her ill. Now the woman's lip is trembling and for an alarming moment it seems she is intent on making a scene. Mr Foster takes her arm and steers her gently towards the car. As they walk, he turns with a grimace of apology and mouths over his shoulder, "Sorry!" Aloud he says, "Time to be off. Congratulations to you both. Splendid news, I say. See you next month, Creed."

"Is she alright?" I whisper under my breath.

"Mad as a box of snakes," Ian whispers back, and we both laugh. As the car pulls away he puts his arm around my waist, and I lean against him, feeling how solid he is, how comforting. The two of us walk together back into the house: the estanciero and the future Mrs Creed.

Marta, Part I:
First winter, June 1920

The estancia

The night my mistress died, it was snowing. When everyone was asleep, I went to the bunkhouse to find my gaucho, and we crept away together, searching like two mice for a corner to make our nest. The snow was so deep it came over my boots, but I didn't care, because he and I would be warm together.

Sometimes I think about how my life would have turned out if I hadn't left the house to find him. If I hadn't crept through the scullery mouse-quiet, late, late in the night, after everyone was asleep. If instead I had spent that night beside the nursery fire, or in my bed at the top of the house. I would have heard my master dreaming. I would have run downstairs to quiet him, together with my mistress. She would still be alive and I would still be caring for my little man.

As soon as I came through the kitchen door, I heard voices. There was no light, save the last red embers of the fire. I was used to darkness. I was used to the sound of the Señor's dreams and the murmur of my mistress trying to calm him. But this time, I could hear crashes and gasps, and I was afraid my little man had climbed out of his bed and fallen down the stairs.

I ran to the dresser for a candle. By then, they were on the landing. Not my little man – my master and my mistress.

I was about to run up the stairs to help, but he raised his arms and gave a great shout and threw her backwards away from him. She shrieked once, as she fell, and the sound made my hair stand on end. Her body thudded down – thud, thud – until she lay all broken at the bottom of the stairs, her arms and legs and hair fanned out like reeds across a lake. I felt the shudder of her breath. As I knelt, I dropped the candle and it went out.

I didn't know if my master was awake then, or asleep and still in his dream. He ran down the stairs, and pulled me to my feet and shook me so hard I felt it in my bones. He kept saying, You saw nothing. Do you hear me? You saw nothing.

I had dropped the candle, so maybe he was right. I wanted to tell him, Stop, we have to help her. But I was shaking too hard to speak. I tried not to think of my mistress spread out and broken on the floor, but the sight of her was trapped inside my head. Even when I shut my eyes and pushed my fists into the sockets, I couldn't make it go away. The Señor was right though, it was better not to speak of what I saw, because that would make it real.

I wanted my mother. I wanted my little man. I wanted to run back outside and find my gaucho and beg him to take me away from that great, dark English house. I wanted to close my eyes and open them and find my mistress sitting up and smiling, and showing me that she was well and whole, not broken into pieces on the floor. I could feel the thread that held me to the world stretch thinner and thinner until I was afraid that it might break and I would disappear.

31.

Laguna Laura

Time ticks and the season slips deeper into summer. Still, ice must be broken in the well come morning, still the relentless wind blows across the pampas, rippling tall silver grasses that bend and flow like water in its path. The brown surface of the plain is rich with sudden splashes of colour. The air is sweet with the scent of clover, tiny white flowers bloom on the mata verde, the calafate bushes are heavy with berries turning blue-black under the sun.

I see little of the men, occupied as they are with the thousands of sheep spread across the estancia as far as the hills. Leo and I feed orphan lambs. I think about Raúl's hands, how they held me at the dance.

We ride together, Leo on his pony, chattering away, his eyes shining. I want to take him in my arms and tell him he will have a mother, perhaps baby brothers and sisters too. I want to ride faster, feel the wind against my face, my hair trailing loose behind me, surrounded by air and space. This newfound freedom takes my breath away.

In the evenings I sit with Ian in his study as he talks of wedding plans, and of the future. Every day, he reminds me that I am to be mistress of the estancia. There is a hunger in his eyes and in his touch: I am both excited and scared by his intensity. I remember Raúl's hands with a strange tinge of longing and regret, and tell myself I have no right to dream of fairy tales.

When the wind blows away the clouds, the sky becomes bright and vast and blue, and it is warm enough to sit on the veranda. One afternoon while Leo sleeps, I rest in a rocking chair, mesmerised by the emptiness of the plain, remembering the shepherds' asado, the flickering fire, the horse breaker's body against mine as we fell together into the grass.

I am awakened from my reverie by Ian's hands resting on my shoulders, his lips nuzzling my hair. I twist round to smile and receive his kiss. Lali stands a little way apart, frowning at the grass below the steps.

"Are you alright, Georgie?" Ian asks. "Have I been neglecting you?" His face brightens. "I've got an idea. Tomorrow, we'll go on a mapping expedition, just you and me."

Lali looks up. "Not tomorrow. There is a meeting with the League."

"You don't need me for that," Ian says, too loudly.

"It is you they want to see."

Ian's lower lip juts out like a petulant child's. Lali's eyes narrow. He takes a step closer, his bear-like frame casting a shadow over my chair. "Come, Señor. This is not the time. You have responsibilities."

"I have responsibilities to Georgie."

It occurs to me that this is no accident, that Ian wants to ride with me precisely because there is a meeting with the League. For a moment, I am excited to think that already I know him well enough to see into his mind. But I don't want to be used as an excuse. I daren't join the argument, but I glance at Lali, trying to signal my support.

Lali ignores me. "Come," he says again. "You can't hide from them." So he too knows what Ian is doing. Ian's face has clouded and I am afraid they will argue. I want to leave but I am trapped between them in my chair.

"I'm not hiding," Ian snaps. "I just don't agree with what they're doing. Look how they treat Green, hovering round him like caranchos. They'll have his land. Mine too, if they get the chance."

"Then don't give them a chance," Lali says. "Green is playing a dangerous game, allowing strikers on his land. The League won't forgive him for that." A pause. "At least he stands up for what he believes in."

He has gone too far. Ian stiffens, and for a second I think he will lash out, but he just runs a hand wearily across his eyes. "You're right. I'm sorry."

I want to hug him, but I can't remind him that he was afraid. Lali does it for me, clapping his huge hands around Ian's shoulders.

"Good," he says. "I will ask Horsebreaker to go with Miss Georgie."

My heart jumps. "Oh no," I hear myself say. "I don't want to be any trouble."

Ian leans over again to kiss my forehead. "You're not any trouble. I don't want you to be bored. Tell you what?" His face brightens. "I'm terribly jealous of that map you gave to Green. Why don't you make me a map, darling, of wherever you end up? That would make me so happy."

*

The sun holds and the sky shimmers blue. Swallows swoop and dive. As the horses trot over the ridge, I hold Ángel back a few paces so I can watch Raúl from behind. He leads me into a broad green valley of tall grass scattered with golden wildflowers, then turns in his saddle and gives me his broad smile – shall we go faster? Ángel stretches forward and the two horses fly side by side over the plain.

We stop at a high ridge in the hills, looking down over a broad lake. "Where are we?" I ask, breathing in the bright air, the rich scents of clover and wild sage in the grass. Last time, when I followed him through the snow, I could not have spoken to him in his mother tongue. Now I can say whatever I want.

"Laguna Laura, Miss. And over there," he waves an arm towards the south, "Pali Aike."

I gaze at vicious outcrops of pockmarked black rock. "Where the Indians say the Devil lives?"

"That's right, Miss."

The horses slither through the long grass to the lake, scattering flamingos. When we pull up beside the water, Raúl stands a little apart. Perhaps he is wary of me, the estanciero's future wife. He can't know that every nerve in my body is alive, every part of my skin prickling with tension. With each breath, I am reaching for him. Ian feels a hundred miles away across the plain. I should not have come.

I flop into the grass with an exaggerated sigh, overreacting to his stillness. "Look at the sky. It's so clear. It's like an opening. No wonder we believe heaven is up there." I am conscious of every movement, surrounded by air and water. I want to explode and scatter into tiny pieces. I want to dissolve into the light. "This is no place for the Devil."

"No, Miss."

He is surly. Angry with Lali, perhaps, for making him ride out with me. Surely he can sense the quiver in my skin, the longing in my eyes. Every part of me is concentrated on him, the air between us solid as a wall.

"Please, Raúl, come. Sit with me. I want to know something."

He moves a few steps closer and stands looking up at the trees. When he takes off his hat and holds it between his hands, I can see sweat on his forehead, the slick of his damp hair. He does not seem angry now, only shy.

"What are you going to do, Raúl, in the future? Are you going to live here forever?" Why wouldn't he? I can't imagine the future holds more for him than the turn of the seasons. But his face lights up.

"I'm going to have my own land, Miss. With horses. There is a man – a great man. His name is Héctor Torres, nobody knows more about horses, and he is going to help me. And the Señor, he has promised to help me too, once the trouble dies down. He will give me some horses to get started."

It is the most he has ever spoken. I sit up, furious with myself for being taken by surprise, for expecting so little of him; jealous, too, of the passion in his voice. Why shouldn't he dream about the future? For a wild moment I imagine myself with him, living on his land, watching as he works, riding beside him over the plain. I am dizzy with longing. I force myself to change the subject.

"The trouble… tell me about it. What is really happening, Raúl?"

He is silent, weighing my words.

"You can tell me the truth," I say, then wonder if it is strange for the estanciero's fiancée to say this to his horse breaker.

Raúl shrugs. "The peons work every day of the year and have nothing to show at the end of it. Nothing to send back to their families. Nothing to hope for in the future."

The future again. I prayed so hard for Ian to rescue me from my own futureless existence; why have I never considered that Ian's workers might have dreams of their own? "But that's not how it is for you?"

"No, Miss. I make some money from the horses."

His breath is shallow, and he holds himself very still.

"It's alright. You can talk to me. It's not disloyal to tell the truth." Although I am terrified now that he will tell me something about Ian.

"What is loyal? I am here for now because of Lali. And because the Señor…" he looks straight at me, and I know he is thinking *your* Señor, "…has promised to help me."

What is loyal? The words stick deep. At least he is telling me something good. But I don't want to think about Ian, or loyalty, instead, I lean back on my elbows and gaze out over the still waters of the lake. I have no idea where to look. Beneath Raúl's gaze, even the smallest breath feels like a performance. The grass is dotted yellow with celandines and as I cast around for something to focus on, I notice among the flowers a nest of soft grey down. Speckled black and white feathers curl over cream-coloured eggs.

"Oh, Raúl, look."

Now he is at my side, quicker than a heartbeat. He is parting the grass with his hands, but his eyes are on my face. "Caiquén."

"Yes."

When I am with him, the land reveals its magic. We kneel in the grass like children, his hands next to mine, alert and still. With each exhalation I can feel the enormity of space between us. I must break the silence, I must move away, but I am caught in the slipstream of his breath. It is no longer possible to remember Spanish, or English, or any other language. My mouth is level with his. It is too late to remember who he is, and who I ought to be.

With infinite slowness I reach down to the nest, take up a feather, and brush it over his hand. He lifts his eyes to mine and takes the feather, raising it to my face, drifting it across my cheek. A tremor runs through me. The feather touches the hollow at the base of my neck, carefully, as if I am something precious and rare. We are still kneeling, facing one another. As I reach to wrap my arms around him, I can think only that this must be some form of prayer: a prayer made, a prayer answered, a prayer understood.

The Story of Jeremy Button

On the first voyage of the Beagle, a Yaghan Indian boy named Orundellico was bought from his family for the price of a mother-of-pearl button. Christened Jeremy Button, he was shipped to England with three others of his tribe, who went by the colourful names of York Minster, Boat Memory and Fuegia Basket. The reluctant convert was taught Spanish and English, and presented at court, before being sent back to Tierra del Fuego on the Beagle to teach the ways of civilization to his Yaghan brethren. The experiment could hardly be called a success: some years later Jemmy Button was implicated in the massacre of English missionaries on Navarino Island.

Poor Mr Button. Why couldn't he have been left alone to fish? He sailed with the Beagle, found his place in the canon alongside Fitzroy and Darwin, and became a murderer in the name of civilization. Civilization, it seems, will always have its casualties.

From *Travels in Patagonia* by Henry O. Chambers

PART THREE

32.

Río Gallegos

In the dim light of the hotel bedroom, Mrs Creed's face has an unearthly lustre. She takes her time dressing for dinner. Hooking and lacing, buttoning and smoothing. Stays, petti-coat, dress and jacket, stockings, neat little shoes. Ribbons, earrings, brooch. I watch her mirrored ghost-face in the glass.

Her preparations are a torment. Now we are here in Río Gallegos, I long to be outside among people, to do all the ordinary things that have vanished from my life since I came to Patagonia. To walk on pavements, shop in a bakery, send a telegram. To forget what I have done. My body still trembles at the memory of Raúl's hands lowering me into the grass. The dark shape of him silhouetted above me, the blue sky behind. My back cold against damp earth, clothes pushed aside, both of us searching, reaching for skin.

Afterwards, a drowsy pulse throbbed between my legs and I curled myself around him as he lay stretched on his back, staring at the sky. When I lifted my head, he raised himself onto his elbow, and with his finger traced the line of my cheek, my neck, my collarbone. I leaned closer and touched his lips with my tongue – how did I find the courage? – and he lowered his mouth to mine. Fleetingly, I wondered how it was that he knew what to do. We barely spoke. Once, he whispered to me in Spanish ¿estás segura? – are you sure? and I arched my back to pull him closer, saying nothing, as if both of us understood that silence was all the protection we had.

A light drizzle began to fall, misting the sky, leaving tiny beads of damp on his hair. When he lifted me to my feet, I leaned against his chest, wanting him to bear the weight of us both.

"We have to leave." The matter of factness in his voice made my heart twist. My words fell loud into the silence.

"I can't bear it."

He frowned, and I watched the furrow in his brow, remembering how I noticed it the day we met, at the port, when he searched the sky for snow. Already I was ashamed of what I'd said. How could I expect him to answer?

"I..." he began, and I could see him struggling for words. His eyes rested on mine and he touched my face, slowly and precisely, his finger scorching my cheek. "I know," he said, and then again, his voice stronger, as if he had found exactly what he meant. "I know you." And I knew that both of us had said the same thing, each in our own way.

At the estancia, we parted in the only way we could. He led the horses out to the corral. I walked through the sticky gate toward the house, and did not look back.

In my bedroom, I examined the grass and mud stains on my clothes. The soiled coat seemed a fitting reminder, though with enough scrubbing, I could make it clean. How could I do the same with my soul? Could I pretend that nothing had happened, that I was the same person who had accepted Ian's proposal? I could pretend, but my body still ached with the weight of Raúl and my heart was heavy with guilt. What had Eddie said? What about those vows, Georgie, that you were so quick to make? I had forgotten myself and all my promises, all lost in light and air and sky. For a few short hours I had felt myself powerful, every part of me open, as if I could reach the heavens with my skin. Raúl had seen it: I know you. But now, curled in my bed, a ragged knot of sensations, I needed to find once more the boundaries of my lost self.

The pull of my own body, the force of my desire, shocked me. I remembered the women at the port in Punta Arenas whose bared teeth and jutting bones had so appalled me, I thought of the girls in the Magdalen refuge at home, of poor Sarah Gerard – *that* woman. How was I different? When I looked in the mirror I saw no alteration in my face and body, no hint of depravity in my eye. I could pretend that nothing had happened, and perhaps that would be enough. I could wash away the stain on my coat and pray and be kind to Ian and Leo. I could make amends. Nobody cared that I had gone to Laguna Laura. Nobody need ever know.

The following day, I went out onto the farm, drawn like a somnambulist toward the horse breaker, but there was no sign of him.

"Where is Raúl?" I asked Lali, praying that he could not see how I – how everything – was altered. Even saying Raúl's name was different.

"He's gone, Miss."

"Gone?" I pretended it was the wind that made me shiver.

Lali seemed oblivious. Perhaps I was a better liar than I knew. "To the summer grazings, Miss."

"Oh. I see." I did not dare ask when he would return.

In the days that followed, I was at the mercy of my body, convulsed with longing and scorched with shame. At any moment my muscles might catch, the breath stop in my throat, heat rise in my face. Then Ian announced meetings with the League, and the Creeds began preparations for a visit to Río Gallegos. I busied myself with packing and sorting, making plans for Leo, who was to remain at the estancia with Pilar. Gradually, the afternoon at Laguna Laura took on a dreamlike quality. The horse breaker had disappeared as if he never existed. Eve's curse arrived like a blessing, and for the first time it dawned on me the danger I had faced. Unanswerable questions broiled inside my head: could I have married Ian and passed off a child as his? Would a doctor have known what I had done? The sight of my blood, and Raúl's absence from the farm, made me wonder if I had imagined the whole episode. All that remained was the throb of my heart whenever I thought of him. I told myself: This is not love. Love is what I have here, with my fiancé. Love is redemption, duty, family, marriage. I closed my mind to Raúl and kissed Leo, hugged and held him until he squirmed in my arms. Ian packed sheepskins and blankets tenderly around my shoulders as I sat in the motor car – no wagon for me this time – and prepared to greet the world as the future Mrs Creed.

*

"Georgie! Wake up. Can you help me with this?" Mrs Creed is holding out her necklace.

"Oh, I'm sorry. Of course."

"What were you thinking? You looked a thousand miles away."

"Oh, nothing." I search for an anchor. "The pearls are lovely."

Her eyes narrow. "This belonged to my mother. It will go to my brother's oldest daughter. I have a brooch which will come to you. You may have it for the wedding."

"Oh no, I didn't mean… I wasn't…" I bend my head and fumble with the clasp. At least embarrassment is a distraction.

"I lent it to Alice," she continues. "When she and Ian were married." At least now she is honest when she dresses me as Alice. I suppose that's progress.

Ian is outside on the stairs, fiddling with his bow tie. I want to throw my arms around his neck to show that I love him, to show myself how sorry I am.

"A few others from the League have arrived tonight," he tells us. "We'll all be dining together." A slight pause. "And Chambers is here."

Mrs Creed sighs. "He's dining too, I suppose?"

"You needn't sit with him, Mother."

"Why are Americans always so boring?" She hooks her arm through Ian's. "Georgie can have Chambers," she says. "The two of them will do very well together."

33.

Dinner

"Creed. My dear friend. How very excellent to see you. And Mrs Creed. Beautiful as ever."

A small man stands at the entrance to the dining room. His voice is high-pitched and twangy, with a strange, extended emphasis on the vowels. Mrs Creed gives him her fingertips. When I hang back, the little man bows again, presenting me with the top of his head.

"And gracious, who is this? Another delightful addition to the party?"

Ian puts an arm around my waist. "Georgie. This is Mr Chambers. Mr Chambers, this is Miss Georgiana Carruthers." A tiny pause. "My fiancée."

"Creed," the little man says again, standing back and scanning me from head to toe. "I must congratulate you. You lucky, lucky man. Why, this is news indeed! Cause for celebration in these trying times." He seizes my hand, putting it to his lips. "Congratulations, my dear. You are entering a mighty family."

"Mr Chambers is an ethnographer, Georgie," says Mrs Creed, without expression.

"An ethnographer?" I say, too loudly. "Wait. Mr Chambers? Mr Henry Chambers? Not Mr Henry O. Chambers the explorer?" The little man inclines his head. "But... I can't believe it." I am babbling. "I've read your book. I love your book."

Chambers bows again. "I am honoured to hear you say so."

"Please stop bowing, Mr Chambers," says Mrs Creed, hooking her hand back through Ian's elbow. "We hardly deserve it and I'm afraid you will do something unfortunate to your back."

"Creed's loss is my gain this evening." Chambers extends his own arm to me with a flourish.

"I can't believe it's really you," I whisper, as he leads me into the dining room.

The table fills up. We are introduced to a Spanish engineer – something to do with oil – and an Argentinian gentleman with an appearance of great wealth and no discernible profession. I am too nervous to remember their names. I find myself almost wishing for the Fosters; even Mrs Foster's downturned mouth would have been a welcome familiarity among all these florid strangers, but perhaps they are not grand enough to be included. I suppress the tiniest glint of satisfaction: what does Mrs Foster think of the governess now?

On the other side of the table is an Englishman. "His name is Frank," Chambers whispers in my ear. "He owns an estancia the size of Kentucky."

"Is he in the Patriotic League?"

"Of course." I wonder if Ian would count him as one of the caranchos. Chambers indicates the silent giant sitting next to Frank. "That one over there deals in furs. Croatian."

My other neighbour is a rosy-faced Englishman named Tupper, who shakes my hand and turns his back. Mrs Tupper leans across from the other side of the table to introduce herself. Her name is Estelle. "You're sweet," she says. "And so good for Ian."

"Really? Thank you." The inward curl of shame. I marvel that nobody seems to notice. I know you.

"Don't look so serious," Estelle replies. "You've obviously cheered him up no end. Maud too. She likes you; I can tell." She lowers her voice. "It must be such a relief to her. After all that awful business with Alice."

"Yes," I murmur, wondering how to change the subject. "So sad."

Estelle raises her eyebrows. "Sad? Yes. Terribly sad. Of course." A pause as she leans closer, a little conspiratorial smile playing at the corners of her mouth. "We're all rooting for Ian, you know, every step of the way."

So the rumours are fair game for dinner party conversation.

"And I expect you'll be relieved about the Fosters," she continues.

"I don't know what you mean."

"You haven't heard? They're going home. Claire Foster wouldn't stop going on about how dangerous everything is, and dropping the most awful hints about..." She stops abruptly. "Robert got quite worried about her." A sideways glance full of unspoken meaning. "She's never known when to stop talking." Estelle glances along the table towards Ian and I follow her gaze, afraid he might overhear. When I look back, someone has taken her attention and she has turned away.

34.

The estancieros

With no one to talk to, I take a sip of wine, and then another. Soon, my glass is empty. As I glance around the table, trying to look interested, Henry Chambers lays a hand on my arm.

"So, Miss Georgie. Tell me how you find it here in town?"

I picture the low wooden buildings lining the main street.

"We have only just arrived. It isn't exactly charming, is it?" He nods in rueful agreement. "You must know its history, I suppose?" I want to appear thoughtful and intelligent, instead I sound hopelessly over-earnest and sycophantic.

Chambers smiles. "I'm not sure this town has much of a history, Miss." I cringe to think how foolish he must find me.

"I suppose I feel like any villager who makes a trip to the great metropolis after the quiet of winter. Rather overwhelmed, and more than a little excited to see so much life."

"So much life?" He leans back in his chair and laughs. "You really have been in the country, haven't you? Mind you, I know what splendid isolation the Creed estate inhabits, so I understand what you mean. Still, it's striking that someone who has travelled halfway round the globe can feel so provincial."

I stiffen. At the far end of the table, Maud Creed is deep in conversation. The hours spent at her dressing table have been put to good use. Chambers follows my eyes.

"You are quite right," he says. "The Creeds are hardly provincial. Isolated, yes, but that's an altogether different thing. I was talking about you."

"Me?"

"I'm sorry. I didn't mean to offend. I chose the wrong word. I wanted to say that you have a quality about you that means you can travel the world and still manage to feel things very simply. It's a gift, believe me. I meant only to praise you."

"Well, it's too late to flatter me now. And I'm not sure I understand the distinction."

"Oh dear." He pushes his glasses back onto his nose. "I have offended you. And I don't know how it happened. What can I do to make amends?"

"I really can't say." I am beginning to feel flustered. Chambers seems to be enjoying my discomfort. I want to ask what an ethnographer actually does, but I am afraid the question will substantiate his already unflattering opinion of me. As I hesitate, he takes up the baton with a simplicity that makes me wish I had been more honest.

"So, I have learned that it is too early for you to form an opinion of your new surroundings. In that case, may I ask how you find life at the estancia?"

I take another sip of wine. Life at the estancia means Raúl. Mr Chambers watches me through his little round glasses as though what I am preparing to say is of immense importance to him. I try not to flinch from the intensity of his gaze.

"I think," I begin, "that it is full of contradictions. I mean, it's enormous and vast and empty. And then you look at the ground and see that it is teeming with life… all insects and tiny creatures. There's hardly anything in the middle. Our lives here seem the same: either we are concerned with vast acreages and hundreds of thousands of sheep, or we are managing tedious tiny details, with very little of the usual diversion that protects us from being swallowed alive or consumed with boredom."

"I see." He is a good listener, watching me with those unblinking eyes. "And what on earth made you come? You were engaged to Creed back in England, I suppose?"

I laugh. "Oh no. I came because it was an adventure. And to look after Leo." He raises an eyebrow, and for the first time I see ahead of me the mortifying prospect of endless repeated explanations. "Yes, I'm the governess. I came because they needed me. I wanted to be needed. And anyway," in a rush of passion, "I couldn't have stayed at home."

He says nothing. I take another drink. The wine seems to be helping, the smooth stem of the glass is comforting in my hand. "Because of the war." How can I speak about the war to this stranger? "I don't know how much you know about it?"

"Not enough, I should imagine."

"Well, the war itself…" How can I explain? "It was like pieces of our lives breaking, one by one. And when it was over, we couldn't go back to how things were, because everything was broken. My…" I falter. The words have jerked their way out in abrupt little spurts. Now they stick in my throat. I can only whisper. "My brothers died." How far away they seem. How is it that I can remember their faces better from photographs than from real life? "There were so many dead men, so many left-over women, they called us – perhaps you know – the newspapers actually called us 'the surplus two million'."

"That must have hurt. It's not as if you did it on purpose."

Despite myself, I smile. "You'd have thought from the papers that the women were a worse problem than the war itself. Yet I was one of the lucky ones."

"Really? How so?"

Am I really going to tell him? "Before the war, I was engaged. To someone else."

"But he died, I suppose?"

I don't have to tell this stranger. But being honest about Eddie somehow mitigates the guilt of the one secret I can never share. "No. He didn't die. He was wounded. Terribly wounded." A pause. I can't look at Chambers' face. "He wanted so badly to be dead. Sometimes, when he wanted it so much, I wanted it for him."

He nods. "I see. No wonder you needed to leave."

The simplicity takes my breath away. "Do you think? Everyone hated me. They couldn't believe I wasn't going to stick with him."

"But why did they hate you? Didn't they understand?"

I shake my head. "Eddie was everybody's darling. The whole village adored him. Probably they all thought I wasn't good enough for him." A bitter little laugh. "Even my own mother doesn't rate me very much." Chambers is gazing at me with a peculiar earnestness. "Almost everybody had lost someone. Women would have gladly given up their lives to nurse their sons and husbands if they'd come back, no matter what state they were in. Especially my mother. She would have done anything. She couldn't understand how I..." I break off, crumbling bread in tiny pieces. How has it happened that I am pouring out my heart to this peculiar little American? I take another sip of wine and force myself to smile. "So, you see. I chose to be a Spanish-speaking explorer rather than an English spinster. Even if I find myself doing not very much, it's a different kind of not much. At least there is meaning in this nothingness."

He raises an eyebrow and glances over at Ian. I have gone too far. Why do I never know when to hold my tongue?

"I mean, obviously I care for Ian. And Leo."

"Obviously."

"And you're quite right. I am from the country. I love the estancia. I am happy to live quietly, and I take pleasure in small things."

"Perhaps it is good to take pleasure in small things after something so vast as a war."

"Yes. Perhaps it is."

"I suppose you worked? During the war, I mean?"

"Yes. Yes, I did. I was a nurse."

"I'm impressed."

"Are you? It's nothing really, it's what everybody did. I'd rather have been a cartographer, like my brother. But women aren't allowed to be cartographers."

"Are they not? That's a shame. I for one would love to see a lady cartographer. Perhaps, Miss, you will be a pioneer in that way too."

"I appreciate your faith in me."

I must have sounded bitter, but he is undeterred.

"If you like maps, there's a particular tribe of people from Tierra del Fuego who might interest you. Their whole mythology is connected to the points of the compass. To the east and west, the rising and setting sun. North is the sea and rain. South, the wind, the snow and the moon. At festivals, men decorate their bodies with coloured lines that correspond." His voice drops to a whisper and I lean closer, gripped. "Imagine your history and your world, etched onto your very being."

I wrestle with the significance of his words. "It's like… being a part of nature itself."

"That's right. Our maps enclose the world. Claim dominion over it. But this is the opposite – the people belong to nature, not the other way around."

I think of pioneers staking their claims. My brothers, mapping the fields of France. Land torn apart for loss and gain. I have never imagined the world could exist in any other way. Chambers' eyes are bright with excitement. A complicity exists between us now, far apart from the others.

"Is it your work, Mr Chambers? To study this mythology?"

"Alas, this is not my work. I learned of it from an esteemed Austrian ethnographer who lives among this particular people and collects their stories. My own project is somewhat different. There is a tribe in the southwest who live entirely from the sea. For thousands of years, they have roamed the coast of Chile and Tierra del Fuego in their canoes. Their harvests are mussels, fish, seals." The words rise and fall, telling a story. "In recent years, the canoe people have found themselves somewhat corralled by the imposition of certain constraints upon their lives."

"What do you mean?" I picture famine, tribal warfare.

"Oh, you know. Government. Missionaries."

"Missionaries?"

"Indeed. Missionaries have strong feelings about this sort of thing." He flicks a glance around the table, and lowers his voice. "As do trappers, estancieros, anyone wanting to make use of traditional coastal hunting grounds." I force myself not to stare at the other diners. "Anyway," Chambers raises his voice again, "my department has sent me to investigate before they completely disappear. A memorial, if you like." He sighs. "With the stroke of a pen, people who have travelled the coasts for thousands of years will be slotted into the expectations of our modern world."

"Won't they be miserable?"

"Yes, they will be miserable. For a nomadic people who have lived their lives along vast stretches of water, this will indeed be a bitter captivity."

"And, maybe I'm being stupid, but isn't this captivity for the land as well?"

"Whatever do you mean?"

He waits for me to stumble ahead with my thoughts. "You said before that the people belong to the land. But this is the opposite. Now the land belongs to people: estancieros, governments. They want to control it."

He smiles. "You're quite right, though I don't think you want to say so in this company. I've changed my mind about you, Miss. I don't think you should follow cartography. I think you should be an ethnographer. Or perhaps both. I can see you at a university."

"A university? Hardly. Where I'm from, not many women go to university." I picture my mother, her friends in the village. "I mean, some do, obviously, but I don't know any."

"Really? It's quite different in my country, you know. Some young ladies even study cartography. If ever you are in the United States, you must look me up and I will show you around my department."

Nobody has ever offered to show me round a university department. I visited Harry once at Oxford, for tea and evensong. We walked through the quads and looked at the pretty buildings.

I am about to accept Mr Chambers' invitation when Frank calls out loudly, "I say, Chambers. Haven't you just come from Buenos Aires? What can you tell us?"

Our complicity is broken. The other diners have no choice but to fall silent. Estelle exchanges a look with her husband, and the silent Croat utters a heavy sigh.

Chambers leans forward to address the whole table.

"Oh, there's not much to tell that you don't already know. I think it's safe to assume the government has the upper hand." Silence. The table waits. The ethnographer has an odd little smile on his face. Perhaps he is enjoying the limelight. "I know you're all terrified of the strike," he continues. "But I can assure you, there's very little stomach for revolution. The army will be here any day."

"Well said, old man." Frank again, slapping his hand jovially against the table. "We're almost home and dry. Then we can get back to business as usual." He raises his glass, looking around for effect, and the assembly applauds. There is a chinking of crystal, a satisfied murmur.

"Here's to the army," Tupper says on my other side, raising his glass. I take a gulp of wine and my stomach lurches. Turning from one speaker to another is making me giddy. I look around the table for water but see only flushed faces, open mouths.

"Let's keep a lid on this, shall we?" This time it is Ian who speaks. "We don't need the army. All it takes is for everyone to stick to the agreement."

"The agreement is over," Tupper says. "Otherwise we'll lose everything we've worked for."

"For Christ's sake, Creed." Frank says. Pink spots have appeared in his cheeks. "It's time to stop making concessions. And put your own bloody house in order, I say, before you start lecturing the rest of us."

"I don't know what you mean." Ian's expression is mutinous, his top lip has disappeared, the lower one jutting out like a child's. If I wasn't so disoriented, I might have wanted to laugh. I scan the table for allies, but expressions are shuttered. Frank's red face is bright with anger.

"Come on, chaps," the Argentinian's voice is poured silk. "Let's save this for tomorrow."

"If we don't hold together now," Tupper says, "we'll blow the whole region out of the water." His watchful little eyes dart from face to face. "I know you don't think so, Chambers, but I swear it'll be nineteen seventeen all over again."

"Do you want to take responsibility for that, Ian?" Frank asks.

"I hardly think I'm that powerful."

"Oh, you don't realise. Anyway, you should be careful. Look what's happened to Green."

There is a sudden silence. "What's happened to Green?" I whisper to Chambers, but he gestures for me to be silent.

"Good God, Frank." This time it is Ian who sounds furious. "We're not going to discuss that here." His hand moves out of sight. Only I know he is pressing his palm against his shaking knee. Nobody speaks. Eyes flicker from side to side, scanning the men and women around the table. Flushed faces and glittering eyes. Over the murmur of conversation from other corners of the dining room, waiters clatter plates, wine swirls, glasses sparkle in the candlelight. Cut glass and sharpened silver, deadly as a gaucho's knife.

Mrs Creed puts down her glass. "Nobody loves the land more than we do. And I believe we've all had plenty of opportunity to witness my son's loyalty to his friends. We are here to celebrate our association, not to disagree with one another. Perhaps one of you would be kind enough to tell me some of the pleasanter things happening in Buenos Aires this spring?"

Relief ripples round the table like an electrical current. Frank breathes out in a long whistle and leans back in his chair. How does she manage to stay calm among all these men? No one has more power than she does. She is magnificent. Unobserved by the others, Ian's eyes flicker to his leg. Henry Chambers gestures to the waiters for more wine. Glasses are filled. Those closest to Mrs Creed press forward to answer her question, the rest begin talking all at once, and the dining room is filled once more with inconsequential chatter.

35

Mr Green

The guests make their way out towards the lobby, the atmosphere strangely inert, as if the energy of the little group has been drained by the hostilities at dinner. Ian's face is white. I hover, hoping for a word alone with Chambers, but Estelle has her hand on the ethnographer's arm.

"Mr Chambers," she is saying, "we were all so busy talking, nobody thought to ask what you are writing about these days?"

"Just finishing another book," Chambers replies. "I've been collating traditional legends and folk stories. An emic perspective on the life and traditions of the Tehuelches. As if anybody cares. It's a rather narrow field of study, I'm afraid, but somebody has to do it."

"Don't pay any attention, Georgie," Estelle says, laughing. "Mr. Chambers is a very great scholar."

"Forgive me," I ask, "but what is an emic perspective?"

"It means from the inside," Chambers replies. "From the point of view of the subject. In this case, the Indians."

Tupper appears at my side. He snorts with laughter and leans over to whisper in my ear. "He's definitely the expert at Indians. Some say he has an Indian wife. Though I've heard rumours it's even worse than that, if you get my drift." Tupper's hot breath smells of wine. I jerk my head away, hoping Chambers has not heard.

We have reached the lobby. Most of the men are already

in the smoking room. Chambers is still speaking. "Not too many of the settlers have troubled themselves with anyone's perspective other than their own. As you can imagine. And the opportunity for such a field of study is running out."

Estelle's eyes open wide. "Why is that, Mr Chambers?"

"Because most of the indigenous people have already died."

"Really? Why?" Estelle sounds as if she is asking about the weather. I picture the canoe people, dying of grief.

"Oh, plenty of reasons," Chambers replies airily. "The usual. Diseases, clothes…"

"What on earth do you mean, clothes?"

"Think about it. If you live outdoors, clothes are no use to you. It's impossible to keep them dry. Much better to use seal blubber. The rain runs off and you're perfectly warm. When the missionaries insisted on covering people in clothes, they were permanently wet and cold. And naked Indians are washed by the rain, they didn't know how to keep clean. Clothes brought from England are riddled with all kinds of European pests and diseases. It's a disaster."

"Told you," whispers Tupper, digging me in the ribs with his elbow. "He prefers them without clothes."

"Really." Mrs Creed is already on the stairs, tapping her fingers on the bannister.

Chambers gives an ironic little bow in her direction. "I was forgetting myself. Anyway, it wasn't all the missionaries' fault. There were political reasons too."

"Political reasons?" I am risking Mrs Creed's displeasure, but somehow I must find a way to speak to Chambers on his own.

"Sure. The government requisitioning land. Collectors requisitioning species. A pound an ear, the going rate used to be. Nothing new there."

I gasp. "Nothing new?"

"Hardly. How do you think the Americas were conquered?"

224

"I've never thought about it," I say slowly.

"It's just progress, my dear," interjects the Argentinian as he passes behind me.

"Progress?" I spin round to face him. "But at whose expense?"

"Progress is always at someone's expense," the Argentinian replies smoothly. "That's what ethnographers are for. To record what would otherwise disappear in its inexorable wake." He bows very low and disappears into the smoking room.

"Well, I don't think it's right." The words come out too loud, childish and petulant. I can feel Mrs Creed glaring. "I mean, what about how the Indians must have felt? An emic perspective," I conclude triumphantly, rather pleased with myself. I can hear my father's gentle sermons from his little Suffolk pulpit. Charity. Kindness. The murmured Amens of his elderly congregation. Comfort, yes, for the weak and the bereaved, but what did his words do to stop the war? Nothing changes, I realise, with a jolt of pain. Progress is indeed inexorable.

Chambers has his hand on the smoking room door. I glance round. Tupper has disappeared after the Argentinian and Estelle has begun a conversation with Mrs Creed on the stairs. I seize the moment to whisper, "Mr Chambers… wait, please. What happened to Mr Green?"

Chambers hesitates.

"Please, Mr Chambers," I plead, and he makes a weak little gesture of concession.

"Your Mr Green sympathised with revolutionaries," he whispers back.

"But… I don't know what that means."

His face is unreadable. "The police took him."

"And?"

"That's it."

He must be teasing me, taking advantage of my ignorance. "Have they put him in prison?"

Chambers sighs. "If only they had. I'm sorry, my dear. Perhaps I shouldn't have told you."

I stare at him helplessly. My head whirls. I feel sick.

"Georgie," Mrs Creed calls.

I need to lie down. I long for Raúl's gentle hands to steady me and keep me safe. "I'm sorry," I reply weakly. "I'm coming up now."

36.

A message to the police

Raúl picks his way through the wreckage of the union building, lifting the smashed remains of chairs and tables, dropping them back onto the floor. Juan Sant is on his knees among the splinters of wood and shreds of paper. A moment later he utters a satisfied "Ah." He prises up the end of a dusty floorboard with his fingertips, reaches down with one arm into the gap in the floor, and hauls out a heavy canvas bag.

"You better hurry," Raúl says. "It's not safe here."

Sant laughs. "Are you worried about me?" Raúl does not return the smile. Since the night Antonio Soto spoke to the workers, he has not come near this place, but now a kind of appalled curiosity has drawn him through the loosely flapping door and into the devastated building. He has no love for the town; he came only to enquire after Héctor Torres. Word has it the legendary horse breaker is mobilising strikers in the north of Santa Cruz, and for a wild moment, Raúl has considered riding north himself in search of his mentor. He feels a shiver of restlessness, tells himself a few more months is not so long to wait.

It was a shock to find Juan Sant crouched amongst the wreckage. By now, everyone knows what happens to strike sympathisers. He can tell Sant is weighing up how far to trust him, and fair enough: as far as the strikers are concerned, he has committed himself to the enemy.

"I can't leave just yet," Sant says at last. "There's still work to be done."

"What are you going to do?"

Sant opens his eyes very wide. "Do you think I'd tell you?"

Raúl laughs in relief. "No." A pause. "But are you going to cause harm?" At once he is angry with himself for giving so much away.

"No harm to any citizens," Juan says, as if sensing Raúl's anxiety.

"I'm glad you say so," Raúl replies. "And I hope no harm will come to you."

"Are you threatening me, che?"

"No. No. I meant it, truly." Raúl is full of hurt. He knows, as surely as if he has seen the future, that whatever Juan Sant is planning will mean the old man's death.

Sant's face softens. "Don't worry about me." He laughs. "Remember, I can't be anything more than dead. Tell whoever it is you care about to stay indoors and all will be well. There is no danger, only a little surprise. Something to confuse the police and make the estancieros jump." He takes Raúl's hand. "And now, my son, you should leave. If the police find you, they'll never believe you're not one of us."

Raúl opens his mouth to speak, but no words come. Juan Sant hoists the heavy canvas bag up onto his back, and is gone.

37

The women march

Word of the army spreads from door to door. Anxiety hangs over the town, a muffled tension showing itself in the distracted faces of the townspeople. The hotel empties.

I am not allowed to attend the meeting with the Patriotic League.

"She is not yet your wife," Mrs Creed hisses at Ian.

I accompany them both as far as the club, and linger outside with Ian. We have had little chance to speak privately since the dinner. I should hug him, give him strength to face the League, but my head is aching and I have no energy for platitudes. He leans forward, expecting a kiss.

"Why didn't you tell me about Mr Green?" I whisper into his ear.

He throws his head up like a startled horse. "God, Georgie. You know how to disturb a man. What a time to bring this up." He lowers his voice. "It's the worst news. Terrible. I knew it would upset you. But you mustn't make a song and dance about it here. People are watching."

Suddenly I am afraid. "Is there going to be a revolution?"

"I don't think so. I hope not. Though when you listen to the others... Foster's so worried he's taken his wife back to Buenos Aires."

It isn't safe. Mrs Foster was right. I remember the sadness in Mr Green's voice when he walked with me in the garden; perhaps he had already chosen his future. The League's friendship is a thinly disguised threat, nothing more. If Ian sticks to the agreement, Frank and Tupper will accuse him of supporting revolutionaries. If he breaks it, he can expect nothing but trouble from the workers he has betrayed. My stomach twists at the thought of the bearded gaucho's vicious knife.

What is loyal? Raúl's words as he stood looking into the sunlight beside Laguna Laura. Oh dear God, if Ian breaks the agreement, what will happen to Raúl?

I should return to the hotel but instead I set off in the opposite direction, along the dusty road. The little town is not so different from the plain it grew out of, each street a rutted expanse of mud. Two children streak between the houses, snatching toys from one another, and I am struck by a painful longing for Leo, to hold his little hand in mine.

I pass the haberdashers and the general store, their bolted wooden fronts a pair of shuttered eyes against the street, and turn onto a muddy path running between low tin-roofed houses with lopsided gates. The path ahead is empty save for a woman in a bright red dress, an unexpected flash of colour against the grey. Even the dogs have disappeared. I falter, overtaken by an inexpressible weariness.

Somewhere in the distance, I become aware of a faint pulsing rhythm: the beat of a drum. My skin prickles. Could this be the army? As the sound approaches, I discern chanting, and an irregular banging, too chaotic, surely, to belong to any organised militia.

The revolution.

I leap a flight of steps onto a wooden porch in a futile attempt to take cover. The noise grows louder and more insistent, the voices oddly high-pitched. A moment later, a crowd erupts around the corner into the street.

It is a band of women. A clattering throng of grey-and-brown. None carry weapons, but many brandish their percussion above their heads: pots and ladles, wooden spoons and copper lids. Some wave banners and flags. All are dressed in working clothes, hair drawn up under kerchiefs and caps, skirts hidden beneath heavy aprons. Small children hold their mothers' hands. Despite the motley assortment of instruments and the cacophony of sound, the procession is orderly and doesn't stray from the path. The women pass without looking at me, and I run behind to see where they will go.

The parade rounds another corner onto a square flanked with shops and warehouses. Windows and doors are flung open, shouts exchanged back and forth. Many of the women are waving and smiling, some are blowing kisses or holding up infants: the men inside must be brothers, husbands, fathers, sons.

There is a shout. A whistle pierces the air. A column of police runs across the square, forming a line in front of the women. The chanting stops, a hush falls over the crowd, one or two of the women closest to the line call out, their voices dissolving uselessly into the wind. The leader of the police waves his sabre and the line pushes forward. His men drag the women, twisting and shrieking, across the square. Batons and sabres rise and fall.

Almost at once, I sense a new surge of movement. Men. Men pouring into the square, wrenching raised batons from policemen's hands, pulling their women aside, until a crack, louder than thunder, brings the scene to silence. A body stumbles backwards and topples into the dust.

Time holds its breath. Then, as if on a signal, the protesters bolt in all directions like rats in a barn, pursued by the police. Sabres flail on backs and heads and faces. An old woman hobbles away, covering her face with her apron. A young man, dripping with sweat, holds his arm at an impossible angle, breathing with an intense concentration of pain.

And then it is over. Everyone is gone. Pots and pans, sticks and banners, flags and shawls, lie abandoned in the dirt. The square quivers. I try not to think of Thomas Green.

Minutes, or maybe hours, tick past. A hand touches my elbow and I cry out as if I have been struck.

It is Henry Chambers. "Miss Georgie. What on God's earth... are you hurt?"

"Did you see?" It is all I can think to say.

"Yes, Miss. I saw." He takes my arm and folds it through his own. "I must send for your fiancé."

"No! Please Mr Chambers... I don't want you to."

He does not insist. "In that case, let us sit for a moment. You're looking very pale, Miss." He guides me to a bench and passes me a handkerchief. When I press it to my face, the smell is sweet and musky, unfamiliar.

"Thank you, Mr Chambers, for rescuing me."

He gives a self-deprecating wave. "Not much of a rescue. The worst was over by the time I came along." I shudder. I don't want to think about the worst. "What were you doing, Miss?"

What was I doing? "I was walking, and the women came... What about you? What were you doing?"

"Me? I was on my way to the prison."

"The prison?"

"My interpreter has been... ahem... detained."

"What did he do?"

"He's a union member, unfortunately. The police are sweeping Santa Cruz. The net they've cast is wide and many fishes are caught in it."

I shake my head in bewilderment. "Will all those men and women go to prison?"

"Most of them will be sprung, if their employers vouch for them. The real revolutionaries will go to Ushuaia – or end up in a pit behind the police station. I'm sorry, Miss," as my eyes widen, "I shouldn't have said that." He shakes his head. "I warned my man to keep his head down. Such is the strength of feeling here these days."

I am no longer listening. "But these are women and children. They didn't do anything. Have they committed a crime?"

"What would you like me to tell you, Miss? They've

supported their husbands in striking against their employers. They've interrupted production."

"Mr Chambers. Please. I am serious. We should do something."

"What shall we do, Miss? Go to the police?" His voice is deadpan.

"Well, surely... We can't just leave them." He does not reply. "My fiancé... he'll do something. He'll speak to the police."

Chambers raises an eyebrow. "Are you an activist, Miss?"

"An activist?" I blink at him. "Of course not."

"That's good. You'd better understand, Miss. If you go around looking for justice, well, people here might think you're an activist." A pause. "Or a revolutionary."

"That's ridiculous."

"Oh, Miss Georgie." His face is full of pity. "You will not be helping your fiancé if you ask him to vouch for these people."

These people? "But... this is..." I break off. I want to say, this is not fair, but I will sound like a child. He has trapped me in his arguments, I want to beat at him with my fists. My father would not have allowed this to happen. I open my mouth to say so and stop short. In the end, for all his kindness, what did my father ever change?

"What can we do? How can we help them?"

"It's not our business to help them." He smiles wryly. "You really don't understand the rules, do you?"

But who makes the rules in a land nobody comes from? Nobody, that is, except the Indians, and they are dead from clothes and disease and hunting, swept aside in the name of progress. Why – why – have I never thought about any of this before?

"You're all for charity, aren't you? Quite the little saint." His eyes open wide behind his glasses. "That's it, isn't it? You'd like to be the one who saves them."

"Well, isn't that better than leaving them in prison?"

"Better, worse, it's not your place to interfere. You can't go around trying to save the poor, Miss. You're on the wrong side."

I shake my head, unable to respond, remembering the basket of toys I carried to Sarah Gerard's little daughter. I had felt so noble, so open-hearted. But what did I do when Sarah came to church with bruises on her face? I waited until it was safe to offer an old teddy and some coloured pencils, then went to Sarah's door in search of my own sainthood. How bitterly she would laugh to see me now. And what about the little boy, Álvaro? I watched him walk about without boots, and when the time came, I did nothing – nothing – to save his life.

There is a thick lump in my throat. The wind picks up once more, shuddering across the street, raising the dust.

38.

Georgie must go home

Restless and alert, the horse breaker prowls the streets, now wishing Juan Sant well, now willing him to fail. Whatever happens, Sant must leave the town. If the police catch him with whatever trouble he is carrying on his back, it will be all over for the old man. By now everyone knows what happened to Green: lashed with wire and beaten, left for a week without food or water until nothing remained of the man he had been. Somehow – without giving Sant away – he must get warning to the Creeds. He cannot allow himself to think of the Englishwoman. When he does, he is lost. The memory of her face, her mouth, her fingers on his skin, makes his belly twist, folds his hands into fists. He wants to slam himself against walls.

He passes the shuttered fronts of El Mercantil and the other stores, sniffing the air like an animal scenting danger. An old-forgotten fear is surfacing, a fear long since buried beneath his life with Lali at the estancia, where the seasons turn, the colts grow into yearlings, the sheep are dipped and marked and shorn. Raúl understands fear. He knows the line between respect and danger when it comes to handling the ferocity of a wild stallion. He knows the terror of a colt with a rope around its neck. One night, out hunting on the open plain, he let the fire go out. When he woke, a black shadow flickered across the darkness and his heart stopped, knowing it was a puma. But this is different: the creeping terror of his childhood. Hunger and cold. Wind on the plain so strong he could not walk or even stand. Not knowing from day to day whether he would live or die.

He circles the grid of streets around the courthouse, gathering resolve and losing it. Slowly, slowly he is heading in the direction of the English hotel. But it is impossible for him to walk inside: he has no excuse to be here. He loiters on the steps kicking at dirt, watching it rise in clouds against his boots. As the dust settles, he becomes aware of a man and a woman crossing the square.

The woman is Georgie.

She is looking straight at him. Her companion is a small gentleman in spectacles; now he bows and withdraws his arm from hers. She must have said something to make him leave.

Coming up the steps, she trips a little and throws out an arm for balance. He catches hold of her, his fingers lingering on her sleeve. The square is empty. Shop fronts and hotel windows wait to see what he will do. Her companion must be watching. And what of Ian Creed? Raúl steps into the shadows at the side of the building, pulling her with him. She opens her mouth to speak, but he puts up his hand to silence her. Tears have tracked a trail through the dust on her cheeks. He wants to put his mouth to her skin, to taste the salt with his tongue. Longing dizzies him.

She is trembling. He must go gently, or he will make her more afraid.

"Tell the Señor you must come home."

"What?" She is still holding his sleeve.

He glances over his shoulder. "Please. You must come home. There are rumours."

"But we can't leave today." The southern sky is already greying as the sun slips away. Crepuscular shafts of light slant through bright gaps in the clouds. "I want to leave," she adds, urgently. "We all do. But Señor Creed is still talking to the other estancieros."

"Then go back inside the hotel. Do nothing. Lock your-selves in your rooms tonight."

Her fingers tighten on his arm and the effort of not placing his hand on hers crushes him. "What is happening? Is it the army?"

"The workers."

"Is it because of what happened in the square? What are they going to do?"

"I don't know. But yes, because of…" He gestures in the direction of the street corner, toward the courthouse and the prison. The tin buildings of the meat-packing plants rise on the northern hills above the town. The wind presses the spindly fingers of sloping trees, inclining like silent watchmen toward the factories. He grips her arms, startled by his own courage. The slope of her shoulders takes his breath away.

Her eyes are locked to his. "Will you speak to Señor Creed?"

"I can't. If I am seen with him, the workers will think I have betrayed them."

She is silent, considering. Anxiety flickers in her eyes like a moth behind glass. Clouds roil overhead.

"Please," he says again. "Don't be afraid. Lock your door tonight. Whatever you hear, stay inside. I promise no harm will come to you. This is the truth. Tomorrow, you must come home."

"I want to," she says, looking straight at him. "Raúl, I want so much to come home."

The wind catches a wisp of her hair, it flutters like strands from a horse's tail caught on a fence in summer. The space between them is as gigantic as the sky over the plain. If he touches her skin, he will be lost. He raises a hand towards her face, then turns and hurries away across the street.

The fox counsels the guanaco

The guanaco used to join the people quite often. He was very curious and wanted to watch what everyone was working on. Every man found this a most desirable state of affairs, for when meat was needed, he would simply kill the guanaco standing beside him. The rest of the guanacos grieved to find one of their number missing; they knew not how or where it had disappeared so suddenly.

At that time Fox and Guanaco were still good friends. The fox was cunning and artful. He had watched exactly how the people secretly killed a guanaco and then ate it. So he asked the guanaco, "Do you know what became of the others in your family?" The guanaco answered, "I do not. All my searching was in vain." The fox continued: "The people here are killing your friends and relatives. Be on your guard and don't go to their huts." Then the guanaco became sad and ran far away from the huts of the people. Since then, it shyly avoids human beings altogether.

From *Travels in Patagonia* by Henry O. Chambers

39.

Fireworks

The explosions begin shortly after midnight. I have been dozing fitfully in a chair, now I run to the window. Doors fly open, citizens stream onto the street below. The sky above is thick with red and grey smoke. When the sound settles, one word rises high above the crowd: ¡Revolución!

There is a hammering at the door. "Georgie. It's me. Ian."

I draw back the bolt. Ian falls against the door and tumbles into the room. A muscle twitches in his cheek.

"Quick! Put on your shawl. They're trying to blow up the town."

"No, Ian. Wait." I fight waves of panic. The explosions are coming from the hills to the north. "Nobody's blowing up the town. It's the factories. Look. The factories."

Ian grabs my shoulders, shaking me so hard my teeth rattle. His eyes are rabid. "It's the revolution. Frank said it. Frank told me and I didn't believe him."

"No, Ian." I tear myself from his grasp and run back to the window. Thick grey smoke hangs over the hills. Men and women are running in all directions, between wagons, horses, cars. A handful stand staring open-mouthed at the sky with the same delight I might have seen at home among country people watching a firework display.

Ian is at my side. I put my hand on his elbow, but he flings out his arm, catching me hard on the jaw. I cry out in pain, cradling my face.

"Please, Ian. It's alright, I promise you. Nothing is going to happen to us. I know."

"How do you know?"

"A message. From… from Lali." Behind the lie, I send Raúl a prayer of gratitude, a recognition that he has risked both the workers and the estancieros to come to me and tell me what to do.

Ian crumples onto the floor and I kneel beside him, wrapping him in my arms, pulling his head against my chest. Around us, the sky is quietening. A few smaller explosions, and then it is over. Nothing remains but a huge grey cloud, fanned out by the wind over the hills, and the red glow of the burning factories. Tiny flakes of ash swirl in the air like snow, covering the rooftops in a soft blanket of grey.

His jaw is still grinding, the muscle pulsing in his cheek. And now I remember why the sound seems so familiar. The hospital. Patients, grinding their teeth, quivering in corners, or crouched like Ian, trembling in my arms. My father taught me to pray for their redemption: *Don't you see, Georgie? These men have witnessed the terrors of the earth. They have practiced evil upon one other in the name of good. Their souls are torn to pieces by what they have done.*

The terrors of the earth. Alice knew: *Fires light behind his eyes, bayonets grow at the ends of his fingers.* What has been witnessed cannot be unseen. I tug my shawl closer around my shoulders and whisper, "Ian, listen. This is not the war. I swear to you, we are not in danger here."

His eyes do not move. Only his jaw works without ceasing. "What are you suggesting, Georgie?"

I recoil from the bitterness in his tone. "It must be dreadful, remembering…"

"You saw injured men in the hospital, didn't you Georgie? Horrible injuries?" I nod, trying to keep my head clear. "Imagine what that looked like at the front. Knee deep in mud." He is breathing heavily, the words sputtering through clenched teeth in little jags and bursts. "I watched people drown, you know. I watched them. Falling off the duckboards. Drowning in mud and gas and wire. Everybody drowning." He bends over for a moment, eyes screwed shut. "Noise so loud. That was a blessing. If I'd heard every scream and every prayer and every curse, I might have jumped right in with them. I might have gone mad." He taps his cheek with a laugh and the sound sickens me. "Sometimes I think I have."

"No, no… of course you haven't." But I am trembling. To think I once envied the strange separation his mind has forged between the present and the past. His eyes have darkened as if possessed by some monster of the war. I wrap myself around him, holding him until his muscles soften, and he leans his head against my shoulder. I lay a hand against his cheek, trying to still the jumping muscles, listening to the noises on the street. My jaw has started to throb. I wonder if there will be a bruise, and what I will say to Mrs Creed.

Mrs Creed.

"Oh God. Ian, your mother. She'll be beside herself." He shakes his head, and I push him away from me, trying to speak calmly. "Ian. Listen. We must go to your mother. We can't leave her on her own. If someone speaks to you in the corridor, ignore them. Keep your head down."

"Righto," he says, and closes his eyes.

I give him a little shake. "I'll go first. I'm going to open the door, and we'll both run. Are you game?"

He nods, with what could be a wink, but is perhaps nothing more than another judder of his cheek. As I open the door, I hear footsteps, thuds and bumps, hotel residents dragging their own bags down the stairs. Escaping the revolution. I draw a deep breath, take his hand in mine, and pull him with me out into the corridor.

40.

The empty farm

I stand beneath the carancho tree, listening to the empty landscape, grateful for the silence. In the stillness of the estancia, I promise myself I will never leave again.

Most of the peons have left to join the strike. Those who remain are surly and uncommunicative and it's clear they won't stay long. Handwritten posters flutter on the walls of the outbuildings or turn to sludge in the puddles. Lali strides across the farm ripping them down, crumpling them in his hands. He watches, with a rifle, after dark.

One day, a wagon arrives with a delivery. Books, ordered half a year ago for Álvaro, back when I believed I had a calling to improve the lives of Ian's workers. I flick through the pages and drop them back into the crate.

Ian and Lali and Raúl shoulder the work of twenty men, riding out for days at a time to the remote summer grazings.

"I hate to leave you," Ian says, putting his arms around me.

"Go," I tell him. "We'll be fine. Nothing can happen to us." I wave my arms, taking in the surrounding emptiness, trying to sound brave.

I concentrate on Leo. We play on the farm as we have always done. We tend the kitchen garden, feed the chickens and hunt for eggs, give slops to the pigs and visit the rabbits. Leo collects feathers to decorate the nursery. Mrs Creed stays in her room, biting her fingernails, watching the plain from her window. Days pass and nobody comes.

One night, I am woken by the galloping of horses: when I run to the window, a troupe of shadows is riding towards the farm. Shouts echo across the yard, silhouettes circle in the moonlight. An assignation. A gaunt shape in an old, crumpled jacket jumps down from his horse to address the gathering before the whole procession wheels round and flies over the ridge, away across the plain. I tiptoe down to the kitchen door, trying not to make a sound, leaping in terror at each creak of the old floorboards. Out in the garden, the crack of a twig echoes through the silence. I hurry from door to door, struggling with heavy, unused bolts. In Ian's study, I search his desk for the key to the gun cabinet. As I reach for the rifle, a pale shadow appears behind me in the glass. I give a shriek and spin round.

"Mrs Creed. You gave me such a fright. I thought you were a ghost."

"What are you doing?"

"The strikers came." The rifle seems pointless now. There is no one left.

"Are they still here?" Her hands pluck convulsively at her throat.

"No. They've gone. They took the rest of the peons with them." I sink into the old armchair, the rifle in my lap, surrounded by the familiar study smells of dogs and pipes and leather. The smells of absent men.

*

Life continues. The house servants cook and clean and care for Leo. I organise the linen cupboards, read to Leo in the nursery. The silent farm reminds me of the war, how it emptied the vicarage, the church, the whole village, of brothers, fathers, husbands, uncles, sons. During the day, I am beset by a weariness so overwhelming I can hardly keep my eyes open, as if a thick curtain has fallen across my mind. At night, I lie awake, listening to the wind howl across the plain. I feel nothing but emptiness: no knocking, no ghosts, only absence, as if the house has lost its heart. I try not to think of Thomas Green. Sometimes I crawl into bed with Leo, and hold him close, listening to his breath. One night, when I creep into the nursery, I find Mrs Creed asleep beside the fire.

The house servants are incapable of managing the farm work. We grit our teeth and feed the animals, keep the closest windmills working as best we can, carry water from the well. All hands on deck. Even Mrs Creed is helping now. I am Álvaro, carrying buckets across the yard, forking hay for the horses. I milk the cows and throw scraps to the pigs. Fingernails crack and splinter, my joints stiffen and my back aches. We battle against the wind with buckets and barrows, while the few remaining horses wander listlessly through the corrals, raising their heads from time to time to whinny for their lost companions. Most of the dogs have gone. One morning, we discover puma tracks and the bloodied remains of a lamb. Despite Mrs Creed's protestations, I take Ángel and, armed with Ian's rifle, ride out onto the plain. By the time I return, my face is blistered from the southern sun.

Mrs Creed is beside herself. "How could you?" she demands. "You might have got lost." I shrug. By now, the surrounding plain is as familiar to me as the house itself. I could never get lost. "You have no idea what you're doing," she continues. "We could all have been killed."

"It was probably me who could have been killed," I say, trying to inject a note of humour. "Anyway, someone has to keep things going. Otherwise, Ian will have a dreadful mess to clear up when he gets back."

"He's got that anyway," she mutters, but I pretend not to hear.

*

We are bending over the water trough, wrestling with the pump and buckets, when a cumulus of dust appears on the horizon. I cock my head to listen, like an animal. The barns are silent, the bunkhouse door creaks open in the wind. Leaves flutter across the yard and settle in puddles, horses stamp and whinny in the corrals.

Watch the horses, Miss. They see more than we do.

But it is too late.

The dust cloud grows and becomes a stampede of hooves, sending the farm horses into a frenzy. Mrs Creed grabs me by the arm.

"Where's the rifle? Quick!"

I stare at her, helpless. She snatches Leo by the hand and the two of them run toward the house. The riders pull up hard at the hitching post.

"Where is the estanciero?" one of them shouts. The servants huddle and clutch each other.

I step forward. "He's not here," I answer, trying to keep my voice steady. "Speak to me." Pilar stifles a little cry, stuffing her hand into her mouth. The scullery maid snatches at my sleeve. Too late, I realise what they already know: a gaucho would have dismounted and announced himself by name. These men are bandits. For an instant, I am afraid my legs will not hold me. I wonder, fleetingly, if Mrs Creed will appear from the house with the rifle and rescue us, then pray that she is safe inside with Leo, all doors bolted.

A rider on a stocky black horse, white-foamed with sweat, gallops to the front of the group and hauls his mount to a standstill. I recognise him immediately: it is the snake-haired revolutionary in the black-and-white hat. He flings out an arm, both lordly and violent, and at his signal men jump down from their horses and run into the barn.

I open my mouth to scream and the sound seems to come from very far away. "Stop. What are you doing? Stop."

Pilar and I clutch each other and watch, helpless, as the men swarm through the buildings and re-emerge dragging barrels of oil and sacks of feed, slitting the throats of shrieking piglets. Blood flows over the yard. They hitch one of their horses to the small farm wagon and pile it high with rabbit cages. The leader raises his rifle and fires into the air, making the horses leap and squeal. They are taking everything, all our supplies. Ignoring Pilar's shouts, I pull myself free and run for the wagon, grabbing at its wooden sides, hauling with all my strength. But the horses are gaining speed and I fall back, panting and useless, as it rackets along the track. The man in the black-and-white hat spurs his horse across the yard towards the corral. He throws open the gate, and the farm horses stream out onto the plain.

At the top of the ridge one of the riders pulls up short, turns, and races back towards the house. In the yard, he reaches down from his horse and picks up Pilar, slinging her over his saddle.

*

With no horses or dogs, no animals left to feed, we bolt the doors, cock the rifle and wait. Pilar's screams echo across the empty yard. The servants cling to one another, weeping. Our nerves are strained with listening, night and day. I join Mrs Creed beside the window, biting my nails to the quick, my eyes gritty from watching the empty, endless plain. Mrs Creed holds Leo tight against her skirt; sometimes a shudder of terror washes over her body and her grip tightens. Leo whines in protest, but she refuses to let go.

Days pass. We wait in silence. When I see horses coming over the ridge, my guts freeze. Then I recognise the riders and fly downstairs to unbolt the door, weeping with relief.

"Did they harm you?" Ian asks. Words catch in my throat when I try to tell him about Pilar, thrown like a rag doll across the bandit's horse.

We walk through the farm, surveying the scattered remains of grain and hay, the smashed fences and blood-be-spattered stones. Ian puts his arm around my shoulders. The purple rings under his eyes are deep bruises and the muscles in his face twitch. He looks broken.

"They've taken our horses and left our sheep to rot. I didn't think it could get any worse, but now..." He rests his head against his horse's sweat-flecked flank. I stand at his side, unable to lift a hand in comfort. The effort of keeping watch has left me as empty as the rusted oilcans strewn behind the outbuildings. There are scratches in the dirt where Pilar kicked and fought as she was lifted off the ground.

"What about the men out at the grazings?" I ask. My mouth is cracked, my throat dry and hoarse. It seems a lifetime since I have spoken. "Did they go with the strike?"

"Most of them. Some love the land too much to leave it, some are too old or mad to care. The younger ones have all gone." He rubs his forehead and a smear of mud spreads across his face. Both of us fall quiet until I can bear the silence no longer.

"Did Lali's boy go with them?"

"What, Horsebreaker? No. He went to town for supplies. He's loyal. He'll never leave. Lali's all he's got."

I turn away behind the horse's shoulder, hiding my face in its mane. "There's no feed left for the horses. We'll have to turn them out."

"Horsebreaker will bring supplies," he replies, without moving. Beneath the dirt, his face is ashen. I gather my own strength and take him by the hand like a child. Together we walk back through the sticky gate to the house.

41

Days of silence

In these days of silence, the sound of horses fills me with both hope and dread. Even the shrieks of dying pigs or the panicked bleating of sheep at the shearing would be preferable to the terrible emptiness of the abandoned farm. When the wind drops, there is nothing to hear but the whine of hinges on the saddle room door and the flapping of broken wire along the fence. The blackened eyes of the bunkhouse remind me of how it once sighed with the cramped breath of the peons. I slink across the yard, trying to avoid the sound of my own footsteps. It sickens me to remember how stupid I was, hoping the peons would love me. Now all I want is a release from the tightness of terror. I want Pilar to come back and Leo to play among the horses. I want Raúl to come, with his soft, calm voice, his gentle hands. I hold my breath, waiting for him to return.

Ian hasn't noticed. He works for hours in his study, his hand wrapped around a tumbler of whisky, shuffling papers and accounts, reckoning his losses. Mrs Creed sits at his side, watching, as if that is enough to protect them both. Lali and I shoulder the responsibilities of the household: I work in the kitchen garden, and roam ever further across the plain, gathering berries from the calafate bushes, while Lali rides out to hunt, bringing home wild rabbits or upland geese for me to pluck and hang on the smokehouse door. Their puckered skins and staring eyes disgust me, but at least we will not starve. And if nothing else, there will always be mutton.

I am digging potatoes when I hear a wagon. I snatch up the rifle, and pray that Leo and Mrs Creed are locked inside the house. When I see Raúl drive into the yard, my legs buckle beneath me. I have imagined this moment so many times, but now he is here I don't know what to do. His eyes rove the yard.

"Raúl's back," I call, but my breath is feeble and the words are lost in the wind.

Ian runs into the yard, his face white.

"It's alright," I shout. "It's Raúl. He's brought supplies."

"I'll get Lali," Ian shouts back. He is gone again. I hear him calling for Lali and his mother.

Raúl unhitches Hero from the back of the wagon, then stops to stare at the desolate buildings, the empty corrals. His home too. His horses. When he catches sight of me, he throws Hero's rein over the hitching post and takes a step in my direction. I stumble forward and his hands hold me steady. I sense the shape of him beneath the thick warmth of his coat.

His eyes, red-rimmed with fatigue, flicker over my shoulder. At any moment, Ian and Lali will be here. We both know it. He steps back and inclines his head slightly, a servant's nod. The deception enrages me. I want to pull him back into my arms.

"Thank God you are safe." With these words, I am telling him everything: about the men, the emptiness, Pilar, how I thought we would all die, how I have prayed for this moment and how now it is here I don't know what to do. I breathe the smell of him, leather and sweat and horse. His face is streaked with dirt and the cuffs of his jacket are edged with something brown and rusty that might be blood. He notices me looking – he notices everything – and moves his hands behind his back.

"What is happening, Raúl?"

"Some things it is better not to know, Miss." His eyes narrow. "Those bastards. They took my horses."

He turns back to Hero to unbuckle the saddle. I stand at his side and pull off the thick sheepskin pads, smoothing my hands over sweat-drenched whorls of hair. Steam rises from the horse's back. Raúl does not look at me, but his fingers hesitate, resting on the leather as if trying to stop time. A shadow passes overhead, a condor perhaps, sweeping the yard and obliterating the sun. He sighs, and lifts the saddle.

I trail behind him through the passage of empty stalls and sheds towards the saddle room. He pauses to wipe a hand over his forehead and I see through his eyes the coils of dusty rope, his own braided reins and lassos and un-oiled leathers hanging on hooks and brackets, all that remains of his beautiful horses. I long to take him in my arms, tell him everything will be as it was. The four walls of the saddle room close around us, a dark safety after the bright open sky above the yard. Raúl catches his breath as I push the bolt across.

Slivers of light stream through cracks in the wooden walls. Dust shimmers. The air quickens. I open my arms to the warmth of him, and part the neck of my blouse to feel his skin against mine. His hands are on my back.

I want nothing more than to be held by him. For as long as I am in his arms, we are safe. But we have no more than a moment. A tiny creature rustles in the dust and straw. Or is it the ghost of Alice Creed watching me betray her husband? Here at the estancia, someone is always watching. Raúl groans as I pull away, pressing my fingers against his lips. Far away, then closer, voices are calling. I hear the sound of running feet.

Raúl is at the door, tearing back the bolt, the screech loud enough to scare the mice and make me leap out of my skin. I throw out a hand and clutch his arm. He tries to pull away, but I grip his sleeve, afraid to let him go.

As the bolt comes free, the door swings open. The Creeds and Lali burst together into the tiny room and stop as one. They must know we had locked ourselves inside. My blouse is untucked, the neck still open. Too late, my hands fly to straighten my collar in a compulsive tell-tale gesture. A shudder runs through all of us, quivering the dust and the cobwebs, shaking the glass in the windowpanes.

Lali's face darkens. I am afraid he will strike Raúl. Ian's dismay is almost comical. At a less horrifying time, I might laugh at the rueful way his eyebrows shoot up as he looks from me to the horse breaker and back again. It is Mrs Creed whose expression frightens me the most: her eyes narrow and her mouth sets in a tight, bitter line.

Nobody moves. When Ian speaks, he looks only at Raúl.

"Get your things. Get out of here." Lali opens his mouth to speak and Ian raises a hand. "Not now."

My heart is beating so fast I might faint. Raúl takes both my hands and bows over them: all the dignity this sordid little scene can afford belongs to him. "Forgive me, Miss. You see I must leave now."

Ian flinches as though the touch has been a blow. "Get out. Before I send for the police."

Raúl turns. Each receding step feels like the end of the world, for myself, for him, for all of us.

Ian's eyes are glazed with shock. He looks lost. "We thought something had happened to you. I shouted. You didn't answer. I thought someone had..." He trails off. I brace myself for the storm, but there is only silence.

Lali speaks first. "Don Ian should go back to the house."

Mrs Creed takes her son's elbow. I start to follow, but a wave of exhaustion knocks me off my feet. I sit down hard on a straw bale, dropping my head into my hands.

Lali stands over me, unmoving. Apology is pointless. I am nothing but flayed skin, raw and exposed before him.

"It's not his fault. It's me... it's all my fault."

He puts a hand up to silence me. "Be very careful, Señorita. You want to be the most important person for everybody. It's a dangerous thing to wish for. I don't think you understand what you have done."

42

The strikers

Lali stands in the long grass outside his bungalow, watching Raúl thread thick stalks of grass through his fingers. He kicks at Raúl's canvas bag.

"How is it that you are so stupid? If you wanted a girl, why didn't you tell me?"

Raúl stabs the stalks between his fingers like knives. "I didn't want a girl."

"No. You wanted this girl."

"It doesn't matter what I wanted."

Lali meets his eye. "I've come to tell you you're not to take Hero."

"What? But Hero's mine."

"Nothing here is yours, you fool."

"Fine. But that's not worthy of him. Perhaps what they say is true after all."

"And that is unworthy of you."

"Is it? You'd defend him all the way to the gallows if you had to. And you'd let her marry him even if he was a murderer. Wouldn't you?"

Lali's fists clench. His face is white with rage but he looks very old. "Don't talk like that. You don't know what you're saying."

Raúl shakes his head. "What does it matter?" He picks up the bag and turns towards the gate. He does not dare look back to see if Lali is watching him go.

The climb over the ridge lasts a lifetime. He cannot remember the last time he left the ranch without a horse. Losing Hero is like losing one of his own limbs. It might as well be – without a horse, he is as good as dead. He walks without looking back, refusing to alter his stride, even when the rain starts to fall and the track turns to mud beneath his boots. The plain stretches ahead of him. He has his boleadoras, and a knife tucked into his belt.

He walks for the rest of the day, doggedly, without breaking his stride, looking always to the horizon. When every part of him is sodden from the rain, he makes camp in a wood under the lee of a small hill, lighting a fire with a few branches of dead calafate. In the half light, he listens to the screeches of the night birds and the wind stirring the bushes.

As night thickens, he is jolted into alertness by a soft footfall and a whistle. Someone is calling in the manner of the gauchos. "Hola. It's I. Juan Sant."

"Juan Sant? For God's sake. What are you doing here?"

"I was waiting for you. But I didn't expect you to travel without your horse. What happened to you?"

Raúl shakes his head.

"It doesn't matter," Sant says, sitting down beside the fire. "I have brought one for you. And we have horses at the camp."

My horses, you bastard, Raúl thinks. "You were so sure of me?"

"I was," the other replies.

"I don't know why. I'm not even sure myself. What makes you think I'll come with you?"

"You have to come," Sant says simply. "How will you get out of here without a horse?"

*

The camp is a silent huddle of resting bodies. The shadowy forms of tethered horses amble among the calafate bushes. There are no fires.

"Some of the strikers have gone over the border," Juan Sant says. "Those of us here have pledged to keep fighting." He passes Raúl a cigarette. "Soto is coming here tonight. He will tell us what to do."

"Nobody tells me what to do."

Sant sighs. "Have it your own way. You can't go anywhere without a horse, and if we give you one, we'll expect you to fight with us."

"You have no right…" Raúl begins, but Sant lays a hand on his arm. "Shhh. Listen." There are murmurs at the edge of the clearing. The old man pushes himself to his feet and disappears into the darkness.

A frisson runs through the camp. Horses lift their heads, whinnying. Someone whistles at the outer edges of the clearing and in the ensuing silence, Raúl hears the double-click of a rifle. Shadows of men slip between the rocks.

A moment later, Sant is back at his side. "Soto is here," he whispers. "Tonight we will decide where next we fight."

"I don't care about Soto," Raúl begins, but Sant only smiles. His face shines in the grey moonlight.

"It's too late now," he says, tugging on Raúl's sleeve in a gesture that is almost childlike. "Quickly. Come with me."

43

Solutions

Maud Creed stands at the drawing room window. Outside on the lawn, Leo tugs on his father's arm, pulling him into some game or other. Ian's face is white.

"So, Georgie. What do you suggest we do now?" Shards of politeness send shivers through the room.

My fingers pluck at my shawl. Tiny specks of wool float listlessly to the floorboards. "Please. Whatever you decide, can we not tell Leo about this? He's done nothing. It's not fair to hurt him." It is all I can think to say.

"You want to talk about what's fair? How dare you? You were ready to take vows, Georgie, or have you forgotten?"

I have been standing at arm's length from myself. Now, with the lash of her tongue, my composure crumbles. "No," I whisper, and the tears catch. "I've not forgotten."

"Oh Georgie. I really thought…" She stops, and shakes her head. "Well, I will make arrangements. You can leave in the morning."

"No! Please, no." Now I am truly afraid, not only for Raúl, but for myself. Where will I go? For a second, wildly, impossibly, I imagine stealing a horse and riding away with Raúl. But he is gone. I pinch the back of my hand hard with my fingernails and a little bubble of blood forms against white skin.

Please, God, let them not send me away.

"So you think you can marry my son and pretend nothing has happened?"

It is as if she has read my mind. I jump. "I don't know. I'm sorry... I don't know."

She is silent, drumming her fingernails on the windowsill, her eyes fixed on her son and grandson. I wait, not daring to move. Is this to be my punishment, not to know what the Creeds will do with me? My ears are ringing with the silence. A breath of wind stirs the room, and a moth flutters against the window. I can hear the whirr of its wings beating against glass. I should faint, or weep, if only to break the stillness. Perhaps if I wept, she would shout at me, or throw me out, and then something would have happened.

At last, she takes a deep breath. I jerk to attention, pressing my hands together to stop them shaking.

"So, Georgie." She turns back to face me. "Let us be very clear. I don't know exactly what you've done and I don't want to know. I would prefer not to see you again, and not to allow you anywhere near my son and grandson." I bow my head and close my eyes against the tears sliding down my cheeks. "But," she continues, "I have reconsidered. We must be pragmatic."

I hold my breath.

"If you leave now, there will be— certain people— who will question why you do not wish to marry my son. Even if we were to put out the truth..." she pauses, and I flinch under her stare. "They will speculate. And we cannot afford speculation. There can be no more rumours." Her voice softens. "I have come to realise, Georgie, that this is not your fault. Terrible events have taken place here, events far beyond our control. You have been exposed to bandits and revolutionaries and that is more than any young woman can be expected to bear. I believe you have suffered a regrettable lapse of judgement due to nervous exhaustion. It is understandable. Forgivable, even. So, we will all forgive you. You will marry as arranged, and none of us will ever speak of this again." A pause. "But do not think, Georgie, that because we can forgive, we will forget. Do you understand?"

And this, apparently, is the end of the interview. Mrs Creed walks out of the room without waiting for an answer. Why should she wait? What alternative do I have but to agree?

I flop onto the armchair, holding my aching head between my hands. The house is silent. Nobody comes. I dare not get up for fear my legs won't hold me. In any case, I can't risk going to my room for fear of meeting the Creeds. The wedding is only a few short weeks away. Marriage will be my salvation. I will stay at the estancia. No need to go creeping back to my old life, or face the world alone. Raúl is gone. He will make a new life for himself, somewhere beyond my reach.

But even as I banish Raúl, I am beset by wild flights of imagination: perhaps he is not gone, perhaps he will return before the wedding to carry me away. What if something should happen to Ian, some kind of accident, and he were to die – instantly, painlessly, of course. Then I would be free. Raúl would hear about it, and he would come for me.

Stop. Stop it. These are the imaginings of a child. I am appalled at my own cruelty. Ian has done nothing – *nothing* – to deserve these terrible thoughts. Mrs Creed is right, I am overwrought, my judgement is not clear. To wish death on another person, I might as well be a murderer myself. *Create a clean heart in me, Oh God, renew a right spirit within me.* I must marry Ian and ask for his forgiveness. He is my redemption. I know, as I have always known, that I must marry him and love him. I must stay here at his side.

*

Much later, when a pale twilight has fallen and the curtains hang like shadowy pillars against the darkening windows, when my body is stiff and cold from hours of stillness, I hear footsteps, and a hand on the door. Ian is standing over me, silhouetted against the light. His breath smells of whisky. As my eyes adjust to the gloom, I can see he is swaying. I struggle to my feet. "Ian. I am so sorry."

"Oh, I'm sure you are." He dashes a hand across his face, and for a moment I am afraid he might cry. Instead, he leans against the wall and folds his arms, watching me. "God, Georgie, I really trusted you. Vicar's daughter. Nurse." A short laugh. "Even after what you told me you did to Eddie. Especially after that. I thought you were like me: a terrible thing happened, you paid the price and all you needed was a second chance. You didn't seem like a…" He pauses, and his mouth curls into a sneer. "Sorry, I can't think of a nice word for someone like you." I shrink into the chair. "I thought… I thought we were well matched, somehow," he continues, "and I was so happy. A second chance for both of us. I should have realised it was too good to be true."

"Ian, please…"

"I'm surprised you dared…" He hesitates.

"I know. It was wrong. I know I've done wrong. I'm so sorry."

"Oh, I wasn't talking about that. I'm not talking about you. I meant, after everything they say about me." He rubs his fists hard against his temples. "So what were you thinking, Georgie? Would you have kissed my stableboy and married me anyway?"

"I don't know. Oh Ian, I'm so sorry. I don't know." But isn't that exactly what his mother is saying I must do? My stomach is a knot of humiliation. I fight to hold back more tears.

"You know," he continues, "if you don't marry me, they'll say you found out. That it's true and you found out."

I have no idea what to say. If I leave, I will ruin him, and myself. I want to save him, but when I see his bloodshot eyes, I remember the hotel bedroom in Río Gallegos, the pain of his hand against my jaw.

"You do believe it, don't you?" he says dully. "You do. Even if you deny it, there's some part of you that thinks I must have been responsible."

"Not like that, Ian."

"No, of course not. Not like that. I'm not a…" He stops. "I was going to say I'm not a monster. But of course I am, aren't I?" He shakes his head and his eyes glisten. "I thought you were here to make me better. To prove to me that I'm not a monster after all."

I say nothing, but I can hear Eddie's hoarse whisper. *The question is, Georgie, which of us is the monster? You, or I?*

Ian presses the heel of his hand against the side of his head as if trying to waken something in his mind. I long to comfort him, but how can I reach across the space between us?

"I keep thinking that one day it'll come back to me," he says. "I'll wake up and remember what happened, what she was doing on the stairs." He hits his fist against his temple, once, then again, harder.

"Stop. Ian, please, stop it." I take his wrists, but he throws his arms up, slapping me away. "Please stop. I'm going to fetch your mother."

"Mother?" He stares at me without recognition. His eyes are blackened sockets in his skull. He shields his face, as if from something bright and terrifying, and I understand at last that whatever has happened to him is more than his mind can bear. How many times, when the dirt blew into eyes and mouth and throat, must he have whispered for his mother in sobs too small for sound? How many times since then has he scrabbled and fought against imaginary burial mounds? What anguish have I caused this fragile, sorrowful man? He offered me freedom and I repaid him with betrayal. A log slips from the grate in a cascade of embers. Ian startles as if he has been struck and sinks to his knees beside the fire.

44

Ir al humo

The chief of police from Río Gallegos arrives in a cloud of dust and a cavalcade of motor cars, followed by several managers and estancieros who drive past the house and disperse into the bungalows.

No sign of Lali. A flash of hope: perhaps he is with Raúl. Moments later, I see him among the estancieros and my heart sinks again, knowing Raúl is alone. One of the passengers looks alarmingly like Henry Chambers. I consider throwing myself on his mercy and begging him to take me away, but when the car draws nearer, the man is a stranger. Tonight all the newcomers will converge on the house for dinner, and I will greet them as Ian's future wife. Well, I had better get used to it.

The police chief has oiled black hair and a thick moustache. "Señor Creed." He speaks in English, but only to Ian. "You and your family are lucky to have escaped without injury. Several of your neighbours have not been so fortunate." He breaks off with a shudder. Pilar is not a member of the family, presumably her misfortune doesn't count. "However," he continues, "I come bearing good news. I am happy to report that by now most of the strikers are in the hands of the army." A sideways glance. "May I speak with you alone?"

Ian gestures wordlessly towards the study. The police chief clicks his feet together and steps inside. Both the Creeds make to follow. The police chief raises an eyebrow at Mrs Creed, who stares at him, stony-faced, until he drops his gaze.

"Send for some tea," she says without looking at me. "Then you can check on Leo. You're not needed here."

"They picked up some stragglers at the boundary," the police chief is saying. "You should inform the army of any you would like returned to the farm."

And the door is shut.

Like animals. He is speaking about them as if they are stray animals to be rounded up and returned. And then, in horror: what if the army has picked up Raúl?

How am I to find out? There are no wives among the passengers, no women for me to befriend, only estancieros and managers. But I have seen how the men admire Maud Creed, how she holds herself their equal, so I prepare myself for dinner as best I can, brushing my tangled hair until it shines, pinching my cheeks to make them glow, rifling impatiently through my meagre wardrobe, searching for a frock least likely to make me look like a governess. But they are all useless, dreary things. In despair, I crumple them into rags and throw them on the floor.

At the last moment, I remember. Alice's dress. Everyone is changing for dinner, nobody notices as I slip along the corridor towards the servants' staircase. No time to care about the ghosts in the attic, though I feel them watching as I throw open the trunk and rifle through the tissue paper. What does Alice think of me now?

In my bedroom I hold up the dress, examining myself i the mirror. It's not exactly an evening dress, but even with its badly repaired hem, Alice's blue silk is more expensive-looking than any of my own clothes. And no longer too tight: my body is thin and sinewy from farm work, elbows and knees sharp-edged. I slip it over my head, and feel Alice herself, waiting to see what I will do. When I look back at the mirror, I am certain she will be there, standing behind me in the glass. The blue silk shimmers.

I regret my decision as soon as I come downstairs. But it is too late, the guests are already entering the dining room. I slip into my seat and grip my shawl tight around my shoulders. The Creeds are seated at each end of the table. Next to Mrs Creed, the police chief. Even if he were to reveal something in conversation, it is unlikely I will be able to hear. The dreadfulness of it all should have sent me running from the room in tears, but there is no time to run or cry. I must try not to attract attention. The dress was a terrible mistake, a stupid, vengeful act, a gauntlet thrown down when I should have made myself invisible. Ian, engrossed in conversation, does not look at me, still, my fingers are trembling, and the shawl slips, just a little. I hasten to cover myself, but the movement, or perhaps the flash of white embroidery on my cuff, has caught Mrs Creed's attention. I see her stiffen, her eyes widen slightly, before she looks away. Ian glances across the table and I freeze, holding the shawl at my neck. I can feel the white scalloped edging catching the candlelight. Ian's knife clatters on his plate.

I force myself to look away. On my right sits a grey-haired estanciero who smells of whisky and speaks little or no English. He does not appear promising, but when both Creeds are once more safely engaged in conversation, I fix a smile on my face and speak softly in Spanish.

"We are so grateful that the police are here to help us, Señor. Can you tell me exactly what they are doing to keep us safe?"

The estanciero drains his glass. "You are perfectly safe, Señorita. The army will dispose of any troublemakers. All of us—" he waves an arm around the table "—can make our wishes known to the colonel."

So it is true. The men sitting at this table will decide who is to be set free. I can only pray they will be merciful. But what of Raúl? If he has been rounded up with the strikers, what chance does he have? I grip my hands together, trying to quell the rising panic. I have no idea yet how this stranger can help me, but this is at least a start. On an impulse, I reach across the table for the carafe and fill his glass. He will think I'm forward, but perhaps the wine will loosen his tongue.

"Is the colonel coming here, Señor?"

The estanciero laughs. "Ah no, Señorita. We must go to him."

Mrs Creed glances in our direction, her attention caught by the estanciero's laughter. She leans across the table with a question, forcing him to turn away. She doesn't want me talking to anyone. On my other side, two managers, deep in conversation, ignore me. I pick up my glass and pretend to be absorbed in my wine.

Mrs Creed's voice, speaking English, rises above the rest. "Yes," she is saying. "It's been terribly difficult. Only yesterday my son was forced to fire another troublemaker."

I hold my breath, listening.

"The man was quite depraved." A theatrical whisper, loud enough for me to hear. "He tried to attack my son's fiancée. Poor Georgie is still shaken." The police chief glances at me and Mrs Creed follows his gaze. Her eyes meet mine. "The dear child was hysterical with shock. Imagine what could have happened... especially after that terrible incident with our nurserymaid."

So this is to be the story. I feel a sudden burn of fury: how dare she use Pilar to add credence to her lies? But if I contradict her, who would believe me? I am hysterical with shock.

What did the old estanciero say? The army will dispose of troublemakers. And the Creeds will use the army to dispose of Raúl. The room swims. I clutch my napkin, terrified I will be sick. Running away is useless, there is nowhere to go. I must stay here, and I must concentrate. First, a gulp of wine, some Dutch courage. I need to find out where

Raúl is, then, how to get there. The rest will have to come later. Mrs Creed has shown me what dissembling looks like. Now, I must dissemble for myself.

I allow the shawl to slip from my shoulders, exposing soft blue silk framing my skin. The grey-haired estanciero, bored with trying to follow conversation in English, turns back in my direction and embarks on a meandering story about his sheep. I sit, smiling, waiting for a chance to interrupt. When at last he pauses to take a drink, I open my eyes very wide.

"It's all so very interesting. But please, my dear Señor, there's something I must know. How long will you all be staying?" I tilt my head to one side and pout a little, feeling stupid. I mustn't lose him. I must find more words. "We see very few visitors, and it is so pleasant to have company."

He smiles. A wolfish gleam appears in his grey eyes. "A young lady like yourself must quickly get bored in a place like this. How long would you like us to stay, Señorita?"

"Oh, Señor. You know it isn't up to me. But I hope your destination isn't too far away?"

"Do you hate so much to say goodbye to your fiancé? Ah, such is young love. I admire your devotion."

He looks past me, trying to catch Ian's attention. Why is he reluctant to say where they are going? The location must be a secret. I have to try harder. All my life I have felt so clumsy, never knowing when to speak and when to hold my tongue, but I can't let that stop me now. Gritting my teeth, I lay my hand lightly on his wrist, sensing his surprise, then pleasure, at the touch of my fingers on his skin. I keep my tone playful, ignoring the white cuff.

"Don't you dare tell Ian I'll miss him. He'll get terribly big-headed." I move a little closer and whisper, "Can't it be our secret?"

He licks his lips. Tiny beads of sweat appear on his forehead and he dabs at them with his napkin. "Believe me, my dear, I will lock any secret of yours securely into my heart."

264

I smile gratefully and he lays his hand over my fingers. His palm is warm and damp. I force myself not to pull away, wriggling my fingers so they intertwine with his.

"Do please tell where you are going. And when you plan to leave." I look up into his face and our eyes meet. "Perhaps I will be able to come too."

He reaches for his glass and gulps the rest of his drink. Without taking my eyes from his face, I pour him another, praying that neither of the Creeds is watching. "Why don't you just whisper it to me. Please, let it be our secret."

He leans closer, his mouth brushing my hair. I can feel his breath, hot and thick with wine. I am closing my mind to him, to the Creeds, to everything but the whispered words. As his voice slips into my ear I nod, just slightly, and press my fingertips once more against his arm.

45

One day's drive to the north

After dinner, I sit alone on the floor of my little room, listening to the shrieks of the night creatures, turning my Bible between my hands, searching for comfort in its familiar pages.

From the end of the earth will I cry until thee when my heart is overwhelmed. Lead me to the rock that is higher than I.

It is a sign, it must be. I mouth to myself the words the grey-haired estanciero whispered into my ear: One day's drive to the north. Another day west, toward the mountains. The farm lies beyond the town. We leave once all the passengers have arrived, probably the day after tomorrow.

What he truly thought to gain by telling me, I can't imagine. A drunken sense of adventure must have spurred him, rather than any real hope. Perhaps, for a lonely man living on a remote farm, the touch of a young girl's hand is enough. Not that it matters. I have the information I wanted – now I must decide what to do with it.

A horse can outpace a car on these roads, and a rider can win precious time by cutting across the plain. My little Ángel is gone, stolen by the bandits, and I have never ridden any other horse, but Hero is here, Raúl's beautiful, long-legged Hero. If I set off tonight, as soon as the house is asleep, it will be hours before anyone notices I am missing. I have no map to guide me, only the words of the old estanciero, but I know which way is north, and once I have turned to the west, I cannot fail to find the mountains. I will have to trust my instincts, like a gaucho. With Hero, a true gaucho's horse, I stand a decent chance of reaching Raúl before anyone can catch up with me. And if I bring Hero, perhaps Raúl will get away.

If I were to set off. It would be the end of everything. But perhaps Alice's dress has ended everything already. I can't move. My mind is working too fast, I recoil from my own thoughts. I lean my head back against the bed, remembering the last time I broke everything that ever mattered.

After the incident with Eddie's wheelchair, I prayed to God to show me an escape. At around the same time, Sarah Gerard – *that* woman – whose little girl died in the pandemic, packed up her home and her remaining children and slipped away, leaving a bunch of wildflowers on her daughter's grave. Sarah Gerard's husband came back from the war: we found him one day, standing beside the tiny stone. The flowers were long withered, nobody had come since Sarah left to pull the weeds or say a prayer.

From the smell, Mr Gerard might as well have held a bottle in his hand, but he was a returning soldier, and my father approached him with his usual courteous smile and outstretched hand.

"Where is she?" Sarah Gerard's husband asked.

My father frowned. "I beg your pardon?"

"My wife. Where is my wife?"

"Your wife? I, ah, I don't think…"

Sarah Gerard's husband turned to me, the question still in his eyes. "I'm sorry," I heard myself say. "I have no idea."

He swayed as if the words had been a blow, lurching closer over me. I thought of Sarah's black eyes and took a step back. But the man crumpled. He dropped his face into his hands and began to wail, a high-pitched keening sound, then collapsed against my father, sobbing like a child.

Like a whisper beneath the sobs, I hear the words I saw in Sarah Gerard's eyes. Go. Get out. While you can. The words fill my ears, my little room. It is not just Sarah who is speaking, beneath the murmuring voices of the wind the curtains lift and reach towards me, a tiny branch scratches against the glass. Alice is here, I am sure of it. Her blue dress, hanging once again in my wardrobe, stirs a little. Alice is here, and she is telling me what to do. I stand up and shake the stiffness from my bones.

*

Hero whickers softly as I slip into the corral. He tosses his head almost knocking me off my feet: after Ángel, he seems enormous. I am afraid he will sense my terror and shy away from me, but with a shrill of indignation, he consents to follow me out into the yard. His hooves ring unnaturally loud against the earth. Every sound echoes in the silence; at any moment we will be discovered. But it is too late to go back. I have kissed Leo for the last time, and said goodbye to the place I thought would be my home.

The horse is impossibly tall. He snorts, the steam of his breath rising in the late chill, and stamps impatiently as I struggle with the saddle and haul myself clumsily onto his back. I remember how effortlessly Raúl's cupped hands lifted me. But it is useless to remember the past, I must think only of what is ahead. Pulling the reins across Hero's neck I whip him up, leaning forward so I can shout against the wind into his flattened ears. He lunges sideways, almost unseating me. I tighten my hands in his mane, clinging on with all my strength, and now we are plummeting over the ridge, across the plain, his long limbs stretched, his neck extended as we whirl away from the road and gallop into the darkness.

*

The first hours are exhilarating. Beyond the outer boundary of the estancia I have no map; like a gaucho, I will have to rely on my sense of direction and the true path of the sun.

Like the people who first lived on this land, before progress arrived to plough their bones into the soil. To the east and west, the rising and setting sun. I must follow my instincts and head north, then west until I sight the Cordillera and discover the direction of the road. I must trust the sun, the moon and the mountains to show me the way.

We press on at our relentless pace. As the darkness turns to grey, guanacos race in step, and ostriches run across our path, their muscular legs striding over the dirt like seven league boots. Hero begins to slow, and I pull him back to a steady gaucho trot. His chest heaves, breath snorts heavily through his nostrils, his shoulders are flecked with foam. Once or twice he stumbles into a dip or over a root and I am flung forward. Each time I manage to cling on, muttering aloud in a continual incantation of prayer. A tepid sun is rising. Ahead lies mile after mile of unbroken ground, undulating softly towards the hills. *Lead me to the rock that is higher than I.*

When the sun is overhead and I am riding on my own shadow, I rein in and allow the horse to rest. The plain stretches around me in a dizzying span of emptiness; the hills seem no closer, nothing more than lavender and purple shadows. The scrubby earth has given way to scattered bushes and short, twisted ñire trees, their penitent shapes stretching bony fingers into the distance like guides.

I slip from Hero's broad back, feeling my legs give way as they meet the soil. The horse snorts and blows as I loosen the girths to let him breathe. I tie the reins to a bush and stretch out flat on the ground, looking at the clouds, trying to catch my breath and contemplate the enormity of what I have done. By now, the Creeds must know that I am gone. Leo will have called for me. Poor little Leo. Any guilt I have left is for him. The Creeds will have listened to the silence, hurried to the nursery, the kitchen, through the garden and out into the yard. They will have searched among the gooseberry and blackcurrant bushes. They will have called out to the barns and outhouses and run up the ridge to look across the plain. Perhaps the grey-haired estanciero has confessed that he revealed the army's secret destination. Maybe Ian and Lali have already set off in the car, hoping to overtake me on the road. I must keep moving. I must find Raúl and vouch for him. That's all. What lies beyond is unimaginable.

Clouds have formed in the darkening sky. A thin drizzle is falling, a mist light enough to land in minute drops on the surface of each hair. Hero throws up his head as if at some unseen danger. I shiver, pulling my cape close. When I tighten the girth, the horse bares his teeth, twisting his head round with flattened ears.

"Don't you snarl at me," I tell him, my voice quivering in the silence. "You might as well save your energy. You'll thank me in the end, when we find him. I'm sorry about the rain." I haul myself back up and spread the cape as wide as I can. "It just means we have to move quicker." But the distance seems impossible, a thousand times farther than I had realised. How could I have miscalculated so badly? The horse lurches forward, jolting my weary body with every step. Cold seeps like poison through my bones.

The heavens open. Rain lashes my cheeks and mingles with my tears.

We gallop until Hero can run no further, then we rest, panting, in the middle of the plain, and gallop again. I am no true horsewoman, I have no idea how far a horse can travel at this speed before it is broken. I know only to push forward as fast as I can. My exhausted mount skids over melting clods of earth, loose rocks and scree. Beyond making for the hills, I have no clear route to follow, so I give rein and allow Hero to twist and turn through the undergrowth, charting what path he pleases. Somewhere ahead must lie the Cordillera, and the mountain road where I will find Raúl. Our progress is a propulsion of legs and arms, wind-whipped hair and mane and tail, the cape billowing out behind us, the effort of my own body driving the horse forward as mechanical as the one-two-three-four gait beneath me. Head down to avoid the rain lashing into my eyes, I see nothing but the ground beneath Hero's hooves. So my mind flies with the horse, blank as a sky full of snow, the animal heaving and blowing, until we come to a dip in the terrain where Hero lurches forward, drops his head almost to the ground, and I, intent on willing him forward with the motion of my own body, am thrown over his shoulders, clutching at mane and saddle and withers, unable to save myself.

46

Candles

The boy in front of Raúl has no coat. His shoulders are sharp as blades through his rain-soaked shirt, and he shivers in the damp air. He holds one hand over his eye where a soldier has slashed at him with a sabre. Blood trickles through his fingers and runs down his arm. Every now and then, he staggers sideways until the nearest guard whips him back into the line. The boy howls. Raúl puts out a hand to steady him. After an hour or so, the boy trips on a stone and topples over the bank at the side of the road. A soldier wheels his horse around and kicks it up the bank, pulling out his pistol as he goes. There is a single shot. A shudder runs through the line.

The men stumble forward. Raúl watches the horses. He tries to imagine Hero's easy stride and pretend it is his own. Sometimes he pictures the Englishwoman, the twist of her hair, the soft curve of her waist. It is her voice that whispers in his ear, don't fall, bide your time, the moment will come – must come – when you can break free. Without her, he could not endure this ragged march. He would rather have ended here on the road, with the boy in the ditch, than march dumbly toward Ushuaia, or whatever awaits them all.

At dusk, the road twists into a grassy track and pinpricks of light glimmer in the distance. An estancia. Horses in the corrals throw up their heads and flicker their ears at the unexpected disturbance. For a moment, Raúl considers trying to crawl under the fence to steal a horse, but the guard at his side will shoot him if he steps out of the line. Wait, he tells himself, be patient. Tonight, when it is dark, will be the time to break free.

The yard smells of kerosene. They pass smoking piles of ash, some with blackened boots on top; once a hand, flung out as if in supplication. One or two of the peons retch into the dust. The soldiers drive them across the yard, past the well, and into the barn.

Raúl is shoved forward, stumbling against those ahead of him, tripping over men sitting on the floor. He finds a space and squats. A candle is pushed into his hands. Half-lit faces glow, long shadows flicker against the walls.

"What are they doing?" whispers the man behind.

Raúl shrugs, but a blond-haired gaucho on his other side says, "If we hold the candles, they can see us. They'll know if we are trying anything."

"What would we try?" the man behind asks.

Raúl twists round so he can see the door. He intends to try something. The barn is filling up. Someone sits down in front of him and looks around. It is Juan Sant.

"So, friend. What do you think now?" Raúl asks, and Sant gives him a wry smile, ghostly in the candlelight.

"I hear Soto is making for the border," someone whispers.

"He is?" Rage rises into Raúl's chest. "He let us surrender and left us to bear the consequences?"

"To be fair, it wasn't his idea," breaks in the yellow-haired European. "Soto wanted to continue. It was the fucking chilotes who voted to give themselves up."

"Not all the chilotes." Raúl's fists clench. "Some of us are still ready to fight."

"What for?" the European asks wearily. He nods his head towards the soldiers standing by the barn doors. "You got a weapon?"

Raúl spits into the dirt. "I'd fight with my fists if I thought the rest of you would join me."

"Very noble, comrade," replies the other. "I'm sorry it's too late for that now."

There is a commotion at the door. A man with long, black hair staggers into the barn and stops, silhouetted against the daylight. One of the guards kicks him in the belly and he doubles over with a grunt. A candle is thrust into his hand. The glow of the tiny flame falls across his eyes and picks out the face above the thick black beard. Juan Sant curses softly.

"El Piemontese," he whispers. "Hola, friend," and the Italian squints into the darkness. There is a rusty stain of dried blood on his temple, but he still wears his black-and-white Ushuaia cap.

"Juan Sant! It's you. I thought you'd run away. I swore if I ever saw you again, I'd kill you."

"Well, now you don't have to. How did you come to be here? You weren't at the camp."

"No." El Piemontese shuffles closer across the floor, his breath sucked in with the pain. "I was heading north, and doing some good work along the way, I can tell you." He sighs. "Shame it was all for nothing."

"Do you have news from the north?"

El Piemontese lowers his voice and leans closer towards Sant. His candle flickers against his face. "Héctor Torres is dead."

"Héctor Torres the horse breaker?" Raúl starts and tries to rise, his candle throwing wild shadows over the seated men.

Sant pulls him back down, whispering, "Shut up. Unless you want to die too. Shut up and listen."

"Torres tried to negotiate with the army. They wrapped him up in wire and left him in a corral for four days," El Piemontese continues. "Then they took off his belt and put him in front of the rifles."

"Why did they take off his belt?" Raúl's hands are fists.

El Piemontese reaches out and takes hold of Raúl's chin, tilting his face toward the light. "What's this? I don't know you, but I swear I've seen you somewhere. What do you want?"

Sant lays a hand hastily on Raúl's arm. "Leave it. Don't start something in here or we'll all be killed."

Raúl shakes his head free. "What does he mean about the belt?" His voice sounds like a child's. Sant softens his grip, letting his hand rest lightly on Raúl's sleeve.

"You don't need to know."

After everything that's happened, Juan Sant is trying to protect him? Raúl looks from El Piemontese's bloody face to the guards standing by the door, and almost laughs out loud.

"Oh come on." El Piemontese's voice is mocking. He must be thinking the same. "Why spare the boy? It's too late for that now." He thrusts his face close to Raúl's with a leering grin. "They do it so the poor bastard will die with his pants around his ankles."

Héctor Torres. Famous throughout Santa Cruz, not only for his skill, but for his fairness and generosity. Rage coils like a spring inside Raúl. He is ready to fight, to take on all these guards to avenge the humiliation of Héctor Torres. Juan Sant swears under his breath and pulls Raúl's head onto his shoulder, holding it there, stroking his hair as if Raúl were a child. El Piemontese laughs. "You think that's bad? Let's wait until tomorrow, shall we?"

By now the barn is full. The soldiers haul the heavy doors together and there is only candlelight, its eerie glow picking out each face. Some of the captives hang their heads or close their eyes, already defeated. Others scan the barn, sending shadows across the walls like ghosts, searching for a way out. Guards stand motionless, watching the flickering faces. The only sound is the breath of a hundred waiting men.

47

Skeleton Mesa

I open my eyes to a sickening ache in my head and the metal taste of blood inside my mouth. Underneath me, the ground is wet and lumpy: it takes a moment to realise I am lying in a puddle. I lift each arm, each leg in turn, testing.

Everything works. I must have bitten my tongue. And now I truly am a fallen woman. I almost laugh out loud, but the sound rings in my ears and amplifies the pain in my head, so I lie back down in my puddle and listen to the rain until it feels safe to sit up and check where I am.

Nothing has changed. The same bushes and knots of grass and little lumps of clotted earth lie scattered across the burnished surface of the rain-washed plain. I might as well have been travelling in circles. Perhaps I have. Hero stands a way off, head down, his back to the rain. One leg is bent at the fetlock, as though it hurts to put weight there. I roll onto hands and knees and push myself cautiously to my feet, shaking out my sodden, shot-heavy cape. Hero rolls his eyes and limps away. Each time I take a step, the horse takes another, until the two of us are some distance apart, facing the hills.

I throw up my hands. "Fine. I'll go by myself then." The horse watches. "I will," I tell him, "I'll leave you here. I was taking you to Raúl, I thought that's what you'd want, but if you won't come, I swear I'll go without you." The horse lays back its ears, listening. I set off in the direction of the hills, feet slopping through mud, trying not to think of my bag, slung over the saddle. Without the horse, I will not survive.

When I risk a cautious look back, Hero is following. I plod on, willing the animal to stay with me. When I stop, Hero stops. In this way, we continue through the rain for what feels like hours, until I can no longer move my aching legs. I pause to catch my breath, looking up into the greying light. This time, the hills seem a little closer, their rust-coloured teeth sharp against the sky. The ground is rising. I stumble on, followed by the horse, until we reach a crest where the plain falls away in a series of rocky outcrops surrounding a mesa.

The rocks offer some protection against the wind. I find an overhang fronted with a spindly tree to keep out the worst of the weather. I am shivering now. If I could only get my bag from the saddle, I could find my matches. Getting hold of the horse is my next challenge. The fact that I have no real idea how to light a fire can wait.

"Watch out, you," I say aloud. "If I get my hands on you, I might be eating horse meat." The horse looks at me with disdain. "Come on," I whisper, holding out a few blades of grass. "Let's help each other. I can take that saddle off you for a start." The horse stands still. I try a step forward, but he moves away, watching. I stop. The last thing I want is to chase Hero away from my camp.

What would Raúl do? I picture him among the yearlings, soothing and murmuring, stilling their fear with his broad hands and gentle words. How would he make Hero come to him? Ripping the bone clasp from the neck of my cape, I hold it out, rattling the pieces in my hands. Hero pricks up his ears. I rattle again, and this time the horse stretches his neck and picks his way towards me. I hold my breath as Hero reaches out to nuzzle at my hand. One second too soon, and I will lose the advantage. Too late, and the horse will realise he has been deceived. As I feel Hero's soft breath blowing into my hand, I slide the other hand forward, and snatch at the trailing rein. Hero flings up his head and backs away, but I cling on and reluctantly he allows me to draw him toward the tree. I secure the reins around the trunk, trying to still my shaking hands. I am weak with hunger and exhaustion. Now I have caught the horse, what little energy I had left is gone. It is no good dwelling on what would have happened if I had failed.

"It'll be worth it, I promise," I tell Hero, unhooking my bag from the saddle. "I'm taking you to Raúl." I fancy the horse's ears flicker at the name. "You see. Raúl. I told you. You'll thank me when we find him." The thought of finding him makes me want to cry.

Hero watches as I pull out my little parcel of food. I did not wish to steal from the Creeds, but how foolish I was to assume one tiny package of bread and biscuits would sustain us both. I try to remain hopeful: after all, the plain is covered in calafate bushes thick with berries, and if I can find a stream, there may be caiquén eggs hidden in the grass. I cup my hands and let the horse nuzzle a biscuit, then break off a small piece for myself.

I lay my matches on a stone and set about gathering wood for a fire. Most of the trees are soaked from the rain, and the matches are damp and unyielding. I struggle until my hands are shaking, and I have to stop and lean against the rocks. The light is failing. It must be very late. Night creatures are shrieking in the gloom. I stare at my little pile of kindling. Seizing the matches, I blow on the heads to dry them and cup my hands around the strike. Hero shifts his feet, a murky shadow against the darkening sky. This time, a match flares. For a second there is a glow of red before the grass blackens and the flame dies away. But now I have hope, I can control my hands. The second strike is true. I lower the match into the twigs, and soon a little fire is blazing as I run back and forth, searching for dry wood to feed the flames.

I have not reckoned on the amount of work it takes to keep the fire alive, but I manage to pull a pile of branches under my rock, praying it will be enough to last the night. I am shivering now, wracked with cold and tiredness, though I dare not take my eyes off the fire. Hero stamps and tosses, ears flat with displeasure. I hope for his sake, the rain will ease. "We both love him," I whisper as I lean against the wall of my little cave, tuck up my knees and pull my cape around me like a tent. "And tomorrow, Hero, I promise, we will find him."

48

Lali will not leave him

The candlelit vigil lasts all night and most of the following day. Towards evening, all the strikers are herded back outside and lined up alongside the barn. Raúl watches the corral, waiting for his moment to run. Most of the peons have given up, they shuffle outside with cast down eyes and shrunken shoulders. He hates their supplicant faces. He hates them almost as much as he hates the soldiers at the door. He will not wait for a firing squad to take his belt. If he is going to die today, then, like El Piemontese, he will die killing.

The colonel strides along the line, looking at faces. Behind him, estancieros or their managers point to one man, then another. Some of the peons are pulled out of the line. There is no sign of Ian Creed or Lali, though surely they are coming. Lali will not leave him to die here. A little stab of pain, a constriction in his heart. Lali will not leave him.

The European next to Raúl is pulled forward, then another gaucho. When the colonel reaches El Piemontese, he leans forward and knocks off the black-and-white cap. El Piemontese spits into the colonel's face. At once, a soldier pulls El Piemontese's head back, another drives a bayonet into his belly. There is a high-pitched choking sound as El Piemontese drops to the ground. His body quivers. The colonel pulls a handkerchief from his pocket and wipes the spittle from his nose and mouth. When he has finished, he looks down at the writhing figure and snaps his fingers.

The first soldier shoots El Piemontese in the head.

The colonel continues down the line until he reaches Juan Sant. He stops again and one of the soldiers whispers into his ear. Raúl holds his breath. The colonel stares hard into Sant's face.

"Juan Sant? We've been looking for you."

"What for?" Sant's eyes are fixed on the ground. He does not flinch. "I've done nothing."

"And yet. Whenever there is trouble, you're always there. Why is that?" The colonel's voice is soft, almost a purr. He raises his hand and the two soldiers step forward. They lift Sant underneath his arms and drag him across the yard away from the rest. He looks like a colt refusing to take the halter, proud and helpless.

The colonel nods his head towards the well.

"No. No, please…" Sant struggles and twists as the soldiers tear off his boots and pants, fasten the rope to his hands and lower him over the low wall beside the bucket. Screams bounce off the narrow walls and echo back up out of the earth. Raúl holds his breath, imagining Sant, his legs hitting the icy water, preparing to drown. There is a cracking sound as the rope jerks to a stop and another scream. Sant must be hanging in the darkness, arms above his head, swinging above the icy water between the black brick walls of the well. One of the soldiers shouts down the shaft.

"Let's see what a night in there will do for you."

A night? Then it is over. Sant will be dead long before they haul him out. In the blackness of the well, it is already night. How many hours will it take? Will the old man try to survive? Will he look up to the circle of daylight above his knotted hands? Will it give him hope? What was it Sant said in the union building in Río Gallegos? The worst thing that can happen to me is death. Now he has found something that is worse.

The line of men has not moved. Every now and again, the silence is broken by a rattle and a shriek inside the well.

Raúl can guess what Sant is doing. He is pushing with his feet against the slippery walls, taking the weight from his wrists and shoulders, perhaps even walking his feet up the wall, the bucket slapping against his chest, trying to wedge himself against the side, until he loses his footing and slithers back down, the snap of the rope sharp against his arms. By now, the wrists will be broken, the shoulders ripped from their sockets. Raúl squeezes his eyes closed. His mind is with Juan Sant, willing him to keep the weight off his arms, to hold his feet clear of the freezing water. He walks the old man up the wall, counting steps. He is dizzy with pain, parched with thirst, here, in the water, unable to drink. Perhaps Sant tries to twist his head to lick some drops from the side of the bucket – a terrible mistake because his feet will slip. Raúl can feel Sant's terror as he scrabbles his feet against the brick. As Raúl counts each step up the wall and slithers and falls and counts and slithers and falls, the tears drop from his eyes. He is Sant, inside the well, calling to the guards for mercy, to the dear Angel, Radowitszky, in his own cold cell, to his mother, long gone and surely dead by now. Raúl stays beside Juan Sant as the old man shrieks and prays, until the pain is more than either of them can bear and there is silence at the bottom of the well.

Back inside the barn, Raúl squats in silence, numb with cold. His mind is empty. He no longer watches the door, waiting for his chance. He no longer believes in chances. Or that Lali is coming to save him.

The following morning, when they haul Juan Sant's body out of the well, ice has formed around his legs. In the corral, the bodies of his fellow revolutionaries hang naked against the fence posts. Raúl is sent onto the hill with the few remaining peons who have not yet been claimed or shot, to dig behind the rocks. He carries Juan Sant to his grave with the blond-haired gaucho he'd sat with in the barn.

"I was two years in the trenches during the war in Europe," the German says. "And never did I see anything like this."

49.

The second day

Early sunlight dazzles on the wet grass and brightens the red and yellow of the wildflowers. From what I can see, Hero's leg is neither better nor worse. I scramble into the saddle and we press on through burnished rocks. The great distance of the plain stretches ahead. Hero moves ever more slowly, his head lowered, his gait awkward as he favours his lame leg. I am afraid he will stumble and throw me again, so I dismount and walk, the horse limping meekly at my side. My lips move in prayer: please God, don't let me die. Let the horse recover so he can carry me. Let me find Raúl. Let him not be captured. Let him not be dead.

I dare not search for water to refill the dwindling reserves in my carafe. I must keep moving in a straight line toward the hills. In yesterday's rain I had only to open my mouth for my thirst to be quenched. Today I will have to drink from puddles. As the sun moves, my prayers become a senseless muttering. The hills seem closer, then further away. The Cordillera floats like an imaginary city, fading in and out of clouds. Shafts of light stab the ground.

It is almost the end of the second day. We are too slow. There is nothing I can do, I will come too late, the Creeds will arrive before me and Raúl will be lost. In the gloom of evening, the hills are almost invisible: lavender fading to purples, greys and blacks. Soon they will disappear completely. But I must look for the trajectory of the setting sun, follow it west towards the Cordillera. Much later, when the plain is in darkness, I crawl into a dip in the earth and curl up against the trunk of a tree. Too weary to light a fire, I lie with my ear against the ground, listening to the scuffle and scurry of small creatures, and once, the rhythm of hooves as a herd of wild horses gallops past, causing Hero to raise his head and call out with a sound that lifts the hair from my skin, and in this way I pass through the few short hours of night.

With morning comes the realisation that the hills are nearer than I thought. I can see the contours of rocks, the outline of trees – and in between, a straight ribbon of grey, flowing north. I have followed the map I carried inside me like a gaucho and I have found the road. I swallow the last of my water, drop the empty carafe and gather Hero's reins in my hand. Together, we press on.

50.

The dog in the river

Ashes float on the wind above the fires, drift down onto faces and are wiped away in streaks of grey and white. Eyes glaze, bloodshot and gritty. Raúl is a beast of burden, repeating over and over to himself the same litany of desperation: if he is digging, he is not dead.

And as long as he is not dead, he can cast his eyes upward, where the condors are wheeling and the rocky tree line waits for him like a promise. He scans the hill, looking for a sign of horses. If he can get to a horse, he will be free.

He watched a dog once, swept away in a burst river, how it scrabbled for a foothold, holding its head above the water, every lunge towards the bank costing a little more of its ebbing strength. Raúl waded in up to his waist and held out a branch: with its last effort, the dog struck out towards the slender lifeline. Raúl leaned as far as he dared, until the river pulled the stick from his hand and floated it away and out of reach. Raúl saw the dog's eyes shutter and glaze over, the muscles in its head slacken. He saw the dog give up hope.

Around him, men walk with shuttered eyes. But Raúl is not yet dead. He wipes the ashes from his face and picks up his shovel once more. Above the hill, the condors wheel and dive.

51.

The estancia

The house with its ribbon of barns and outbuildings lies at the end of a grassy track. A young soldier stands sentry at the gate. What must he think of my filthy dress, my draggled hair?

"No one is to come through here without the colonel's permission."

"I am Señora Creed." My voice is shaking. I wipe my forehead with the back of my hand and force myself to speak slowly. "I fell from my horse. I have come to look for my workers and to vouch for them."

He glances at Hero, back to me. "Allow me to take you to the house, Señora."

"No." The boy recoils from the sharpness in my voice. I ache for a bed, warm clothes, hot food. My legs feel like rags, threatening to give way at every step. "Just some water."

His eyes flicker as he passes me the canteen. The water tastes of metal, but I do not care. He waits until I have finished. "The estancieros have already been here, Señora. They have taken their men. Those who remain are enemies to the land and to its people." The words are a recitation. He too has a tremor in his voice, and his anxiety gives me strength.

"Yes, yes, I know all that. But my manager has not been thorough. We are missing some of our workers. I need to be certain you are not holding men who are of value to us." He falters. Deep shadows ring his eyes, purple eruptions spread across his face. He is a child. I speak more gently. "You won't get into trouble. Tell your superiors to speak to me."

He gulps. His Adam's apple slides up and down the thin neck above his heavy army collar. Dear God, what is happening here to make him so afraid?

I mustn't faint. I can't collapse, not now. I breathe as deeply as I can and lean a hand on the gate. The boy soldier shuffles his feet. "That's right," I say encouragingly, as if speaking to Leo, and he steps aside to let me pass.

I walk as steadily as I can. When I glance back, he has turned away, pretending he never saw me. I slip off the path into the mata negra bushes and double over, waiting until the dizziness subsides. I tie Hero to one of the bushes and tell him to wait for me. His head hangs down. I am afraid he is too exhausted and too lame to be of use, but he is all we have.

Tall trees stand sentinel along the track. At the end I can see the house, long and white against the dark brown-and-green of the hillside. Behind it lies a windowless barn, an intricate web of fences, a series of sheep pens abutting the corrals. In front, a row of motor cars. I had imagined some sort of prison building, an army official, the quick stamping of a document. Instead, I am faced with a house full of estancieros. If they have heard Mrs Creed's accusations against Raúl, they will not help me. Why – *why* – have I not expected this?

I hurry along the track, keeping close to the trees. The shock of these unexpected surroundings has jolted me awake and sharpened my senses. There is nobody I can turn to for help. If Raúl is here, I must find him by myself.

From time to time I hear the crack of a rifle. Figures on the hillside move between little columns of smoke. There is a smell of burning oil, compounded with a sweet stench that turns my stomach: I know it from the hospital. I press my palms over my nose and mouth. Please God. You've brought me this far. Don't let me fail now. And another prayer, to Raúl, carrying me forward: Wait for me. I am coming.

The yard is silent. Flurries of ash rise like snowflakes on the wind, swirl and fall again. A bucket lies beside the well. I peep through the heavy doors into the barn: empty, save for hundreds of candle stubs, scattered across the floor.

Dear God, is Raúl still alive? Where is he? Take me to him.

High up on the hillside, the shapes of men move back and forth.

52.

She is coming

Sun glints on Raúl's face, drying sweat that runs from his hair down into his eyes. His hands are slippery and raw. When he stops to wipe his arm across his forehead, there is blood. Still, with each step, he scans the hillside, waiting for his moment.

He and a skinny peon with long hair carry a body between them. The peon's clothes are torn and bloody. His face is grey with ash and his eyes are dead, like the dog in the river. He stumbles against a rock and the body slips. A soldier shouts, points his rifle. Raúl lowers his end of their burden – the head – towards the ground, just enough to catch his breath, to look at the hill.

A shadow catches his eye at the edge of the path. At first he thinks it must be a condor passing overhead, but whatever it is stays close to the ground, cautious as an animal, but too awkward: no animal would give itself away like that. Out of nowhere comes a memory of the Englishwoman, breathing life into his aching muscles and broken skin. He crouches, rubs his hands against his eyes. A quiver of excitement rises in his belly, like watching a troupe of wild horses in the distance. The soldier with the rifle is approaching, but he doesn't care.

53.

Up on the hill

The hill path jags its way steeply between rocky outcrops and clumps of undergrowth towards the soldiers and their captives. My feet stumble over every root and stone. At the top, I crouch behind a heap of rocks to catch my breath and gather my nerve. Some of the peons are digging, others lug sacks between them, tipping the sacks into narrow trenches between smoking piles of earth. Dig and lug and tip. I recognise the same sweet stench from earlier and press fistfuls of herbs and sweet grass against my nose. Soldiers stand watching, rifles cocked.

And there he is, almost in front of me. Raúl.

I have to look twice. His beautiful face is blackened with dirt and blood, the skin around his mouth broken and bruised. But it is Raúl. I pick myself up from my hiding place and walk out into the open.

Dazed peons drop their loads to stare. The soldiers snap to attention and point their rifles at my chest. The shovel falls from Raúl's hand. I swear I can hear his heart pounding, or perhaps it is my own.

A soldier pulls at my arm. Another jabs at me with his rifle.

"What are you doing?" I shout. I am sick with fear. "How dare you? I am Señora Creed. I am here to vouch for my men."

The soldier's eyes glitter, cold as the metal of his gun. If I say the wrong thing now, Raúl will die and I will die with him. Gaunt peons watch, their arms slack at their sides. I want to tell them, I will help you, Ian will get you out of here, but I know it is a lie. There is no one to help them and nothing I can do. The rifle is still pointing at my chest.

My mouth is so dry that when I speak, the words won't come. I have to start again. "My manager made a mistake. I am here to vouch for this man."

"You are wrong, Señora. These men are revolutionaries."

"They don't look like revolutionaries to me."

He shrugs. "The estancieros have given their instructions to the colonel."

Ian has signed Raúl's death sentence. And the colonel will see that execution is carried out. Anger sharpens my voice. "It's a mistake. This man is a valuable horse breaker. The estanciero will not be happy if something happens to him." A pause. "The colonel will not be happy."

A flicker of anxiety crosses the soldier's face. Despite his rifle, he is as fearful as the boy at the gate. He shrugs and glances round at his colleagues. When they look away, he waves us towards the path. The peons watch. I can't look at them. The estancieros have given their instructions to the colonel: soon the graves these men are digging will be their own.

Raúl and I stumble together down the hill. The soldiers stand at the top, watching, their rifles pointed at Raúl's back. With every step I am afraid I will fall and they will shoot me on the ground.

As soon as I can, I pull Raúl off the path, behind the rocks. His face is smeared with blood and ash.

"Hero is near the gate." A silent prayer to the horse: Please, be brave enough, strong enough, to carry Raúl away. "Go," I tell him. "Hurry." With every heartbeat I am waiting for the soldiers to open fire. I am ready to throw myself in front of rifles. But there is only silence.

He touches his hand to my face.

I want to take his hand and not let go. But we both know that if I delay him, he is doomed.

He ducks his head, twists round and is gone. I watch him disappear among the trees. If he can get through the gate and out onto the plain, if Hero can carry him away, perhaps he will be safe.

*

A metal flask presses against my lips, brandy burns at the back of my throat. Blankets, more brandy. Voices come and go.

After Raúl stumbled away, I waited, then went to the house and knocked on the door. What else was I supposed to do? I had no horse, no money, and nowhere else to turn.

The house was almost empty. Most of the estancieros and their managers had already departed, taking with them any workers they wished to keep. Among the few who remained were the Creeds. They were waiting for me. The sight of them made me tremble. If Ian had not caught me, I would have fallen.

The Creeds give me laudanum. Images of Álvaro float in my mind, his slack mouth and rolling eyes. Although I have no strength, I struggle and push away the cup. When I open my mouth to scream, someone tips back my head and I choke as the drug slides down my throat. My head swims. Ian crouches at my side and I cower from him. If he gives me more laudanum, I will die. Perhaps he will send me to the hillside and kill me there.

I must have spoken aloud because he answers sharply.

"For God's sake, Georgie, I'm trying to take care of you. I'm taking you to the doctor." He carries my slack body down the stairs, out through a back door. He doesn't want anyone to see me. Another dead wife.

Lali is standing beside the motor car. I want to weep for our shared loss, but his face is stony. "Do not think you can run away again."

Run away? I had not considered it. I can barely move my limbs. "You could have vouched for him."

Lali's eyes narrow. His fists clench, and for a moment I am afraid he might strike me. But when he speaks it is without expression. "My boy is gone. Don Ian is out of his mind. And still you blame everybody but yourself?"

Ian drives me to the town. My teeth are chattering so hard I have to hold my jaw between my hands. The doctor gives me more laudanum, too much. I try to tell him about Álvaro, but his hands force my mouth open as if I am an animal. He calls for his wife to watch me; she sits in a chair at my side. I am afraid she is waiting for me to die and I cling to her hands, begging her to bring something to make me sick. A child's voice calls out in a nearby room, and I struggle to sit up, thinking it must be Leo, but perhaps it is Álvaro warning me about the laudanum. The woman disappears and comes back with my mother. Kneel, Georgie. Kneel and pray. Beg for God's mercy. But the sheets pin my arms tight against my sides and instead of God I see Raúl among the trees, the soldiers chasing and Ian pointing his rifle. Blood runs in rivers across the plain.

In the evening, the doctor's wife gives me water and my head clears. When she slips out of the room to check on her children, I put on my boots and walk out of the house.

The Legend of the Yasi-Yateré

The Yasi-Yateré (or Jasy-Jateré as he is also known) is a magical child with blue eyes and blond hair. He lives among the trees and can sometimes be seen at dusk. He lures children into the forest with wild honey, making beautiful noises like a bird, but if they follow him, they lose their wits and are never seen again. This is a Paraguayan story, but some believe its origins lie in Patagonia. Long ago an Englishman came here with his family. He had two sons – and one was kidnapped by Indians. Years went by, and nothing was ever heard of the lad. Then, one day, a traveller to the region noticed a blond boy working in a mine. He was struck by the difference between this boy and his Indian fellow workers. Later, the traveller happened to stay with the English family who had lost their son and he was struck once more – this time by the likeness he discerned between the remaining son and the young man he had seen at the mine. And so, in this way, the lost boy was returned to his family. But it was too late. The child they had lost was no longer there in the young man. He could neither sleep in a bed nor eat at a table. One day, he slipped away into the forest, and was never seen again. He is probably the Yasi-Yateré. His civilised self is the one who lost his wits and disappeared. The wild spirit is all that remains. Perhaps the legend is a way of telling us about the wild spirit inside everyone. A warning that we could all become this boy, lost to the magic of the forest.

From *Travels in Patagonia* by Henry O. Chambers

PART FOUR

54.

The women

The town is nothing but a few dirt streets, a scatter of houses. I wander through the margins like a ghost. I thought I knew about grief, but this is different. Raúl is gone and I will never know if he is alive or dead.

Inside the boliche, men are drinking and playing cards. A woman stands in the doorway. She reminds me of the estancia laundry women: tired eyes and heavy, rounded shoulders, a thick waist beneath her cheap-looking coat. Something about the yellow loops of ribbon in her black hair seems familiar. The colours make my head ache.

"Are you alright?"

Tears spring in my eyes. I had not expected kindness here. "I fell... I've lost my horse."

The woman nods. "Are you looking for a place to stay?" Is it so obvious? Through the doorway of the boliche, tables are strewn with glasses, men lean across the bar. The woman raises her eyebrows. "You don't have to go in there," she says. "You can come with me."

Her name is Teresa. She leads me through an alley between the buildings to a dark little house with a front made of corrugated iron and an atmosphere not quite of neglect, but of carelessness. Doubt seeps into the corners of my mind.

Once inside, Teresa settles me on a chaise in the entrance hall, disappears behind a curtain, and returns with a cup of matico. Something in the drink makes me drowsy and uncertain. I am possessed by an unutterable tiredness, I want to lie down and weep for all the futures that are lost. My life on the estancia. Little Leo. Raúl. Teresa shushes me, and strokes my tangled hair.

The house is unexpectedly hot. When I've drunk the tea, Teresa pushes me into a small drawing room, thick with cheap scent and cigarette smoke. A thin girl with dreadful, pockmarked skin is sitting on a sofa. She looks up in open-mouthed surprise and giggles, then catches my eye, and puts a hand over her mouth. She is missing several teeth. The mocking laughter scratches: her face is familiar, like a painting seen somewhere long ago, or a story I can't remember.

"I know you," she says. "What country did you come from?"

"England."

"England?" Her eyes are sharp and do not smile. "I hate English people."

It is enough. I know her now. She is the mad girl from Punta Arenas.

A tall woman stands by the window, looking out. "Verónica." Teresa calls, and the two women exchange a glance. This room hurts my eyes. The fire crackles and spits in the grate, I can feel sweat glimmering on my cheeks and trickling between my breasts. The tall woman named Verónica drops the curtain and comes to face me, lifting my chin between her thumb and fingers. I jerk my head away. Behind me, Teresa is blocking my route to the door. This is no refuge. I have walked into a trap.

"I have to go," I say, and the mad girl giggles.

"Oh no, lady," she says. "Maybe you have to stay and look at something you're not supposed to see."

"Don't mind her," Teresa says. "She says stupid things, but she doesn't mean it."

"Oh, I mean it." The girl's expression darkens.

I remember that look of recognition from Punta Arenas.

"I don't know you," I say quickly.

She stares at me for a long moment. "I hate English people."

There is a knock at the door and we both jump. Verónica jerks her head. The mad girl makes a face, but gets up without a word. When she returns, she is holding a child by the wrist.

"My mamá says to tell you there's soldiers in the town."

"Soldiers?" The women shift and flutter like birds.

"The ones who came for the strikers."

"Run and fetch your mamá, and the other girls," Verónica says sharply. "Be quick."

An unspoken urgency ripples through the room. The mad girl smiles, her eyes narrowing into slits. She makes a coarse gesture, rubbing her thumb and fingers together: money. I must have made a sound because all the women turn to face me.

"Oh, lady," the mad girl says. "Don't you like soldiers? Are you scared you'll have to look at something you're not supposed to see?" Her mocking laughter makes my skin curl. Her dress is open at the back and the bony knobs of her spine poke savagely through bare skin. Teresa makes a face and taps the side of her head.

"Soldiers?" I say. "The ones who killed the strikers?" My voice sounds distant, as if someone else is speaking. I am not even sure if I have uttered the words aloud.

Verónica turns. "What do you know about that?"

The mad girl points at Teresa. "Her husband was in the strike." She puts her finger to her temple, fires an imaginary trigger. "Bang." I jump as if she has fired a real gun. I am back on the hill among the rifle shots. Somewhere on the plain, Raúl is running for his life.

Teresa turns away, fists pressed against her eyes. "I don't want anything to do with soldiers."

Verónica rounds on her. "Are you crazy? What about your precious boy? What's he going to eat if you have nothing to do with them?" Teresa drops her gaze. Her face is round and soft, but her dress is threadbare and her eyes droop with exhaustion. She has a son, a precious boy. My heart contracts, remembering Leo.

"I'm not going with soldiers," the mad girl says, as if she's making an announcement.

"Oh God. Not you too. What's wrong with you?" Verónica rolls her eyes.

The girl's body tightens. She makes a hissing sound, animal and defensive. "My gaucho."

Verónica is shaking her head. "Oh come on, both of you. You want to play politics? Don't you want to eat?"

"Politics or food?" the mad girl says, her eyes glittering. "I eat politics."

"That's because you're stupid," Verónica replies, and the girl's fingers curl into claws. Nobody moves. She falters, balls her hands into fists, hits them against her own temples. "That's better," Verónica says evenly.

I am swaying with dizziness and fear. I understand nothing except that the soldiers are coming to this house. Blood crashes through my body as if trying to escape. I must slip away – now – before they notice. I cast my eyes around the room, but the mad girl is at my side.

"Oh no," she says, and there is menace in her tone. "There's no way out for you."

Someone rattles at the door.

"Open up!" a man's voice calls. "Lady artistas, we've got good business for you."

More shouts and laughter.

"Hey – don't keep us waiting. We've got doorknobs for you to polish."

Is it so simple? Can these men take off their uniforms and forget what they have done?

Somehow the mad girl agrees with me. "I won't go with soldiers," she mutters. Her face is white and she is trembling. With each rap at the door, she jumps. Is this deranged creature my only ally?

"The soldiers shot people," I tell her. My heart is pounding so hard I can hardly catch my breath. "So many people. They burned the bodies on the hill." I picture the old men, covered in ash. Where are they now? Where is Raúl? The women stare at me as if I have spoken in tongues.

The knocking is louder. The shouts and laughter have become a chant: "Let us in. Let us in."

Verónica takes a deep breath, then marches into the hallway and plants herself in front of the door. "Go away!" she shouts. "We're closed!" The others cling to her like frightened children.

A moment of silence, followed by jeers and boos. "You must be joking," calls a voice.

"She'd better be," shouts a second. "Come on, ladies – we can help you open up."

More laughter, and then another voice rising above the rest, harsher, more impatient. "Stop playing games."

The chant begins again, quicker this time, more urgent. There is a hammering at the door.

"They won't leave," Verónica says. "We'll have to go out."

"We can't." Teresa's eyes are wild with terror.

"What if they break the door?" the mad girl whispers. All the earlier bravado is gone; she is a grey rag of fear.

"We have to go out," Verónica says again. "If they break the door, it'll be too late."

I turn to her. "Do you have a rifle?"

"Are you crazy? They'd hang us."

"Then what else?"

What else? In the kitchen, we pull out brooms and mops, long-handled pots and pans. We gather in front of the door, holding our breath, glancing from one to the other. If the soldiers are carrying weapons, we will all die. When Henry Chambers asked if I was an activist, I was appalled. Now it seems I am to die a striker.

Verónica raises a broomstick above her head, the mad girl bares her teeth. We pull back the bolts, tear open the door. The soldiers falter, wrong-footed. I recognise the baby-faced adolescent from the gate. As the women run forward, someone is shouting, "You bastards! You murdering bastards! We don't fuck murderers!" I pick up the refrain. "We don't fuck murderers." A stranger has taken my body and my voice. I am wild with shouting. I am waving my saucepan, feeling thuds and cries as my paltry weapon connects with faces, shoulders, heads and arms. Each blow I am striking is for Raúl. For the old men on the hillside. For Pilar and the women of Río Gallegos. For Raúl, for Raúl, for Raúl. I swear and run and hit and shout until I am hoarse and my limbs are shaking from the effort. The curses of the soldiers fade as they stagger backwards, fending off the blows, then turn and run away.

55.

Seeing a ghost

We are still breathless when the police arrive. A few bystanders watch as we are led away. Some laugh and point, once a stone skims past my head. If any feel solidarity with our cause, they do not show themselves. I want to explain, to tell them I should not be here, that this is a mistake. But it is too late. I have no friends left to help me.

The prison is a series of tin sheds: no candle, no furniture, just a covered bucket, and a stale smell of sweat and filth. I am separated from the other women and sit alone and shaking on the dirt floor. From time to time, I hear a scrape or a shout, and once a scream that raises the hair at the back of my neck. I am desperately thirsty, my mouth dry and claggy from the laudanum. The drug would be a blessed relief now. I hold my breath against the smell and will myself not to be sick. I pray that Raúl is out on the plain, far away from here. Is he lighting a fire, or catching a rabbit? Has he crossed the border into Chile? Is he free?

A man's head pokes through the door and I blink in the grey light, calling out to shadows. "Please... could I have some water?"

"You want water?"

I am nodding – yes, please, water. I want to explain who I am, that I shouldn't be here, but the door is already closing.

Footsteps again. He is back. The key in the lock, the door scraping as he pushes it open. He is holding a heavy jug in both hands. Thank God. I struggle to my feet, ease out my aching joints. The man smiles. He swings the jug back, just a little, then jolts it forward, sending a sheet of freezing water into my face. The icy blast knocks the breath from my body, I choke on a scream and stumble backwards against the wall. The guard laughs as he flings the empty jug past me into the cell. It bounces off the floor and rolls to a stop at my feet, the last dregs of water pooling on the dirt floor.

I stand, blinking, opening and closing my mouth. There is nothing in the cell, no blanket or shawl to dry or wrap myself against the cold. My teeth begin to chatter. Soon I am shivering uncontrollably. And so I pass the night.

In the grey light of morning, I cower from the sound of the key in the door once more. Everything aches. This time, the guard puts the jug down on the floor. I snatch it up and drink deeply, water running down my face.

He points to me, and to the open door. I stare at him, stupid with fear, and he tilts his head sarcastically. I stumble out of the cell, my body shrinking from the bitter cold. With each step I am sure he will snatch me from behind, or shoot me in the back, but he does not touch me. We reach what looks like an office, a solid wooden hut with proper windows, and he stands back to let me through.

Inside, seated on a chair, is Maud Creed.

She looks weary, more gaunt than I remember, with a paper-like thinness. For a moment, I feel sorry for her. Some part of her was extinguished when the bandits destroyed the farm.

"So it is you," she says.

"What do you want?" I don't know what else to say.

"What do you think? To get you out of here."

"How did you know I was here?"

She rolls her eyes. "The doctor informed the police that you were missing. They alerted us as soon as they brought you in."

"You knew I was here? You let me stay all night?"

"You have been very stupid," she says. "I thought this was the safest place for you. Somewhere you can't run away from. At least you had a room to yourself."

A room to myself. I wrap my arms around my frozen body. She is right, though. I would sooner run away again than go anywhere with her. "I'm not coming back with you."

"No, you're not. It's too late for that." Her mouth is a thin, hard line. "You are going back to England. I have arranged a passage for you."

So I am to be returned, like a parcel. To my father's sorrow and my mother's scorn. To the judgement of my village.

"Am I to just... go? Now?"

"Everything is arranged. I have a wagon waiting." She looks me up and down, taking in my ragged dress. "I will see that you are provided for in Punta Arenas."

It seems there is nothing more to say. Nothing about my flight from the estancia, nothing about Raúl. What else could I expect from Maud Creed? She opens the office door and gestures for me to follow. It is time to creep away and go home.

As we round the corner between the buildings, we come face to face with two policemen. The mad girl hangs between their arms. Her expression is glazed, her lip split and bloody, but when she sees us, her eyes become focused, wide and dark with fear. Her slack body stiffens like a hunted animal and she shrinks against her predators. At the sight of her, Mrs Creed falters at my side. She grips my arm and I twist beneath the pain. An electric terror pulses between the two women. It is as if each of them has seen a ghost.

"Stop." Mrs Creed jerks her head towards the office. "Take her in there. Wait for me." The girl is whimpering. Nobody moves. They look between each other, resentful of the Englishwoman's tone. Her voice rises. "I said, take her inside." Her eyes flicker between me and the girl.

The policemen scuff their feet. They think she wants to

rescue their captive. They have not seen what I can see: the terror in the mad girl's eyes.

Mrs Creed propels me across the yard, checking back over her shoulder. By the time we reach the gate, she is almost running. A wagon waits on the street outside, so like the one that first brought me from Punta Arenas that I cry out aloud at the sight of it, half-believing I will see Raúl himself busy with the harness.

"Quick," she says. "Get in," and I scramble up inside. Already she is turning, hastening back across the yard. My heart twists for the mad girl.

The driver is an old man in a heavy coat, his hat pulled down low over his face. He avoids my eyes as he closes the canvas flap. No sitting up on the bench this time, waiting for Raúl to nudge my arm and show me the magic of the plain. No promise at the end of the journey, only the interminable passage back to England, and then – what? Where will I go? Who will give me refuge now? Seated in the darkness, I wait for the wagon to jolt forward into another life.

56.

The wagon

We haven't gone far when the driver calls out to steady the horses, and the wagon eases to a stop. I hear the heavy thud as he jumps down from the bench, the slow pace of his footsteps. He is coming to kill me. How stupid I was to imagine Mrs Creed would let me go so easily. But then I hear a stream of liquid splashing against the side of the road, and a moment later he pulls open the flap, holding out an empty hand to help me down. Dizzy with relief, I slip away from the wagon into a small clump of bushes where I too can relieve myself. When I emerge, he is waiting calmly beside the horses, smoking a cigarette.

"What is your name?"

"Tomás."

Tomás. He seems gentle, and decent enough. I remember asking Raúl the same question, hearing his name for the first time.

The horses stamp and swish their tails. Tomás glances in their direction with a frown. The nearest animal throws up its head, ears flat, and whickers softly. Watch the horses, Miss. Nothing stirs, but still they lay back their ears and snort the air as if something has unsettled them. Tomás catches my eye and shrugs.

*

The wagon jolts between the rocks and potholes. I have no

idea how many hours have passed when I become aware of movement, a shuffling and scraping. The mass of baskets and canvas piled in the corner shifts, and I shrink against the bench, liquid with terror. I was right: Mrs Creed has sent a murderer to kill me and throw my body out onto the plain for the caranchos. The dark mass rises. The blankets are thrown off, I am on my feet, shrieking, and we are facing each other in the grey light. Hands are reaching toward my throat. I make out a face pinched and marked with scars, an open mouth filled with terrible, blackened teeth. It is the mad girl.

"Shut up," she hisses. "You are so stupid. Why do you make so much noise?" The wagon does not stop: if the old man has heard my cries, he does not care. She shoves me down onto the bench. "Where are you going?" she asks urgently. "Where?"

"Punta Arenas."

"Why?"

It seems a ridiculous question. "I'm going to England. How did you get out of the prison?"

Her lips twitch. "First she wants you, then she wants me. Why should they give her everything she wants? They didn't like the greedy lady."

Of course they didn't like her, I saw it in their faces. So while Mrs Creed threw me into the wagon, the girl was allowed to slip free.

"Aren't you scared she'll come after you?" I needn't have asked. It is obvious. "Has she tried to find you before?"

The girl shakes her head. "She thought I was dead."

So it's true. I know who she is.

"She let you go," I say slowly. "She put you out on the plain. She thought you would die."

But Marta is shaking her head. "Not her. Him."

"Ian?" Surely not. "But I thought…"

"You thought it was the old Señora? Oh, English lady, you think you know everything, but you are wrong."

310

"I don't know what you mean." I draw myself up, stiff against her contempt. I've never doubted the story Ian told me when we stood together on the attic stairs: Marta spread rumours because she was simple, and a liar, so Mrs Creed turned her out. Now I'm looking at her. Simple, yes, of that I have no doubt, and almost certainly a liar, but she is shaking her head – no, no, no.

"I didn't see anything," she says.

"Are you sure?"

She stiffens. "Don't ask me. I didn't see anything."

"Marta, listen…" She flinches. "You are Marta, aren't you?" She shakes her head, burying her face in her hands as if to push the name away. "Listen to me. If you didn't see anything, there's no reason to be afraid."

She laughs, a strange, high-pitched sound. She really is mad. I am alone in this wagon with a madwoman. What if she was responsible for Alice's death? She presses her face close to mine, and I recoil from the stench of her breath.

"If he sees you with me, he'll kill you too."

"Nobody's going to kill me. They're sending me back to England." But my skin shrinks and my heart beats faster.

"I didn't see anything." She thrusts her head forward on her neck. Her eyes narrow. "You didn't see. If you say a word to anyone, I'll find you and I'll kill you. You didn't see."

"Oh God." I try to take her hands but she bats me away. "Did Ian say this? Did he say this to you?"

But I don't need her to tell me. I have seen her fear, and Maud Creed's. I know what she will answer, and I know it to be true.

57.

The cemetery

The guesthouse outside Punta Arenas is tiny, little more than a cabin. I am to wait here until the boat is in dock, then Tomás will take me to the port, where I will collect my ticket from the shipping office and board the steamer. Whatever has happened to Raúl, I will never know. I will slink home in shame. Or vanish forever, like Sarah Gerard, becoming nothing but a memory.

Tomás is to sleep in the wagon, where Marta is still hidden beneath the blankets. I am afraid that when he discovers her, he will chase her away, but my fears are unfounded: at night, I hear him groaning over her in the darkness. In the morning, she smells worse than ever. She has taken to pulling out her eyelashes, her eyes as raw and swollen as her shredded fingers. While Tomás cares for the horses, I bring bread out to the wagon from my breakfast table and fetch a basin of water so she can wash. She gives me her strange, cunning smile, slips her hand into her bodice, and holds a handful of grimy notes just beyond my reach.

"Oh, Marta. You didn't steal it?"

"Mine." She snatches it away with a hiss.

As the days pass, I watch her gathering spoils like a carancho. Inside her clothes she secretes a rusted coin and a bent pin; beneath the filthy pile of skins and furs where she has made her nest, I find an old tin cup. On our third night, she shows me the vicious, glittering blade of Tomás's knife.

"For God's sake. You think he won't come looking?" Now we have Tomás to be afraid of as well. But her eyes glitter as she thrusts the blade towards me – what can he do, when she's the one holding the knife? I flinch from her and she laughs.

*

A message arrives from Punta Arenas: the boat has docked and I am to leave the guesthouse. With the messenger comes an envelope containing an unexpected sum of money. I am shocked and almost grateful until I realise this must be for my work as Leo's governess. Mrs Creed is buying my silence. Or perhaps she just likes to be correct. The thought makes me want to laugh.

Tomás wants to drive me directly to the ship as instructed, but Marta begs him to conceal her, and the wagon, somewhere on the outskirts of the port. She refuses to explain, but I know she is afraid to see the Creeds. Their discussion erupts into a heated argument. I intervene to suggest that the Creeds may not be happy to hear Tomás has allowed Marta to travel with me, a logic he accepts without question. It is his idea that we should leave her at the cemetery.

I can't imagine how this can be a solution until we pass beneath the gate into an endless grid of paths and avenues lined with dense, sculpted cypress bushes that stand guard over layer upon layer of graves and monuments and mausolea. The cemetery is a city in miniature, a perfect place to hide. I stand among elaborate monuments blazoned with the names of Braun and Blanchard, Menéndez and Kusanovic: all of Europe seems to have found its way to this cold corner of the earth. When I look up from the graves, Marta has already disappeared to hide among the trees. I will never see her again. God willing, I will board the ship today.

*

The bustle of the port makes me dizzy. As I walk to the shipping office, I am afraid I might fall. All I have to do is collect my ticket and get on the boat. There is no reason for this terrible foreboding, yet with every step I feel I am drawing closer to some impending danger. As if in agreement, the heavens open. The crowd murmurs, parting around me as passengers run for cover. Water drips down my cheeks, rain rattles on the tin roof of the shipping office. As I pull my sodden shawl back from my face, someone takes my arm from behind. I cry out aloud and spin round. It is the ethnographer, Henry Chambers. There is no surprise in his expression. Clearly, he is expecting to see me.

58.

Henry Chambers

"Georgie. How very excellent. I knew you had to be here somewhere." Chambers' hand is outstretched in greeting. I cast around for an escape, but there is nowhere to hide. "So good to see you," he continues. "I've already told Creed we must have dinner at the club. Not that I'm here for long, you understand. Will you stay until the wedding? I'm sure you have a million things to think of, not to mention this current project, which I imagine you'll be in charge of, will you not?" The barrage of words leaves me blinking and bemused. He breaks off with a frown. "But look at you. You're quite soaked. And your hands are frozen. What on earth was Creed thinking, sending you out here without an umbrella?"

"Mr Chambers," I manage. "I…" What must he think of me? He cocks his head like a sparrow and I squirm beneath his gaze. "Mr Chambers. Is Ian here?"

"Oh, I met him by the road. He said you've come for the new governess."

There is to be a new governess? Of course. Ian and I talked about this. I picture her driving with Ian to the estancia, unpacking her trunk, listening to the wind in the corridors. Will Mrs Creed dress her in Alice's clothes and prepare a place for her in Ian's bed?

A cloud crosses Chambers' face: he has sensed my anxiety. "Is something wrong, Miss? Have you caught a chill?"

"No. Not at all. Mr Chambers... I must leave. Please excuse me."

He takes my arm. "I can't let you go without an umbrella, you'll catch your death. At least let me escort you back to the motor car."

There is nothing for it. He won't leave me alone. "Mr Chambers, I'm not here with Ian. I have broken with the Creeds. I'm on my way back to England."

He drops my arm. The rudeness of the gesture is almost comical. I watch the struggle in his face, the realisation that Ian has avoided telling him the truth.

At last, he says simply, "I'm very sorry to hear it." Those searching eyes glimmer behind his little round glasses. "I imagine you won't want to talk much about that. But what do you intend to do? If I remember correctly, you had excellent reasons for leaving England in the first place."

"I'll find another position." My whole barren future, summed up in those few words.

"Not a lady cartographer, then?"

"Sadly not. Though I don't think my life with the Creeds would have allowed for that either."

He laughs. "You're quite the one, Miss Georgie. Between ourselves and the gatepost, I suspect you are destined for greater things than you ever could have achieved with the Creeds. You don't have to tell me anything," he continues, "but I'm a good listener, and a willing friend."

The unexpected kindness is overwhelming. "Oh, I'm sorry," he cries. "I didn't mean to upset you."

"It's not that." I am breathless with the effort of speech. "It's just... your friendship means a great deal to me."

"You may count on it."

I manage a smile. "It seems you are rescuing me again, Mr Chambers."

"Oh, I'm not sure I'm doing any rescuing, Miss. Once more, I seem to have arrived somewhat after the main event. Although, I do wish there was something I could do. I am curious to know how much enthusiasm you have for returning to England?"

This time I almost laugh aloud. "Enthusiasm has nothing to do with it, Mr Chambers. I really don't have a choice."

"Ah," he says, his eyes bright behind his glasses. "But perhaps you do. I've an idea, you see. Just a thought, you understand, a suggestion…"

"Please, Mr Chambers." I can't bear the prevarication. There is a rising excitement in him as if he is building to some great announcement.

"You remember my project? I might have mentioned it to you in Río Gallegos, the canoe people?"

What did Chambers tell me in Río Gallegos? I haven't even thought to ask what he is doing here at the port. But he has been kind. "Oh. Yes. Of course."

"Well," he says. "Perhaps…" he hesitates. "It's an outlandish idea to be sure, but I wonder if you might care to stay. To work for me? It would be a formal position," he adds hastily. "Quite above board." As he speaks, he pulls out his card, scribbles something on the back and presses it into my hand. "If the weather holds, I intend to sail tonight. First stop, Wellington Island. I will stay in the region for at least a year, but you of course would be free to leave whenever you choose."

I stare at him, turning his card over between my fingers. He is offering a different future, an escape. I could stay in Patagonia. For a moment, I am lightheaded with the prospect of salvation. And if I stay, I might one day hear word of Raúl.

But first there is the new governess. I can't leave without warning her, and, when I do, Maud Creed will proclaim me a liar and a criminal. My reputation will be lost, Mr Chambers will hear how far I have fallen, and he will withdraw his offer.

"You are truly kind. I am grateful for your faith in me, though I've done nothing to deserve it. I want so badly to accept… but it's too late for that now."

"Of course." The disappointment is palpable. He thinks I am afraid.

"Mr Chambers, I know you are my friend. But you are also a friend to the Creeds." He raises his eyebrows, and I remember how Mrs Creed mocked him in Rio Gallegos. "I thought I would leave quietly, but there is someone I must speak to before I go, and it will be ruinous for me. You of all people know what it means to tell a truth nobody wants to hear." I see the hurt flash across his face, and remember the unkind jokes of the estancieros. "My reputation will not withstand whatever the Creeds say about me. You will hear terrible things, and you'll be relieved I didn't accept your offer."

He lays his hand over mine. "I don't listen to gossip and I don't much care for conformity. Whatever your reputation, believe me, I am capable of forming my own opinion. And – I appreciate my allies."

It occurs to me that if Tupper's insinuations are correct, Mr Chambers might stand to gain a great deal from my friendship. His own reputation is perhaps more fragile than I had thought.

"Remember," he says, carefully, "you would be disappearing into the wilderness. No one need know where you have gone."

No one need know. His offer is true sanctuary. But even now, the new governess is seated in Ian's car. How can I leave without warning her?

"I won't forget your faith in me, Mr Chambers. Truly, I wish I could come with you." And, with a sudden flash of courage, "Do you know, if things had been different, I would have liked to join your expedition, not just as your assistant, but as your cartographer."

He sighs. "Oh, Miss. It is cruel of you to suggest something so perfect, only to snatch it away."

I have dared to say it only because I have nothing left to lose. All my foolish dreams have vanished, flicked from the surface of the land. Soon, I will be on the boat, sailing home towards nothing. It is too late for all of us, except – perhaps – the new governess.

59.

The new governess

The port is not large. It is not long before I see Ian, striding through the rain as if it doesn't exist. Next to him, a young woman clutches her coat and dodges puddles, trying to keep pace. What has brought her to this wild place? Some shame or other, like my own, or is she simply seeking adventure and a new life? I am overwhelmed with sorrow, remembering the estancia, and the future I thought I'd found.

I hurry across the road, then falter. What am I to say? And how can I persuade her to listen? In front of me, a noisy group of travellers jostles into the street, running from the rain. Ian turns to look and I am caught in his gaze. He freezes, then leans over to murmur something in the young woman's ear. Handing her his umbrella, he points her towards the motor car and stands squarely between us, feet planted in the puddles, blocking her view.

"Hello, Georgie." A hollow laugh. "You haunt me, really you do." It used to be Alice who haunted him. Am I too a ghost? "What are you up to now? Have you come to ruin my life again?"

That same plaintive voice. It's true that I have ruined his life. And yet. I glance over his shoulder towards the governess. At once, his eyes cloud with anger. "My God. What are you planning this time? What are you going to do?"

Rain pours between us. Earth dissolves in streams beneath my feet. He has read my mind. "You can say what you like, Georgie. No one will listen to you. We all know what you are." He's right, but that can't stop me. And we both know the rumours will do their work. "I won't let you," he says uncertainly, and then again, with steel in his voice, "I won't let you." His blue eyes darken to a glittering intensity. I am caught in his gaze, and before I can move, he has snatched my wrist. I shriek and pull away, slithering in the mud. He lunges again, and I remember Río Gallegos, the way his fist slammed against my cheek. It is too late to search for words. I run.

Rain soaks my skirt and slashes at my legs as I weave between the buildings. When I look back, he is following. I round a corner and find myself on a deserted stretch of sand, a wasteland littered with broken boats and piles of rubbish. He mustn't catch me here. I swerve back towards the road, hoping to hide among the wagons and motor cars.

The streets and alleys beyond the port are deserted, shops and houses shuttered against the weather. My chest is hurting, I have a stitch in my side and cramps in my legs. I stop in shadows to catch my breath, and hear his voice calling me through the rain.

"Georgie. Please stop. I just want to talk to you." Then later, with an edge of anger, "Georgie. This is ridiculous. Just stop."

I pick myself up and run again, cursing myself for leaving the port. I never thought he would follow me this far.

I have zigzagged north and east and north. Somewhere here must be the cemetery, full of places to hide. With a last effort of will, I lengthen my stride until I find the gate. Once inside, I hurry along the domed cypress bushes that line the path until I find one thick enough to push my way through the branches and press myself against its dark trunk, breathing as silently as I can, my heart hammering loud against my ribs. Through the dreadful crashing of blood in my ears I listen for footsteps, but I hear nothing more than the lash of rain against the gravel.

I wait for as long as I can bear. I am sick with fear, but not just of Ian. I have come too far from the port: what if the ship sails without me? I dare not risk the wide avenues leading to the main entrance, instead I double back and forth between the most overgrown and desolate pathways until I reach the farthest edge of the cemetery. Here, I must leave the shelter of the gravestones and make for the road.

I am almost at the gate when I hear his voice, a ragged shout behind me. He must be out of breath from following, wiping the rain from his eyes to search for the slip of a dress, the whisk of a figure around corners.

On one side, I am trapped by the cemetery wall. On the other, a row of trees guards high, ornate tombs topped with angels on pedestals. I could hide in there, among the angels, but it is too late, he is too close. There is nothing for it. I turn and he is here.

He stops an arm's length away, as if to show he will not hurt me. But the familiar muscle is working in his jaw, and his hands are clenched into fists. I can feel the wildness of his fear. I am close enough to see his eyes, a monster's eyes, blazing with shrapnel and shells and machine gun fire. Is this the wild, divided soul that Alice saw the night she fled?

He lunges forward – or perhaps he merely takes a step and slips in the mud. I'll never know because I am shrieking aloud, and he too is shouting, his hands flailing toward my face. And through the rain one of the angels is leaping from its tomb and flying towards us, wings spread wide, teeth bared, landing on his shoulders. He staggers forward under the weight, knocking me aside, and when I lift my head I see the creature clinging to his back, and it is Marta.

He twists and curses, but she is wrapped tight around him. It takes all his force to prise her fingers from his neck and throw her off. She hits the ground in a crumpled thud, throwing up spray. He hurls himself after her. I am screaming, but before I can reach him, Marta's arm swings out and up and out again. A black line is drawn across his throat.

He lets go of her and opens his mouth as if to speak, but a gush of blood bubbles between his lips. Marta crouches in the mud like an animal, her face fixed in a snarl of rage and fear. In her hand is Tomás's gaucho knife.

I'm a nurse, I know what to do – put pressure on the wound to stop the blood, carotid artery; clear the airways, help him breathe, trachea. But already it is too late. Blood pours into puddles, mingling with the rain. I did this. I led him here to be murdered by an avenging angel, a monster of his own creation. I must be feverish, or insane, to have such thoughts. Is this what killing does? It makes you mad. Marta is mad, and so am I, and both of us have killed him. But it is he, Ian, who has destroyed himself.

"Quick." She is on her feet, pointing towards the gate. But I can't move, I can only watch as she hooks her hands under Ian's shoulders and hauls at him with all her strength. His body resists for a moment, then gives way and slithers over the wet grass. Within moments he has disappeared into a thick patch of mud and weeds. I see her bending over his chest. She must be covering him. Not that it will make a difference. The feral dogs and wild creatures of Punta Arenas will find him before nightfall.

The knife is still lying on the path. She kicks it into a drain, clutching her bodice in a small protective gesture. Rain washes the bloodstains from her dress.

She grabs my hand: "Move."

I allow her to pull me along the path. Rain drips from the cypress trees. Our footprints fill with water, soften, and disappear.

At the road she pauses, looking to left and right, sniffing the air like an animal. I am terrified she is going to leave me, but her hand tightens around mine. We walk hand-in-hand along the broad avenue – slowly, slowly – until we reach an alleyway leading in the direction of the port, where we slip round the corner and, by some silently agreed communion, run until we can run no more, then stop in an empty doorway, doubled over, heaving for breath.

In the distance, a ship's horn blares. The steamer. I should board now, I should leave Patagonia before anyone notices that Ian is missing. As for Marta, she was never here. She could disappear, just as she did before. Both of us can vanish.

Nothing – and everything – has changed. Until this moment, I was lost. Now I know what to do. With a detachment that feels like freedom, I pull the ticket out of my pocket and press it into Marta's hand, folding her fingers over it, out of the rain.

"Quick. It's for the ship. Run."

She doesn't understand. She looks at the ticket, and at my face.

"Hurry." I tell her. "I don't want it. Go north."

She shudders. Without a word, she is gone, running towards the port, vanishing into the rain. I picture her hurrying along the jetty, clutching my ticket. She is Georgie now. Perhaps she pauses as she is about to step on board to pull something from her bodice and wave it in the air like a handkerchief in a signal of triumph and farewell, and perhaps it is Ian's wallet.

60.

Gone

Georgie Carruthers has gone. She will set sail for England and vanish one day into the bright skies of Buenos Aires or Montevideo, never to be heard of again. The thought is so vast, so terrifying, my legs begin to shake.

The rain is slowing now, nothing but a soft drizzle, the kind that falls up instead of down, caressing your face and sitting in tiny beads on top of your hair. The earth has turned to mud. Water streams off every surface. Rain pouring from the gutters has created little rivers braiding in and out of one another on their way toward the sea. I can't stay here: Mrs Creed will be roaming the port, searching for her missing son.

Everything has changed. The governess is safe. The good people of Punta Arenas will gather around Mrs Creed and Leo, and they will be safe too. Marta has vanished into a new life. Now it is my turn to become somebody new. I am free to go: there is nothing to stop me from disappearing with Mr Chambers into the Chilean fjords, losing my old self forever among the tangle of channels and islands and dark green mountains where the Andes tumble down and break into the sea. Nothing can stop me from imagining Raúl. Perhaps he has escaped. Perhaps he will make a farm for himself with horses. And perhaps, one day, I will find him.

A thin haze of rain remains in the air, softening the dark grey water. I pull my shawl over my head and hurry along the docks, slipping between the passengers like a ghost. Men haul packages aboard small boats that bob between the waves. Somewhere, Mr Chambers sits in his cabin, dreaming of the canoe people.

The ferry's horn sounds. I am running down the jetty; hands reach out to pull me aboard. Someone wraps a blanket around my shoulders. Waves whip froth as we pull away from the shore, heading for open water. Tiny fires burn like souls in the darkness, defiant against the weather and the sea.

THE END

326

Acknowledgements

Broken Horses has been a long time in the making and there are many people to thank. Without you, this book would not exist.

Everyone who has contributed to the making of the book: My publisher, Lynn Michell for your generosity, belief, and skill in making Broken Horses the best it could be.
Ayana Playle for your eagle eyes and thoughtful questions.
Adelaida Monguillot for your skilful, sympathetic advice regarding the social context, language and history of this story.
Leigh Forbes for making the book beautiful.
Nick Ross for generous design advice and support. I learned so much!
Mark Radley for endless patience and support.
Richard Ogle for kind advice on cover design.
Django Pinter for your beautiful cover design and map.

The mentors who have supported me along the way. Your skill, wisdom and insight are second to none. You've all been so generous with your time and your encouragement.
Jonathan Ruppin for believing in me, and pushing me always to do better.
Helen Thomas for helping me dig deeper into this story (and myself), than I had ever thought possible.

Andrew Wille for driving me mad with unanswerable questions - far better than giving me any answers. And for providing the design hotline.
Stephanie Butland for showing me the best way to travel from A to B (not via C!).
Fiona Melrose for sage and kind advice.
Tom Harvey for helping me realise I couldn't give up.

Thanks are also due to:
The readers who accompanied me through the development of the novel, who generously read and re-read, advised and discussed, listened and engaged in endless conversations along the way: Hannah Hulme-Hunter, Anne O'Leary, my partners-in-writing Katherine Quarmby and Tom Shakespeare, and Claudette Williams, Kate Thorman, Janet Dulin Jones and the rest of the Veritas Vincit writers' group.
My further readers: Eva Blechová, Janie Beales, Emma Cater, Christine Gettins, Lesley Bond, Jane Saunders, Jo Le Grice and Matt Milner. You gave me the encouragement I needed to keep going.
Christine Gettins for reading, supporting and championing me from the beginning.
Jo Unwin, who listened patiently.
Anna Caig, Jane Saunders and Lesley Thomas for helping me get this story out into the world.
Helena Scott for emergency grammar solutions.
Debi Alper for wise advice.
Fiona Petheram for helping me with difficult choices.
Caro Gervay for beautiful photographs.
Gill King for being ready to walk into a publishing house on my behalf.
Tim Robbins, Eleanor Anstruther, Avril Joy, Emma-Claire Sweeney, Fiona Melrose, Stephanie Butland, Katharine Quarmby, Danny Scheinmann and Patrick O'Donoghue for your generous support in advocating for this story and telling the world about the book.

Christopher, Jeremy and Alexander Dick of Estancia Rio Penitente, Magellanes, Chile, for sharing your history and knowledge with such warmth and generosity. Your loving care for the land and its creatures is impeccable – and you have the most beautiful horses I've ever seen.
Raúl Ivan Sanchez, who drove me to the workers' memorial in El Calafate.
Estancia Coy Aike for my first introduction to the wonderful world of the estancias.
The gaucho at Hostería El Galpón Del Glaciar, who advised me on gaucho vocabulary.

Others who supported my research:
Cathie Campbell
The Huntingdon Library
Margaret Gurowitz, chief historian at Johnson and Johnson
Victoria Webb at the Wellcome collection
Arts Council England for the generous DYCP grant that enabled me to develop my craft and complete this novel.

Of the many, many fascinating books and articles I read, museums I visited and films I watched while researching this story, these two authors were my constant companions for more than a decade:
Osvaldo Bayer, Argentinian historian, whose extraordinary work La Patagonia Rebelde became my foundational text.
Francisco Coloane, Chilean writer, whose beautiful stories showed me the way.

And finally - thank you to my family. You supported my writing with patience, and travelled with me to Patagonia. Jack, you read every single version of the manuscript and helped me wrangle every decision. Django, you filmed Patagonia for me from the back of a horse, drew the map and designed the cover of this book. Alfie: you supported and believed in me. I owe you all so much. Here, I run out of words.

www.ingramcontent.com/pod-product-compliance
Lightning Source LLC
Chambersburg PA
CBHW030936120726
47906CB00002B/594